ELIJAH'S MERMAID

Also by Essie Fox

The Somnambulist

ELIJAH'S MERMAID

ESSIE FOX

First published in Great Britain in 2012 by Orion Books,
an imprint of The Orion Publishing Group Ltd
Orion House, 5 Upper Saint Martin's Lane
London WC2H 9EA

An Hachette UK Company

1 3 5 7 9 10 8 6 4 2

A CIP catalogue record for this book is
available from the British Library.

ISBN (Hardback) 978 1 4091 2334 7
ISBN (Trade Paperback) 978 1 4091 2335 4
ISBN (Ebook) 978 1 4091 2336 1

Typeset at The Spartan Press Ltd,
Lymington, Hants

Printed in Great Britain by Clays Ltd, St Ives plc

The Orion Publishing Group's policy is to use papers that are natural,
renewable and recyclable products and made from wood grown in sustainable
forests. The logging and manufacturing processes are expected to
conform to the environmental regulations of the country of origin.

www.orionbooks.co.uk

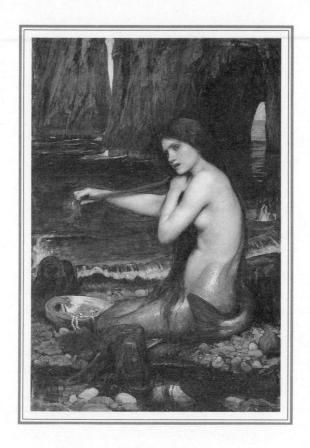

A Mermaid

by John William Waterhouse

To

William Henry Bengry
The kindest heart I was blessed to know
and

Hazel and Bossy Davies
Who always welcomed me into their home,
and led me past many a field and stream in the
village of Kingsland in Herefordshire

Acknowledgements

With heartfelt thanks to Isobel Dixon, my agent,
and Kate Mills, my editor.

PART ONE

Sand turns traitor, and betrays the footstep that has passed over it; water gives back to the tell-tale surface the body that has drowned . . .

From *No Name* by Wilkie Collins

*In Which We Are Introduced To Pearl And Learn
Of Those Momentous Events That Occurred
At The Time Of Her 'Finding'*

Article taken from *The Times* newspaper: May 1850

MYSTERIOUS DEATH. – Late on Thursday evening, Mr.
Davies, deputy coroner, held a lengthened enquiry at The
Eight Bells public-house in Chelsea, touching the circumstances attending the death of an apparently respectable
woman, name unknown, whose body was found floating in
the River Thames off Millbank on the morning of Monday
last. It appeared from the evidence of the witnesses examined, that about midnight on Sunday the police patrol saw a
woman whose dress exactly corresponded with that worn by
the deceased, who appeared to be carrying a bundle of cloth
while walking along Cheyne Walk in the direction of
Battersea Bridge. William Taylor, also of the Thames
Police, stated that he had found the deceased at around
6 o'clock on Monday morning. The woman appeared to be
about twenty years of age, five foot six or seven inches high,
very thin with fine features and abundant fair hair.
Advertisements, with a description of the body and the
articles found upon it, had been inserted in several of the
papers, but as yet no relatives or friends have come forward
for identification. On the body were found expensive articles
of dress. There was no hat or bonnet. A black velvet cloak
was trimmed with black ostrich feathers. A cream silk dress
had beneath two petticoats trimmed with lace, both white.
Stays were fastened in front by steel clasps below which
were a white muslin chemise and white silk stockings.

3

There was no money found on the person. All pockets had been filled with coals and bits of wood apparently collected at the water's edge, leading to the belief that the deceased had committed suicide. Mr. Baker and Mr. Hodgeson, two surgeons of Chelsea Royal hospital, by direction of the deputy coroner, made *post mortem* examination of the corpse upon which no injuries were found. The whole of the organs were found quite healthy though the condition of the womb indicated a recent childbirth. The lungs indicated death by suffocation. The jury, in the absence of any clearer evidence, returned a verdict of 'Found drowned'.

PEARL

Deep with the first dead . . . secret in the
unmourning water of the riding Thames

Dylan Thomas

That May night of my 'birth', of my finding, many marvels and wonders were seen, and every one of them noted down in Mrs Hibbert's Book of Events. Thus –

There was a cabman who worked Cremorne Gardens who, come to the end of his shift for the night, was about to head home across Battersea Bridge when he saw an angel flying by. In the moonlight her ebony wings glistened silver, snapping and billowing out through the air, and two black feathers floated down to brush, like a kiss, against his cheek.

A warehouse nightwatchman at St Katharine Docks swore blind to have heard a mermaid's song, and such a sweet melody it was, ringing clear as a bell through the dense fogged air. A waterman down Wandsworth way claimed to have seen a nymph that dawn. He told how her hair shimmered over black waters, a rippling fan of gold.

And then, there was the comet, described by so many that night; its tail a streaking fire of light as it followed the sinuous bend of the Thames, until its arcing trajectory plunged far out in the sea beyond Margate, at which point there was nothing left to see but a rising plume of fizzing steam.

I doubt that any such tales were true; more likely to have been conjured up by Mrs Hibbert's warped genius – Mrs Hibbert, pronounced Mrs 'eebair', who held court in the House of the Mermaids, a most prestigious Chelsea abode which overlooked the River Thames, from where she concocted fantastical bait with which to lure the clientele through the doors of her *maison de tolerance*. And with every one of them being toffs – aristo-crats, barristers, men of the cloth – to retain their investment in her house she indulged those gentlemen's every whim. She offered a glittering palace of dreams where they could dab the finest whores who played the part of dutiful wives, but without any matrimonial bonds.

Privately, she called them dupes. *The things they will believe, ma chère!* But then she was very persuasive and I was never more beguiled than when hearing my very own story told, with Mrs Hibbert's dulcet tones as soothing as any lullaby – *You were sent to us from the mermaids.*

I used to squeeze my eyes tight shut to try and imagine the scene that night, as glassy as a daguerreotype, a picture exposed in the melting dawn when the street lamps flickered like smouldering ash, when the river was blurred with silver mists.

And now, almost twenty years later, I have made my return to Cheyne Walk, where the winter air is a cold damp gauze, so thick that when I lift a hand it could belong to anyone, I could be standing anywhere, and nothing else alive to hear but the muted snorts and clanging stamps of the horses hitched to a waiting cab. And through their jingling harness song comes Mrs Hibbert's whispering, the hiss of a memory long since passed that still has the power to pierce my heart, which is suddenly beating so very much faster, and I find myself dizzy, having to lean forward, hands clutching the splintering jetty rail, ears filled with the slip-slopping song of the Thames – as if Time itself is ebbing there.

Those swirling small eddies around wooden piers create a dreamy hypnotic state and gradually my heart is lulled, and gradually it starts to slow, a solace not unfamiliar to me though more usually found in a sticky brown syrup rather than the mud and the filth of the river. But I must try not to think of that; the

6

tincture's slow burn in the back of my throat, the tingling fire as it sings in my veins, and how it may still be weaving its dreams, because when I lift my eyes once more the sky has grown dark with a million stars and the milky light of a low full moon is gleaming down on Battersea Bridge; the looming carcass of mouldering wood which creaks and groans as if alive, and through that almost animal sound I hear it so clearly – the fluttering snap of some feathered wings, the sudden hollow splashing thud, the wailing horn of a distant tug as mournful as any funeral bell.

Why does that blast make me shiver? Does it tell of another bride for the Thames, another poor wretch who has been sucked down into his cruel embracing arms until there is nothing left to see but a bubbling phosphorescence of death – as thick and grey as Satan's seed? Has such an event been spied by the mudlarks, those foragers heading towards me now? They look like some ghostly Greek chorus wreathed in rags of drifting fog, crooked backs hunched beneath their bulging sacks as, oblivious to the noxious stench of oily floating turds around, long hooks prod and scrape through the oozing ditch to glean lumps of sea coal and iron and wood; the pitiful harvest on which they live. Do they see what looks like a diamond of light, the spectral orb of a lantern affixed to the bobbing prow of a scull now emerging from under the bridge's gloom? As it draws nearer I find myself thinking – how strange, how incongruous it is that the man who toils at those clumsy oars should be wearing what looks like a fur-collared coat, and perched on his head is a tall silk hat which, despite the brim falling forward, concealing the upper part of his face, cannot disguise his identity.

I would know this gentleman anywhere. Tip Thomas – Mrs Hibbert's 'fancy man', her procurer, her pimp, her scavenger – who now, with his paddles being set down, pushes back the brim of his tifter (that sly little 'tip' for which he is named) while fixing me with the scheming leer that betrays the mask he prefers to show; the clear blue gaze of the pretty boy who could charm all the birds right down from the trees, who barters with

7

punters and tickles the whores – who might now be charming the fish from the sea. Or has he been looking for mermaids again? Or has he been dredging up the drowned?

Tip once told me such business is lucrative, with rewards coming from the authorities, better still from the medical men who are always in need of another corpse, another fresh body to pin on their tables, to rip and dissect then stitch back up; no more use, no more soul than a sewer rat.

Tip is as cunning and quick as a rat. One lurching dip and his craft is moored, and he stands in the shallows at its side where the sluggish tide is rising round. He pulls a small silver flask from his pocket, deftly unscrewing its lid, knocking back a long slug then exhaling a sigh as the bottle is stoppered and stashed again. '*It helps keep up the spirits, dear.*' And now, with his courage quite restored – slowly, almost tenderly – Tip Thomas stoops forward and lifts his catch, embracing what might be a bundle of rags, and while wading towards me, towards the shore, his pace is very leisurely – though what cause has he to hurry now, having found the thing he was searching for, able to savour each squelching step as his boots trudge their progress through gravelled sludge?

There is a moment I fear him lost, dissolved in the shadows beneath the pier's boards until . . . Can you hear it, that *shlump, shlump, shlump*? That is the sound of Tip Thomas's feet, a steady ascension up wooden steps. And look! He is here! He is right by my side, and the street lamp's glimmer is lighting him up like a bauble on a Christmas tree. But what *is* this gift, this queer fish that he holds? Something soft and pale fleshed is nestling there, lodged between sacking and minky fur collar. And yet, there is no fishy odour. No metallic, glistening lustre of scales, nor the usual bloated decay of the drowned who stare through blind and jellied eyes. When Tip draws back his coat's lapel to reveal his living treasure's face I see it has eyes, green and glistening, and a tiny pink mouth like a shell that opens and whimpers and dribbles with slime before letting out a plaintive whine. And when that creature kicks and squirms the foot of an infant child is revealed – though you might almost think it a little frog, the flesh between toes so wrinkled and webbed.

Tip Thomas is not the least bit repulsed by such an odd deformity. He makes a low sort of shushing sound, and I try not to flinch when that rancid and gin-fumy breath of his prickles like ice against my cheek – when common sense tells me that it should be warm – when the very blood almost stagnates in my veins to hear his crowing mantra, '*God bless your sweet little orphaned soul. Did she think I was going to let you go? A gift from Heaven you are to me. A pearl dropped into me waiting hands.*'

His hands? I wonder, what about mine? What will he do if I hold them out? Will he give her to me? Will he let me save this undrowned child from what is to be her destiny? But I must be taking leave of my senses even to contemplate such a thing, for this is Tip Thomas and he has no conscience, no bleeding heart for compassion to prick. Tip Thomas has only ever cared for what is waiting across the street, where behind iron gates and high brick walls that are topped with shards of broken glass an undraped window glows with light, and there, in its centre, as if on a stage, I see a woman's silhouette – and the silhouette is lifting one arm, as if she is waving – or beckoning.

I know that is Mrs Hibbert. I know that she beckons to Tip, not me, because I am the ghost neither one of them sees. I stand in their future looking back to witness the time of my genesis. And that was a time passing strange, don't you think, as strange as any myth they wove, when they called me the Wondrous Water Child, the Living Jewel from the Oyster Beds, Spawned from the Loins of Old Father Thames and the Fishy Womb of his Mermaid Bride?

But the truth always was more prosaic than that. The truth is that I was the bastard child saved from the river by Tip that night when my mother drowned herself for shame. And the only name I have ever known is the one Mrs Hibbert chose to bestow. And the very first memory I have is the sound of her lulling, lilting voice as she called for me to enter a room with lovely pictures all over the walls, walls painted with silvers, blues and greens, with fishes, and mermaids with golden hair – hair wreathed with ribbons, with stars, with pearls.

My hair was once yellow and curling. I wore a crown of shells. Beneath lace skirts my legs were bare, no stockings or shoes to hide my feet, the stubby wedges where toes should be, tingling and cold on the marble tiles. I wanted to run back upstairs to my room but I knew Tip Thomas was standing close, his lips twisted into a snide grimace between whiskers as pale as walrus tusks, and the daggers of his fingernails digging down through the flesh of my shoulders, and me more frightened of riling him than whatever was waiting in that room, from where Mrs Hibbert coaxed again – '*Come, ma chère . . . ma petite nymphe.*'

Mrs Hibbert held out her black-gloved hands and crooned through the mesh of her thick black veils, '*Come play with my friends, my pretty Pearl.*'

Those Historical Documents Pertaining To The Births Of Lily And Elijah Lamb: The Twins Who When Babes Were Deposited At The Doors Of The Foundling Hospital

FREDERICK HALL, PUBLISHER
41 Burlington Row
London

May 7th 1855

AUGUSTUS, DEAR FRIEND,

I hardly know how to commence this post which is proving to be the most onerous task, and far be it from my intention to wish to cause you more distress than that you have already suffered during these past five years. It still fills my heart with grief and guilt to think I encouraged your dear boy to London to work with me in the publishing business. They say that fifty thousand souls were lost in that outbreak of cholera, and still no explanation known, whether the miasma of the air or the corruption of water supplies. Alas, I have grown too jaded to care what those quibbling scientists next debate. If only I could go back in time and offer myself to the pestilence, to give my life instead of his.

I pray now that God will steady my hand as I come to relate some further news that has bearing upon your son's personal affairs, and by that a direct connection with you. Believe me, Augustus, for too many nights I have struggled with my conscience, debating whether it is right to burden you with such intelligence. And yet, I do feel that it is my bound duty to relate what has recently come to light — that during the year he spent in my house, Gabriel succumbed to the lure of romance. His actions were not without consequence.

The young woman in question went by the name of Isabella di Marco and, as you may surmise, was descended from Italian stock. I know of some details regarding her background, and for reasons that will soon enough be apparent, such as that in 1848 she left her homeland and set sail for England along with her father, himself an artist who had hoped for some prospect of work here in London. But he suffered a fatal seizure while their ship was still at sea. Isabella arrived here entirely alone, and being less than twenty years and of a most pleasing appearance then, was at no small peril of being abused by reprobates who seek to inveigle those innocents whose very trust and naivety mark them out as the prey for debauchery. Even so, the girl's future was duly safeguarded when she happened to meet with a friend of mine – a virtuous man who had volunteered to work with the Dockside Nightbird Mission, a charitable Christian enterprise which strives to find occupation for all repentant homeless souls. I have two girls in the kitchens here, as amenable and diligent as those sent from exclusive agencies. But Isabella was a cut above, being refined and well educated, fluent in English and French as well as her native Italian tongue. When my acquaintance first brought her here he suggested she might be employed 'upstairs', helping to translate those foreign works that we often buy in from overseas – mainly short stories and travelogues to feature in the magazines which prove to be more and more popular, really the most lucrative business.

But I digress from the point in hand.

As I am sure you have now deduced it was through their mutual employment in the offices of Hall & Co. that an intimacy came to develop between the two young people. With both of them lodging in my apartments I should have been more vigilant to the signs of a growing affection. But the passions of youth flow very strong, and at times they can be devious, and though I believe they may have wed, events conspired to dash such hopes.

With the tragedy of Gabriel's death, and that coming so close on the loss of her father, Isabella could not, would not, be consoled. Within a month she departed my house without so much as a parting word. And now, there is the further distress of having discovered the reason why – the shame which befell that poor sweet wretch.

You may ask how I happen to come by such news when over five years have since elapsed. My dear friend, I confess it is the result of the strangest of coincidences, which only makes me more convinced that Sacred Providence is at work.

Of all those charities I support the very dearest to my heart is Coram's Foundling Hospital, to which orphanage I make an annual donation along with a great many books – many of your own titles among them. Only last week, when visiting, I was invited to stay on a while to observe the boys and their marching band, and afterwards the refectory where they partake of their midday meal – though I hardly consider such a show to be classed as 'entertainment'. If I wished to see keepers throw buns to bears I would visit the zoological gardens. I do not find it dignified, no matter what Lady This or Lord That happen to be in attendance. As such I made my excuses to leave, though barely gone past the clerk's office door when faced with two bawling infants and the nurse who struggled to hold them, who, when questioned, gave me the harassed reply that only that morning, the siblings – twins, a boy and a girl – had been returned from their foster home.

The smallest of the children here are farmed out until the age of five by which time they are deemed suitably mature to join the institution's life. However, when in the Foundling the sexes must be separate. Boys in the west wing, girls in the east, and the chapel to separate between. And that was the knotty problem here, for the little girl screamed merry hell, refusing to let her brother go, clinging on to his arm like a limpet.

Of course, I went to offer assistance, only to find myself struck dumb when viewing those siblings' features. So familiar were they – so sure was my mind that I made some more formal enquiries, though how tiresome and protracted they were, my patience and nerves stretched to breaking point while waiting in that office, and whatever discoveries then ensued not without a little bribery. But that is by the by. Corruption is blessed when the outcome is moral. The point is that armed with a good enough guess at the probable date of admission and the fact that twins must be somewhat rare, I found myself viewing the relevant file and in that the petitioning

13

document where I read with the very heaviest heart the name of Isabella di Marco, and alongside that of Gabriel Lamb, he divulged as the children's father, and the place in which he and Isabella had first come to be acquainted was listed as being Burlington Row, at the offices of Hall & Co. Finally there was the fact that Gabriel Lamb was now deceased, leaving the mother in no fit state to support dependent infants.

And that, my dearest friend, is why I am now obliged to pass on such momentous news, though should you wish to ignore it, fearing the consequential slur on your own good reputation, then you may safely be assured that your grandchildren are in excellent hands and that both will be schooled for respectable trades with which to support their future lives – the boy trained for agricultural work, the military, or the navy – the girl for domestic service.

I only urge you to swiftly decide on whichever course you think best to take.

I am, as ever, Your own True Friend,

FREDERICK

May 20th 1855. Adopted and removed from the Foundling Hospital, one male and one female infant, sibling twins, known as Elijah and Lily.

Name and Condition of the person adopting the children – Mr Augustus Lamb, widower. Occupation, Author. Residence, Kingsland House, Kingsland, Herefordshire.

References:- the Reverend John Preece, Bloomsbury, and Mr Frederick Hall, Book and Magazine Publisher, Burlington Row, London.

LILY

Clear and cool, clear and cool.
By laughing shallow, and dreaming pool;
Cool and clear, cool and clear,
By shining shingle, and foaming weir;
Under the crag where the ouzel sings,
And the ivied wall where the church bell rings,
Undefiled, for the undefiled;
Play by me, bathe in me, mother and child.

From *The Water-Babies* by Charles Kingsley

Received: A Blank Child. Those four little words headed up the receipt given out whenever an infant was left in the care of the Foundling Hospital, become a blank canvas from which to erase every trace of inherited sin and shame.

Only today did I find our own, and the letter once penned by Frederick Hall, along with the adoption slip made out in the name of Augustus Lamb – Augustus Lamb, his dearest friend – Augustus Lamb, our grandfather – the man we always called Papa.

Now, all of those items are battered and yellow, having been hidden away for years in a box of antique ivory, concealed in a notebook with thick marbled covers, covers with colours all swirling like water – a remnant from those days gone by when Papa still used to write things down, beguiling the young with his fairy tales, the adventures through which his mind constantly swam – although now his mind is a murky confusion where the world is viewed through a shifting lens, and no matter how often he tries to reweave them the threads of his memory dissolve. What ran with luminous colours before has dried to a trickle of thick grey sludge; as black as the ink that filled his pen, that now lies unused, impotent on his desk.

'Lily, is that you?' Papa's earthbound voice is croaked with sleep. 'What are you doing over there?'

I look up from his desk with a nervous smile, feeling guilty for prying where I should not and hurriedly slipping that handful of papers back into the covers of the book – because Papa seems angry to see me there, and so I try to reassure, 'You've been dozing, Papa. I've been looking at all our old treasures.'

This ivory box contains the charms which once inspired Papa's dreams. A white scallop shell. A child's milk tooth. The shadowgraph picture of a fern: a silhouette drawn by the pencil of nature, leaving white where there should be blackness, leaving black where there should be white – an alternative version of the truth. There is a beetle's metallic gleam. A goose's quill. A dragonfly, its green wings a delicate webbing of gauze, so fine they would crumble away into dust if anyone dared to touch them now.

Papa has no inclination to try. He only grunts his stern reply, 'Burn them, Lily. Burn them all!'

Of course, he does not mean it. He is confused again. His gnarled and trembling fingers pluck at the shawl that lies across his lap, and his rheumy blue eyes are staring out, well beyond the world of the ivory box and into the artificial gloom – though goodness knows what he can see when so little light ever enters this room owing to the many layers of dust that have settled like ice on the windowpanes, and the ivy that smothers the house façade, penetrating the mortar and rotting the frames, even the wainscoting nailed to the walls. Month by month it encroaches more. One morning I fully expect to wake and find ourselves trapped in its dark embrace; imprisoned inside our own castle, locked up in a fairy tale. And perhaps that is what Papa desires, to sleep and forget for a hundred years. But I do not, and so I plead while standing and walking to his side, 'Can we not cut the ivy back this year?'

His answer is always the same, though remarkably lucid and prompt today. 'You may do as you wish when I'm gone. I like it like this. It keeps the outside world away . . . and what about the birds . . . the nests? What about the rose?'

Ah yes, what about the rose?

Some years before she died, long before my brother and I were born, long before Papa came to find us in London, his wife had planted a climbing rose, and however short-lived its blooms may be, the big blowsy petals as white as snow have stems inextricably entwined with the vigorous growth of that monstrous vine. How could we think to chop it down? How could we think to cause Papa distress when it is all that he can do to cling on to what's left of past happiness, though he rarely ever mentions his wife, and the same with Gabriel – their son – both of them sleeping side by side in a grave in the village churchyard.

One time, when Elijah and I were small, only living in Kingsland a very short time, I remember standing in front of a grave as Papa explained that from that day on our name would be Lamb, the same as the one carved there on the stone before which he placed a single rose, afterwards taking our hands in his as he knelt in a quiet contemplation – which seemed to go on for a *very* long time – and soon growing bored and restless with that, I gazed to the top of the church's grey tower where an old iron weathercock was perched. I liked to see it spin around, but that day there was barely any breeze, nothing to disturb the humid air that circled Elijah, and Papa, and me, that seemed to hold us in its spell, until my brother suddenly asked, 'Is our mother buried here as well?'

'No.' Papa's voice was blunt. No fanciful stories to weave that day. 'I'm afraid no one knows where your mother is.'

'*So . . . who gives her flowers?*' I thought, but did not say the words, already sensing Papa's response. She had no grave. She had no face, not in the way our father did, because every day we could look at him in the oval-framed portrait that hung on the wall right next to the desk where Papa worked. And Gabriel had been such a pretty child, the same age as us when that picture was made, with curling fair hair and the palest grey eyes – eyes very much like Elijah's were. But apart from that one distinction our decidedly darker appearances must surely have favoured our mother instead, and reminded of her by Elijah's words, I felt a burning ache in my throat, dragging my fingers away from Papa's and ignoring my brother's plaintive shouts when running past weathered stone angels and crosses, on through the whine of the churchyard gate, and over the field, then the rickety bridge that spanned the stream at the end of our gardens – and from there I burst in through the open door to where Papa's housekeeper, Ellen Page, was taking a nap by the kitchen range.

Her frizzy white head was lolling back. Wrinkled cheeks were two mottled slabs of meat either side of a mouth that was drooling and slack – whereas, when awake, it was always clamped in the thinnest thread of a smiling grimace, not due to any lack of warmth but because Ellen Page was adamant that: 'there's no Tom, Dick or Harry shall see how deficient my ivories'.

But Elijah and I had seen them, being obsessed with teeth at the time, having just begun to lose our own. One day we'd found her snoring, when we'd left Papa working and went to the kitchen, tiptoeing close to Ellen's chair, inhaling her sour and peppery breath and the rising reek of mustard and lard from the embrocation she often applied for the easing of her rheumatical knees. Holding our breath, we peered inside, be-tween the lips then hanging loose. We poked with our fingers and prodded her gums. All pink and slimy with spittle they were. And we counted five black rotting stumps – those same stumps to make a rare public appearance on the day when I came running back from graveyard, when Ellen woke with a snuffling grunt before scooping me up to sit in her lap while she dabbed at my cheeks with her apron hems, and her voice, which was usually stern and gruff, only crooning when she smiled and asked, 'Why . . . what's this, Little Lily? What's happened to make my best girl cry?'

I spluttered an answer through snot and tears. 'Papa took us to visit our father's grave, and then . . .'

'Ah, your father . . .' She heaved a great sigh. 'Gabriel was the dearest child. If only he'd never grown up and left us. And his mother, Rose Lamb . . . a mere slip of a girl when she died, she was. A good twenty years younger than Mr Lamb . . . the most gentle of souls who walked God's earth. I dare say that's why God claimed her back, another angel to grace his clouds, though his greed nearly sent your poor grandfather mad. I've never known a man to grieve as he did when he lost her life like that . . . so soon after bearing their only child. And now, Rose and Gabriel joined again, sleeping fast within that grave.'

'But . . .' I tugged at a strand of hair that was dangling loose from one of my plaits, sucking it hard between my lips before continuing with my thoughts, 'If they're only sleeping, why can't they come back and sleep here in the house? Why do dead people have to go under the ground?'

'You'll swallow that hair and clog up your lungs. It'll wrap itself around your heart – tighter and tighter until it stops beating . . . and then you'll be under the ground as well.' Ellen let out a wheezy groan and I feared her lungs were full of hair when she set me back down on the red-tiled floor, smoothing the creases out of my skirts and giving my skinny rump a pat before struggling to stand herself and say, 'And haven't I got enough washing to do! Who wants mouldy old bones hanging round in the house, rotting and festering under the sheets? When a body dies, the soul flies out and . . .' She paused for a while and stroked my head, before hobbling off towards the sink, glancing back over her shoulder to say, 'and of those of us left to toil below I shall need to get on and look sharpish, my girl. Mr Lamb and your brother will soon be back and I've not even started to peel these spuds. Here I am nattering, letting things slip, getting slower with every passing day. Never grow up, Lily. Always stay young. This old age and decay is a terrible thing.'

This old age and decay is a terrible thing. Such words meant all too little then. How could they when I was new and eternal, when the world turned around me – me and Elijah. But I think of them very often now, especially here in the study where my heart sinks to see the damp seeping in and the peeling of the papered walls, and a wet black mould is rotting the drapes, and I fear for the books piled up on the shelves; so many spines with Papa's name.

Sometimes, at night, when the doctor has been to give the injection to help Papa sleep, allowing his frail body to lay off its shaking, I have taken to coming back down again, led on by the flickering light of my candle and the wuthering wind that moans soft in the hearth. An eerie sound it is. When I was a little child I used to think it was calling my name. But I am no longer so whimsical. I barely even notice it, my disembodied chimney friend, the accompaniment to my lonely task of pulling the books from Papa's shelves, dusting the covers, then flicking through pages as I search for the signs of insidious worms; silent as the illness that eats through his mind, silent as the spiders that watch from their cobwebs which drip like lace from the ceiling rose, its plaster still stained a tarry brown from those years when Papa worked below while puffing and sucking his pipe of tobacco.

Now that pipe is unplugged and cold. It lies on his desk, at the side of his pen, like the relics of one who is already dead. But Papa's spirit is fighting on, sometimes swimming up to the surface again, and then we have much better days when we think of new stories, and I write them down, and on good afternoons we might walk through the gardens, even as far as the stream at its end, and if he is tired or stumbling there is always the big bath chair to push him through the country lanes, even as far as the village again – though Papa increasingly gets upset, the outside world too quixotic for him.

Last week when a stranger passed by on his horse, Papa thought him a knight off to slaughter a dragon. He thought the decrepit old yellow dog that lies outside the Angel Inn, its head on its paws, its tail thumping the ground – the most benign of greetings for us – was the monstrous hellhound Cerberus. Papa struck out with his stick, only thinking to try and protect himself, but the creature cowered and whined so loud that those villagers drinking inside the bar, who had always been courteous before, came running outside to curse and berate, saying high time we put the old man away.

Can they really think him mad? Would they lock him away with the lunatics? Such a prospect only fills me with dread for I have seen what goes on in these places. And the doctor assures us it won't come to that. And Papa is still the dearest old man with the kindest heart I am blessed to know, and every day I pray to God that he goes on believing that I am his friend – even if that friend is disguised in his mind as an angel – a princess – a mermaid.

And now, there is only the sweetest smile when Papa lifts his trembling hand, his fingertips fluttering over my cheek, when he says, 'My Lily . . . my own little Lily . . . what would I have done without you and Elijah? You brought me so many treasures. You saved me from drowning in myself.'

I bend forward. I kiss his cheek, white-stubbled and scratchy against my lips, and my voice nearly breaks when I make the reply, 'It was you, Papa. It was *you* saved us. Me . . . and Elijah.'

'Saved?' In no more than that short space of time, his yellowed, bloodshot eyes grow dim. 'Elijah? Who is Elijah?'

I draw a deep breath and I take his hand, and I speak as I've done so often before, in the language he likes to hear the most, '*Once upon a time . . .*'

Once upon a time, when I was no more than five years old, I found myself gazing up at a man with dishevelled grey hair and sparkling eyes that were spilling with tears as he stared back down, and although I have no recollection of uttering one single word I really didn't need to speak because my brother was there at my side, my hand clutching on to his for dear life as we stood in an enormous room with very high ceilings and very dark walls, walls covered all over with great gilt frames where I felt myself quite overwhelmed, struck dumb while my brother's fluting tones voiced what was then our mutual thought, which was simply the question, 'Who are you?'

'I suppose you must call me your grandfather.' On that answer the man's face cracked wide in a smile. But then everyone smiled when they looked at Elijah, for even as a little boy my brother was very beautiful, with his glossy dark hair and his plump honeyed cheek, and so cheery a disposition then.

I never possessed my brother's charm, and even though people used to say that my features might resemble his it was always as an afterthought. There were too many subtle differences, and the tiniest differences alter much. To this day I still recall the shock when I first saw myself in a photograph because *that* little girl, all grainy and blurred, was much thinner than I could ever be, with a cast of suspicion in narrowed eyes, and the hair that fell straight around her face was lifeless and lank when compared to her brother's – although Papa insisted the camera lied, that in the world of reality my hair *'always shimmered like ribbons of silk'*, and my eyes *'sometimes brown and sometimes green, were flecked with drops of molten gold, like a shower of rain on a sunlit day'*.

Dear Papa. He could be very fanciful, but even that quaint, queer turn of phrase did little to console the child who wanted her eyes to resemble her brother's; a liquid silver, very pale. And she wanted a nose a little less snub, and a mouth less likely to purse in a frown whenever she stood on tiptoes and peered into one of the mirrors that hung like veiled windows in Papa's house; the windows that once you smeared a hand through all the layers of dust and grime (that Ellen Page too rarely cleaned) always refused to lie.

And then there were other hidden reflections, the secrets unfolding one page at a time, half-truths that would take many years to tell – with Papa resolved to keep us cocooned, well away from the rest of the outside world. So, the only friends we really knew were very much older than ourselves, being Papa, and Ellen, and then Uncle Freddie, who came to visit every May to celebrate our adoption month – no one knowing the actual date of our birth.

How we loved to see Freddie walk in through the door, not least because those occasions heralded great improvements in Ellen Page's culinary skills when she slaved at the kitchen range for days, baking cakes and all manner of fancy things, though as years passed by I began to suspect that the true extent of her enterprise was based on something more profound than mere hospitality. Ellen was a spinster, and Freddie was a bachelor who possessed an imposing, rakish style to which, even I, a little girl, was not entirely immune.

Unlike Papa, whose own unruly locks had been grey since the very first day we met – with Freddie a good decade younger, his hair was still as black as jet, cut short to his head and slickly oiled, except for two wings of silver that grew at the side of each temple. Ellen said that was most distinguishing. She thought the same of his moustache, being as close to a work of art as any whiskery thing could be. When Elijah and I were still small enough to clamber up his trouser legs, we would sit on Uncle Freddie's knees and twiddle the stiffly pointed ends into the most elaborate shapes, at which our uncle only laughed, quite prepared to tolerate those acts. But then Freddie held such affection for us, and the visits he made to Herefordshire must have taken a considerable toll on his personal and business commitments – although he never stayed the night but lodged in a Leominster hotel, ready to catch the early train to London the following morning.

One day a year. That's all we had, but a day of great excitement it was, for Uncle Freddie never arrived without being armed with wonderful gifts: tops and marbles, kaleidoscopes, a

Noah's Ark for Elijah once, with all sorts of carved wooden animals, a great many of which ended up on display in the rooms of the doll's house he gave to me – along with the miniature furniture, and the miniature porcelain people too: a gentleman with a black moustache, and his black-haired wife with her rosy cheeks, and their two little children, a boy and a girl, both as near in size and shape as twins. The perfect family.

But our household was not in that 'perfect' mould. A wonder we ever survived at all, with Papa always engrossed in his work, and having very little sense when it came to life's practicalities, such as when to eat or when to sleep, and the need to wash and the need to dress, at which Ellen Page would mutter on, 'If not for my tending and administrations, waiting hand, foot and finger on you, Mr Lamb, then you'd probably fade away into thin air . . . you three would be knocking on Heaven's Gates.'

To be honest, we thought she would win that race, always moaning and groaning about her age. And Papa could be an awful tease, once saying he'd seen the church registry and there it was clearly written down that Ellen Page was one hundred and ten! Well, Elijah and I could not believe that anyone lived as long as that – unless they were in the Bible and sailed on Noah's Ark, unless they dabbled in wicked spells, their souls being sold to the Devil in Hell. And Ellen did have a long hooked nose and a wart growing out at the side of that, and a bristly hair on the end of her chin. And when she was angry and pointed her finger you felt as if you were being cursed.

She pointed at Papa at least once a week, usually when she threatened to leave, shouting, 'Mr Lamb! You show no respect . . . and I wouldn't be here at all, you know, if not for your dear wife's dying wish that I should take good care of you . . . and what do I get for my loyalty, but these raggle-taggle gypsies to keep, and where you got them . . . well, let's just say that with all of the gossip around these days it's as well I'm past the breeding age, and . . .'

Once Ellen started she'd never stop, and should Papa ever dare to suggest that he hire someone more 'biddable' she would only start to sniffle and cry, asking how he could think to consider such things when she had become so attached to us, at which Papa would shake his head while exhaling a weary sigh of relief – or was it exasperation?

Still, whether Ellen was a witch or our very own Angel of the Hearth, she exerted *some* power over Papa, for following one of her worst tirades – I think that episode with her teeth – when she said that Elijah should go to school, '*up Lucton way, like Gabriel. He can board there and learn his manners, and what's more he'll stop leading his sister astray. Never known such a girl for trouble and scrapes . . .*' well, in answer to that Papa gave a nod and then stared at the portrait of his son with the gravest expression on his face. 'I see I shall have to consider this.'

A horrible claw of cold spiked fear was gripping and twisting in my bowels. I stamped my foot and shouted, 'No! You can't send my brother away to school!'

But Elijah, he said nothing at first, only reached out to hold my hand, his own then shaking, gripping hard when he looked up at Papa to make his plea. 'Let me stay, with you and Lily. I like it here at Kingsland House. I promise to leave Ellen's teeth alone.'

Papa said he would think on the matter some more – that every bad act had a consequence and that was a lesson we needed to learn – and a night of little sleep ensued during which I fretted terribly until Papa rattled my bed the next morning and then did the same to Elijah's, telling us both to wash and dress, to go down to the kitchen for breakfast, and then to sit at his study desk while he peered over half-moon spectacles (that always slipped down to the tip of his nose) and announced that a verdict had been reached – that Elijah should stay at home with me, with both of us spending every day taking our lessons in Papa's 'school'.

We were so relieved and grateful, really the most assiduous pupils, and Papa taught us all those things that useful children ought to know. He encouraged us to write and draw (Elijah had such a gift for art), our best efforts stitched into little books and placed on the shelves beside his own. But when our studying time was done, when the big marble clock on the mantel struck out its twelve long twanging chimes, Papa would shoo us on our way, leaving him there to work in peace, lighting the pipe only ever smoked when he set about his writing work. There at the desk he would puff and suck while we sniffed out the yeastier fragrance of Ellen Page's fresh-baked bread, wolfing down buttery slices that were melting with dripping or sugar or jam before running out to the gardens to play, only blowing back in much later on if it rained, or if we were hungry again, when Ellen would groan at the state of our clothes, or crush up brews of snails and worms to smother all over the bruises gained when climbing walls or the branches of trees while searching for Treasures and Magic Things – things with which to inspire more of Papa's tales. There might be a bird's nest with blue speckled eggs, or the fragile skeleton of a mouse. Or the dewy white bud of a rambling rose.

It was on such a mission, one day in spring, that our mermaid obsession first began. I think we were eight or nine by then, and the weather warm and so cloying with pollen that it caught and tickled the back of your throat. Elijah was running on ahead, leading me across the lawns and into the darker, denser parts where the overgrown bushes created a tunnel, where drifts of feathery dandelion seeds wafted slowly round our heads. Papa once told us those seed heads were fairies. But now we were older and wiser. We knew they were only bits of fluff and, anyway, that afternoon, our minds were fixed on more watery things.

Elijah had found an empty jar and knotted some string around the rim to create a sort of dipping trap, intending to place it in the stream. Until recently we'd avoided that place, mainly because of Ellen's tale that if you happened to go too near you might hear the pitiful wailing cry of a lingering ghost from years gone by, when a village woman lost her mind and drowned her newborn baby.

Papa insisted it wasn't true, that story only Ellen's way of ensuring we didn't go too near and risk becoming drowned ourselves – about which he seemed to have no such qualms. But I doubt anything could have stopped us, our curiosity inflamed after reading the latest magazine that Uncle Freddie sent each week, the one called *As Every Day Goes By*. That latest instalment contained a new story – the one about Tom, a little boy with whom we felt some allegiance ourselves, with him being of a similar age, and having no parents of his own, and never once attending school but living instead with Mr Grimes – a man who was nowhere as kind as Papa, who forced Tom to work as a chimney sweep, climbing into the darkest stacks where the air was smoky and made him choke. And, once, when employed at a big country house, Tom found himself lost in the maze of flues, emerging in a bedroom hearth where he really had no right to be, where he saw – *the most beautiful little girl . . . Her cheeks were almost as white as the pillow, and her hair was like threads of gold spread all about over the bed.*

What a lovely vision Tom thought that to be. But when the girl's nursemaid stormed into the room and made a great fuss to see him there, and being smeared with so much black that he looked like a monkey instead of a boy, poor Tom had to jump through a window and scramble down the trunk of a tree before heading off through the gardens and fields, eventually coming to a stream where he tried to wash all the filth away. But somehow he must have fallen asleep, and perhaps he had drowned in that water because when he came to wake again his chimney-sweep body had disappeared. Tom had shrunk to be less than four inches long and his neck was frilled with a ruff of gills, turned into a water-baby – of which very many were said to exist, if you only knew how and where to look.

Elijah and I looked very hard. We were determined to find one. I lay on my front with my chin in my hands, peering over the edge of the shingled bank as I watched my brother scramble down, clutching that jam jar in his hands. Through the thrum of the zithering insects around I heard the soft rush of the stream below, and the thin bleat of sheep in the field near by, and I heard my brother's excited breaths when he stooped to immerse his trap in the water, and very soon afterwards tugged it back – when I sprang to my knees, crying out, 'Let me see! Let me see what you've caught.'

Very gingerly, he lifted the jar, holding it high to show me before setting it down upon the grass, where, once it appeared to be secure and with one of us either side of the prize, Elijah on tiptoes, me lying down, we pressed our noses against glass walls, absorbed in the living creatures there – not water-babies, just three little fish that darted through swirls of settling silt. And when that residue had cleared I could see right through to Elijah's face, the curve of the jar distorting his features, making him appear to be under the water. One eye was magnified, too large, glistening, bright as a diamond, with lashes like spiders that crawled on his cheek, which was flushed, which was dusted with freckles and dirt, and while wondering if mine looked the same, lost in a moment's reverie, my brother's features disappeared.

I couldn't imagine where he'd gone, sitting up very fast, feeling oddly bereft – startled to hear the voice that squeaked, 'Lily . . . help! I've fallen into the stream. I've turned into a water-baby!'

What magic was this? With a thumping heart, I crawled forward and peered back down into the stream, where something went plop, and then again, a little splash of water.

'Elijah!' I gasped, my heart in a flutter of panic by then. 'Come back to me . . . you'll be washed away.'

'Fetch the jar . . . I'll try to swim inside.'

No sooner had I turned my back to reach for the jar as Elijah asked than I realised how suspiciously close my brother's voice had been just then, coming as it did from under the bank where some of the rock had eroded away and formed a natural hollow – and where I suddenly recalled that Elijah had hidden himself before, one day when we'd played at Hide and Seek.

And that's when I thought of a trick of my own, creeping

back with the jar clutched in my hands and trying not to make a sound as I squinted down through a fence of ferns to see a small brown hand emerge, and that hand flung a pebble into the stream, and another plipping splash was made, after which I stretched out with both my arms and tipped the jar above the spot where I thought Elijah's head might be – though only a dribbling spill it was, just enough to give him a bit of a shock, not so much as to risk the little fish.

'Found you, Elijah Lamb!' The giggles were bubbling up in my breast to see my brother's expression then. Crawling out from his hiding place, he was blinking and pushing the hair from his eyes, the wetness gleaming black as jet as it clung to his lids, his cheeks, his mouth; the latter a great big 'O' of surprise before some of that water dribbled in and Elijah was trying to spit it out, spluttering, coughing, laughing too. 'Ugh . . . that tastes disgusting!'

'A real water-baby would like the taste! A real water-baby likes the wet.' I set the jar back down on the grass, cupped my chin in my hands again and wiggled my feet back and forth in the air while Elijah began to busy himself with tugging at his boots and socks and then rolled up his trouser hems before standing and wading into the stream, an innocent paddle, or so it seemed, until he looked back with an impish grin and then began to kick about so that splashes of water were arching high, raining on me, on the grass around – which caused me to hurriedly shuffle away, all too wary of Ellen's pointing ire if that morning's clean clothes should be grubbed and spoiled. And when I was making that escape my elbow knocked the jar of fish, and I had to fling myself back down in an effort to set it straight again, and too late before I realised that my new white smock was soaking wet, smeared with stains of grass and mud. But seeing those three little fish, still safe, the flick of their tails and glinting scales, I soon forgot about Ellen's threats because something so thrilling had entered my mind, I called down to my brother excitedly, 'Stop splashing, Elijah . . . what do you think? Perhaps water-babies don't *really* exist, but we *could* try and catch a mermaid . . . that is if they don't only live in the sea?'

Elijah, whose feet were now becalmed, was half-smiling, half-frowning at such a suggestion until he replied with great certainty, 'Last year, when Freddie visited, he said this stream runs into a river, and that river runs all the way to the sea. So, a mermaid *could* swim as far as here . . . if she wasn't too big . . . if she wanted to.'

'She might,' I agreed through a moment of tentative creeping doubt, '*if* she swam too far . . . if she lost her way. Shall we take these fish to Papa? Shall we see what Papa says?'

As it turned out I was right not to fret. Ellen Page never mentioned the state of my dress. And Papa, well, the gift of our fish inspired him to write a new fairy tale, though when that was published up in a book he had to make it longer, and the ending became much happier. But this is the story he told that day –

There was once a lovely mermaid child who left her papa in his palace of shells in the depths of the darkest ocean. He had pleaded and begged for her to stay, for she was the most precious thing he possessed. But she had such a yearning in her heart to see the airy light of the sun and to feel its warmth upon her face. So, one day, when her father was sleeping fast, the mermaid swam to the top of the waves and played with dolphins and gossiped with gulls, and rode on the foamy backs of white horses – until they all dissolved away, being so very far from home and by then having come to the mouth of a river.

There, the mermaid glimpsed a dragonfly, a creature she'd never seen before, and she found herself longing to stroke its wings, which were coloured a vivid turquoise hue, like the blue of the sky and the green of sea, like an oily, lustrous, precious jewel – a jewel she might give to her papa.

Wherever that insect hovered next, the little mermaid followed it. She battled the river's downstream flow, heading past ships and bustling towns, then into the quieter countryside where each day the banks grew narrower, where each day the water grew shallower, until there was barely enough of it left to cover the mermaid's silver tail, which by then had begun to scorch away, for the hot summer sun was beating down, the stream dried to a ditch of gluey mud. She wept salty tears 'til she had no more, and those tears left a crusting trail on her cheeks, as if slugs and snails had been crawling there. Her breaths grew faint and her heart grew slow, and with its last beat she gazed up at the sky, where she saw the dragonfly again, and this time it hovered so very close that the tips of her fingers could touch its wings around which the air seemed to sparkle and whirl, a strange iridescence of glistening light, as blue as the sky and as green as the sea – in which she would never swim again.

Papa's stories could be somewhat cautionary. The moral of that one was not hard to see. Better to be safe and stay at home, however beguiling the world might seem. But all through that summer *our* world was the stream, to which we returned most every day to dip our toes in liquid green and to stare at the ribbons of wavering light that shone on the water's surface – where there might be the glint of a mermaid's tail. And that hollow in the rocky bank, where Elijah had hidden himself from me, we imagined a sort of grotto where a mermaid might happily make her home, well away from other prying eyes, or the hard cruel glare of the midday sun. We decorated our stony den with old shards of china and bird-pecked snails – and when Uncle Freddie had seen it, a week later he sent us a basket, and that basket full of straw and shells, all smelling fresh, of salt and the sea, and attached to the handle a note which read: *Something to entice your mermaid home.*

What a cherished gift it was. We used the straw to make a bed upon which the mermaid might rest her head, and then we sorted every shell, going by colour and size and shape, which Elijah then glued to the grotto walls, and all sorts of patterns he made there; flowers and stars and suns and moons. But still our mermaid didn't come.

And so, like two scavenging magpies, we sought yet more to coax her. We 'borrowed' a string of milky pearls from a dusty box in an upstairs room that had once belonged to our grandmother. We gathered twigs and fir cones and feathers. We paddled about in the water for hours until our feet were cold and numb, careful to step on no dead baby's bones as we looked for the prettiest of the stones that lay in the oozy slime below. But when they were plucked dripping into the air, although some of them glistened like mother-of-pearl, gleaming the loveliest blues and greens, every one of them dried to the dullest grey.

A backward sort of alchemy.

PEARL

'The story of our lives, from year to year' – Shakespeare

AS EVERY DAY GOES BY

A Weekly Journal.
Conducted by
Frederick Hall

Title page from the popular magazine *As Every Day Goes By*

A strange and contrary thing it is that with the passing of the years I almost look forward to those nights, always the last of every month, when Mrs Hibbert entertains her most important gentlemen swells. To be honest, they all seem a bit dillo to me. There's that red-faced lush, Lord Whatshisname, and Sir Rummy Old Cove who likes nothing more than to play a game of Blind Man's Buff while wandering round in his underwear. *Come closer, my dear. Come sit on my knee. Let me stick you with my little pin.*

Mrs Hibbert says he's harmless enough, but she won't have me sit on anyone's knees, whatever the needful they're offering. She watches as keen as any hawk from behind those swaying veils of hers – though I always think she must see the world through the thickest pea-souper in history! Anyway, any nonsense, she'll blow right up, and then what a hubbub and shindy there is! Cook says that when she's in a mood not even the devil could hold up a candle. No one dares to contradict Madam – and the slaveys, what lip-lashings they get when preparing the house for those monthly events, when the hall's marble floor is rubbed with milk, buffed up until it gleams like glass. And the kitchens, you can't imagine how busy, with Cook toiling down there for hours on end, scraping and grating and whipping away, her temper and tongue as sharp as knives. But oh, so many lovely tastes in the hot sticky gloom of those low arched walls, with the air all fuggy from bubbling pans, and the sheets that drip on the ropes by the hearth – a hearth so big you could stand inside if not for the fire that always roars – for the laundry work it never stops, with the slaveys washing and pressing the linen, surrounded by wafting lavender scents as they chatter about the music halls. They often sing the latest songs, and when they do Cook's cat will purr – the big ginger cat which sits by the range – though that creature is kind to none but its mistress, and best you never try to stroke for its claws will lash out and tear your flesh. More than once that creature has drawn my blood.

''E's not a pet . . . 'e's a mouser!' Cook always used to chide before I grew wise to his fickle ways, when I would cry at the sting of my wounds until soothed by the taste of the almond cakes that she would stuff into my mouth, '*to feed my hungry little bird*'.

A wonder I am not as fat as a pig, just like Miss Louisa is these days, with her eyes of blue glass and her round pink cheeks and all those lardy puffing rolls exuding around her elbows and knees, and great squashy bosoms like marshmallow pillows that spring uncontained from the top of her corset, which is often the only thing she wears as she wobbles her way down the basement stairs – when those moments of peckishness come on between one visitor and the next. Louisa has many visitors. She is always in great demand, and to keep up her strength and her ample frame Mrs Hibbert has said that she may peck whenever, whatever it is she wants – iced cream and fruit puddings, pastries and honey; a veritable banquet every day.

But Cook does not like the whores coming down, preferring to send trays up to their rooms. Cook does not like Louisa at all, and Cook can be just as tart as a plum – such as today when Louisa was sitting beside the fire eating some sugar-dipped buttery bread, her thunderous thighs splayed over a bench, and all dimpled they were, all marbled white, and in the kitchen's dingy light she looked what you might call Rubenesque. Cook had been staring a good long while before curling her lip and commenting, 'You fuck for nothing but food. How Mrs Hibbert sustains your greed is a constant mystery to me!'

At first, Louisa gave no reply, only a long and arrogant stare. She slowly continued to chew her bread as if contemplating what best to say, which was, 'I don't mean to stick around here for long. I aims to find me a gentleman, like my mate Sally Hamilton did, when she married her German count . . . had three thousand pounds settled annually and her very own villa in Saint John's Wood, and a nice little stipend for Hibbert and Tip . . . so everyone's happy in the end. Everyone gets their retirement home, in Margate or Gravesend or Whitstable. And what's more . . .' she tilted her double chins, 'in case you are still wondering, the men fuck me because they like me fat . . . they don't want a skinny old drab like you, a raddled old witch whose best days are spent!'

At that point I thought it best to run, knowing that altercation might very well end in a punching match, an event which sometimes does occur when people get their danders up. But while I was passing Louisa's side I made the mistake of reaching out to grab at a crust on the edge of her plate, and I thought she was trying to snatch it back, only rather than that she caught hold of my arm, a lopsided smile on those scarlet lips when, 'Look at this darling, darling girl. Would you believe it . . .' She grinned at Cook, as if they were now the best of friends. 'This dainty little slip of a thing could have been me a few years ago . . .' She jabbed a finger against my chest as if to emphasise her point. 'Nothing more than skin and bone!'

Her free hand was cupping the back of my neck, pulling me closer when she said, 'Come on, Pearly. Give us a kiss.'

Her pouting lips slobbered wetly on mine, greasy they were,

and grittily sweet. I flinched back and wiped a hand to my mouth to spit out the taste while she carried on, 'Don't you go and take any offence, my dear. You're welcome to have a poke at me and play on Cupid's kettledrums. Aren't you curious, to see how my diddeys feel, what you've got to look forward to one day, when you finally start to fill out a bit?'

Next thing she was pressing my hand to her breast, the flesh soft and doughy, repulsive to me, and perhaps that thought had shown in my eyes for she let my hand drop, and the malice barely concealed in hers when she asked, 'How old *are* you, Miss Prim and Proper?'

'Fourteen.'

'Fourteen! Gracious Lud! D'you hear that, Cook? The nipper looks barely past ten to me!' And then, 'Oh . . .' as blue eyes grew rounder, 'will you hark at that. Am I green or what? Oh Lord, I'll say. I'm as green as that cabbage you're chopping today!'

The vast hams of her arms were lifted, hands dramatically smacking her mouth when she leered at me with a knowing nod. 'So, Miss Silver Bells and Cockle Shells and Pretty Maids all in a Row is already over the age of consent. I'll wager in the next six months that little muff won't be as tight.'

'Won't you shut your head!' Cook snapped her response, thrusting out her chopping knife, its blade glinting red in the light of the fire as it pointed towards Louisa's face. 'You know the rules as well as me. No more of this dirty, grubby talk . . . not when we've got Miss Pearl around. Mrs Hibbert doesn't like it.'

'Just saying . . . what I've heard from the horse's mouth.'

'From Madam?' Cook enquired, less certain now, every tendon strained in her scrawny jaw.

'No . . . you noodle, Mr Mary Ann . . . the queen who *really* rules this house.'

'Tip Thomas, that posturing mandrake! She should flog him . . . and you as well!'

'Well, that could be Madame H's forte. The Cheyne Walk

Mistress of Flagellation, though what a queer breed of man it is who likes the flick of the governess's stick. Oh well,' Louisa gave her lazy smile, 'there's one thing I've learned . . . it takes all sorts.'

'It certainly does. And *your* sort should learn to shut her mouth or else get it filled with a knuckle pie and . . .'

I didn't linger to hear any more, and really that was just as well because Mrs Hibbert was up in my room, already waiting to dress my hair. But Louisa's words, that mention of Tip, still rang in my mind when, an hour or so later, I stood below the mermaid walls, where a table was littered with all that remained of Cook's spiced beef, and béchamel fowl, and lobster salads, and turkey poulets, and the air was wreathed in the serpents of lust puffed out from the mouths that sucked cigars – through which fug I trembled as I walked, my crown of silk flowers and silver shells tinkling like fairy bells. I took a deep breath to steady myself when I read from the big leather Book of Events – which Mrs Hibbert placed in my hands, always opened at the appropriate page – *That night of my birth, of my finding, many wonders and marvels were seen . . .*

In truth, I know every word by heart, so often have I spoken them since Mrs Hibbert first taught me to read when I was only four years old, when, if I ever grew tired or distracted, and especially if I lifted my hands and tried to raise the hems of her veils to see what face might be concealed, she would tap at my hand and reprimand, 'Curiosity killed the cat! Get on with your studies and always remember this, ma chère. To be pretty is never enough. We must strive to be extraordinaire! Only then can we hope to escape our fate.'

Well, whatever my fate might happen to be, tonight I was not extraordinaire. I stumbled too often over the words. All the time I was fretting and wondering, *Why do these men come to look at me . . . to hear the story of my birth? Can it be true, what Louisa says?*

I began to feel faint and very hot, and then Mrs Hibbert was at my side, leading me out, into the hall and up through the warren of service stairs until I was back in my crow's-nest room.

I like my room. I feel safe up here. The walls are a trellis of rosebuds. I have a purple velvet chair in which I can sit to read or sew. I have a desk and shelves of books, and my closet spills over with lace and silks, with cashmere and mousseline de laine. My bed is something fit for a queen, being made of brass and very ornate, and that is where I obediently lay while Mrs Hibbert said her goodnight, setting my crown back on its hook before stroking my forehead and kissing my cheek, a caress always married with the scent of aniseed, or cloves or mint, and the smell of the gentlemen's cigars, and something less pleasant – I don't know what – infused in the brush of those chiffon veils. She gives me a spoonful of 'Murgatroyde's Mixture'. A sweet and syrupy tincture it is. She calls it *Mother's Blessing. Something to help our Pearl sleep tight, undisturbed by the house's 'goings on'*.

But these days it seems to have little effect, even though I strive to make the pretence, whispering my sleepy goodnight, yawning and fluttering my eyes – and the moment Mrs Hibbert has gone I reach underneath my pillows and pull out *As Every Day Goes By* – which is now my favourite magazine with its stories serialised each week; with all those eerie real-life tales that appear beneath the banner that asks, '*Is it Possible?*'

Cook gives me all her old copies. Mrs Hibbert would tut if she knew. She prefers me to read things like *Woman's World* with advice on fashion and etiquette, all the latest musical arrangements to play on the parlour piano or harp, with pictures of devoted wives who pose as angels of the hearth alongside their perfect children, inside their perfect homes. But Cook says we are all fallen angels here, and better not to dream of lives that have no bearing on our own – which is why I like *As Every Day*. And those pages *are* educational. The things I have learned. You would be amazed! Did you know there are hogs living wild in the sewers, breeding as fast as rats, and rats that grow to the size of dogs that would tear out your throat and

38

drain your blood if you so much as dared to cross their paths? And tonight I was reading of Spring Heeled Jack – a supernatural being who once caused a spate of hysteria among half the women of London town, tormenting them with his blazing red eyes and his fingers like claws and a mouth that could vomit blue tongues of fire. Imagine being confronted by that! The ugliest of customers! *A Murderer. A demon from Hell!* Well, that's what all the headlines said. But never once was that devil caught because of the springs that were fixed to his boots, that gave him the power to fly over walls, after nobbling his victims half out of their wits – and some of them really did go mad, thereafter committed as lunatics.

The stories are stashed back under my pillow. But I am awake. I cannot sleep. What is that creaking outside the door? I hold my breath when it opens up. A golden light comes trickling in. Watery circles lap over the ceiling. Watery shadows creep over the walls. I freeze at a jingle-jangling sound, a faint scratching patter across the boards, then the sudden weight on the end of the bed which causes the mattress to dip right down. For a moment there I almost scream. I am thinking – *Jack has come for me!*

Oh, this is no supernatural beast, whatever the aura of menace that seeps from his every pore. I know that dial all too well and I know that low and mellifluous voice when he spouts his soft enquiry, 'Are you sleeping, or are you pretending again? Won't you wake for the present Tip's brought tonight?'

He's always coming in at night bringing me his midnight gifts, posies of flowers, old books of verse, a wooden box full of Turkish Delight: sweet fragrance of honey, lemon and rose seeping out through the tissue paper's folds. Those jellies melt upon your tongue like something sent from Paradise. But I only eat them when he's gone. Only then do I stop pretending sleep, squinting through the narrowed slits of my eyes to make out his silhouette on the bed as he sighs and lowers his head in his hands, getting corned from the gin in his pocket flask before leaving his tributes for me to find, nestled like eggs in the folds of the quilt, the dipping little womb of silk that proves Tip Thomas was really there, not some goblin conjured from laudanum dreams.

I know when I am dreaming, all of those tumbling, dancing forms. I know I am awake, not dreaming now, while holding the sheets up tight to my throat, peering through the murky gloom and answering with as much hard brass as that in my metal bedstead, 'Get out of my room! You've no right to be here!'

'Oh, Pearl,' he groans in mock despair, 'we are an impertinent little minx. Why would you speak to your saviour so, the one who found you as a babe? Don't you think it's time to offer Tip some token of your gratitude . . . to warm the cockles of his heart?'

His hands are fumbling on the stand – hands with long nails – nails like knives – eventually finding the tinder box, striking it, lighting the candle stump. And, through the sudden flaring flame, I see what is perched on the bedstead's end, the glisten of red in two brown eyes, eyes like a child's, curious, round, but set in the face of a wrinkled old man. A thick-lipped, grinning, rubbery mouth. A head that is covered in tufts of grey where two pink ears are sticking out. It puts me in mind of an incubus, one of those little imps from Hell that sit on a sleeping maiden's breast until every breath in her lungs is spent.

'I don't like it. Take it away.' Hard to conceal the fear in my voice as my eyes are dragged from that monkey to Tip where, above the pale tusks of his moustache – Piccadilly Weepers, they are called – the sharply angled bones of his face are sheened with the faintest glisten of sweat, stuck with some strands of fine fair hair. Cook says that he gets her to help with its washing, scrubbing in ashes and yellow flowers, trying to lighten it up yet more. She says that where Tip and his hair are concerned he is as vain as any girl. She swears that he's got all his minerals; that Tip's lithe frame and elegant limbs might be perfumed and clad in velvet and lace, but his muscles are wiry and strong as an ox. She said she once saw him strike a whore who had dared to call him a nancy boy, who had laughed at the way he pinked his cheeks. She said that girl's cheeks were soon blushing redder, dripping with blood from the scratches Tip made, which never really healed again, an infection set in with scarring welts. And, soon after that, she disappeared.

I am thinking of that caution now, of how only a fool would rile Tip, when he suddenly tears the sheets from my grasp, whipping them back so very fast that I am unable to struggle or shout, my mouth still open wide in shock when Tip murmurs, as if he is thinking aloud, every hushed word of his questioning given the gravest consideration, 'Hmm . . . so she doesn't like her gift! What it is to have a thankless child . . . sharper than any serpent's tooth! These creatures don't come cheap, you know. I had it stolen specially . . . one of Senor Rosci's Edu-cated Monkeys. It'll jiggle its pizzle on demand. It'll do it right now . . . would she like to see?'

Tip is grinning, his head cocked to one side. 'Oh dear, have I gone and upset my Pearl? Why, she has turned as white as death. Still, some gentlemen like the consumptive type, the morbidly delicious girls. Or perhaps we could tie some wings on your back and have you play the cherub child, flitting around with a tray of cigars. In the New Jerusalem Company of Learning, Love and Liberty they have a girl who does just that . . . and a nice way to get yourself broken in, used to all the establishment's ways.'

As if such threats are not bad enough, I nearly jump out of my skin with fright when something is dropped from Tip Thomas's hand to rattle loudly on the boards – the chain attached to the monkey's neck – though Tip doesn't seem to notice the fact that his little ape has broken free. His eyes are intent on me instead, leering, yellow as a wolf's when caught in the glim of the candle's flame. Hook hands then lower to cradle my foot, to stroke the webbed flesh between the toes – that caress going on for a very long time, during which I hold my breath again and stare at the grime beneath ridged nails. The

sight of them is vile, but compulsive. I almost swoon with the
sheer relief when he lowers my foot to the mattress again, as
gently as if it is made of glass, after which he reaches for one of
my hands and asks, oh so tenderly, 'Well . . . my sweet, it's
almost time. Tell me, does she have you prepared?'

'Does who have me prepared? Prepared for what?'

'Mrs H. Has she told of our plans to sell?'

'Mrs Hibbert will *never* do that to me!' I try to be brave, but
inside I am quaking. 'She says I am precious . . . as loved as a
daughter.'

'Oh, my naive little ladybird. None are so deaf as they will
not hear. You know if the price is high enough Mrs Hibbert
would sell her mortal soul. She would certainly sell a daughter!'

He drops my hand with a sneering grin and a horrible chill
runs through my veins, but oddly enough that gives me the
courage to ask what no one has ever told, 'Am I Mrs Hibbert's
daughter?'

'What's this, are we growing curious? Has Pearl been trying
to work it out . . . whose womb *she* might have sprung from . . .
whose tit once gave her suck?'

Did someone give me suck? I'd never considered such a
thing. If it was Mrs Hibbert, if *she* was my mother, then surely
I'd know – surely I would remember.

My breathless brave response was made. 'I know it's all flam
and fabrication . . . everything written up in the Book of
Events.'

Tip chuckles softly when he says, 'The sorry tale of a mermaid dead. And Mrs Hibbert might really be French. I might
be the Queen of Sheba. It's all to whip up the trade, ma chère.'
And then, somewhat more thoughtfully, still staring through
pale and glittering eyes, 'If Madame H is to capitalise then she
must act without delay, leading you into her temple and laying
you down on her altar of love, sacrificing your virgin blood to
the devils she worships so fervently . . . Monsieur Mammon
and Madame Amour.'

'A sacrifice?'

'Mais oui, ma chère! A little death . . . a little blood. Do you bleed already, Pearl?'

I am spooked. My heart thuds as fast as a drum. Through trembling breaths I manage to say, 'Get out! Take your horrible monkey too. Get out, or I'll scream. I'll call Mrs Hibbert. I'll . . .'

'*I'll call Mrs Hibbert.*' He mimics. He taunts, 'My, my . . . what a spitfire we've bred. I have to say I admire your pluck, but then I've heard it all before. And there's really no point. You know she won't hear . . . too busy holding court downstairs . . . an evening of literature with her friends. A chapter or two of *The Birchen Bouquet* . . . or is it *The Romance of Chastisement* tonight?'

I have seen those books upon her shelves. The ones *she* reads to the gentlemen. She does not let me look inside but they are all exquisitely bound, and the lovely gilt letters, and the covers so worn they are furred, soft as velvet – unlike Tip's nails, which graze my wrist when he grabs so hard that I wince and struggle to pull away, while he hisses, 'She's down there. I'm up here with you and I'll only go when I'm good and done . . . when we've had us a bit of beano.'

His loosens his grip but I can't relax. I see through the dipping dancing light how Tip's angry features are suddenly ugly, his breaths coming much too heavy and fast when one of his hands slips beneath my shift, sharp fingers caressing my inner thighs, scratching and needling the flesh.

'No!' I am determined to scream, but his free hand is pressed against my mouth, his wispy moustache tickling soft on my cheek when he lowers his lips very close to my ear, his tone become softer, despite its threat. 'Yes! You are mine as much as hers. A mutual investment you were, a long speculation that risk we took. Now the risk has paid off, and the market is prime and . . .' A momentary wave of concern is washing across his features at a dull, repetitive thudding sound from somewhere low down beside the door, whether inside or out it is hard to tell.

Has someone come to save me?

No, my heart sinks. It is only that monkey, squatting down on its haunches in velvety shadows, one hand tugging fast on the lollipop that is standing proud as the mast of a ship. I know this performance is something obscene, that innate suspicion only confirmed by Tip's smirk when observing his pet at play. How I wish that would keep him entertained, but too soon his face leers back at me and so close there is barely an inch in between us, and those fingers still held between my thighs begin to crawl yet higher. I gasp. I think of a spider there, its black legs raking in small teasing circles until I hardly dare to imagine where they might try to venture next, when Tip whispers wetly in my ear, 'I should indoctrinate you now . . . give you a taste of the Venus arts.' His nails dig deeper, a pain so intense that I struggle and twist to free my head, at which point the fingers below are extracted and Tip is trying to gag me again, this time with both hands pressed over my face so that I am unable to breathe or speak, still forced to listen to his threats. 'You won't lose any value, you know . . . even if I do choose to fuck you tonight. I'll have the quack come and stitch you back up . . . then sell your virtue all over again. Goes on all the time in me Limehouse gaff . . . which is where you'll end up if you don't comply, sold on to the syphilitic old goats who think they'll be cured by a virgin fuck. Why, I've been some-what oozy meself of late. We could try out the cure, right here, right now. No?' He raises a questioning brow. 'Pearl's not in the mood for a tickle?'

I think he teases. I hope he teases. But what he says next is too horrible – 'And when your cunt's all coopered out, there's always the lascars and dockers around, the opium addicts too addled to care as to where they dip their filthy quills. In the end, you'll wish I'd let you drown. You'll probably finish the job yourself.'

When that revolting speech is done, his hands are lifted away from my mouth and all I can do is gasp for breath. The bile is rising in my throat. I have to struggle to swallow it down. And what a pathetic show of bravado when I beat my fists against his chest, when he laughs and turns his back on my hatred, his footsteps springy and silent as they pad towards the bedroom door, only glancing back again when he hears the crash upon the boards – the mirror framed in seashells that I snatch from my nightstand and fling his way. A hundred broken pieces of glass. A hundred twinkling shards of light. A hundred daggers to pierce his heart, if only I had the pluck to try. And Tip has an answer, he always does. 'Merde! What has she gone and done? That's seven years bad luck for Pearl.'

He clicks his tongue for the monkey to follow. A rattle as chains drag through the glass, as the beast leaps into its master's arms, and there it is cradled like a babe while Tip Thomas makes his soft farewell. 'Shall we call that Pearl's first lesson in love . . . a little taster for us both . . . a warning that she should never forget exactly where her loyalties lie? And not a word to Madam H. Least said is soonest mended.'

Today, I have not left my room. I hardly slept a wink all night, my knees folded tightly up to my chest, trying to rock the fear away, afraid of the seven years ahead when I looked at the shattered glass on the floor – when I wondered whether Tip would return to finish what he started. I have not had the heart to dress. I am wearing no more than my shimmy now as I stand at my window and grasp the bars, the ones put there when I was a babe, in case I should try to climb and fall. But I don't feel safe here any more. I feel like a prisoner in a gaol. And the watcher, 'the doorman' who guards the gate, the one who keeps the ruffians out . . . is he also there to keep me in?

I breathe the lilac blossom's scent, the sap of the trees on the pavement edge. Above them the air is singing and blue and only the faintest sewage smell, and there on the opposite banks of the Thames, the Wandsworth fields are picturesque, with sheep like little dots of white, and a church spire that points all the way up to Heaven. And even in shadows beneath the bridge where the water is rippling, black as lead, here and there the sun is glittering; flickering flashes of gold and green which reflect the steamboats sailing by, all of them decked in coloured flags as they ferry the visitors to Cremorne.

Cremorne is the place where, these past few weeks, after all these years of being confined and playing no part in the real world, Mrs Hibbert has taken to walking me out. In Cremorne she converses with gentlemen who press their lips to her black-gloved hands, upon whom she bestows her *cartes de visite* – though why she must advertise the house when Tip Thomas brings trade from the gentlemen's clubs and, every night when it is dark, so many cabs draw up outside? Very often I stand here and watch, seeing all those vaguely familiar men, always coming and going, coming and going – and Sarah, who is one of the maids, the one who mostly cares for me, insists there is not the capacity for increasing the visitors' numbers. 'Why, any more top hats in that hall and Mrs Hibbert shall need a new whore . . . and even if she had a mind, I ask you, Miss Pearl, where is the room?'

I think of that now and my head starts to whirl. Mrs Hibbert has always called me her favourite, the one for whom she has great expectations. She has said I shall never work in this house. She has said I shall never be one of her whores. And yet—

And yet, in my heart, I have known what must happen for some time. I sleep here at the top of the house, and under the strictest instructions to go up and down by the service stairs and never use those at the front of the house, the ones which the gentlemen frequent. But I am not stupid, or deaf, or blind. I hear all the thumping of bedsteads on walls, all the sighings and moans that spill under doors, and sometimes those sounds invade my dreams – and once I rose from the warmth of my bed to walk along the corridor where two enormous Chinese jars stand either side of the curtain there, the curtain that conceals the stairs that lead the way to the floor below. I pushed it aside and went on down. I crouched before a closed-up door and pressed my hands against the wood, my fingers spread wide on that barrier as I peered through a keyhole to see a room that was dimly lit with sputtering jets which glimmered on marble washstands and mirrors, illuminating the naked flesh of the man and woman sleeping there. A tangle of limbs on an unmade bed, and might that be the alabaster face of Mrs Hibbert, the house madam? I'd never seen such features before, so languorous and sensual. Such a potent animal air there was of alluring seduction and decadence. With those swags of red velvet draped around she might be an actress on a stage. The star of this miniature theatre. The queen of a sultan's harem. Scheherazade come to vibrant life from a scene in *The Arabian Nights*. Really, it seemed like a fairy tale with those pictures all around the walls – a woman who lay with a white-necked swan, a woman with legs astride a bull, its horns wound with garlands of flowers and shells, much like the little crown I wear.

I have never forgotten that scene, even though I am older and wiser now, even though I know that fairy tales can only be illusions of art. And I know there can be a 'consequence' for acting out such fancy games – and that is why the doctor comes, regular as clockwork, once a month, to sit at the scrubbed kitchen table where he looks for disease and dresses wounds inflicted by clients with tastes too exotic – though I've heard the gossip in the house, how he has some peculiar tastes of his own, but before his reward is handed out he is entirely professional. He offers potions for those 'indisposed' to make their moon bloods flow again. He hands out bottles of 'Collis Brown' to soothe the nerves of those who cry, and jars with vinegar sponges inside, pickled as if they are gherkins, and what they call 'ballons boudruches', which Sarah says are the bladders of pigs, but prettily tied at the top with red ribbons. I cannot be sure what they use them for, but I know it is something to do with 'down there' – the private tackle between the legs that monkeys and men like to fiddle with.

I hope no one tries to fiddle with me. I hope there are no syphilitic old goats, because sometimes the doctor's potions fail and sometimes a pretty face is scabbed, or a narrow waist begins to swell until it can no longer be concealed, and Tip takes the belly plea away, and who knows where to, but I think I do now. I think it must be 'down Limehouse way'.

I have learned not to get too fond or attached. There are only two constant things in this house. One is Mrs Hibbert. The other is Tip.

And now, Mrs Hibbert is at my door. I hear the hushing of her veils and the snapping crunching of her feet as they tread the shards of broken glass. She does not ask me why it is there, only murmurs gruffly under her breath, something about Sarah coming up, to sweep the mess, to clean the room. She extends an arm of thin black silk. She caresses my cheek with a silk-gloved hand and her voice is as clear as a tolling bell when she says that I must wash and dress, because we are to walk in Cremorne again.

I don't answer. I keep looking out of the window.

I am gasping, gasping. I cannot breathe.

ANOTHER LETTER FROM FREDERICK HALL
53 Burlington Row

Tuesday, April 19th 1864

DEAR FRIEND, AUGUSTUS

Forgive the delay in sending news. As you will note from this letter's address, I have recently up-sticked, as they say, though only the shortest of distances, leaving my lodgings 'above the shop' for one of the houses opposite. The intention has been to create more space. You would not believe the growth in trade – as your next remittance will demonstrate!

But far more important is the fact that, within these new walls and without the sad ghosts of memories past, you might feel yourself somewhat more inclined to accept an invitation; for the country mouse to visit the town, when I thought we could make a trip to Cremorne, where, as you will see from the cutting enclosed, a 'mermaid' is to be displayed during this coming month of May. I beg you refrain from telling the twins, even though they are well beyond the age when such things could be viewed as 'actual'. Even so I should like to surprise them. And it is very fitting, do you not think, considering your latest published work? What could be more appropriate!

However, I shall not press this point. Should you choose to decline nothing more will be said and I shall content myself once more with making my annual pilgrimage to the rural splendour of Kingsland House.

I am, as ever, Your Own True Friend,

FREDERICK HALL

LILY

So mind all fast young gentlemen, who journey to Cremorne,
Or any other gardens, or where crinoline is worn,
Do not propose to wed strange girls, however well they dress,
Or else like me you perhaps may get in such another mess,
Be sure you know her station well, before you say you'll wed her,
A little care is just as good, as good and a great deal better.

Final verse of the popular song 'As Good and a Great Deal Better'

It promised to be a glorious day, though only twenty-four hours before when we'd waited on Leominster station the air had been dreary, drizzling, grey. Not that anything could have dampened our spirits, even if the train was late, the minutes dragging on like hours, during which we had amused ourselves by viewing the posters on platform walls. One was headed up with the words *'Times Past'* and depicted a cart and a shabby horse driven by a curmudgeonly looking old man. (I suppose it was cruel that we giggled so – but that man did look very much like Papa.) The one at its side, *'Times Present'*, that showed a gleaming passenger train with great puffs of steam rising up above and the faces of passengers peering out, every one of them young, smiling, gay. To be honest, I couldn't stop smiling. I was breathless with all the excitement, though as it turned out we might just as well have travelled to London town by cart, for even when the train arrived the journey proved to be dreadfully slow, the engine crawling to a stop at every station on the route, quite belying Ellen's fears that the motion and velocity would cause such a pressure inside our brains as to risk a fatal injury – a nosebleed at the very least!

Papa had laughed and called her mad to entertain such notions. Even so, when I think about it now, perhaps Ellen Page was right to fret. Perhaps she had some second sight, some premonition of danger to come, a suspicion of Papa being ill? It's obvious now, the way he'd been tired and distracted for months, hardly lifting his pen to write a word and then, when he did, his hand trembling so that writing was nigh on impossible. Still, any fellow passengers who peered through the glass of our carriage door might only assume him in perfect health; a wholly distinguished gentleman whose long grey hair and beard were trimmed and whose suit, despite smelling of mothballs and mould if you happened to venture a little too near, was pressed so sharp it might cut like a knife – as sharp as Ellen's warnings, which kept playing again and again in my mind, as if she was really there on the train. And I think she would have been, you know, if only she'd been invited. A nod and a wink from Frederick Hall and Ellen Page would fly to the moon, she would face any peril life threw head-on – instead of which she waved us off with those premonitions of doom and gloom rattling like bullets off her tongue –

'You be sure to be careful and keep your wits. There's folk there in London who'd slash your throat for the sake of no more than a penny apiece. There's thieves who'll try to chop off your hair and sell it to barbers for making wigs. And don't you go trusting any strange men' – that said with a serious nod at me – 'there's more than one innocent country lass been flattered and charmed, then dragged to her ruin . . . her brains all addled by drugs or booze, her virtue in tatters before the next crow of the morning cock.'

When she said that Elijah laughed, and then blushed as red as a beetroot, though the joke was entirely lost on me, but the rest of her cautions continued to nag until my brother touched my hand, murmuring, so as not to wake Papa, who by then was dozing at my side, his head rolling gently forward in time with the rocking of the train, 'Little sister . . .' My brother's eyes shone silver within the dark frame of his lashes, and he offered his most mischievous smile. 'You look as timid as a mouse. But really, you shouldn't be worried at all! What does Ellen know of London life . . . except what she reads in magazines?'

He had recently taken to calling me 'little', having grown four inches taller that year, his new trousers already too short in the hem, no material left to let down again. But I didn't mind, and I had to agree, because it was true that Ellen Page had never gone anywhere very much beyond our village church or shop.

'And, of course, Uncle Freddie will be there to meet us.' The words ran smoothly off my tongue, though with every chugging lurch of the carriage my toes were wriggling round in my boots and I fidgeted back and forth in my seat. But then, as the day faded into mauve shadows, I must have dropped off to sleep as well, my cheek pressed hard to the window glass – until jolted awake with such a fright when the engine's whistle screeched so loud and I tried to look out of the window again and all I could see was cold black glass with reflections of me, and Elijah, and Papa, each one of us a silvery ghost beyond which a rolling bank of steam was flecked with glowing cinders – all that fire and whiteness through which we stepped in something of a weary daze when, at very nearly midnight, we found ourselves on the platform edge – and there was Freddie, just as he'd said, holding his arms out to greet us, as if to embrace the whole wide world.

What grandeur there was in Freddie's world! What immensely tall buildings. What breadth of streets that seemed to run on for evermore. I felt as if my head might explode from the rumbling clang of the iron-hooped wheels, and the stamping of the horses' hooves, all of the shouting and shrieking laughter that issued from those still out and about who worked or played in the hours of dark, with our own drowsy Kingsland left behind as still and quiet and dark as a grave – whereas London had lamps to gild your way, to sputter and hiss like serpents' tongues. And then, how peculiar it was to stand in a street where every tall brick building resembled the model that Freddie once gave to me, that still stood beside my bed at home – with its grand double frontage, square windows each side and a canopied porch above wide stone steps.

In London, in the world of reality, two maids, very neat in black and white, were already waiting at the door ready to carry our bags upstairs while Elijah followed Freddie in. But me – I lingered outside a while, waiting for Papa, who seemed to have fallen into a trance while gazing out across the street. He was staring at another house – exactly like Freddie's in every way except it was seeped in darkness, and there on the door was a large brass plaque, the dull metal faintly glimmering in a street lamp's sputtering glow of gas.

'What are you looking at, Papa?' I shivered while threading my fingers through his.

His voice sounded flat and exhausted. 'The offices of Hall & Co. I thought . . . for a moment he might be there. I thought I saw Gabriel looking out. But of course,' he tried to force a smile, 'that is completely ridiculous. No more than an old man's fancy.'

'Oh!' I could barely conceal my surprise. Papa told us that Freddie had moved, no longer living in the house from which his publishing business was run, but I had no idea it might be so close – the place where my parents once lived and worked, and—

And that made me feel terribly guilty, for in all the excitement of coming to London I had not once stopped to consider them, or the fact that Papa would think of his son; the father I had never known and who, however heartless it sounds, I found it very hard to mourn. I really felt no bond at all. I always thought more of my mother. But Papa still grieved, of course he did, and I saw the sorrow in his eyes when he turned to me and squeezed my hand, and I laid my head on his shoulder a while, until he eventually turned his back on that unlit memorial to lead me up the pristine steps and into a hall that blazed with light – and so vibrantly coloured those flocked walls that Ellen Page would no doubt fear the destruction of our optic nerves, not to mention the risk of a fainting fit, with the flaring flames in those hissing jets sure to suck all the oxygen out of the air.

I found myself yawning and desperate for sleep when Freddie suggested we go and eat – a cold collation in the dining room – and it looked like a banquet fit for a king.

Who could eat at such a time, almost one o'clock in the morning? The answer was Elijah, who still looked as fresh as a daisy, announcing himself to be ravenous. (In those days he could eat from dawn 'til dusk and still find room for something else.) But I had no appetite at all, already filled with a sense of discomfort, an odd sort of loss as I held Papa's hand – and how weary he looked to be just then, such a ragged, throaty edge to his voice when he said, 'Freddie . . . it is rather late. I should prefer to find my bed.'

Freddie did not argue, leading the way up two flights of stairs until we all stood on a landing where a door was opened and then closed up, with Papa disappeared behind.

I didn't know what to do. Papa had not even said goodnight. Should I knock to ensure that he was well, or—

Freddie interrupted my thoughts, now having opened another door, the one standing opposite Papa's, announcing that this room contained my bed. His moustache tickled stiff against my cheek when he stooped forward to plant his kiss, his breath smelling oddly fiery and sweet when he murmured in his deep brown voice, 'Sleep well, my dear. Tomorrow we all need to be our best. There is quite a surprise I have in mind.'

'A surprise!' Elijah was grinning at me.

'Indeed, a surprise!' Freddie echoed his words, and before I could think to blink or yawn my uncle had stepped away from me, he and Elijah descending the stairs to make their way back to the dining room – though at the turn of the landing below Freddie looked back and softly called, 'If you wake . . . if you need me during the night, my room is on the floor below . . . the one situated beneath your own.'

I had no idea where Elijah was sleeping. Like Papa, he had not said goodnight and thinking of that I lifted a hand to touch my face, to where Freddie's caress was tingling still and where, normally, Papa's kiss would be. I felt myself oddly hot and flushed, slightly afraid to be alone, grown invisible on that upstairs hall. I felt as if all of Papa's grief had leaked from his heart and under his door to form a puddle at my feet.

Such confusion when I opened my eyes, unable to think where I could be; red flowery walls, and chintzy chairs, and the paint-work a gleaming emerald green – and a maid setting down a cup of hot chocolate, brightly announcing while next engaged in folding and sweeping back shutters and drapes, 'I've been sent up to wake you. The others are already downstairs.' And then, when heading out again, she looked back from the door with a sniff of disdain. 'I do 'ope you're not the flaky type, or you might get an 'eadache from sleeping in 'ere. But then, Mr Hall likes it cheerful and lively, what with being so lively and cheerful 'imself . . . a man of extravagant, colourful tastes.'

I quite liked the room myself, though in the harsh glare of daylight I suppose it was rather gaudy. The thing that had unnerved me more was that maid being so familiar. But I very soon forgot about that, only wondering what the day might bring, quickly washed and dressed and heading downstairs from where masculine voices were rising up, and Uncle Freddie's the loudest with words like 'printers' and 'new publications', all the business that he was discussing with Papa.

The dining room was at the front of the house, very formal, rather gloomy and chill with its thick damask drapes and panels of lace preventing any view beyond – particularly the house standing opposite, the offices of Hall & Co., the door of which I fervently hoped we should never have cause to enter – knowing now how that would upset Papa, and not wanting to stir any memories that were better kept quiet, kept buried. And, on a somewhat cheerier note, those curtains created a barrier so that any of us who sat within were safely concealed from the street's prying eyes – which was probably just as well with Freddie like a beacon in red, wearing a paisley smoking gown, and a sleeping cap with tassels of silk that hung very jauntily on one side. It made him look louche and theatrical. It made him look like a magician, the ensemble carried off with style – even if it would seem ridiculous on anyone less confident.

Elijah and Papa were both attired in the same Sunday best from the day before, both seated on the left of our host at one end of a dark polished table. There, I thought Papa looked somehow diminished and no less exhausted than he had been when going to bed the previous night. His eyes were like two swollen bags of blood, his expression strained and very pale – but Elijah – my brother was nothing but smiles when glancing up to see me there, and Freddie – he was much the same, patting the empty chair on his right, saying, 'Ah, and here is Lily. Our sleeping beauty wakes!'

'Did a prince come to kiss her?' My brother grinned though I pretended not to hear, smiling at Freddie and saying 'Hello!' when I made a twirling entrance, two hands held wide to show off my shawl – a lovely embroidered Chinese silk that my uncle had sent some weeks before, though I felt much less sure of the yards of blue muslin that seemed to protrude a good yard ahead and lifted too high above the ground by the wooden cage of my crinoline. Such a contraption it was. But the draper in Leominster, he would insist that it was quite 'the London thing', showing me several fashion plates in which ladies appeared to float like bells. I felt more like a bobbing boat, and I dreaded more teasing to come from Elijah, but my brother was much too busy to look, what with having to do all that eating again, chewing great mouthfuls of kippers and eggs.

Once seated and offered a plate of the same I found I still lacked appetite and only nibbled a corner of toast, almost feeling as if I had two heads – the one full of worry about Papa, the other fizzing up with excitement, wondering what the day might hold – what Freddie's mysterious surprise could be. And almost as if he could read my mind Uncle Freddie set down his knife and fork and gave a small cough to clear his throat, which must have been some sort of cue, for one of his maids then entered the room and there on her tray was a brown paper parcel – which Freddie placed into my hands.

'What is it, Lily?' My brother set down his cutlery while I tore my way through the wrappings. He looked on with curiosity, his eyes grown wide and the twitch of a smile to see me uncover two brand-new editions of Papa's mermaid storybook which, after much deliberation, had been titled *Of Lost Mermaids ~ and Other Salty Wanderings*. It had proved to be very popular, now having sold for several years; this new edition with green leather bindings, the letters and patterns embossed in gold, and its surface as soft as velvet when stroked beneath my fingertips. In excitement I handed the spare to Elijah, my arms stretched across the tabletop before settling back in my chair again to flick through the pages of my own, where I saw my name as clear as day right there on the dedication page, and underneath it, there was my brother's, and something that made me cry out loud, exclaiming, 'Elijah! Did you know?'

As he swallowed the food that remained in his mouth the surprise on his face soon answered that, no, he really had no idea that some of his pictures were printed inside, those swirling visions in sepia tones that my brother had worked on the previous year, that Ellen Page had considered dull – she always preferring a vase of pink rosebuds, or a robin's nest filled with forget-me-nots, the sort of pretty clichéd thing that Elijah might have painted once, when he was very much younger, when Ellen liked to save each one and pin them on our kitchen walls. But Papa was Elijah's champion, encouraging originality, taking Ellen Page to task for making such blinkered crude remarks. And although I knew nothing about such things I did know those pictures were beautiful – menacing, dark, but beautiful, each beginning with simple pencil lines upon which the washes of colour were built, creating such depth and translucence – all now reproduced in this brand-new book, the sight of which rendered my brother dumb, blushing to his very roots when Uncle Freddie smiled and said, 'Dear boy, you should be immensely proud. Everyone here at Hall & Co. has been most impressed with your workmanship . . . so much so that we might discuss future commissions. And perhaps we should think to get you enrolled you in the Royal Society of Artists . . . at the very least to arrange for a tutor. It's not only the education. It's the contacts you'll make along the way, all so crucial to forging a future career.'

'Oh, Uncle . . . that would be wonderful!' Elijah's eyes glittered with excitement, bathed in his uncle's adoring gaze. But to think of my brother going away – well, mine were cast down in sudden dismay, pricked with the sharpest sting of tears. I can only say I was much relieved when Papa made the stern intervention, 'Freddie, the boy is but fourteen years.'

'Why, Millais was less than that when he trained at the Royal Academy and . . .' Freddie's challenge was boldly begun, though soon broken off with a lengthy sigh, after which came his earnest apology. 'Ah . . . Augustus. Forgive me. I grow too enthused and forget myself. I shall simply count my blessings that Elijah and Lily are here today . . . not to mention yourself, my dear old friend!'

The tinny tinkle of porcelain alerted my senses to Papa's nerves, for his hands were shaking violently while pouring some coffee into his cup. He looked down at his plate, his breaths too loud. He did not attempt to return Freddie's smile. And me, I did try to look cheerful but my heart felt as heavy as lead in my breast because for the very first time in my life I realised there would come a day when my brother might think to go away, to leave me alone in Kingsland House.

But how fickle the sorrows of youth can be, because even that cloud on the distant horizon melted away into clear blue skies when Freddie took my hand in his and announced we should make a trip to Cremorne.

*

Freddie was paying at the gate. Papa loitered a little way off, and Elijah and I were standing between, me fidgety, shuffling from foot to foot while glancing back towards the pier and the steamboat from which we had disembarked, having sailed all the way from Hungerford Bridge with the engine vibrating and rumbling below, and a flutter of flags and bells above and the constant shouts of 'Creeee-morne! Creee-morne!' I was sad when we puttered to a halt, the vessel then banging against the pier's landing so hard that I had to clutch Freddie's arm until the violent rocking stopped and, at last, we were able to disembark and return to the safety of firm, dry land where, crushed in with a small tide of humanity, we streamed along the riverside path – and then caught our very first sight of the gardens – and just like a heaven it seemed to me, with everything manicured, shining, green, and that day in May so very warm I would gladly have kicked off my stockings and shoes and paddled about in the fountains. But there would be no dilly-dallying. Freddie had ordered a table for lunch, marching us off towards the hotel, where, thankfully, there was cold ginger beer to wash down the devilled kidneys, the platters with lobster and shrimp on ice, followed by sorbets and coffees and cakes which left me so bloated and full inside I thought I should never eat again – which was when Uncle Freddie drew out his gold watch, springing up from his seat to make the announcement, 'Come along . . . come along! We must be off. We don't want to miss the aquatic displays!'

Next thing, the human dynamo had whirled us through a theatre's doors, where we were amazed to see a stage made up of a huge glass aquarium. The audience was rather thin, barely numbering more than twenty souls, but each of us 'oohed' and 'aahed' with glee when presented with '*The Beckwith Frog* . . . one of *the world's finest acrobats*', who dived into the water, gyrating among all the goldfish and eels, or else walked back and forth on his hands while consuming a bottle of milk in one – all the time with his head completely submerged!

'You didn't get that in Kingsland!' Elijah nudged my side

and laughed, and too soon the spectacular came to an end and a man called Professor Beckwith appeared – he being the human frog's trainer – and once he and his protégé had bowed, sated with our hurrahs and pattering claps, the professor proclaimed two other shows for the audience's delectation that day. I was sorely tempted by the sound of Signor Rosci's 'Educated Monkeys', which were due to perform on the lawns at three, though all thoughts of that wonder were soon eclipsed when he spoke about the mermaid tent, and what was enticingly described as being '*half beautiful woman, half fish, upon whom even the doctors cannot agree. Go, see, and decide for yourself* '.

Could he really mean a mermaid . . . an actual living mermaid? I itched for the chance to 'see and decide', my head bobbing first to the left, then the right, begging with Freddie and then Papa, 'Oh, may we go . . . may we go and see?'

Elijah was silent. A serious frown. Had my eagerness caused him embarrassment? But surely he was as keen as me, for his legs were doing that jiggling thing, and his cheeks were flushing red again. By contrast, Papa looked rather grey when he patted my arm absent-mindedly. 'Of course, my dear . . . of course, you must go. But if you don't mind I shall wait elsewhere . . . perhaps take some tea in the open air.'

I wondered whether I should stay with Papa. I wondered at least for a moment or two – but to see those tickets in Freddie's hand, and to see the twinkle in his eye when he said, 'Why don't you two go on ahead. Augustus and I will follow' – well, I wanted to throw myself into his arms, giddy and breathless, crying out, 'Oh . . . thank you, thank you, Freddie! This is the *most* perfect day!'

Elijah took the tickets and my hands grabbed his jacket tails as we made our way through the theatre doors, then on towards a red and white tent where we ducked between some canvas flaps to stand in a sort of vestibule – and no one there but my brother and me, gasping for breath before turning around to peer through the murk of the candlelit gloom, until hearing a low and husky voice. 'Well . . . let's be 'aving yer tickets, then.'

What I'd thought to be a little child was in fact a woman, very short of limb and wide of jaw, which hinted at something masculine, as did the furrowing lines of her brow above two deep-set staring eyes. There were heart-shaped patches stuck on her cheeks. She wore the most elaborate wig, like something you'd see in a Hogarth cartoon in that series they call 'The Rake's Progress', of which Papa had several engravings framed back in our hall at Kingsland House – though it always made me rather sad to see the poor rake ending up as he did, paying for his life of debauchery while confined in a house of lunatics.

I imagined that dwarf might be insane, being dressed in a miniature ballgown festooned with red ribbons, white feathers and pearls. What did *she* have to do with a mermaid? But, despite me standing there gawping like an idiot country bumpkin, she was doing some ogling herself, a good long look at Elijah Lamb before making a little curtsy when taking the tickets from his hand, proclaiming with a knowing wink, ''Allo, my very 'andsome sir . . . I am the Fairy Titania.'

More like a Tattyiana, holding that splintery stick in her hand with a crumpled glittery star on the end, and those battered white wings fixed on to her back which were stitched all over with tarnished bells, though they did make the prettiest tinkling sounds when she performed a merry dance; white feathers and towering wig of curls trembling most precariously. I feared the ensemble might collapse to land up on the sawdust at her feet. I wanted to laugh but wasn't sure whether that dance was supposed to be comical, when she waved her wand about in the air and then gave Elijah's thigh a tap, glancing up at him coquettishly before – at long last – proceeding to lead us towards the exhibits.

Once again, I followed my brother, on into a tunnel where canvas walls were gloriously daubed with paintings of Neptune and mermaids and narwhals, seahorses, serpents and hideous monsters – but all of them somewhat grimy as if they had once seen better days, as if a jolly good dip in the ocean would not go far amiss. Titania pointed her wand at a sign which read, *The*

61

Incredible Talking Fish, which, as far I could tell, was no more than a big brown carp in a tank, and who but the world's most gullible child would believe her gruff explanation that this creature was 'a phenomenon' in that it could dance upon its tail while acting out entire scenes from three of Shakespeare's finest plays!

Truly, the mind did boggle. All we could see was a gulping mouth, and when Elijah nudged my arm I had to hold my hands to mine to stop the laughter splurging out, the same with *The Gentleman Oyster, who sits smoking his yard of clay all day*, and that no more than two hinged shells clamped around a tiny pipe which, I think, when the dwarf slipped under the canvas, she must have been blowing on herself, or perhaps she was working some miniature bellows to create those belching puffs of smoke. When she re-emerged, quite out of breath, she raised her wand to lure our eyes to what was on top of a wooden plinth, what I thought the stuffed trunk of an elephant. But no, how wrong could I have been, for this particular delight was 'the genuine pizzle of a whale', of which Titania seemed very fond, stretching on tiptoes while dimpled arms stroked up and down its rubbery length – which surely measured as much as three feet! And all the while she smirked at Elijah, licking her lips lasciviously before, to our mutual relief, there were sounds of muffled voices behind and the fairy Titania waddled off, leaving us entirely alone to view the next exhibits.

They were of the pickled variety. The first was a two-headed white salamander by which we were mildly intrigued. But the next contained something so shocking to see it fairly took my breath away – two foetuses labelled as *Water-Babe Twins* whose pale flesh shone with such a transparency you could see the mapping of veins beneath. But despite their size, which was very small, it seemed that those siblings were perfectly formed, except for the thick band of gristly skin which joined them together at their breasts, along with the heart those beings shared – which looked like a shrivelled brown walnut.

Of course, I can only speak for myself, I really don't know

how Elijah felt, but I found it strange to contemplate that those tiny dead infants could look serene, as if they were only sleeping, and at any moment they might chance to wake, though if they did happen to open their eyes the nature of their deformity would mean that all they ever saw was the mirror of each other's face.

I couldn't drag *my* eyes away, standing there as if in a dream, observing every detail as if through the lens of a microscope, every pale and wavering strand of hair that formed the down upon their skin, every single tiny finger and toe – and something so pathetic to say but I felt myself on the brink of tears, wishing that Papa was there to explain. But, for then, it was only Elijah and me – and Elijah was reaching for my hand, his fingers curling tight through mine, tugging hard when he started to lead me off, as he murmured, 'Come on, little sister. Don't let's look at this any longer. Let's find the mermaid . . .'

'*If* she exists,' I butted in, and then laughed at Elijah's one raised brow, the wryest of smiles upon his lips indicating that, much the same as mine, his expectations were very low. Even so we carried on towards the ornate banner that spelled *The Wonder of the Southern Seas*, and beyond that no more than two or three candles to glisten over the spectacle – though, honestly, if you saw what we saw, well, pitch darkness would have been preferable.

I felt cheated. I felt disappointed, staring back at my brother, aghast when I asked, 'A mermaid . . . is *that* a real mermaid?'

The creature displayed was clearly a fraud and rendered even less palatable by what was placed on either side – the stuffed turtle, the morose staring sturgeons suspended from wires in empty glass tanks, and the tank with the mermaid just as dry, with dusty wax weeds and anemones and the base of the thing that was lying upon them, the thing that purported to be a live mermaid, looking to be even more desiccated than the husks of dead flies that were littered around, black legs pointing upwards like stiffened threads, black undersides gleaming with rainbows of light which put me in mind of a dragonfly's wings; such a lustrous swimming of blues and greens – but too soon that reverie came to an end because one of the insects, still being alive, made a zigzagging flight around the container, creating a horrible, high buzzing whine which rendered me yet more anxious still, relieved when the music came to an end, the fly settled on one of the mildewed panes and its legs crawling stealthily over the glass until it stopped, right in front of my eyes. Still, I tried to focus on that rather than what was lying beyond, my words coming hushed and incredulous. 'How could anyone think *her* beautiful?'

A short pause before my brother replied, and I heard the tremor in his voice, those days almost as deep as a man's with only the slightest grating break to betray the child he'd recently been, who, not so very long ago, had shared his sister's foolish belief that a mermaid might actually exist. 'She looks more like a devil.'

As we stood there, side by side, transfixed, I saw our reflections in the glass, superimposed on what lay within, such an ugly preposterous thing. Have you ever seen pictures of shrunken heads, their eyes all bulging, their noses flat, mouths distorted in lipless rictus grins, with teeth like razors, filed to points? Think of orange hair, like wool, a few strands hanging limp from a balding skull. And, as if such a sight were not bad enough, picture two flaccid shrivelled breasts, a pair of thin and withered arms, the skeletal fingers, the hands like claws. Think of its flesh as tough as tanned leather, an abdomen bloating below narrow shoulders stitched on to the carcass of a fish – a giant fish with a hard ridged spine and some shrivelled torn fins sticking out at the sides, and there, at the very end, a few scorched feathers in lieu of a tail.

That was the horror we saw that day. That was why I gripped Elijah's arm, a sliding sense of dread inside when I heard that sudden trickling sound, though I don't know whether he heard it too, and I never did ask him at the time, fearing my brother might think me mad, for such a peculiar thing it was to stand in the warmth and the dark of that tent, to know that the sun was shining outside with barely a cloud to blight the sky, and yet to hear those drip drip drips, and the air within that mermaid's tank suddenly swirling, as if filled with water, and through that eerie liquid lens something to make the blood freeze in my veins – because I would have sworn that the mermaid moved – or was it only a trick of the light, the shimmering of the candles' gleam? I was put in mind of a fairy tale, the one about a mischievous sprite who once made a mirror infused with bad magic, and that mirror possessed the power to cause '*all that was good and beautiful when it was reflected therein, to look poor and mean . . . magnified and increased in ugliness. In this mirror the most beautiful landscapes looked like boiled spinach, and the best persons were turned into frights, or appeared to stand on their heads; their faces so distorted that they were not to be recognised . . .*'

When the Beckwith Frog stood on his head the weight of the water distorted his features, just like those of the mermaid now. But, instead of becoming ugly, her monkey face had been transformed into that of a lovely girl, a girl dressed entirely in white, whose small hands were lifted to the glass, both palms pressed flat against it.

In truth, no magic had caused such a change for that vision was perfectly human. The girl on the opposite side of the tank must simply have followed us into the tent, as silent and lithe as a spirit child – and apparently no less shocked than us for she gasped at the mermaid, and then she swooned, and the watery sounds that filled my ears were drowned by the crushing hush of silks. And there she was, slumped in a puddle of fabric, the ripples of her unbound hair spreading like threads of gold around – and I found myself thinking of Tom the Sweep, before he became a water-babe, when he entered a room that he should not, when he saw a girl who he should not. I lifted a hand to my brow, where some brown wisping strands escaped my hat, the rest of my hair damp and limp beneath. And while I stood there, glued to the spot, my ever gallant brother rushed to the fainting maiden's side, kneeling down, one hand cradling and lifting her head as she let out a trembling little sigh –

though it might well have been a siren's song – the sigh that stole my brother's heart.

I knew it, you see. I knew he was lost, though no actual words were spoken, but something intense, some thrum in the air, when her green eyes flickered open again and gazed straight up, straight into his. I wondered whether that sudden faint had been nothing more than a devious act, if Elijah had simply been seduced by the pretty looks of a cunning thief who might, at that very moment, be dipping her fingers into his pockets, or did she hold a knife in her hand, about to slash my brother's throat? All those dire warnings from Ellen Page! They buzzed like wasps inside my head as I shuffled back into the shadowed gloom to conceal myself from what I viewed, feeling embarrassed, as if an intruder – until hearing some shuffling sounds elsewhere, at which the girl gave a sudden groan, a flashing of fear passing over her features before she struggled to stand again, brushing the creases and dust from her gown – just as two other people appeared.

One was Uncle Freddie – and there at his side was not Papa but a woman dressed in nothing but black, a neckline high and demure at her throat, where the only relief was the twinkling glimpse of the links of a narrow golden chain. Above that her face was concealed by veils. Not an inch of her flesh was visible, her arms and hands also encased in layers of glossy satin cloth. Impossible to tell her age. She was very slender and erect though unusually rigid in her stance, which made me suppose she must be quite old. When one of her hands touched Freddie's arm the movement was oddly staccato, and yet so familiar her approach I could only assume they had met before. And then, when turning away from him, her black fingers plucked at the sleeve of the girl, though it might be the claw of a swooping crow when it snatches a piece of carrion.

She hissed, '*Viens ici!*' – at which order her victim's stance was compliant, allowing that woman to draw her round, almost as if being led in a dance. And when both were facing Freddie again, even though it was hard to see very well, I had the distinct impression that behind her netted layers of veils the crow might well have been smiling. For his part, Uncle Freddie did nothing but stare, and for such a long time I bit my tongue, almost on the verge of blurting, *You keep looking at that you'll wear it out.* But something in his expression deterred me for he looked so terribly serious, perspiration dribbling over his brow, on past the greying hair at his temples, down over his ruddy cheeks and neck – and when I finally *did* say his name, when he eventually answered me, his voice sounded different, much too tense, 'Why, Lily . . . Elijah . . . there you are! Augustus was still feeling a little faint. I dare say it's this blasted heat. I've left him resting in some shade.'

'Oh, poor Papa. It is very hot. Why, this girl . . . she fainted too. She . . .' Suddenly indecisive and pausing, my words were replaced by the veiled apparition, her voice assured and very smooth, her tone slightly foreign and musical when she turned my way and asked, 'Do you refer to my ward?'

I nodded my assent, really too nervous to do much else, very glad when she addressed Freddie again. 'Ah . . . you see how she is. Did I not say? Such refinement is prone to fragility. A tender flower . . . so quietly raised.'

'Indeed, a remarkably pretty child.' Freddie continued to stare at the girl, who appeared to be looking straight through him, her green eyes glazed and empty, except for the flicker of candlelight that made them glitter like emeralds when the woman who held her arm replied, '*Bon!* You have the finest taste, and how fortuitous this encounter! Clearly, fate has intervened in the hope that I might make amends . . . our last transaction too tragic by far.'

What could she mean by that? What past did she and Freddie share? But no time to consider the riddle more, for the woman seemed to glance my way, veils swaying around like an inky mist through which her words were lightly voiced. 'But, I see you are otherwise engaged. We shall not delay you a moment more . . . only to give you my *carte de visite.*'

At that she dipped a black-gloved hand into the black-beaded reticule that dangled from her slender waist, from which she extracted a small white card. The sepia tones of a photograph. The glint of gold borders embossed at the edges. The tightest of smiles on Freddie's lips when he slipped it within his jacket's breast pocket.

Nothing more was said. The woman led the girl away. Titania came prancing back and Uncle Freddie glanced down at the dwarf with barely concealed disgust on his face. A good job he did not cast his eye on the horror that lay in that mermaid tank, instead of which he strode right past, and we followed without another word, no sound but the crunching of our feet on the sand of the exit tunnel floor, where a small way ahead more tent flaps opened up and I saw a vivid slant of light in the centre of which were two female forms, one very tall, one shorter, both of them wavering silhouettes.

When we emerged from darkness to light, squinting at the glare of the lowering sun, that mismatched pair had disappeared. Freddie walked all the faster, pushing his way through the milling crowds, through an avenue of spreading trees where the leaves danced above us from silver to green, where there was a table with several spare seats at which Papa was sitting, drinking some tea – smiling, insisting himself quite well, and just as if to prove the point one of his feet was tapping along to the strains of an orchestra playing near by.

The bandstand below a towering pagoda – something alluringly oriental – was surrounded by wooden decking, upon which some couples were starting to dance, and a wonderful vision I thought that to be, and all that was needed to lure my thoughts from what had occurred in the mermaid tent.

Freddie's humour was also restored after that cryptic exchange of his with the mysterious woman in black. Now, all charm and beaming smiles, he said, 'Ah, what larks! The polka! What a glamorous picture of beauty and youth!' And catching the eye of a white-aproned waiter, he called out, 'Champagne! Yes, it *must* be champagne. After all,' he offered Elijah a wink, 'this *is* the twins' special day . . . that is,' he glanced at Papa, questioning, much less confident, 'so long as Augustus approves?'

Papa looked benign and nodded assent. 'I can't see that one glass could do any harm . . . though hard to believe it has been a decade since we were all in London last . . . since that day when I came to the orphanage. *Tempus fugit.*' He heaved a great sigh, at which my mind was filled again with what Freddie had mentioned at breakfast – about Elijah coming to London.

Again the thought of growing up was something I didn't want to face. But then Elijah was changing fast, that transition more than physical, for in the blinking of an eye my usually cheery brother seemed to be cast in an evil spell, become brooding and silent, slumped over the table at my side, his expression really very glum.

And Papa – why was his hand trembling again, so much so that he tried to conceal the fact by holding it in his jacket's folds? But I'd noticed – if no one else had done – and I'd noticed how subdued he was. I felt sure he would rather have been at home with its peace and quiet and solitude – which right then seemed a million miles away, with Freddie waving his arm about and shouting at two passing gentlemen, 'Samuel . . . Samuel Beresford!'

In a flash he was standing to make introductions. 'You already know Augustus . . . and these are my dearest two young friends . . . Lily and Elijah Lamb.'

'Hello, Freddie . . . what a surprise!' Considerably younger than Freddie or Papa, my uncle's new friend appeared to be suffering greatly from the heat. He carried his jacket across one arm. His shirtsleeves were rolled to the elbows. He wore a top hat, very shiny it was, as shiny as his gleaming brow, against which was plastered some sweat-damp hair – a lovely glossy chestnut hue. He wasn't exactly handsome. His nose, though straight, was a little too large, and his chin perhaps too prominent. But those brown eyes were filled with such friendly light, and his smile was as bright as his paisley cravat. And how jaunty those peg-top trousers! I supposed he must be some 'dandy' type, and he carried the whole ensemble off with such a degree of swagger – until his nose began to twitch as if he'd been sniffing the pepper pot, his features contorting into a sneeze which was spluttered into a handkerchief, though, when that fit was over and done, he continued much as he had before – and in only slightly nasal tones, 'How delightful . . . to meet the twins today! Freddie often mentions you.'

He was very charming. I felt only drab. My blue muslin dress might be good enough to wear of a Sunday in Kingsland church. But here, in London, here in Cremorne among all the shimmering colours and light, and compared to that girl in the mermaid tent, I was surely as dull as a little brown moth in a house of exotic butterflies. For the very first time I was relieved to be wearing the cage of my crinoline. At least *something* about me was fashionable, even if it was not visible!

'Cremorne is an idyll, is it not?' Uncle Freddie was in his element. 'I love to come here whenever I can, well away from the city's grime and smog. They say a few hours spent here in the gardens works better than any medicine, that the atmosphere expands the lungs . . . as much as the imagination.' With a rumbling chuckle deep in his throat, he turned to smile at his friend again, and he on the verge of another sneeze – 'Don't you agree, Mr Beresford?'

I didn't mean to laugh. I don't think Mr Beresford took offence, giving his nose another wipe before saying, 'Forgive me . . . this wretched hay fever. I find the month of May in Cremorne not at all conducive to *my* health.'

Intense dark eyes held me quite rapt, even if they were somewhat reddened by then, and I started to grow very flustered and hot, wanting to fidget and squirm in my seat, relieved when his gaze moved on to Papa, who spoke with genuine warmth in his voice. 'Sam, I would hardly have known you! It's been too long since last we met, when I came to the office of Hall & Co. But Freddie's been passing on the news . . . all about your promotion in the firm. From errand boy to editor. I must offer my congratulations!'

'And I am delighted to meet *you* again . . . I've always admired your children's books.' The younger man glanced at some empty chairs. 'Are you expecting any more guests? Freddie always draws a crowd.'

'There was one,' Elijah broke in. Did he look expectant or petulant? Perhaps he was hoping to learn her name, the fainting girl who he had held when stating so very suddenly, 'Someone Freddie met in the mermaid tent.'

'Oh . . . speaking of mermaids,' Samuel Beresford went on, 'you must meet my cousin, Osborne Black . . . why, he's only come to the gardens today in the hope of seeing that display.'

He glanced back, calling out to the other man, who still dallied a little way behind, scuffing his feet upon the grass and looking decidedly churlish, perhaps peeved to have been ignored so long. And what a strange couple they seemed to make, with Mr Black's dress much more austere, his jacket shiny and worn at the elbows, and the front of it – what?– was it streaked with paint? He was older than Samuel Beresford, looking to be in middle age, and something too predatory in dark eyes which were set in a tanned and rugged face, around which was a growth of coppery beard, thick and bushy, so tangled with knots I wondered if it had been groomed in a year – the same with the hair upon his head.

'Ah yes . . . the artist Osborne Black!' Uncle Freddie seemed somewhat less enthused. 'We once worked together on *The Germ*.'

'*The Germ*!' I exclaimed, just as the younger man sneezed again.

'A magazine,' Uncle Freddie explained.

'Goodness,' I tried to suppress a laugh, 'it sounds as if you might catch a disease simply by picking the covers up.'

'An infection soon eradicated!' Uncle Freddie continued with the theme. 'And like many a classified disease it has . . . or had . . . a much longer scientific name. In this case, *Thoughts toward Nature in Poetry, Literature and Art.*'

At this Mr Black's voice was found. It was deep and measured and gravelly with the trace of a northern accent. 'The name was intended to describe a seed – the growth of creative ideas, if you will. At the time Mr Hall was most generous, advising on printing costs and such. But the venture was always doomed to fail. No more than four issues published . . . so much bickering, boorish behaviour . . . those poets as bad as a bunch of old spinsters.'

Uncle Freddie raised a questioning brow. 'Yes, the seedling shrivelled and died, and Mr Rossetti perhaps better employed with his painting than his poetry. And you, Mr Black . . .' the artist received a knowing glance, 'are perhaps above the lowly task of providing illustration work. But, enough of such matters for now . . . won't you join us and share a glass of champagne?'

Freddie's invitation was a command, hardly pausing for breath before going on, 'Elijah, Lily . . . now you know that Osborne Black is an artist, and Samuel employed on my magazines, as editor, writer, whatever we need, not to mention his famous recipes, which are written . . .'

'Under a pseudonym . . .' Samuel Beresford interrupted, giving an enigmatic smile while one finger tapped at the side of his nose. I feared that might set off another eruption but for then everything remained quite calm, leaving him able to carry on, a false expression of shock when he said, 'Mr Hall. You should not be divulging *Mrs* Beresford's secrets. What would our trusted readers think? What of the rumours of royal connections which have helped to boost circulation so? We really should be more discreet.'

Freddie's answering smile was equally wry. 'I doubt *Mr* Beresford ever so much as brewed himself a pot of tea. Still, he makes an adequate journalist.'

'A journalist who would rather be as fine a writer as Mr Lamb.' The younger man was serious in his flattery of dear Papa, who, very much like my brother then, was making me feel uncomfortable, too quiet, too introspective by far – become more like strangers than family.

'Thank you,' Papa replied at last, extending his hand to the painter, 'and I am most honoured to meet Osborne Black, having read a great deal of his recent success . . . the sea studies in particular. One review praised the use of colour and light as reminiscent of Turner's art.'

Mr Black condescended – or so it seemed – to reach over a hand and shake Papa's, and I saw that his shirt cuffs were grubby and frayed, the flesh thickly furred with more auburn hair, and his fingers rather stubby and thick. You would never think him the artistic type – his cousin perhaps, but no – not him.

'Yes,' the stern Mr Black went on, 'that was the general consensus . . . that my work was too derivative. Not one spark of Turner's genius.'

'Forgive me, I meant no insult.' Papa was clearly taken aback.

'Oh, it is no matter,' the artist replied. 'Those critics were right. I need to expand my horizons, to create something different . . . something new.'

While proclaiming this ambition, rather than following Samuel's lead and taking one of the vacant seats, Mr Black simply lowered himself to the grass, stretching out his long and muscular legs with the trousers quite worn into holes at the knees – at which I began to consider that he must represent those impoverished types who live all their lives in a garret, starving to death for the sake of art.

'Osborne has a calling, you see,' Samuel Beresford was explaining. 'He's recently back from the Holy Land, having hoped to seek inspiration there . . . to work in the clarity of light that they say is so extraordinary.'

'And has he returned with *extraordinary* works?' Uncle Freddie's tone was sceptical.

'No.' Osborne Black's response was sharp, that single word spoken while looking down, thick fingers engaged in the delicate task of plucking a single blade of grass, which was then placed between his lips, upon which he sucked when he glanced back up, his eyes almost black between slitted lids. 'But, I believe I shall make some . . . based on the time I spent at sea, not what I saw in that desolate land.'

'Do you know Holman Hunt?' Papa leaned forward with interest. 'Those paintings he made in Palestine were . . .'

'Cynical and commercial.' Osborne Black exhaled a sigh while raising his eyes to the heavens, as if this was a subject that bored him to death. 'I know him in passing, of course. But we have very little in common these days. The Brethren never accepted me.'

'The Brethren?' Did he mean priests or monks, what with all of this talk of the Holy Land?

'The Brotherhood of the Pre-Raphaelites.' Papa turned my way to explain. 'You have seen some of Mr Hunt's work, my dear . . . that print of *The Scapegoat* which hangs in our church?'

'Oh, yes!' That *was* a desolate scene. Such a sparse and barren landscape where you practically felt the white glare of the sun beating down on the back of the lonely goat stuck fast in some mud at the edge of a lake. Was Jesus, the saviour, waiting near by, about to help the goat escape – or was that goat a symbol of Christ, his life sacrificed for the sake of ours? I never could make up my mind, always thinking that painting less about hope, more about suffering and death, and I found myself speaking my thoughts aloud. 'Mr Black, I hope that your new works will be happier than Mr Hunt's.'

'Who knows. I shall have to find my muse.' He fixed me in his brooding stare and I felt myself somehow too exposed, as if he could see all the way to my soul, very glad when Freddie touched my hand, when I felt protected and safe again, when he said, 'Don't let Osborne Black bully you, dear. He is what they call a *serious* painter . . . and one who has the luxury of paying for any model he needs, of working whenever, wherever he wants . . . on *whatever* might take his fancy.'

Freddie had stressed the word *serious*, and not, I felt, for praise's sake but simply to highlight the irony of one who

seemed quite unable to do much more than glower belliger-
ence, whose next response was equally blunt: 'Mr Hall is
correct. Happily, with my parents being dead, I have independ-
ence, and I have wealth.'

He was certainly straight to the point! For a while, the
conversation flagged with no one quite sure how best to
respond, though Samuel Beresford did try, addressing Elijah
more trivially, attempting to draw my brother out with, 'Have
you been up in the hot-air balloon? I hear it affords the most
wonderful view.'

'No,' was Elijah's succinct reply, not appearing the least bit
interested.

'No,' I was all enthusiasm, 'but a hot-air balloon sounds
wonderful!' I was thinking that nothing could be more appealing than to go flying up into the sky with Samuel Beresford at
my side, though such hopes were soon deflated when – 'No . . .'
said Uncle Freddie, determined to stop such silliness, a puff of
smoke escaping his lips, having just lit a small cigar, 'the
balloon is not flying today.'

Hard to hide my disappointment, though I was not dismayed
for long, seeking Samuel Beresford's eye once more. 'But we
did see the Beckwith Frog . . . before going on to the mermaid
tent.'

'Oh, yes . . .' He sniffed. 'Well, that sounds to be most
appropriate, considering your grandfather's latest book . . .
and Elijah's illustrations. Your brother is quite a prodigy!
But . . .' his smile was all for me, 'you must tell what you
thought of the mermaid today.'

'She is perfectly horrible!' I said.

'Hideous.' Uncle Freddie scowled. 'Nothing but an
abomination!' But then, thankfully, the waiter arrived, and
Freddie was all smiles again, exclaiming, 'Ah . . . more glasses.
More bottles, young man. Our numbers have grown. This will
not suffice.'

That first cork made a disappointing pop and hardly any fizz
rose up. But Freddie still toasted our special day and everyone

raised a glass to clink, except for Osborne Black, that is. He remained unresponsive on the grass, even when Papa made the suggestion that the artist might come and visit one day – should he ever wish to paint rural scenes and chance to be in the vicinity of the village of Kingsland, in Herefordshire.

I cringed to see Papa so rudely ignored. But then, I was also concerned for Elijah, my brother by then staring back at some bushes, and, curious to follow his gaze, just for a moment I thought her back – the girl we'd seen in the mermaid tent. Two female shapes. One tall. One short. Both blurred by the shadows of trees around. But as they entered the path of the sun it was clear that the older woman here could not have been more different, decked in clothes that gleamed as bright as the wings of a bird of paradise, and the child being dragged along in her wake was hardly more than nine or ten, yellow hair not hanging loose at her back but a clustering mop of ringlets that fell across her dimpled cheeks. She was dressed like a miniature adult, her gown cut too low to be decent, and her face painted up with the carmine paste so that innocent features appeared depraved. And something too hectic about the flush that shone through the woman's powdered cheeks, beneath which the skin was pitted and grey, through which two glazed and bloodshot eyes first alighted on Elijah. But then, she seemed to change her mind, her glance moving on to Papa as she squawked in drunken, slurring tones, 'Now, sir . . . you look a little glum. Do you fancy my Miss Curious? I guarantee she'll cheer you up, and she's awful lonely, so she is, and we have us some private chambers near by . . . if you'd care to come and play with her. It's only a little way to walk.'

A push from her vulgar guardian and the child stepped forward and reached out a hand, and the fingers which curled around Papa's were bloody and scabbed, bitten down to the quicks. By contrast his looked like gnarled pieces of wood, with blue-slugged veins and sparse grey hairs – and that trembling started up again, even worse than it had been before.

A terrible moment that was, during which we were shocked

and could only look on until Mr Black jumped up from the grass, such expletives ringing from his mouth, shouting – no, screaming, 'Away with you. Filthy harlots! Jezebels! Little wonder they call this place Sodom on Thames!'

The intruders went scurrying back to the bushes with Osborne Black still giving chase like the devil about to claim their souls – during which Uncle Freddie, if anything, seemed to be somewhat amused. 'Surely a stern but quiet word would have been more appropriate!'

Samuel Beresford appeared to be only embarrassed, blushing and stuttering, 'Oh . . . Oh dear, Mr Lamb. How unfortunate . . . how very . . . how . . .'

When the young man's words trailed off Papa was speaking in his place, and almost as fierce as Osborne Black when glaring at Freddie with vitriol. 'This decadent place! This life you lead!'

Thank goodness he thought to stop when he did. I dreaded to think what might come next. I hated to see Papa upset, but so frosty was the atmosphere and Freddie now looking decidedly rattled, standing up, his cigar being thrown to the floor, stubbed out with the heel of his shoe when he said, 'Augustus . . . I do apologise. Such things are said to go on, of course, but only much later . . . only at night.'

He was waving his arm for the waiter again, calling for him to bring the bill, afterwards reaching into his pocket to find the notes with which to pay when that card he'd received in the mermaid tent was dislodged and fluttered to the ground, to land in the debris of his cigar.

Three people attempted to pick it up. The first was Uncle Freddie himself, but his sudden haste caused him to stumble, catching his foot on the leg of his chair. The second was Elijah, beside whose seat the item lay. And, finally, there was Osborne Black, who by then had stomped back to the table's edge, who proved to be the most agile by far when ducking down to snatch it up. And when he was standing erect again, when glancing at what was in his hand, there was such a strange look upon his face at whatever might have been printed there, the words which, despite my proximity, were far too small for me to read – though I did see the grainy photograph. It was a portrait of the girl who'd fainted in the mermaid tent.

And that was when he left us – that rude man whose nature suited his name, for even when silent, not ranting and railing, Osborne Black possessed the sort of persona that darkened the very air around, infecting the spirit of anyone near, and an aura so strong I could almost believe it had a sound all to itself. A low vibrating note it was, a humming of dissatisfaction, mournful and wanting – but wanting what? Perhaps it was what he had seen on that card, his expression become unreadable, and a hard sort of blankness filling his eyes when he bade us all a curt goodbye, saying he needed some exercise and would walk back home by the river path.

'How odd.' Samuel Beresford looked confused while watching his cousin disappear. 'We walked all the way from Chiswick before. We took the path along the Thames. But still, it must be at least ten miles . . . and to do it all over again in this heat! I'm sure my legs will be aching for days. I wonder if Osborne ever rests.'

'Chiswick is west. Mr Black turned east.' Uncle Freddie gave his blunt response.

All too soon we were travelling east as well, though when Uncle Freddie hailed a cab (to save us taking the omnibus, for which I was very grateful, that vehicle heaving with passengers and all those waiting in the queue having to clamber up on top, and how the ladies managed the steps with their skirts snagged and billowing around!) I cared not one jot where Chiswick lay, but was sad to leave Samuel Beresford, who, in the moments before our goodbyes, had taken my hand in both of his, the palm turned upwards to meet his lips when brushed with the sweetest, softest kiss – an act that quite took my breath away.

As we clattered away from the King's Road gates I squeezed my fingers into a fist, trying to hold that kiss inside. I strained to look back through the cab's smeared glass and watched Mr

Beresford walk away, only wishing he might glance back once more, to wave at me before heading back through Cremorne Gardens' iron gates, his form slowly melting into the dusk where the lovely pagoda twinkled with lights and the strains of the orchestra drifted out, and a wafting perfume from bushes near by, where white flowers were gleaming as bright as stars.

But, he didn't turn. He didn't wave. All too soon my giddy excitement was lost, brought back to my senses when I recalled that those fragrant bushes held little romance, only a painted woman and child. And when I glanced up at Elijah I felt quite as glum as my brother looked. Had he also seen the face on that card – the one that Osborne Black snatched up? I hoped he had not for I sensed that it augured something bad, that nothing was quite as it seemed to be. And perhaps it was due to that glass of champagne but I found myself feeling nauseous. No more sweet floral odours, only sweat from the horses, and piss from the horses, though I should be used to such farmyard smells with plenty of muck in the countryside. But, in London, that perfume was too intense, as if every passenger in our cab had managed to step in a turd on the pavement, and that mess still stuck to the soles of our shoes, firmly refusing to fade away.

This was the place of my genesis – mine and Elijah's too. And yet, what had 'made us' seemed alien. The shop doorways where drunkards reeled and sprawled. The ragged infants who crouched in the gutters, picking through rotting vegetables. The young girls who sold flowers by theatre doors, like the one whose fingers touched Papa's.

I held Papa's hand the following night when we stood on Leominster station again, when it seemed we had never been away – except that I felt like a wrung-out rag with hardly the strength to carry my bag as we made our way to the waiting trap. One more hour of rattling along, we descended the valley where Kingsland lay, where thin drifts of fog flowed over the fields, wreathing the hedgerows that lined the road. With the horse's hooves muffled, as if bound in cloth, we passed all the houses we knew so well, some black-and-white timbered, some new red brick. There was the post office. There was the church, and the public house where windows glowed, a welcoming light spilling over the path to illuminate the stone in the verge – the one that looked like a miniature grave and to which, when we were younger, Elijah and I were often drawn, thinking it might be a shrine for our mother, that she might still be living in the town engraved on its worn mossed surface, beneath which an arrow pointed the way: *London ~ 100 miles.*

Now, I might have thought it more, with London as far away as the moon, and when our journey came to an end, when Elijah and I pulled down the bags while Papa paid the driver, we trudged side by side up the winding drive and there at its end was Papa's house, even then overgrown with its ivy façade, and what ghosts looked back through those black-latticed windows to watch when Elijah touched my arm, and murmured his question in my ear, 'Lily, do you feel as if you belong . . . as if Kingsland House is still your home?'

'Yes! Don't you?' I froze inside. Did I really want to hear his reply?

'I don't know. When we were in London I kept thinking about our parents. And then, that girl in the mermaid tent . . . I wanted to stay . . . to be part of their world. Won't you tell me that you understand?'

'Elijah!' What pangs of jealousy I felt when giving him my swift retort. 'You know if you went it would break Papa's heart. You know he would worry, and . . .'

Papa's footsteps came crunching behind, heading on past us and into the porch. A long time he spent fiddling with the lock, twice dropping the keys down to the ground before he could let us into the house in which, I hoped, with the coming of dawn, our lives might go on as they had before.

But they didn't.

Elijah remained discontented, become strangely distant and secretive. Papa said nothing, but Ellen did. Ellen said, 'Don't you worry about it, Miss Lily. It's just that still waters run deep.

It's just that your brother is growing up. We all change. No one ever stays the same.'

I knew that Ellen Page was right. From that very first night back in Kingsland House I felt my old life leaking away. I felt as if I was dissolving, becoming something less than the whole, just as I had when Papa proclaimed that Elijah and I should stop sharing a bed, when he had taken me by the hand and shown me what, from that day on, was to be my very own separate room. A white iron bedstead. A patchwork quilt. Rosebuds sprigged across the walls. But I wanted none of such prettiness, and I cried every night for weeks on end. I missed my brother terribly. I missed his warmth. I missed his smell. I would press my fingers against the wall, knowing he lay on the other side, and sometimes I knocked and he would knock back, our own reassuring secret code that would lull me back to sleep again. But then, as the months and years went by, more often than not the answer was silence, and then I would creep from beneath my sheets and walk along the shadowed hall, praying for hinges not to whine when I twisted the cold iron knob of the door that opened into my brother's room, and if he was facing towards me then, and if his shutters had not been closed, and the night not overcast with cloud, then I might chance to see him quite clearly – his black hair against the white pillow, the red of his lips, the brown of his cheek, all lustred by moonbeams, a silvery white. I could stand there and watch him for hours like that, like a mother who doted on her child – and sometimes I crept into his bed and wrapped my arms around him, and felt his breaths upon my cheek – until the time Elijah woke, when he nudged me and whispered, 'Lily, is that you? Go back to your room.'

'But, Elijah . . .'

'I'm tired. This bed's too small for the two of us.'

I said nothing more. I did as he said. I left his room and closed the door. He didn't need me as I needed him. And when we returned from London I felt that loss again, the pillow damp beneath my cheek as I lay in my bed, in my unlit room. And when I finally did go to sleep I dreamed of that medical specimen jar that had been on display in the freak-show tent, the one that contained the pickled twins – the twins who, when in their mother's womb, had shared one living, beating heart.

I woke with such a sudden start, wondering whether those twins could have ever survived with their flesh being fused together like that. And when they were born were they already dead, or had they been smothered then and there by the midwife, who saw their deformity, who considered their murder the kindest thing? Had she wrapped those two freaks in a blanket, concealed from their mother's weeping eyes? Had she sold their remains to a travelling fair? Or had their own parents done such a thing, cruelly disposing of their babes, not caring to give them a Christian grave, not caring to think of their fragile flesh as being condemned for evermore to float in a yellow limbo land?

PEARL

Strong and free, strong and free,
The floodgates are open, away to the sea,
Free and strong, free and strong,
Cleansing my streams as I hurry along,
To the golden sands, and the leaping bar,
And the taintless tide that awaits me afar.
As I lose myself in the infinite main,
Like a soul that has sinned and is pardoned again.
Undefiled, for the undefiled;
Play by me, bathe in me, mother and child.

From *The Water-Babies* by Charles Kingsley

A week it has been, since that day in Cremorne, since the night when Tip Thomas came to my room to ask if I had been 'prepared', since when I have been waiting, every day staring out of this window to gaze at the river and street below, where so many gentlemen come and go. I watch them. I wonder, *Is it now?*

This evening an answer is made at last when Mrs Hibbert appears at my door. The delicate rustle of black silk skirts followed by heavy thudding feet when Sarah the maid pokes her head round the door, announcing through raspy laboured breaths, 'Mrs Hibbert . . . the doctor is already here . . . I've left him waiting downstairs, in the hall. And the lawyer, he said to say he's done . . . only needing to get the signatures.'

'*Bon!* What is the doctor's name?' Mrs Hibbert's voice is thin and strained.

83

'Fat Evans!' is Sarah's stark response.

'Ah . . . him.' Mrs Hibbert bows her head, her attitude more urgent when she lifts a hand and points at the maid, 'Depêche-toi! You may tell him to come on up, but . . .' she continues in faltering tones, 'no need to tell Tip . . . at least, not yet.'

A clap clap clap of silk-clad hands and Sarah is gone, the door slammed behind, creating a draught that catches in Mrs Hibbert's veils. *Hush*, they seem to be saying to me, until she coughs and breaks the spell, such a harsh and rattling sound it is, and when she begins to speak again her voice is oddly querulous. 'Pearl . . . I can no longer pretend. The time has come for you to leave. It is not what I wish, but I think . . . I think this arrangement will be for the best.'

'So . . .' I cannot begin to take it in. It is a shock. It is all too soon. 'So, what Tip said . . . so, I really must . . . so . . .' And then I am pleading, down on my knees. I can almost hear the crack of my heart when I think, *Who will tell me stories now? Who will give me Mother's Blessing? Who will tell me I am extraordinary?*

I am stunned. I am hardly 'there' at all when she drags me up and towards the bed where she pours out a spoonful of Murgatroyde's Mixture. But no promise of sleep and sweet dreams tonight. This is to remedy my nerves, to ease my panic and distress when more footsteps tread the creaking boards.

This doctor is not the usual one who comes to visit the kitchens each month. He is fat. His face is filmed with sweat. He is a panting, swanking crow. He speaks as if I am a senseless glock when requesting my bloomers are removed, that I spread my legs so that he can examine my private parts more easily. I lie on the bed like a lump of meat, almost weeping with the embarrassment – the way he is staring at my sex. I wince and give a strangled cry when I feel his fingers retracing the flesh that Tip Thomas invaded some nights before. He grins and I notice a dribble of slime running out from the corner of his mouth when he spouts, 'This intrusion is nothing, my dear. My client needs to be satisfied that you are all they say you are.

From now on you must learn to be brave and endure. No need for these whimpering complaints. In time you will find there is pleasure, not pain.'

But he lies to me, because there is pain. A prodding jab that makes me squirm, gritting my teeth at his meddling. But then the intrusion is done on the fly, almost over before it is begun. And now this man is looking down while wiping his hands on a handkerchief. That cloth is removed from his pocket with such a swaggering flourish I think he may be a magician about to conjure up a dove. But a dove is the symbol of godliness. There is nothing godly about this cove, who glances towards Mrs Hibbert again, who is standing at the end of the bed. When he nods his jowls are wobbling. Two sweaty red jellies on a plate when he says, 'Bene. She is intact. All appears to be in order . . . as far I can tell. Of course, I can't swear her free of disease.'

I'd like to tell him to sling his hook when he goes on to query the marks on my thighs where Tip Thomas's nails went needling. He asks, 'These imperfections . . . are there more . . . apart from the creature's feet? An unfortunate indication of sin . . .'

He breaks off. Mrs Hibbert inhales a breath, so sharp that her veils suck hard to her lips – through which she makes the convincing lie, 'The child scratches herself in her sleep, and the chats such a plague this warm weather too. We've had all the older mattresses burned, the bedsteads carried outside to the garden for scrubbing with the sulphur soap.'

The doctor gives the slightest of frowns. A curt bow and then he takes his leave, and the next little act in this charade is when Mrs Hibbert tells me to rise, to replace my bloomers and pull down my shimmy before she leads me out to the hall, on through the heavy velvet drapes and past the guarding Chinese jars, down, down, down through the labyrinth of stairs until we pass her study doors.

Here the walls are aheave with shelves of books, and I try to concentrate on those, but the first is too ironic to bear with its title of *Randiana – The Amatory Experiences of a Surgeon*.

Below those shelves there is her desk, before which her

screever is scribbling, blotting then holding some papers out, asking for my moniker, asking whether I understand that – *In this entitlement deed, I, Pearl, do hereby agree that I give myself into the care and protection of* . . . (and at this point the paper is empty, awaiting who knows what name) *and to confirm that I am a virgin, as verified by a physician, and that as of this day, 15th May, 1864, I have reached the age of fourteen years and have therefore attained the age of consent.*

Beneath that there is an addendum clause which says that should I disappoint, or my services no longer be required before I reach my majority, then Mrs Hibbert will have first refusal to take me back into the House of the Mermaids at half the original rate of exchange, thus resuming her role as my guardian. I can only assume that as time goes by, when my husband – whoever that man might be – has finally tired of his chavy bride then my value might lessen considerably.

Despite the humiliation my voice remains steady, solemn and low, as if I am swearing a marriage oath, though the papers are trembling in my hand and I hardly know whether to scream my dissent or to fling myself down on to the floor, to curl into a tiny ball and close my eyes and make the wish that this is nothing but a dream, a story for Mrs Hibbert to tell when she next opens up her Book of Events and makes a note of expenses incurred – with meticulous columns of numbers that list the lawyer's and the doctor's fees, all to be set against profits raised; the push for my virginity.

A sob erupts from the back of my throat – at which she tells the lawyer to leave, and only when we are alone, the study door closed with a gentle thud, does Mrs Hibbert reach for my arm. At the same time her other hand lifts the veils – and so shocking is this revelation that I feel as I if have been clocked, a pain in my breast and a cry in my throat that comes as no more than a feeble 'Oh!' through which I hear her shrill demand, 'Pearl . . . Look at me! Look at my face!'

I refuse. I jerk my head away and I hardly notice the door open up, only starting at the drawl of a voice grown much too familiar. 'Oh dear . . . not that dial on show again. Is there really any need? Such horrors will send the poor creature mad!'

He whiffs of gin and laudanum, no doubt on the ran-tan for hours and hours, almost falling over on his arse when Mrs Hibbert lashes out. But he only laughs, quite unperturbed, as if he is used to this countenance. And such a strange trinity we make when he rests his hand upon her arm and, after a moment's silence, Mrs Hibbert demands of me again, 'Look at me, Pearl. Look . . . I insist!'

One glance, one brief moment has been enough to know that the image wrapped up in my heart, the one in which Mrs Hibbert lay naked and lush on an unmade bed, soft white arms entwined with a gentleman's – that that was no more than a fanciful whim. The reality is a hideous thing, to see the elegant 'widowed' Madame as vile as that freak in the mermaid tent.

I want to bolt, but she has me trapped, her hand like a claw upon my arm, such a note of sadness in her voice. 'Don't be afraid, ma chère. I did not always look like this. Once, I was . . .' Black fingers release their hold on me to caress the lace that bands her throat and the golden chain always hanging there, upon which is linked a small brass key, though what it might fit I have never known. From there black fingers grasp my chin, forcing it up so that I must see, as she says, 'I was as pretty as you in my time. But all too soon this curse began . . . this creeping mask of the syphilis. *This* is how you must remember me, the monster who stands before you now.'

A welling of sorrow in my breast, all at once too tight; too constricted. From what sort of face had she once looked out through these eyes that are neither blue nor grey? Now, her brow is a mass of uneven lumps. Half the flesh of her nose has been eaten away. On one side of her mouth the lips are curled as if they belong to a snarling dog; a permanent sneer of blackened gums. All that remains of the hair on her head are one or two tufting ribbons of grey, as fragile and fine as spun gossamer. She might have been dug up from a grave. She might have lain there for a hundred years.

'Pearl . . .' Her voice drags me back to my senses; that lovely voice much softer now, but an undisguised note of authority when she says, 'Look at my ruin. Look at what remains . . . and only made worse by the toxic brews that I slathered on in the early years, all of the quacks' miraculous cures that ate as deep into my purse as my flesh. My last resort was the use of this veil . . . though it does add a certain je ne sais quoi.' Her chuckle is throaty and bitter. 'I removed myself from the public eye and found some new employment here. I made myself a mystery while awaiting the final one of death . . . the summons that comes to us all in the end, though perhaps the cloven-footed old goat won't be able to see me under these . . . won't force *me* to jump from . . .'

'Hush, old woman!' Tip hisses his warning.

To be honest I had forgotten him here, still focusing on the single word that has struck such a dagger of fear through my mind, recalling Tip's tales of raddled old men being cured of the pox by a virgin fuck.

'Syphilis?' My heart is racing. My flesh is cold, dreading to think of that ravaged face as simply a mirror of my own; the future I have to look forward to. But at last I find the courage to ask, 'Am I really to be sold . . . given to some diseased old lush?'

I start to cry. The tears stream hot across my cheeks where I suddenly feel the slap of silk. Not too hard – after all, the flesh of the peach is spoiled when bruised – but pressure enough to shut me up before her fingers swiftly drop, renewing their grip on my arm once more while Tip Thomas releases his hold on her and begins to pace around the room, sighing his exasperation, running a hand through his long fair hair, eyes darting from us to the door again when he warns, 'I knew there'd be trouble . . . all of these years you've been spoiling the girl, cosseted and moddley-coddleyed and . . .'

'Tais toi, tais toi!' She spins round, spitting her answer back at him. 'You! What would *you* have done instead? Would you be so happy to damn her soul, the same as . . .'

As what? I am never told for she breaks off mid-sentence to face me again, the harshness of peppermint scent on her breath mixed with the noxious stink of decay as her twisted lips whisper close to my ear as if not wishing Tip to hear, 'Pearl, you must believe, ma chère. What I do this evening I do for you . . . to give you some hope . . . to escape this house.'

'But this is my home, living here with you. Mrs Hibbert, please . . . what else do I know?'

She draws away from my embrace. 'There is a great deal you do not know. But you will learn. We all do in the end. I give you this chance to be redeemed . . . to be free of me . . . to be free of Tip. I want you to be respectable, to grow up and make your own choices in life. This night will find your protector and patron and . . .'

'And,' Tip interrupts, 'one who is able to pay the fees, to reimburse your expenses here.'

Beneath Mrs Hibbert's Medusa glare, a wonder Tip does not turn to stone as she swiftly counters his remark. 'Safe from those who might seek to lay *other* claims, who might try to take you for their own . . . then share you with *anyone* who pays.'

At this, she takes my hands in hers, 'If I could change these things, I would. This is the best I can do for you now. In time, I think you will understand.'

'But I *don't* understand.' I wrench my hands free. 'Why can't *you* go on protecting me?'

'It would be crueller to let you stay. I know *everything* that goes on in this house.' She flings another acid glance towards where Tip is standing now, resting his arm on the back of a chair, perfectly languid and nonchalant, and almost a smile on his rouged red lips when Mrs Hibbert carries on, 'Men are like dogs, driven by their noses and tails! *That* dog will chase you to Hell if you stay.'

'Then make *him* go. I shall miss it here. Mrs Hibbert, please . . . I shall miss you.'

She groans. 'I shall miss you, ma chère. How could I not after all of these years. But now it is time to unlock the cage and let the little bird fly free.'

'Shall this melodrama go on all night? Shall we cancel the main performance and invite our guests to this jolly instead?' Tip's derision cuts sharp through the air. 'Just get on and tell her the truth . . . just tell her that times is hard, ma chère.'

She takes a step back, away from me, visibly stiffening her pose before she draws those veils back down and spends some moments arranging their folds until no one would guess at what lies beneath, or that Mrs Hibbert conceals a heart, or how her eyes burn red with tears.

'Pearl . . .' her voice is controlled again, 'you are soon to meet your protector. But while the lawyer deals with him there are others arriving here tonight who have paid a great deal to attend your sale . . . to bid for your virginity, which was in fact the original plan before an alternative arose. To postpone or cancel the main event would only cause us detriment. We need to protect this house's name, the belief in our integrity. What- ever may go on to occur, you must only remember the deal has been struck. The man who has bought you awaits elsewhere. He is not so old . . . and . . .' She pauses now, as if pondering how best to continue. 'I believe him to have certain passions and needs, but not the ones you might expect.'

'You might say the same of me!' Quick as a shadow Tip Thomas is back, taking my arm in his sharp claw hands and dragging me towards the door while Mrs Hibbert calls behind, 'Go, ma chère, and remember my words. Deceive them all. Be extraordinaire!'

I have no slippers on my feet, my ugly webbed toes are on display as Tip leads me across the hall's tiled floor and on through the room with the muralled walls, and into the big glass orangery, a procession as slow and decorous as in those romantic tales I've read – of a father leading his daughter to church, to meet her groom on her wedding day. We pass all the pots of lacy ferns that form a green aisle on either side in a room as darkly lit as a church. And here is the congregation, though I do not dare to look their way. I keep my eyes fixed straight ahead. I think the drug must be taking its hold for I find myself to be oddly soothed by the splash of the fountain, like music, hypnotic, and when tiny droplets of water spray out they shimmer like crystals on my arms. I look at those jewels and start to shake when I hear Tip Thomas murmuring, 'Don't think I'll forget you. Whatever she says . . . wherever you happen to go tonight. You know you'll *never* be free of me. You're my queen bee. You're my honey trap. I found you before, and I'll bring you back. When the old queen is dead . . . and it won't be long.'

I give Tip Thomas my sullen response, swearing the oath he does not want to hear. 'I'd rather die than suffer that. I hate you, and I always will.'

'Oh, how she breaks my heart.' He laughs. 'Well, be plucky and smile at the toffs instead.'

I nearly jump out of my skin right then, at the echoing patter of all the claps that bounce back and forth on the crystal walls when the veiled madame appears again, following us through that aisle of green to do what she's done so often before, when she places the crown of shells on my head. And that is when I lift my eyes to see the audience around, all the raddled brows and drooping cheeks, the eyes that leer through sunken lids as those coves lounge like sultans on Turkish divans where low japanned tables hold pineapples, and cut-glass goblets are filled with champagne, and iced silver platters hold mountains of oysters, and beside them the painted wooden stands made to resemble Negro boys, each one with a turban on top of his head, and really very little else, except for the trays held high in their hands, upon which are pipes carved as dragons or snakes, and ebony boxes filled with tobacco, or snuff, or cigars, or opium.

How lavish this hospitality. How pungent the vases of lilies around, though the perfume makes me nauseous. It makes me think of the rotting flesh that ribboned Mrs Hibbert's face; even more so the cloying scent of the candles which, when a door opens elsewhere in the house, dip and smoke alarmingly. Flames shudder and glisten on sweating brows, on all the slimy bear-greased heads; enough oil there to form a small slick in the Thames.

Some of these punters I recognise from all of the monthly dinners before. Others are new, lured in by the cards, from those times Mrs Hibbert walked me out, none of them knowing themselves a mug, that the deal has already been signed and sealed, when the black widow's voice rings out like a bell as she tells the old tale – for the very last time – all the wonders and miracles of my birth – *There once was a cabman who worked Cremorne Gardens who, come to the end of his shift for the night, was about to head home across Battersea Bridge when he saw an angel flying by* . . .

In the glimmer of dark glass above I imagine black feathers floating down. I am dazzled by my reflection there, my face haloed in gold from the candles around, my arms raised high above my head with its garland of rosebuds and silver shells.

Another attack of nausea. I squeeze my eyes shut and swallow hard, trying to keep myself grounded and calm, trying to pretend I am elsewhere, perhaps even rising up into the air and melting through the crystal panes, clutching on to the hands of my mirrored twin as the two of us fly as high as the stars, grasping the tail of a meteor as it streaks its way to Margate beach. I can almost believe the racket true, that I am the spawn of a mermaid's womb, a changeling washed up in the oyster beds, gleaming and white and innocent, as pure as the pearls after which I was named, now trapped in this tissue of vile deceits spun out to the lawyers and bankers and lords, the officers from Birdcage Walk, every one of them contemplating my price while somewhere else, in another room, Mrs Hibbert's whores are patiently waiting to compensate those who will be disappointed. I can hear their twittering laughter. I can hear a piano starting up. And I think of the white cockatoo in its cage, its crested head being cocked to one side as it balances on one grey scaled leg. Gripped in its talons there is a nut. *Crunch.*

Snap, the shell will crack, a sound that always makes me flinch – though tonight I hear only the plash of the fountain, and the rustle of Mrs Hibbert's skirts as she walks past divans and offers each man a new *carte de visite* upon which to write his numbers down. And when everyone has completed that task, Tip Thomas gathers in the bids, and Mrs Hibbert stands at my side about to announce the auction results.

I see my own face looking out from the picture clutched tight in those silk-sheathed hands, a photograph taken last Christmas Eve when she had a man come into the house, to set up his tent and camera stand. For advertising purposes, that's what Mrs Hibbert said at the time, providing her most popular whores with mementoes to offer their clientele. But mine . . . I thought my portrait to be a private remembrance for her, not a means of luring in new trade with the promise in that ornate print: *A unique opportunity to possess one of Nature's rarest jewels.*

If I am a jewel, that jewel is black. If I had been spawned by the River Thames then how much of its filth have I swallowed down, and how much of it oozes from me still? My belly aches, as if full of grit, the grit you might find in an oyster shell, an invisible but constant reminder that whatever my outward appearance may be, however shiny and new I might seem, deep down I will never be clean again.

Mrs Hibbert calls a name. Someone stands and when I dare to look I see through a spinning tunnel of fear something I cannot comprehend, because this is the gardener employed at the house, the old man who comes three times a week to tend all the ferns that grow around, the old codger who, for this one night, has been dressed like a toff in a dinner suit, though he looks like he'll choke on that white silk cravat, like a murderer condemned to wear a noose, when his warty hot hand is holding mine and Mrs Hibbert leads us out, back through the room with the mermaid walls where the whores all sit in silence now.

Some eyes are hard as granite. Others are damp and glittering. I walk past them and try not to look. I cannot begin to say goodbye, and too soon I am in the study again, and there the

93

old stooge goes on his way, a brown paper package clutched in his hands, and Mrs Hibbert helps me to dress in the clothes that someone has brought down, and in no time at all we pass the baize, descending to the basement floor. But the kitchens are strangely quiet tonight. No cook. No slaveys singing songs. It is as if some plague has struck and every doomed body has been whisked off, except for Mrs Hibbert and me – and the man who is lurking beside the hearth, who steps out of the shadows where sheets drip grey like sobbing wraiths, when he reaches to take my hand in his, when he says,

'You are my mermaid.'

And now, some months later, he says it again. A candle flickers at his side, trembling in the concentrated breaths of the man who draws me on his page, though I try my best not to meet his gaze in case he has somehow been transformed – turned into one of those lecherous gents whose lustful eyes all fed on me that last night in the House of the Mermaids. To think of them still makes me shiver, though that could be the air down here, so cold and clinging and furtive it is, and the blackness, it seeps into my mind, and there is a moment my memory freezes. I cannot remember where I am . . . what *are* these walls, all patterned with shells?

Ah yes – we are in the grotto, and once, or so Osborne told me, these shells would be coloured and lustrous, but now every one is a uniform grey, sooted with oil from the lamps around.

None of the lamps are lit today, but this is how Osborne prefers to be. He likes this darkness through which his voice is growling and echoing around, repeating itself again and again: *My mermaid. Mermaid. Mermaid.*

This is how he is when he works. I try to grow used to his serious ways, how he constantly mutters under his breath, things like, 'I must . . . I *will* get this right. To think that I found you . . . only by chance . . . I knew, when I saw that calling card . . . when I saw your picture in Cremorne. It was a sign . . . don't you see? Your destiny to be my muse.'

He is as deep as Australia.

Somewhere, outside and above us, the wind is wuthering. It might almost be the sound of the sea with the faint cutting cry of the gulls overhead. I miss the beach, all our walks on the sands; sunlight and watery wind in my eyes. Down here I am blind as a sewer rat, hidden away in this warren of tunnels, hired out for Osborne's exclusive use.

'Who built it . . .' I wonder, 'this cave of shells?'

'No one knows, but they all like to make a guess. It could be a rich man's indulgence, a folly created in Regency times. Or it could be an ancient temple, and the ledge upon which you are lying right now might once have been the altar stone where virgins were brought to be sacrificed.'

Like a story from *As Every Day Goes By*, like one of Tip Thomas's horrible threats? What if these shells have tasted blood! It makes me afraid to think such things, for Osborne does have some peculiar whims. Would the ticket collector hear me scream – with him at the top of the steep stone steps that lead on down to this grotto's depths? What ancient magic might they hold, all these cockles and muscles and oysters and whelks to which Osborne points, as if chanting a spell: 'This panel depicts the tree of life. This is a rose . . . a phallus . . . a serpent . . . this one here, this is the horn of a ram.'

I see only hearts, and flowers, and stars.

There were stars in the skies on the night we left London; and me near to fainting from nerves and exhaustion by the time we entered the hotel doors. Osborne requested adjoining rooms, but the bleary-eyed receptionist stammered his earnest apologies, because he could only offer one, at which Osborne grew brusque and came up with the lie to make such an arrangement respectable. He said he was my father.

A key was taken, a door opened up, and he sat in a chair by a window and necked down a bottle of brandy. Even so, when slurring drunk, he still behaved as a father would. He did not lay one hand on me – at least not until the morning came when I'd spent the whole night awake at his side, trying not to move a single inch for fear of disturbing his snoring sleep, my nose assailed by his hot sour breaths until he turned over and lay on his side, when he dragged off the sheets and left me cold.

Come the dawn, it was freezing the balls of brass monkeys. I didn't feel up to snuff at all, and my heart was really very low to see the soiled walls and the tarnished jets, the curtains too skimpy to draw quite closed; nothing at all like the opulence to be found in the House of the Mermaids. And when I finally did nod off it was only to wake with a jerking gasp at the banshee screeching of the gulls that perched on the window's balcony – and then the weight of Osborne's hand when he pushed some hair away from my brow, when I heard the thudding thump of my heart, my mind a panicking whirling ask of, *Will it be now? Will it be now?*

When he raised himself up on an elbow I focused my gaze on his fingers. No one would think they belong to an artist. They are stubby and thick, and the backs of his hands are downed with a bearish coppery hair. I thought I should swoon and take a turn when he tugged at the ribbon of my shift and then pushed the fabric below my breasts. One thumb painted an invisible line to circle a tautening nipple. He brought his bearded lips to mine, a scratching and tickling it was, and more inhalations of rancid breaths as I tried not to cringe, as I tried not to retch, but oh so relieved when he flinched away, as if something in me was repulsive to him.

How contrary I was when that act of rejection seemed to be worse than whatever I'd dreaded might happen next, because what if he came to change his mind and decided he did not want me now? What if he returned me to Cheyne Walk? Would Mrs Hibbert give me to Tip? Would Tip take me off to his Limehouse gaff?

My turn to shudder then, watching as he sat on the mattress edge, his feet like the roots of two great trees, his back hunching forward, as still as a statue, until his brusque apology. 'I'm sorry. I can't . . . I . . .'

His face twisted back to look over one shoulder, and I saw

the tears that ran from his eyes, like diamonds they glittered on his skin until lost in the thicket of his beard. And it was a queerly intimate thing when he reached to touch my cheek again, when my own hand also rose, my fingers curled on top of his, and I felt so peculiar just then. I felt as if I was a mother who sought to console her suffering child.

Today, in this temple, I feel that again, a response to the vulnerable note in his voice when he stares from behind his easel and asks – oh, so solicitously – 'Are you cold? Are you comfortable?'

I force myself to make a smile and stare right back into his eyes, gleaming, intense in the candle's glow as he works with his pencil and charcoal sticks to capture the nuance of light and shade – what he calls a 'chiaroscuro' effect. I try not to fidget or change my pose, though, really, if the truth be told, the blanket on which I am lying affords very little protection against the damp now rising up. My hands and feet are growing numb, my legs all a-tingle with sharp pins and needles, unable to move for the wrappings of silk to emulate my fish's tail. But my eyes – my eyes are all my own, still able to turn as they look to the left and then to the right, on up to the little circle of light that leaks through a hole cut into the dome that rises above this cavernous space. Could it be the circle of my escape?

Osborne pauses in his work. Perhaps he senses my discontent. Perhaps the sketch does not go well. He is standing and then he is groaning, his arms stretching high above his head. And then the looming shape of his hand, stained fingers clenching his charcoal stick, so tight that his knuckles grow white with the strain when he holds it level to measure my features; the length of my nose, the width of my brow. Any moment that stick might snap in two. He might snap me in two, like a blade of grass. And, as if he possesses some animal sense, as if he is able to smell my fear, he purrs his deep and growling assurance, 'Don't be frightened. You must never be frightened. I have no intention of causing you harm.'

Then why did you buy me? What do you want? Is it only to have me to pose like this?

He says it again, 'My mermaid.'

I want to say, No, I am just a girl . . . just a girl who has webbing between her toes. Mrs Hibbert has made a mug of you with the spouting of all her fantastical lies.

He says, 'If I could spare you discomfort . . . but I have to capture this scene more precisely. It will be dramatic, don't you see? The mermaid sleeping in her cave. Everything gleaming, black and gold.'

So earnest he looks, his brow deeply furrowed in stern concentration, below which the whites of his eyes are streaked red, the lids around them bruised and bagged. Are mine the same, after all the upheaval and change in my life, every night only snatching at drifts of sleep, always lying awake and wondering, *Will it be now? Will it be now?*

When I do sleep, I dream of a day in Cremorne, of a mermaid, a mummified leathery freak – not warm and alive as the boy had been, the boy who held me in his arms, the boy with dark and curling hair, and nothing of malice or greed in his eyes, the palest eyes I have ever seen. How I wish I'd been able to ask his name. How I should have liked to tell him mine. How I should have liked to be his friend. But, of course, such things are impossible. I am not like other girls. Mrs Hibbert and Tip have made sure of that.

And yet, I have not been defiled. I am still the virgin child who was secretly handed to Osborne Black – Osborne Black, who whisked me away in a cab, which ferried us off to a railway station, from where we boarded a late-night train. And how strange that the omen did come true when we followed the trail of the meteor and ended up at Margate beach, a place that I shall be sad to leave – with the sands and the candy-striped swimming huts, and the steamers putt-putting, tooting past. Sometimes I think this little town might be busier even than London with the thronging of crowds on the promenade, and the ting-a-ling bell of the omnibus when it stops beside the big town clock – and that clock with the chimes that strike the hour, like the bells from the church across the Thames that I always heard in Cheyne Walk.

I miss the House of the Mermaids.

Living with Osborne can be too quiet, especially since we left the hotel when he rented a cottage, high up on some cliffs, all craggy, with narrow ledges and pathways, overlooking a lonely shingled beach. On each of these blue summer mornings he leaves me there and walks into the town to fetch fresh rolls and papers and milk. He brings me a cup of café au lait to drink while he opens the windows wide to let in the bracing salt sea air. And before I dress he starts his work. He sketches me while I lie in the bed, every part of my body, from every angle. But since that first morning, in the hotel, he has never tried to touch my flesh.

Still, this is a kind of honeymoon, a holiday, I suppose you would say. I have ridden the donkeys on the beach. I have collected pebbles in baskets, picked from the frothy white foam on the sand. I have eaten dishes of jellied eels while watching the Punch and Judy shows. But such childish pleasures all came to an end that day when the weather began so warm, when Osborne woke me up at dawn and, with no other souls near by, we descended the steep winding path to the shore and stripped off our clothes and went into the sea.

It was marvellous, that feeling, though at first I only gasped for breath, not expecting the water to be so chill. But I soon grew used to the temperature, and Osborne said he would teach me to swim, and how thrilling it was to be floating like that, first held in his arms and then free, on my own, though the moment I found myself out of my depth, touching a foot to the shelf of sand – which suddenly was no longer there – I started to panic and thought I would drown, flailing around as the swell pulled me down, until Osborne's hands gripped my hips again and lifted me, holding me high in his arms while I spluttered and blinked the salt from my eyes, while I laughed and said, 'Osborne . . . you look like King Neptune!'

And he did, with that great wild beard of his, and the water running through his hair, streaming over his face and into his mouth. He smiled and carried me back to the shore. He set me down upon the sand. He said, 'You are my mermaid.'

It was then I noticed the swelling of flesh as it rose through the shadowed mass of dark hair, his cock no longer concealed by his drawers, the wet cotton become translucent. Strange to say, but I wasn't unduly concerned. I did not think it augured lust, only excitement to be on that beach, to be at one with the elements. I no longer had the slightest fear that his motives and passions were less than artistic. So, when he asked me to pose again, I was perfectly happy to follow his lead, stripping off my clinging shift and spreading it over a rock near by, upon which to lie lest the heat of the stone try to scold my flesh – for already the sun burned in the sky.

Osborne fished for ribbons of seaweed. He draped them over my hair and breasts. He asked me to lift a shell in my hands, and hold it up against one ear. And it seemed I heard the whole wide world, its every living thrilling breath, while I watched little rivulets winding their way through the zigzagging furrows etched wet in the sand, all the froth-flecked wavelets that nibbled my toes as I gazed into the depths of a pool that was formed by rocks that circled round. The water's surface rippled and danced. Beneath it the scuttle of small brown crabs, and a starfish, bright red, and the darting black fish that played hide and seek through the shifting ferns – waving ferns that might be a mermaid's hair.

I suppose I was too intent on that, and Osborne on his sketching work, to notice the bloke descending the path, that receptionist from our old hotel who'd arrived with some of Osborne's mail. I turned to see the sprays of sand thrown up behind his running feet, the shingle stones crunching, scattered like rain, falling as hard as the shouts of abuse, words about Incest, Lust and Shame. And I don't know why but I thought of a story that I'd once read. *The Water-Babies*, I think it was called. I really hadn't liked it, what with all that talk of sewers and slime, of mothers and children defiled by sin.

Mortified, on the brink of tears, I was desperately trying to gather my clothes, attempting to cover myself again, though Osborne showed no urgency, slowly setting down his work before standing there, naked and shameless; his fists clenched like rocks against his sides before lifting them in a threatening pose. Really, he looked ridiculous, posturing like some burly, bare-knuckled prizefighter, and such blind aggression in his eyes that our visitor turned on his heels and ran.

Back at the cottage we found all the letters, torn up and scattered beside the door. Some of the windows had been smashed. Osborne groaned to see that wanton destruction. He set his bag down on the step. He lifted an arm to shield his eyes when he turned to stare out across the sea, where the sun's reflection was dazzling, a wavering line of the sheerest gold that drew your eye over the water's depths to where, on the distant horizon, the blurred sails of a boat could just be seen.

I said, 'I don't care. I was happy today.'

He spoke as if I wasn't there, reciting some lines from a poem he knew, 'A light upon the shining sea – the Bridegroom with his bride!' His voice became tight with emotion. 'Why should we endure these insults . . . all of these narrow, pathetic minds? They're philistines. They know nothing of art. They fester in false piety . . . when you are pure, when you are . . .'

He broke off. He looked back at me again, and such a yearning in his voice. 'Would you like to go away from here . . . to a place where the sun shines for most of the year, more beaches, more grottos, and wonderful paintings, and no one to question our being together?'

He didn't wait for my reply but then his mind was already made. And now, while arrangements are finalised, we keep ourselves away from the sands. Osborne brings me here, to this grotto instead, where he pays to ensure no prying eyes, where the slab of damp stone strikes up through my bones, where I am cold and miserable. But Osborne must work. He says he must work, or else be consumed by the darkness again, and then he is driven to madness.

And what can I say as an answer to that, when this grotto is nothing but darkness?

PART TWO

LILY

That face, of Love's all penetrative spell
Amulet, talisman and oracle –
Betwixt the sun and moon a mystery.

From *'Astarte Syriaca'* by Dante Gabriel Rossetti

Six years had passed by. Six years and we had not seen Freddie, not once since that visit to Cremorne. And although Papa could never be drawn on any precise explanation it was not hard to guess at the cause; most surely Uncle Freddie's bid to lure Elijah away from us, and whatever the motivation, however sincere his intent had been regarding my brother's future, I knew his behaviour was tactless – considering that Papa's only son had been lost while in London, in Freddie's care.

Not that Papa was a vengeful man. Neither was he prone to flights of superstition, but I sensed he preferred not to give fate the chance of repeating itself all over again. And although his decision to make that break was personal, it was never professional. On the matter of publishing his books, Papa's links were retained with Hall & Co. – but via the postal service. His manuscripts were all copied out (more often than not in my own hand) and then wrapped in sheets of brown paper and sent off to Burlington Row.

Now and then Elijah and I included personal letters too, to thank Freddie for the gifts he sent – for me lovely perfumes and jewellery and lace, the most ornate of hats and shawls in which I would waft around the house, or cause the old ladies' jaws to drop when visiting the village shop, as la-di-da as anything when requesting a twist of sugar or tea.

For Elijah there were more practical things: paints, brushes, charcoals, sketching blocks – as if not to let my brother forget that Freddie foresaw his future in art, even though Elijah showed no further interest in illustrating Papa's books. And sometimes, he simply disappeared, not showing his face again for days, which caused Papa and I a great deal of distress – until we heard from Ellen Page that Elijah was working out in the fields, picking hops, or making hay, or busy with sowing his own wild oats. Well, I may not have fully appreciated the true implication of her words but I could not help but register the moony-faced girls who looked his way whenever we went to Sunday church. And it wasn't that I was jealous as such, but whenever Elijah was not around I missed him more than I could say, and I hoped any money he might have earned was not being saved for a train fare to London – because then he might never return again.

Even those times when he was at home he rarely emerged from his bedroom, what with all of the drawing and painting he did. Now and then I was invited in, my brother sketching my likeness while I lay on his bed and read a book, and sometimes I read the words out loud as if that imaginary stream of thought could build a wall around us both, or perhaps it was between us, negating the need for him to speak, to tell me about his adventuring; those new games from which Lily Lamb was excluded.

But I knew some secrets in his mind. Those times when I laid my book aside and sneaked a glance over his shoulder, curious to judge how his work progressed, when more often than not I would chance to see not an image of myself at all but a lovely girl with glass-green eyes and long waving tresses of golden hair. *She* did not smile at him in church. *She* did not work in the fields around. No one in our parts looked like that – though as far as Elijah was concerned, it was almost as if he truly believed that by drawing her likeness again and again, by some magic she might yet materialise, right under our noses in Kingsland House.

There were times when I truly wished she would. She might warm that secret discontent, the splinter of ice in Elijah's heart which did not truly start to melt until the year when we reached seventeen, when two gifts arrived which opened the doors that led us into 'other worlds' – and those doors, for a little while at least, drew my brother back to mine.

That May Uncle Freddie sent two wooden boxes. The one labelled up for me was what they call a stereoscope with tantalising instructions that promised the gift of binocular vision. When you looked through the lenses on the front and into the darkness of the cube, whatever the photographs placed inside – my selection included Italian scenes, the Roman Colosseum, the bridges of Venice – they all had the illusion of real height and depth as if in a three-dimensional form, only in Lilliputian dimensions.

Elijah and I loved those pictures. We longed to see such places ourselves. We imagined our mother being there, and perhaps that is what Uncle Freddie intended, to keep her memory alive – though such fancies did not amuse Papa, who thought Freddie was up to old tricks again.

Elijah's box was much larger. It had gleaming brass handles on either side and was set on a kind of trolley, with wheels. Inside was a camera and tripod stand, and a tent to place on top of that which would form a portable darkroom in which to process any slides whenever the photographer was out and about. There were shelves with buckled leather straps to secure all the flasks for the chemicals. There were trays for fixing and 'washing off'. In short everything that he might need to create a 'flying studio' without which, from that day on, my brother was rarely seen; his paraphernalia dragged behind when taking pictures of village life, or roaming through the fields and lanes in search of more natural subjects.

When the various techniques had been mastered Elijah's compositions were wonderful. Such depths of shadow and luminous light created with wet collodian, and though Ellen Page only tutted and scowled when her scullery sink and pantry store were sequestered as a 'development' room – the windows gloomed with dark red paint, the shelves now lined with more glass jars full of volatile liquids which were stinking of ether and alcohol, with a spirit lamp over which to concoct the magical photographic brews – well, for all the old woman's dire mutterings of explosions and deaths from noxious fumes, she became as enthralled as Elijah was, next to me his most ardent assistant and aiding all his experiments – preparing the albumen paper for prints with coatings of egg whites mixed with salt (and so many jars of lemon curd being made from any unused yolks that we had to give most of them away!). She really didn't mind a jot that her aprons were blotted with sepia stains. With such gusto did she fling herself into sourcing the costumes and all of the props used for creating his 'classical scenes', even deigning to wrap herself in sheets and to wear a false beard upon her chin when she posed as the ancient Methuselah, who was said to have lived nine hundred years, which I think was Elijah's private joke, remembering that time when we were young when Papa had teased and we believed that Ellen Page was one hundred and ten.

Not even Papa was immune to the lure of the camera's magic eye. He posed as Don Quixote, the hero sitting alone in his study and dreaming of empty victories – for which he wore trousers cut off at the knees to give the effect of pantaloons, stuffed into which was a nightshift of mine, the one with voluminous puffing sleeves. (Not one of Freddie's favourite gifts.) As a backdrop we pinned up some old damask that we'd found in one of the attic trunks, and I painted a windmill to hang on the wall while Elijah made armour from papier mâché; a breastplate and helmet that looked most convincing, and a lance that he'd carved from a fallen branch. The greyhound that lay at Papa's feet had been loaned from Ellen's sister, whose husband once used it for hunting down rabbits, though of late it did little but sleep and snore, growling and farting whenever disturbed – whenever the shadows became too dense for a picture's exposure to be assured, when Elijah would set a lighted match to a twisted strip of magnesium, the unpredictable flare of white creating a spluttering fizzing sound.

Fizz! Elijah was taking my picture, or rather he fiddled with his reflector and yet more strips of magnesium which either refused to light at all or sizzled ineffectively to leave the air hanging thick and grey with acrid fumes of swirling smoke.

I was to be an Ophelia – inspired by the painting by Everett Millais, the one in which Hamlet's doomed mad love was depicted as drowned in a flower-strewn brook though, for reasons of practicality, I did not pose in our garden stream despite Elijah doing his best to try and persuade me otherwise. We had settled instead on the open tomb (that looked like a horse's water trough, only in this case it was perfectly dry) which was built against one gloomy wall inside the Volka Chapel; a small annexe attached to the church's main porch, just large enough for the camera to stand and beside which Elijah was tightly crammed, right next to the chapel's altar.

Outside it was sultry, a hot August day, but I shivered in that cold dank tomb. I was doing my best to look mournful – and dead. Both of my eyes were tightly closed. Both of my hands were crossed at my breast, which was sheathed in the finest muslin cloth; an old dress from another attic trunk that had once belonged to our grandmother, wrapped up in white paper, perfectly preserved, and fitting as if it was made for me. I wondered what age she had been when she wore it – if she had also been twenty years.

When I'd asked Papa he could not recall. Papa was starting to forget.

I tried to forget Ellen's story about the Volka Chapel tomb – saying that it once held the bones of a nameless woman and newborn babe. But in one of his rambling sermons when I was still a little girl, the vicar had distinctly said that the tomb had never been used at all, but was what they call a 'symbolic' grave, a memorial for the Wars of the Roses when, in the battle of Mortimer's Cross – a field, no more than a mile away – over four thousand men were slain. It had been a time of great tragedy but one of signs and wonders too, for that day came a portent magical in those moments before the battle commenced, when all of the soldiers were praying to God to make their side victorious, after which the heavens began to glow with the light of not one, but several suns.

A 'parhelion' – that is the scientific term. A sun dog the more poetic. But then, being so young at the time, I imagined an actual dog in the sky, and only when walking back home with Papa, when I must have mentioned such a thing, did he throw back his head and laugh and say, 'Now, Lily, *that* would be a sight to see! Such an occurrence is very rare, but nothing to do with a real dog, and certainly not a miracle . . . whatever the vicar chooses to think. It happens when the air is cold and crystals of ice form high in the clouds, and when the sun shines through them, and *if* all the angles of light are just so, then the rays begin to diffract and spread, much as they do when a rainbow appears. But instead of seeing an arch in the sky those soldiers saw many coloured stars. They say to look on such things brings luck and I dare say it did for the Yorkists that day – all those soldiers who carried battle flags embroidered with symbols of the sun.'

'Well . . .' I pondered a little while, 'that *sounds* like a miracle to me!'

'It does! And I wish I could have been there.' Elijah, very quiet 'til then, now spoke while staring up at the skies, which that Sunday hung dense with a low grey cloud – and much too warm for any ice. 'Will you tell us more stories like that, Papa?'

Papa reached out and took our hands, and with one of us standing on either side he tilted his head to look up at the sky and recited some lines from a Shakespeare play –

Three glorious suns, each one a perfect sun;
Not separated with the racking clouds,

But sever'd in a pale clear-shining sky.
See, see! They join, embrace, and seem to kiss,
As if they vow'd some league inviolable:
Now are they but one lamp, one light, one sun.
In this the heaven figures some event.

'What funny words!' Elijah said. 'What a funny thing . . . for suns to kiss – and why did those men fight over Rose? Was our grandmother really so very old?' And then, without a moment's pause, he leaned across Papa and kissed my lips, and I screwed up my face and batted him off, complaining loudly in mock disgust while Papa just stood there, staring up, and—

That memory rushed vividly into my mind when I lay stiff and cold in the empty tomb, while Elijah coughed and waved his arms to dissipate the magnesium smoke and a bright ray of sunlight came shafting in through the Volka Chapel's window. I had to squint through slitted eyes while concentrating on holding my breath, trying hard not to sneeze from the scent of the flowers that Elijah had placed around my 'corpse', a few of their stems threaded into my hair, out of which little insects were crawling, tickling over my forehead and cheeks. Unable to stand one moment more I lifted my hands to brush them off, at which my brother sighed with frustration. 'Lily, you're fidgeting again. Now the exposure's bound to be blurred. You'll look like a ghost . . . half disappeared, or some goddess from the Orient with twenty pairs of arms.'

A second slide was set in place. The cap of the camera was removed and I stiffened myself not to move an inch even though my nose continued to itch and, for some reason, I don't know why, while Elijah counted the seconds down I found myself musing on Freddie's friend, the one called Samuel Beresford, and how he had sneezed again and again when plagued by the pollen in Cremorne. But such thoughts were interrupted when I heard the sharp thudding of footsteps on gravel and I made the hushed whisper while rising up, scattering petals all around, 'Elijah . . . someone's coming. What if it's the vicar?'

My brother froze, then muttered low, 'He's supposed to be in Leominster . . . visiting the hospital. Ellen asked at the rectory yesterday.'

'We'll be in trouble if he's not. Quick! Kneel down. We'll say we've been praying. We'll say we've been collecting these flowers to put on the family grave.'

'But what about the camera?'

I had no answer to that, hastily snatching up the blooms and, as the state of our panic increased, as the footsteps grew louder upon the path – oh, what a relief it was to see none but Ellen Page herself, a wrinkled brown potato face peeping around the porch's door, panting and puffing when she said, 'Come on home, you two. There's visitors! I've already set the kettle to boil but . . .'

'Is it Freddie?' Such spontaneous excitement there was in my voice at the thought of seeing my uncle again.

'No.' Ellen returned the sternest frown. 'Some gentleman calls himself Osbert . . . or was it Oswald? Oswald Black?'

'Osborne Black!' Elijah broke in. 'Lily, you must remember. The artist we met that day in Cremorne.'

'Oh . . . yes.' I remembered *him* very well, but what was he doing at Kingsland House?

'You must hurry and come,' Ellen pressed again. 'Mr Lamb was most insistent.'

Worrying then about Papa, I left Ellen with Elijah, she helping to pack his camera box as I headed off through the churchyard gate and ran over the field that led to our house, and soon, having crossed the stream's wooden bridge, I arrived at the end of the gardens, waiting a moment to catch my breath and brushing down my flimsy gown while peering through tangles of shrubbery to see Papa standing within the frame of the drawing room's veranda doors – and Papa must have seen me there, calling out with a tremor in his voice, 'Lily . . . is that you? Where have you been?'

Of late, any unexpected events caused our grandfather undue distress, setting off that shaking in his hand – and now it was back, grown more pronounced when Osborne Black appeared at his side – though I wondered if I would have known him again, without Ellen's previous intelligence. His broad muscled figure was much the same, though perhaps he was running a little to fat; a fact not entirely undisguised by the finely tailored jacket he wore, beneath that black trousers, striped with green, and no crumples or streaks of paint that day. His hair had been neatly cut and oiled; a dark gleaming red in the afternoon light. And the great bushy tangle of beard and moustache that he'd sported when we previously met had been trimmed to expose an unsmiling mouth, all at once sullen but sensual. To be honest, while walking towards them both, I felt as unnerved as Papa looked, my eyes become locked with Osborne Black's when I heard the deep resonance in his voice, still edged with the bluntness of northern tones, 'Miss Lamb, I presume? Well, *you've* certainly changed. I remember a skinny, plain mouse of a girl.'

I blushed and hoped he could not see that I wore no shift or petticoats beneath my ancient muslin dress. I was not so skinny any more.

'Please, excuse my husband's bluntness.' The next voice I heard was lilting and low, those admonishing words softly spoken as another emerged from the house's dark shadows. 'It is Osborne's way to speak plainly.'

This time the eyes that stared were green, and whereas *he* dressed conventionally her apparel, like mine, was anything but. Having also disposed of stiff corset constraints, her slender frame was only enhanced by the narrow flowing shift she wore, a shape reminiscent of classical Greece rather than any English belle. Turquoise silk draped from her breasts where a placket was richly embroidered in gold, below which some criss-crossing ribbons were tied.

She could have stepped out of a painting. If she was a fragrance, if she had a smell, then it would be lemons and jasmine. She looked so sleek that she might have been frosted, and the darkness of ivy and blossoming white of the rose that trailed round the drawing-room doors provided the perfect foil to accentuate her milky skin. Her eyes were like jewels, like emeralds, against which the lushness of gardens around seemed only to fade to a dullish grey. Such a sensual fragility, so lovely she was. There could never be two who looked like that – like the face upon the *carte de visite* that an artist once stole from Frederick Hall—

She had called Osborne Black her husband!

My dazed state of shock was fractured when 'Oh,' she exhaled a sudden gasp, just as Elijah and Ellen appeared; the old woman scuttling off to the kitchens, my brother still pulling his camera box, the wheels being jolted behind on the lawns making a dull sort of thudding sound while the vessels inside it tinkled and chimed, while Mr Black watched and Mr Black smiled. 'Ah, this must be Elijah Lamb! Your grandfather has shown me some of your work. I must say I find myself impressed.'

Elijah – who looked rather slovenly then with shirt tails pulled loose above trouser tops, and his hair become snagged with willow leaves – stopped short in his tracks and appeared confused, glancing first at the artist and then his wife, his mind surely filled with the same memories that had recently flooded back through mine. *The freak-show tent. The fainting girl* – the girl who was now a young woman, though that woman could easily pass as a child, and how sweetly serene the smile she gave when Papa next ventured to make introductions.

'Elijah, Lily . . . I'm sure you recall Mr Osborne Black? That day in Cremorne when . . .' He paused, and looked terribly anxious, perhaps thinking himself of the moment when a child had reached over and touched his hand – how aggressive the artist's reaction had been. But at last he continued more forcefully, 'And this is Pearl . . . Mrs Black . . . his wife. They are going to stay for a cup of tea.'

He suggested we sit at the big garden table, to which Ellen

Page soon brought a tray, and I started to pour her over-stewed brew into the very best china cups – and such a grating on my nerves, cringing inside at the rattling sound when I passed those cups and saucers round, worse still when Mr Osborne Black began to stir his sugar spoon, scraping and scraping the base of his cup. There was some cake, but very dry. Only Osborne Black accepted a slice. I found his slobbering mastication to be intensely irritating, yet further dismayed at the catch in my voice when I turned to address the artist's wife. 'Mrs Black, it has been such a long time since we made that visit to Cremorne. I fear my memory grows dim. Were you also there, in the gardens that day?'

She lowered her gaze to the table and said, 'Please, you must call me Pearl. And, no, I have never been to Cremorne. I was raised by my parents in . . .'

'I met my wife in Italy.' Brushing crumbs from his lips with the back of his hand, Osborne Black made his brusque inter-vention. He lied more easily than she. 'That is where my recent paintings were made . . . the ones of the mermaids, with Pearl as my muse. But now, with my fame here in England, we saw no reason to stay away.'

Papa asked, 'Are you living in London now?'

'We are currently residing in a hotel but shall soon move on to my Chiswick home . . . Dolphin House situated upon Thames Mall.'

'Oh, dolphins!' I exclaimed, gaining courage through the momentum of words. 'Do dolphins ever swim in the Thames? My grandfather once wrote a book about a mermaid who did just that. My brother created some illustrations, and –' really my persistence was terrier-like; a wonder that I had the nerve – 'did you go on to see the stuffed mermaid that day . . . that day when we met you in Cremorne? She really was repulsive. A wonder some people didn't faint.'

I gasped at the sharp and sudden pain when my ankle was struck by Elijah's foot, but no stopping the flow that had begun, for Papa continued after me, 'I think, before they leave, our guests should be presented with a copy of *Salty Wanderings*. And perhaps they would also like to see the original illustrations.'

'Thank you, Mr Lamb,' Pearl Black was all grace, 'I should like that very much. When I was younger we took all the weekly magazines and some of your stories were serialised, but I don't think I know that particular one.' And then, as if realising some error, she hastily added, 'My family had all the journals sent over from England to Italy. Of course, they were always out of date.'

She offered Papa the sweetest of smiles. It might almost have been flirtatious, but something too desperate in her glance when it fell upon Elijah again, where I thought it lingered a little too long, and Elijah held hers, just the same, his cheeks very red against dark curls that still framed his perfect features then.

Osborne Black appeared not to have noticed, too busy with speaking to me and Papa. 'No, Miss Lamb, I did not see the mermaid. And kind though it is to offer, viewing illustrations for children's books is not the point of my visit today.'

'The point?' Papa's tone was cautious.

'We met Frederick Hall last week . . . an affair at the Royal Academy. It was he who happened to mention your grandson's gift with photography, reminding me of your kind invitation to come and visit Kingsland House.'

Concern washed over Papa's face. 'Freddie always did have a good memory.'

An uncomfortable silence followed, until Elijah eventually said, and with only the slightest catch in his voice, which I dare say no one noticed but me, 'You must tell us, Mr Black . . . how is Uncle Freddie? We have not seen him in such a long time.'

'And your cousin,' I said, 'Samuel Beresford. Is he also married now?'

Whatever devil possessed me that day, being so eager to hear the news, not only of Frederick Hall but of a man met the once before – and to ask such a question, so openly!

'Frederick Hall is as he ever was. And Samuel . . . I really have no idea. I imagine he still works for Hall & Co. He's never struck me as a man of ambition. Too much of the dilettante. Too spoiled by his mother to think to wed. But then, he and I have not met in years, not since that afternoon in Cremorne.'

'Mr Black, you have strayed from the point of your visit,' Papa broke in, his voice tremulous, to which Osborne Black gave the swift reply, 'Indeed I have, and it is to ask if Elijah might come to work with me . . . assisting in my painting work and also employing his camera skills.' All at once he was urgent and passionate, his gaze fully intent on Elijah. 'Photographs can be invaluable as a reference for the artist's eye, as an aid to truth and fidelity. Do you see what I mean? Do you not agree?'

'Osborne?' His wife's features were drained of all colour. 'You made no mention of this before.'

Deep lines of irritation furrowed the artist's brow when turning then to answer his wife, 'Frederick Hall and I talked for some time on this subject . . . or was your butterfly mind elsewhere?'

'But you said you must work in complete isolation. You said . . .'

'I *need* a studio assistant.'

'But surely I can help.'

Her husband's groan was too audible, his patronising answer low. 'Pearl, this is hardly the time or place for dissent. You are my muse. You are *nothing* else!'

She lowered her eyes like a guilty child, seeming to shrink into herself, and meanwhile her husband turned to Elijah. 'Well, what do you think? As my wife says, I'm a plain-speaking man and from what I have seen of your work today, you have talent enough to suit my needs.'

Elijah glanced swiftly at Papa – Papa, whose voice was strained and thin, who reached out a hand to touch a white rose that was growing against the wall near by when he said, 'How can I stand in your way?'

My ears filled with the droning buzz of a wasp as it circled some fallen crumbs of cake, little sugary stones on the tabletop.

'Papa . . .' That was Elijah's voice. 'Papa, I think I should like to take up Mr Black's kind offer.'

'I shall need to know before we leave.' Osborne Black made his rude interruption, apparently not in the least concerned at Papa's visible show of distress. And perhaps Papa was right not to argue. Perhaps he knew – the same as me – that whatever we said to the contrary, Elijah would want to go away, that this was an opportunity of which most could only think to dream. But even so, there was something wrong – wrong with this husband – wrong with his wife – this young wife who suddenly caught my eye and made the suggestion which, afterwards, I came to think must have been an attempt to warn us – 'Shall we go for a walk, in the gardens, leave the gentlemen to their discussions? Your brother has much to consider . . . many more questions he needs to ask.'

She had a question for me as well, asked when we walked across the lawns. She said in her lovely lilting voice, 'Is that the sound of water?'

'Yes . . . a stream. Would you like to see?'

She smiled her assent and soon we were ducking through branches of willow, stepping over the clumps of white bog lilies before she knelt down among some ferns, removing her shoes and then standing again, silk skirts hitched high above her knees, at which I quickly averted my eyes, for how brazenly she showed her flesh.

The water was shallow that summer. Where she paddled, a silty mud swirled round, clearing again when she stood quite still and leaned forward to peer at the spot where some shells still adhered to the damp mossed walls.

'You have your own grotto!' She smiled back through the dappling shadows until suddenly flinching, as if in pain. For a moment or two she bit down on her lip before letting out a lingering sigh, and then that guarded note in her voice when she murmured, 'Osborne must not see this place. He would only want to paint me here.'

'I remember before, when we first met your husband in Cremorne . . . I remember him talking about the sea.'

'The sea . . . streams and rivers . . . any form of water . . . and always painting me as a mermaid. For private collectors, for galleries. You would not believe the sums they pay. But he keeps far more than he ever sells.'

She looked down to where water was lapping her ankles. It might be liquid manacles, the silver circling the flesh, so white that it took on a greenish hue from the vegetation grown around, enclosing us both within its cage. She held me in the cage of her eyes. She asked in a very solemn voice, 'Do you not find that strange, to paint the same person, to set the same scene again and again?'

'I suppose it must be romantic, to inspire an artist, to be his muse.'

'But strange,' she persisted stubbornly.

I stared at this creature who stood in our stream, thinking back to the time when the grotto was made, when Uncle Freddie sent us shells. Now, he had sent the mermaid too. But the mermaid was never meant to stay – only there to entice my brother away.

I thought back to Papa's fairy tale and how the ending had to be changed when, instead of dying all alone, when the mermaid reached out with her fingertips to brush them against the dragonfly's wings – *the air all around her fractured like glass, a splintering shimmer of blues and greens, and through the lustrous gleam of that magic the insect transformed into something quite other, becoming a merman who lay in the stream, who held her gently in his arms and kissed her parched and cracking lips. The sweetness of his salty breath filled her lonely soul with bliss. And then, with a great splashing flick of his tail the dry dam of that muddy stream was breached, and together they drifted on down to the river and from there all the way to the sea.*

Was the merman her father, or lover? That question only

then occurred as Pearl splashed her way to the shingle shore, soon having clambered back up the bank and sitting again among the ferns, where she used skirt hems to dry her feet. And that's when I noticed her toes were webbed, quite stunned to see such a deformity in one who was otherwise perfect – indeed so surprised that it took a while to register that the green of her gown was streaked with stains of vibrant red.

'Your foot . . .' I said, 'it's bleeding.'

She touched a finger to her heel, afterwards lifting it close to her face, staring a while at the glistening wet. 'It's almost stopped. I think I stepped on a broken shell. It's nothing. I rarely feel much pain.'

She slipped her shoes back onto her feet – during which the question gushed from my lips, 'Will you go back to London now?'

'Yes, Osborne is desperate to work again, while we still have the summer months ahead. The house in Chiswick has been repaired. The roof had been leaking . . . among other things. A great deal of water damage done. Do you . . .' She was standing by then, her eyes very serious when she asked, 'Do you think your brother will come . . . only . . .' She paused, her expression grave. 'Only Osborne can be such a passionate man. About his art, I mean. But also . . .' She broke off and we heard the toll of the church's bell, a sound that carried across the field – five doleful chimes to strike the hour, after which she spoke more hurriedly. 'Is that the time? I must get back. Osborne will wonder where I am.'

'It must be very flattering, to have so attentive a husband.'

Why did I say that, too forward by far? I was testing her. I was also intrigued as to how such a marriage had come about.

Her answer was oddly matter-of-fact. 'Handsome is as hand-some does.'

The bearishly handsome Osborne Black was admiring Elijah's photographs, those which were framed on our drawing-room walls. With so many shadows draped around the three men in that room looked like silhouettes, every trace of colour and light leached out. Mr Black and Papa were then engrossed in some new conversation, but Elijah must have sensed our return for he turned and walked back to the garden doors where he stared beyond me to gaze at Pearl, who followed on the lawns behind. And it lasted no more than a moment – that look between the two of them – but it was enough for me to know that she also remembered a day in Cremorne.

In the ivy a blackbird was singing. I looked up, past the glossy dark spread of the leaves, my eyes narrowed against the glare of the sun, which hung very low, like an orb of fire.

They say you should never look at the sun, and perhaps my eyes were damaged then, for what else could explain that blurring mist and the wondrous sign that then occurred, when it seemed that not one but two stars shone down.

See, see! They seem to kiss . . . the heaven figures some event.

PEARL

Six years I have been with Osborne Black. I am twenty years old. He is forty-one. The difference does not seem as great as it did when he blagged me away from Cheyne Walk, when all of the lies and pretence began.

That first summer we spent in Margate, and then we travelled on to France, and from there we went to Italy, where Osborne took rooms in a Florence hotel: such lovely rooms; and every one bathed in the Arno's glow. You could sit there and watch all the rippling shadows, the river's flickering dance on the walls. You could think yourself to be immersed.

In Florence he still told any who asked that I was his daughter, my mother long dead. He did not encourage friendships. We kept ourselves to ourselves. He said I must learn to be seen and not heard and to cleanse my tongue of obscenities, and if I forgot he would shout and scold, 'You might look like an angel . . . you sound like a whore!' He took to punishing my indiscretions, slapping my cheek so very hard that it would redden up and burn. He would snatch at my wrist and pinch the

122

flesh, which bruised into black and purple welts. I didn't care for those manacles. They made me feel like Osborne's slave. I soon took to learning what was allowed – holding my tongue, biting down on my lip. No more *fuck me's!* or *Blooming 'ells!* I could imitate the plummy toffs who used to visit in Cheyne Walk. I knew a smattering of French. But even that was not enough because Osborne went off and bought a book, the one with advice on etiquette – how to talk, how to eat, to be modest and meek, and all bound in the leather covers of *The Manners of Young Ladies, Abroad or at Watering Places*. Well, we were certainly abroad, and Osborne liked anywhere watery, but I hated those worn old pages with their petty and prudish suggestions. I imagined what Fat Louisa might say to – '*a lady should never join in any rude plays that will subject her to be kissed or handled in any way by gentlemen; ie: If a hand reaches out to admire a breast pin, draw back and take it off for inspection.*'

I'd seen hands reach out for more than pins, and a secret is only a secret when you don't have anyone to tell. And anyway, who did I have to tell, my lips as mute as the mermaid who sold her tongue to a wicked witch? I had no friend but Osborne Black, and he never really talked to me, only rabbited on about his art. *My* past was to be a closed-up book. My present was nothing but bland repetition, soon taking on the firm routine whereby every evening we dined alone, and every day we wandered the city, often finding our way to the Boboli gardens. There Osborne made countless sketches of me, and I felt myself lost in another world, such verdant plantings, such glorious fountains with statues of nymphs and ancient gods rising up from the depths of slimed green pools – as romantic as any one of the paintings adorning the walls in Cheyne Walk. I liked the stone dwarf, grotesquely fat, his tiny genitals exposed while sitting astride a turtle's shell. Osborne liked the grottos, all decorated with coral and shells, and more mythical figures half-born from stone, and every one guarded over by Neptune; the tyrant, long haired and long bearded, his trident held high in threatening hands – much as Osborne had looked on Margate beach.

During the first dank Florentine winter, too cold for us to walk for long, Osborne's obsession with churches began. Even though he observed no religion as such he was as serious as a don, studying the paintings and statues while I stood obediently at his side, inhaling all the odours around – the ripe stench of lilies, the sweat from hot bodies, the beeswax exuding from candles and polish – smells just like those in the House of the Mermaids – except there were nuns instead of whores. I watched all their slow processions. I listened to their beautiful songs, not bawdy tunes from the music halls but prayers, soft and hushed as a mantra. I felt safe in those sacred palaces, all the pillars of sculpted marble, all the altars dressed in opulent lace, the gleaming gold crosses, the saints and apostles, and everywhere I looked there was Mary. Mary the mother – no mermaid, no whore – and her face bathed in harlequin colours of light which broke through the stained-glass lights above, to wash every one of my sins away.

A more secular Madonna we found on the walls of the Uffizi Gallery, where the painting that Osborne admired the most was called *The Birth of Venus*. And again, I was nostalgic, thinking too much of Cheyne Walk when I saw that goddess born from the sea, rising up from the womb of a scallop shell, her cheeks faintly flushed, one coy hand at her breasts, and only long strands of golden hair to protect her modesty below. She was blessed by the flowers that drifted around. She was clean. She was white. She had not been dragged from the filthy Thames, tarred with the mud of the oyster beds.

'Who is she?' I asked in a whispered awe, quite as entranced as Osborne then.

'Simonetta Vespucci,' he mumbled back. 'She was renowned for her beauty. Botticelli painted her constantly. He was devastated when she died. I believe she was only twenty-three.'

'That is sad. That is much too young to die.'

'Why sad . . . when he made her immortal, forever preserved

in his paintings? This is how I would like to paint you . . . to make *you* something remarkable.'

A tingling shiver of memory: *You must be extraordinaire.*

I still missed Mrs Hibbert, no matter how Osborne indulged me then, always buying clothes and jewels, and silks for my embroidery. How cosseted I was. Why, the slightest little sniffle resulted in a doctor called, and no expense was ever spared for whatever tonics, tinctures or creams might be prescribed to cure my ills – whether real, or in Osborne's fancy. So overprotective this 'father' of mine.

I suppose, in that, he remains the same. But in other ways his affections have changed. While his girth grows thicker each passing year, his belly more pouched, his muscles more slack, he has begun to restrict my food. Sometimes I have nothing to chew but toke – and no butter or jam to give it taste. He does not want my limbs too round. He does not want my breasts too large. He hates the sight of my hair, down there. Whenever he paints me as a nymph he insists I shave it all away, 'to resemble the smooth pudenda of Italian marble goddesses'.

How it prickles and itches when growing back in. It is like a constant reminder of shame. Do you know that in Latin pudenda means shame? I read that one day, in another book. And shame was the very emotion I felt when my monthly moon bloods first began, confused and not knowing what best to do, and Osborne's behaviour shocking, his face turning almost blue with rage, shouting at the top of his voice, 'You stink like a whore. You stink like death! Get out of my sight until you're clean.'

That one change in me wrought many in him, and no matter how often I washed and bathed I knew I would never be clean enough. He did not love me as he had. From then on, once a month, I was cloistered away in my room like a nun, weeping alone at the aching cramps and craving for sugared indulgences like the sweetly melting almond cakes that Cook used to feed me in Cheyne Walk.

But then came the time when someone else would choose to

indulge such appetites, even if Osborne Black did not, because Osborne thought cakes would make me fat.

It started just over two years ago. Osborne said he was tired of our hotel. He leased a small secluded house set in the city's outskirts. He no longer took me out walking. No more visits to gardens or galleries. No more crowded, bustling, sunlit streets where men called from doorways, or whistled and winked whenever we passed their market stalls, or stared with black and glittering eyes through the incense in churches which coiled around, causing Osborne to bristle and stiffen with rage.

He never called or whistled for me. He only looked when he painted – more often than not in our courtyard, which smelled of roses and lemon trees. There was a pool with golden fish, and loggias tangled with dripping vines to conceal us from carnal, prying eyes – except for those of Angelo, the ten-year-old son of the housekeeper, who arrived with her every morning when he worked in the garden and swept the leaves. He had the face of an angel, a pink-cheeked imp with tousled curls, like a painting by Caravaggio. I teased him. I called him my *putto* – one of those luscious cherub boys that cluster in every religious scene, that make you want to pick them up and kiss their bee-stung, pouting lips.

Osborne was just as fond of the boy, soon employed to assist him with his work, from then on sleeping in the studio, fetching his master's food and wine, learning to crush the plants or stones to make up the pigments for the paints. He began to prepare the canvases too, which Osborne was often too quick to discard because when a painting did not go well he thought nothing of taking up a knife and slashing a whole month's work to shreds.

I suppose, with such behaviour in mind, I should have been wiser, I should have restricted my shows of affection, in return for which Angelo brought me gifts – those delicious cakes that his mother baked; pandoro wrapped in white paper parcels, flavoured with orange and looking like starfish, or the buttery moist gubana with all sorts of sticky fruits inside. I hid each one away in my room, eating at night, in darkness, relishing every secret bite, always careful not to leave a crumb in case Osborne chanced to see the sheets – though he rarely left his studio, or else went out and about alone, meeting with the agent he employed to ship the best of his work back home, along with the artefacts he bought; mostly old paintings and sculptures. From such evenings he would often return with his face deeply flushed, his breath stinking of wine, or drenched in an alien perfume. It hung around, on his skin, in his hair. I knew it well from Cheyne Walk. It was the smell of sex and sin.

One such night, when I'd heard him going out, feeling restless myself and unable to sleep, I left my room to wander the house, coming at last to the studio door, where I looked in to see little Angelo, still working there by candlelight, cleaning the brushes, palettes and knives that Osborne had used for his work that day – all those hours when Angelo's curious eyes had shifted between what appeared on the canvas and my living, three-dimensional form. And perhaps a whore's blood did run in my veins for I never felt any embarrassment, but then I'd posed naked so often before, simply grown used to passing the time with reading books, or stitching my patterns of gold on silk, my mind wandering off into reveries. And, during that particular day, my reverie had been to wish for something different to occur, to relieve the aching tedium of the unchanging daily routine of my life. We should all take care what we wish for.

Angelo's wish was to paint, and even when his master said that the boy lacked any talent, there was nothing could subdue his desire. So that night, when I stood in the open door, when Angelo looked back and saw me there, he smiled and asked in his piping voice, 'Signora, you mind . . . you sit? I make picture? Osborne, be 'appy, you think?'

How could I think to say no? I let my nightgown fall to the floor and arranged myself on the sofa. I swear there was nothing more – though, perhaps, had the boy been older – had Angelo

127

been any bolder. But such a day would never come. Osborne Black made sure of that.

The light was dim and fading fast. Long shadows were curdled over the drapes, over the paintings propped against walls, over me, and over Angelo. The boy was silent, immersed in his work. I think I must have fallen asleep – suddenly waking in alarm to see Osborne standing in the room, then tearing the paper from Angelo's hand and, who knows what possessed the man, bellowing like some raging bull, lunging forward, his fists beating down on my head – until Angelo, little Angelo, tried in vain to stop the onslaught, and by then I was cowering on the floor, my arms curled up to protect my head, and through the ringing in my ears I heard a piercing, high-pitched scream, glancing up to see two blurred Angelos, two gaping wounds where one eye had been – two Osbornes beside him with blood on their hands, with blood on the tips of the knives they held.

Somehow I managed to stand, staggering to a table and grabbing on to that for support, where I heard Osborne's voice coming low and dull, and lacking in any emotion at all when he gave me a look of sheer contempt and said, 'Cover yourself, you filthy whore. Get out of my sight and go upstairs.'

Afraid to imagine what might come next, I snatched up my gown. I was leaving the room, when I stopped to look back for one last time, to view the callous efficiency with which Osborne stooped to take up a cloth and to wipe the blood from Angelo's face, and Angelo standing there mute and limp, whimpering in that bear's embrace, his unmarred cheek pressed firm and hard against his master's belly.

My head was throbbing, was swimming. I hardly know how I found the strength to walk back upstairs to my room again, where I saw my face in the looking glass, already bruised and swelling. But nothing compared to Angelo, for whose sake I knelt down and tried to pray, pressing my forehead against the boards and weeping until my tears ran dry – until Osborne Black was there in the door, towering above while telling me that he had called in a doctor, that Angelo's eye had been removed, the wound well cleaned and now stitched up, the boy taken back to his mother's house. 'There will be no further consequence. Financial arrangements have been made.'

'No consequence?' I could not believe that Osborne could be as callous as that, inflamed by my anger and crying out, 'When Angelo must bear the brand of your spite until his dying day!'

Only then did Osborne show any sorrow, collapsing to his knees at my side, where he rocked back and forth like a man possessed, burying his face in those monstrous hands, and his moans barely comprehensible. 'He knows . . . I'm sorry. I thought he'd betrayed me.'

'Betrayed you? But he's just a boy!'

'He betrayed my love. My trust in him.' Osborne's bloodshot eyes met mine, filled with self-pitying anguish for which I could feel no sympathy. In truth, I would gladly have struck the man, clocked him then and there with my own bare hands. But I didn't, because I was afraid. His mood could change as fast as the wind – just as it did in my room right then, all remorse in his voice too soon replaced with, 'Forget him. Forget about Angelo. It's time we thought of going home. You're old enough to pass off as a wife. Start packing. We'll leave in the morning.'

And that was that. We left Italy. I said no goodbye to Angelo. I never thought to see him again – which is why it came as such a shock, when we'd been back in London for less than a month, when we went to the Royal Academy, as vulgar as any penny gaff with such a chattering thronging crowd, all flimflam girls and square-rigged men who leered from beneath their tifters at me while I stood below Osborne's painting, and that lifted well above 'the line', which pleased my husband inordinately, having complained of years gone by when his work had been hidden away in dark corners. I wished I was in a dark corner, away from all the scandalised stares, all the prudish disapproving frowns of the ladies who huddled with fluttering fans, who had surely recognised my face in the picture called *The Libertine*.

There I was, a mermaid again, this time rising up in a river, my hair and flesh wet with droplets of water, water that glistened like sparks and pearls. And there, on the bank, lying down in the grass and reaching out with extended arms, the fingers of one of his plump little hands tweaking the tip of my nipple, was a Cupid who looked just like Angelo – a perfect Cupid with two brown eyes.

I was all too aware of Osborne's smile, how cruel and calculated it was when he watched for my reaction then – and me hardly being able to breathe, lonely and heartsick with all of the grief when I bolted and pushed my way through the crowds.

At last I was standing outside, turning round in slow circles, at something of a loss to find myself in the entrance court. The blazing of torches. The queuing of cabs which went rattling out through the high arched gates, and leading to what? My freedom? But where could I go? How could I survive? Could I return to Cheyne Walk to live in Mrs Hibbert's house? Since coming back to England I kept dreaming about her, all of the time. I had written some letters, but how could I send them? What if the wrong hooks opened them up? What if the touch of black silk gloves was replaced by jagged fingernails?

A touch on my arm made me start in alarm. A man's deep voice, not Osborne Black's: 'Can I offer you some assistance? My name is Frederick Hall. I saw you leave the gallery. I thought you looked to be distressed.'

His face was vaguely familiar. A thick head of lustrous steel-grey hair. An airy self-possession he had. A smile exuding confidence. Had we met that night in the gallery, or was it— Yes, I had him now! One of the gentlemen in Cremorne, with the whisky-veined cheeks of a lushington, the sort Mrs Hibbert took pains to befriend – though before another word was said Osborne appeared on my other side, glaring at me as he waved for a cab – which this Mr Hall then asked to share.

To tell you the truth I was almost glad. Less chance of receiving a reprimand for daring to spoil Osborne's grand hour of triumph, though any delay could not last long. The hotel was barely ten minutes away, during which I was fretting in silence while this Mr Hall – who might be another painter, or perhaps he was a dealer, for I sensed him and Osborne not strangers – became intent on enquiring what price *The Libertine* might be to buy.

I wondered how much he'd stump up for it, but Osborne said it was not for sale, of profound 'sentimental value' to him – at which I felt nauseous all over again while Mr Hall expressed disappointment but suggested the painting could be mass-reproduced, an independent profit raised with the sale of limited-edition prints. 'You need only create the engraving . . . a copy of the work, which may then be viewed in every home while you retain the original.'

'I have no time for such things as that!' Osborne's answer was rudely snapped, until giving the matter a little more thought. 'But, I suppose . . . if I had an assistant. Is there anyone you might suggest?'

Mr Hall then mentioned a friend of his. It was someone who, by all accounts, Osborne had met several years before. 'Do you remember Augustus Lamb, and his grandson, Elijah . . . a gifted young man with a very fine eye, and now gaining skill in photography? He has sent me examples of his work. Really, the most stunning visions. Pastoral idylls of fields and streams and . . .'

While Mr Hall was wittering on, I turned my face to the window, hoping that way to hide my tears. Such a stone of grief was lodged in my heart at the memory of Angelo, but through that came the niggling question: *Do I know that name? Augustus Lamb?*

Suddenly, I turned to ask, 'Would that be the writer Augustus Lamb? The writer of fairy tales?'

'Indeed it is,' Mr Hall replied. 'And I am Mr Lamb's publisher . . . though we've met too infrequently of late.'

He looked down at his lap, become morose, his moustache glinting silver when caught by the light of each street lamp we passed along the way until our journey came to an end, halting at Claridge's white-pillared porch, where Mr Hall was the first to get out, extending his hand very gallantly while assisting me down to the pavement. Osborne soon followed on behind, and such a scowl upon his face – I felt sure he was going to start a row. But before such a fear could be realised the porter stepped forward and spoke in his ear, some message about a note from his dealer being left with the hotel receptionist.

While 'my husband' strode on through the hotel doors as if he'd forgotten my presence there, Mr Hall snatched his moment to talk with me. 'Mrs Black, must I really call you that? I hardly think it suits. And I feel this journey has been too short, passing by in the merest blink of an eye . . . almost as fast as the past six years, since the day I first saw you in Cremorne.'

He had remembered me! I was shocked, but I stared back into his eyes, too tired and upset to think to lie when I replied, 'My name is Pearl.'

He took my hand in his again. His lips brushed the skin in a gentle caress, before, 'Ah . . . how appropriate. The pearl thrown down among us swine. My dear, should you tire of Osborne Black then . . .'

'Don't you know how unlucky a pearl can be? Pearls represent tears and misery.'

He smiled at my stark interruption. Above his dark eye a brow was arched. 'I'm sure *you* could bring much happiness. How the Italians must have adored you . . . and how charming their natural tongue must sound when issued from lips as sweet as yours. I have always found its rhythm seductive. The language makes me think of love.'

I thought his tone too suggestive by far, and the words that almost slipped my tongue were not Italian at all, rather, '*Shut your face and all your sauce!*' But then, I remembered my lessons well, all those texts that advised on etiquette. My lips remained politely closed, and what a relief when Osborne returned, his big feet stamping heavy on pavement slabs while Frederick Hall continued with, 'You have an enchanting wife, Mr Black. Pray do tell me how you came to meet?'

'I painted her portrait.' Osborne was blunt.

'And then you took her as your bride.' Mr Hall fixed me in his gaze again. 'Are there any more like you, Mrs Black? Do you have any relatives near by?'

'No!' My voice was wavering, all confidence lost with Osborne's return. 'No one but my husband.'

'Forgive my persistence, but are you sure? I once saw a girl who might well be your twin, her picture impressed on a *carte de visite*. Who could ever forget such a face as that? And the name on that card . . .' He narrowed his eyes. 'Could that name have been something like Hibbert?'

'I know of no such name.' Osborne was coldly dismissive. 'Whoever these Hibbert people are, there is no connection with my wife.'

But before he could think to drag me away Mr Hall placed his hand on Osborne's sleeve, not lifting it until he was done. 'I'm so glad we met again tonight. You know how much I admire your work, even if you do refuse to sell. But, in time, you might think on the matter again. Markets and tastes can fluctuate. Fame and fashion can be such fickle things.'

Nothing more was said. We left Mr Hall beside the cab and entered the hotel's vestibule, and all that night, alone in my bed, I tossed and turned and fretted to think of what Mr Hall might know of me. I imagined that Osborne must feel the same, but what a surprise when the morning came, when he looked in at my bedroom door and made the blithe announcement, 'It's clear that you've not been well of late . . . the stress of the journey from Italy, and London in summer can be so oppressive, not to mention the noses and gossips around. The builders have almost finished in Chiswick. But, until then, I think a trip to the country, to visit with Augustus Lamb. You'd like that, wouldn't you . . . to meet an author whose work you admire?'

A day later we met with the author, and Elijah and Lily, his grandchildren. She – Lily – she gave me a curious smile – though I didn't remember her at all. But Elijah – Elijah – *that* is his name, the boy I once saw in the mermaid tent!

Now I sit in the cage of this railway carriage, alone again with Osborne Black. The cut on my foot is stinging and sore. I try to ignore it, pretending to sleep, but through the corner of one eye I can see the fast blurring of steep grassy sidings, the green of the trees, the green of the fields – the world that is Elijah Lamb.

'Pearl.' Osborne is calling my name.

I don't want to answer or look at the man, to feel myself trapped like an insect in amber.

'Here . . .' he goes on, 'I have something for you.' He draws a book out of his pocket. 'A good omen, don't you agree? To think that my new assistant will be sharing my interest in mermaids.'

He tosses the book high into the air. It lands with a thud on the seat at my side. I lift it and open the green embossed covers and look at the pictures instead of the words. My fingers trace the elegant lines. Every one has been drawn by Elijah Lamb. And inside my head I am silently chanting, the words repeating, again and again in time with the engine's rattling drum –

I want him to come. I don't want him to come.
I want him to come. I don't want him to come.
I want him to come . . . I am frightened.
I am frightened because he will.

LILY

His image in the dusk she seem'd to see,
And to the silence made a gentle moan,
Spreading her perfect arms upon the air,
And on her couch low murmuring, 'Where? O where?'

From 'Isabella; or, The Pot of Basil' by John Keats

He went. I always knew he would. The days before were torturous – watching him packing and making arrangements, receiving letters from Osborne Black, and seeing how anxious Papa was I tried to hide my own distress by wandering off to be alone, more often than not going down to the stream.

I was there when Elijah found me, late in the day on that last afternoon. I'd been sitting quite still among the ferns when I startled to hear him call my name, hurriedly lifting up my skirts to wipe at the tears running down my face, which were dribbling salty and warm on my lips, through which I blurted the sudden sob, 'Oh, Elijah, I'm going to miss you so much.'

'Little sister . . . please don't cry!' My brother knelt down, very close at my side. The sketchbook that he'd held in his hands was dropped to the ground with a muted thud over which he carried on his plea. 'I'm not going away to the ends of the earth. I'll come back and see you in Kingsland House . . . and I'm sure you'll be able to visit me.'

When I still didn't dare to face him, he cupped my chin in one of his hands and as soft as a lover's were his words, though I was reminded far too much of the night we'd returned from London before, when he said, 'Won't you tell me that you understand . . . even if you don't? Won't you try and give me your blessing?'

'I do understand. I think I do. In your place I would probably do the same. And . . .' I paused before going on, 'Pearl Black is very beautiful.'

My brother gave no answer to that. For a while there was only our silent farewell, the trickling song of the stream in our ears, our breaths coming heavy and steady, in rhythm, and our thoughts – for I'm sure they were also entwined – all full of our recent visitor. I recalled our visit to the stream, and the way she had exposed her legs without the slightest pang of shame, and the pale down of hairs that had glistened there, and how ugly and thick the dark growth of my own. I thought of the way she'd looked at me when drying the water and blood from her foot, and—

And Elijah broke my reverie. 'Do you mind if I draw you . . . here, by our stream? Something of my sister for me to keep, to look at whenever I miss her most. My dreaming lady of the ferns.'

He asked me to sit with my hands in my lap, and when he had finished he showed me why. In his drawing I held a small glass jar – a jar with some string knotted round its rim. And inside was some water, all swirling with silt, and through that murk there swam three fish.

Did he miss me? I missed him terribly. At night I behaved as I had when a child. I lay in my bed and pressed my fingers against the wall, pretending that he was still *that* close, still there, still on the other side. But Elijah's room was empty. The sheets on his bed were cold, though there was that time when I thought him back, waking at the creaking of feet on the boards and the twanging groan of the mattress springs – and when I got up and went to look, what I thought was Elijah was only Papa, sitting there on the end of the bed, hunched over and holding his head in his hands.

Most nights there was nothing more to hear than the rustle

of ivy on windowpanes, and so often my dreams would be of that vine – a dream where a demon was trapped in its core, something dark and evil at its heart that was gradually waking and stirring to life. Green sap pumped like blood into gnarled dry roots which were twisting and tearing up from the soil as the house bricks cracked and opened up, as branches extended like outstretched arms, at the end of which tendrils were sharp as nails. Tap, tap, tap. They beat at my window glass. Scratch, scratch, scratch. They burrowed down into my thoughts. They hissed in my ear, like poison – at which I would wake in a shivering sweat, my heart thumping wildly in my breast, seeing the eyes of Osborne Black – eyes full of a jealous burning spite which glittered with little tongues of fire. But the strange thing was, when morning came I could never recall what those secrets had been. I heard no more than the cooing of pigeons, or the church's muted clanging bell, and I hoped for a blast of the post-man's horn to announce that some mail had been left in the box that was fixed to the wall by our main front gates – into which, hardly more than week elapsed, my brother's very first letter dropped.

How eager I was for the news from Thames Mall, where Elijah now resided. I must have read a hundred times that Dolphin House was –

the last of many fine residences with a frontage of trees and high hedges to further shield its privacy, although the house is only disturbed by those intent on visiting, of which there have been none at all since the day of my arrival here. A peculiar quiet air it has, almost of rural isolation despite the breweries around and the river traffic sailing by.

The interior is very opulent, and everywhere Osborne's paintings hang. Almost all are water-themed which suits the decoration well. There are windows stained in blues and greens, the same with the hallway's ceramic tiles, which Osborne says his grandfather sourced when employed by the East India Company. There is a stuffed peacock with tail feathers fanned. There are antique statues in marble and bronze, Turkish carpets. Satsuma vases. An enormous fretwork marriage chest inlaid with ivory and gold, now adapted for use as a sedan.

I closed my eyes. I tried to imagine I was there, standing in that hallway, right next to my brother's side – the same when he wrote about Chiswick House, a grand Italianate villa that was, in the grounds of which Osborne was setting a painting –

where we come and go at will, by means of a gate in the garden walls for which Osborne holds a set of keys – some arrangement he has with the owners, though as yet I have never met them.

Elijah said Osborne's studio was a newly built construction where the plaster was barely dry on the walls, but –

full of a glorious natural light, and most unlike the rest of the house where rooms are kept shuttered and steeped in gloom. Tall glass doors allow access to the lawns and from there on down to the river Thames. Many storage rooms are hidden away behind the wooden panelling to house Osborne's props and materials. One leads into a passageway and that to my very own 'darkroom', its sinks plumbed with water for washing the plates, and shelves set above for the chemicals. Ellen Page would be most impressed to see the camera I work with here, being far more advanced than that at home. Osborne has spared no expense whatsoever. I feel myself very 'professional'.

I think what tugged the most at my heart was when Elijah wrote to describe the Sunday he met Uncle Freddie for lunch, when they ate a roast chicken at the Bell, a public house on Strand on the Green – a riverside walk near Dolphin House. Afterwards, they followed that towpath to cross the bridge that spanned the Thames, just on the other side of which they found the Botanical Gardens of Kew. Elijah said Freddie had been most keen to go and view the tropical palms, and my brother sent me the studies he'd made – a banana, a pawpaw, a mango – and the Latin names inscribed beneath all copied from labels fixed on to the plants. And there was Uncle Freddie too, as dapper as he had ever been, sitting down on a bench with his long legs crossed, and wearing a very tall top hat.

I did not show that letter to Papa, who still blamed his old friend for setting the trap and luring Elijah away from him, who now seemed to bear such a virulent grudge it was best not to mention Freddie's name.

A week later, another envelope came. But that proved to be disappointing, containing only the briefest of notes – and the same with the next – and the one after that. And then they all stopped. Ten weeks, and no more letters came – though I wrote to Chiswick religiously, every Sunday afternoon, with sections dictated by Papa too, who by then could hardly hold a pen, with his tremors becoming so severe.

Not knowing what had caused the blight, the doctor suspected a passing depression for which he suggested the Malvern Cure. But Papa refused to be convinced that being half-drowned in a vat of cold water could help revive anyone's spirit or health, whether or not Mr Darwin did! So, the doctor prescribed a tonic instead with a fancy French label attached on the front, with swirling gold letters that spelled out the words: *BROMOCARPINE ~ Traitement des afflictions nerveuses.*

To my mind, that tincture made Papa worse, bringing on strange hallucinations, though the doctor insisted that those were signs of the ailment being purged from within, for which he then gave an antidote, which was some injections of opium after which the shaking did lessen some, but Papa was left in a dreamy state, unless ridden with sudden spasms and cramps, after which his whole body would freeze and lock, his fingers curled into rigid claws.

Poor Papa. It was as if he had been cursed – and what would we have done without Ellen Page, who nursed him as if her very own, and no task too vile or oppressive to bear. Not that she couldn't still act the witch and, one day, when Papa was sleeping, when I went to sit in the kitchen with her, both of us sharing a pot of tea, she fixed me with her bird-like eyes and pronounced, 'That quack don't know his arse from his elbow, driving around in a flashy gig . . . far more intent on impressing you than trying to cure poor Mr Lamb. Hmm,' she sniffed and tilted her chin, 'I could do the job as well as him, handing out bottles of laudanum and charging a guinea a pop on his bill, when the pharmacist sells the very same for less than a shilling, I'll have you know. I could tell that doctor a thing or two. I've seen others beset with such symptoms before. To my mind there's no pill or potion on earth that will make your grandfather well again. He's got the shaking palsy he has. There's not a moment of doubt in my mind. I've seen it coming on for years just as it did with my father before. I know that mask he sometimes wears . . . his face all blank and staring. That's how they all seem to go in the end.'

'The shaking palsy? What does that mean?'

'It means . . .' and at this she reached over the table, one bony hand clasped either side of my face as if not to let me fall apart when the shock of her diagnosis was made, 'it means he's going to get much worse, worse in his body as well as his mind. He might even come to forget who you are, and . . .'

'Stop it. Stop it!' I shouted back, pulling away from her embrace, no longer able or willing to listen to such a dire prediction as that. I flung my cup of tea to the floor and then, stooping down to collect the smashed china, sliced open a finger on one of the shards. A bead of red welled up like a ruby before trickling over my wrist and the soft white flesh of my inner arm, and I found myself thinking about Pearl Black and how, when she'd paddled in our stream, her foot had been cut on a broken shell – such a strangely formed foot with its white-webbed toes – those toes upon which, even now, my brother might be gazing. Or were his grey eyes lost in hers so green, forgetting Papa, forgetting me?

Heaving dry sobs of lonely resentment, I crouched there and rocked like a thing gone mad, until I was calm, when I looked up at Ellen and started to plead, 'What can I do? I want things to be as they were before, with Papa well, with Elijah back home. I don't even know if he's happy or sad, or whether he's safe, or . . .' *Or what?* When I tried to picture Elijah his features were blurred and indistinct, lost in some drifting sea of mist that went by the name of Dolphin House.

'Well, missy,' Ellen took my hand, and only the slightest catch in her voice when she said, 'now you've got that self-pitying out, you'd best let me see to that cut of yours before you get blood all over my floor. And then you can fetch a pen and some paper and write to your Uncle Freddie in London . . . see what *he* has to say on the matter. There'll be some explanation, I'm bound. Letters get lost in the mail, you know. People get ill and . . .'

'If Elijah was ill . . . if he was so ill that he couldn't write, then wouldn't the Blacks have let us know?'

'You'd think so.' Ellen's eyes were narrowed to slits, the crow's feet around creased to tiny pleats, and her voice very gruff when she carried on, 'From the little I've seen of *that* gentleman, I'd not trust him as far as I'd throw him. And there's something not right between him and his wife. I noticed Elijah gawping that day. I know when a couple are smitten . . . or not. Moths might be drawn around a flame, but a flame is fire and fire burns. I warned Mr Lamb and he called me deluded. But you mark my words. You see if I'm wrong!'

Something was wrong, that was for sure, and while Ellen bandaged up my hand, while I bit on my tongue at the stinging pain, I thought of Elijah, I thought of Pearl, and those longing, intimate, yearning looks that had passed between the two of them.

I told Papa that I had written to Freddie. I wrote to Osborne Black as well, politely asking for news of my brother. The artist never did reply, but Freddie responded within a few days, and in the form of a telegram – TRAVELLED TO CHISWICK. BLACKS

GONE AWAY. INFORMED ELIJAH BEEN DISMISSED. MAKING
FURTHER ENQUIRIES.

Why had Elijah been dismissed? And where on earth could
my brother have gone – if not to Freddie in Burlington Row – if
not home to us in Kingsland? Could there have been an
accident, on the train, coming back to Herefordshire?

Papa tried to allay my fears. 'Don't worry, Lily. We would
have heard of a rail disaster. People don't simply disappear. We
must write again . . . to Osborne Black. We must . . . we
must . . .' As so often he started to lose his thread, eventually
whining like a child, just as I'd done with Ellen before, 'Oh,
Lily . . . what can have occurred? What can we do . . . what can
we do?'

The telegram dropped from my hands to the floor when I ran
to kneel at Papa's side, and I – I felt strangely composed when I
took his shaking hands in mine and said, '*I* can do something,
Papa. I can travel to London. I can go to Thames Mall. I'm sure
Freddie will help me to look for Elijah and . . .'

Papa began to moan, a high keen, almost like an animal.
'Lily, don't go. Not you as well. Frederick Hall stole my only
son before. He stole my . . . he stole . . .'

'You'll be all right, Papa. Ellen is here.'

'It's not that. It's not me. I shall worry for you. I lost Gabriel.
Now Elijah too. What if he's dead? What if . . .'

'Papa!' I shouted through my tears. 'You must never ever say
such things! Elijah's not dead. I would know if he was. But
something is wrong, and I must try and find him. Please, Papa.
I have to go.'

Oh, such a clamour at Paddington station, clinging on to my
bag for grim life, enveloped in steamy clouds of smut through
which I was jostled this way and that, and very nearly knocked
off my feet by a porter hurrying past with his trolley. But with
my balance and vision restored I saw Uncle Freddie, right there
on the platform, and just as he'd looked all those years before
but for the loss of the black in his hair, those silver streaks now

everywhere. How happy I was to see him, dropping my bag, rushing forward, embraced again in my uncle's arms while inhaling his perfume of leather and spice – and feeling like a child again until overcome with embarrassment to have acted with such abandon, to see his expression of surprise when he held me back at his full arms' length, taking some time to appraise my looks before exclaiming with a smile, 'Lily . . . but, how you've altered! My dear, you're quite grown up.'

For a moment or two he disappeared, retrieving my bag from the platform edge, but continued when he swiftly returned, 'You must be exhausted from such a long journey, and the weather tonight so bitterly cold. Come . . . we must get you into the warm.'

I must have dozed off in the cab, only waking again at our lurching halt, when Uncle Freddie was touching my hand, saying, 'Lily. Wake up. Here we are. Back home again, in Burlington Row.'

'Home?' I was yawning, rubbing my eyes, thinking: *This isn't home. Home is Papa!* Such a panic there was in my mind, for a moment not knowing Freddie's house, with its tall iron railings like prison walls. And still confused and shivering when Freddie assisted me down to the pavement, from where I found my eyes were drawn to look at the house standing opposite, just as Papa's had been that time before, and just as before that house was in darkness, such a contrast to Freddie's, all colour and light, and a brand-new maid to take my things – very young, very pretty I thought she was.

I took Freddie's arm and he led me upstairs and into his private sitting room – a room not seen last time I came – a room that spread over the front of the house, with bookcases lining two of the walls, with newspapers and magazines spilling out almost everywhere, from cupboards, and drawers, in piles on the floor, and any walls that might be bare were covered in paintings, sketches and prints; mostly scenes from classical literature; what I now recognised as Pre-Raphaelite works.

There was one much smaller than the rest, its frame far less extravagant and, hidden away at the room's far end, it was very much in shadow, but its glass caught a shiver of gaslight, drawing my curiosity. I peered at a woman embracing a pot, and that pot embellished with human skulls. I suppose it sounds rather morbid, but I knew what it represented, that image being taken from a tale in *The Decameron*. Papa kept a copy on his shelves, and I often used to pull it down, my fingers flicking through to the page which held such a resonance for me – simply because the heroine's name was the same as that of my mother. But even if that had not been so, who could have failed to find themselves moved by the tragic tale of a girl who had spurned an elderly suitor, only then to discover her young lover murdered, and concealing his severed head inside a pot of basil, that plant thereafter cherished and mourned as if it was her lover's shrine.

The image hanging on Freddie's wall was enhanced by a little inscription on brass –

ISABELLA; OR, THE POT OF BASIL

SHE WEEPS ALONE FOR PLEASURES NOT TO BE . . .
AND THEN, INSTEAD OF LOVE, O MISERY!

Still silently mouthing those sorry lines, I turned to see Freddie observing me and looking not himself at all, his expression too fixed, too serious – his thoughts no doubt on Elijah, though no mention had yet been made of my brother, and the atmosphere was very tense as I walked back towards the marble surround within which a fire burned vigorously, a blast of hot air rising up like a friend to gleam on the fender and mirror above, before which was a marble clock and a bust of Queen Victoria, and two brightly plumed birds in tall glass domes. The velvet green chairs either side of that hearth were very capacious and cluttered with cushions, and into that feathery embrace I was happy to sink when the maid came in, setting down a silver tray, and upon that a silver coffee pot, and two china cups beside a plate which contained the daintiest little cakes. But Freddie had other refreshment in mind. When she'd gone he opened a chiffonier, drawing out a decanter and two crystal glasses, pouring out two measures of ruby-red wine and offering one to me while insisting, 'Drink this, my dear . . . it will do you good. We'll soon have your cockles warmed up again.'

I suppose he was right, for the hot spreading glow of the port in my belly went some small way to thawing my bones, and while shuffling cold feet back and forth on the rug I watched Freddie down his glass in one, before filling it up to the brim again, then taking the chair set opposite mine. He placed both bottle and glass in the grate, and with firelight gleaming over his features I noticed how my uncle had aged. There was that greyness in his hair, and his face was bloated yet deeply lined, the flesh of his cheeks almost porridgy – and something else was different too, something so subtle I couldn't define it, though you might almost say he looked haunted, gazing at me through swollen lids in which bloodshot eyes stared, too intense, grown moist when my uncle leaned forward again, his voice coming earnest but hesitant. 'Little Lily. How you have come to resemble . . .'

He broke off with a heavy sigh, reaching down for the glass from which he gulped until nothing remained but the wine's grainy dregs, and meanwhile I was presuming that, like so many other people of late, Freddie had been about to say that I'd come to resemble Elijah – but had then decided to hold his tongue. Even so, in that mirror placed over his hearth all that I'd seen reflected back was a plain young woman whose face was too drawn, whose eyes were almost too big, too black, the skin around them bruised with exhaustion. If anyone, I resembled Papa, and thinking of him, I said very bluntly, 'Do you know about Papa? He's terribly ill . . . and he worries about Elijah so. The doctor thinks it is his nerves. But, Ellen . . . she calls that nonsense. Ellen says . . .'

'He was like that before . . .' Freddie made his brisk

intervention, 'when Gabriel was taken. And now,' he held a hand to his brow, 'and now, thanks to me, it must happen again.'

'Thanks to you?' A cold band of iron gripped my heart. After all, Gabriel had long been dead. What on earth could Uncle Freddie mean?

'I invited you to Cremorne where we met with Osborne Black that day, and more recently, seeing the artist again and hearing how he sought an assistant . . . it was I who recommended Elijah. I knew. I knew what might happen. I won't insult you by lying. I *hoped* that it would, that Elijah would come, allowing me to see him again. Oh, Lily . . . six years!' He thumped a fist on the arm of his chair and a small bloom of dust went rising up. 'You can't know how much I've missed you both.'

His response was very dramatic. I wanted to say that we'd missed him too, and we had, it was true – from time to time. But I had more urgent things in mind, seeking to steer Uncle Freddie's thoughts on to more practical matters again when I asked, 'What happened, when you went to Thames Mall . . . when you went to enquire about Osborne Black?'

'I was told he had gone travelling and intended to be away for months. Naturally, I assumed Elijah was with him, but the servant then said he had been dismissed, an event that occurred some weeks before . . . and how furious Osborne had been at the time, though she couldn't say what it was about. Anyway,' Freddie paused, pouring out what little was left of the wine, the coffee and cakes still completely ignored, 'I have placed advertisements in the press appealing for information. And Sam . . .'

'Samuel Beresford?'

'The very same. He has agreed to come with us tomorrow when we travel again to the house on Thames Mall.'

'Oh!' I had not expected that, my rising excitement to hear his name immediately quelled by the ominous sense of being

146

thwarted in our search, and before it had even chanced to begin. 'But is there any point . . . if the Blacks really have gone away?'

'*If* Osborne Black has gone away then he has left his wife at home. And that is something I very much doubt.'

'You saw Pearl? Did she say anything?' My heart was thudding hard and fast. Was it the thought of seeing her . . . or was it Samuel Beresford?

'We had no opportunity to speak. But when I was leaving, just at the gate, I heard a tapping sound above . . . a window at the side of the house which was fitted with bars and . . .'

'You're sure it was her?'

Uncle Freddie frowned and closed his eyes. 'I met her this summer . . . an art exhibition, when the Blacks first returned from Italy. Once seen, who could forget that face?'

'I have seen her for myself, you know!' My retort was sharp. But then I remembered that day in Cremorne when we first saw Pearl in the mermaid's tent.

Had Freddie forgotten that?

My uncle stared solemnly into the flames as if reliving some vision there, before saying, 'The poor creature looked terribly ill, no more than a ghost of her former self. It was well past three in the afternoon and yet, as far as I could tell, she was wearing no more than a sleeping shift. She held a finger to her lips, as if begging me not to betray her there. And then she threw something down to the path, after which she simply disappeared . . . as if she'd never been there at all. But I had the proof in what she'd thrown. The sort of stone you might find on a beach, and wrapped around that was some paper upon which she'd written a message.'

'What did she write?' My question was barely a whisper: of hope, of fear, of anxiety.

'I have it here.' Freddie stood up and went to a desk, opening a drawer from which he extracted a crumpled page, and when he had placed that in my hands it took no more than a second or two to read what Pearl had written down – *He knows. He lies. He is here.*

'Who knows what? Who is here?' I mumbled the words as if to myself. 'Does she mean Osborne Black, or Elijah?'

'That is what we need to discover. It is very little to go on. Only these scribbled cryptic lines. No proof of a crime, no . . .'

'No body?' My voice was too loud as, unconsciously, I scrunched Pearl's note in my clenched hand before flinging it down into the hearth, where a stray ember caught and the paper blazed up, shrinking and charring before our eyes; our only scrap of evidence lost, at which I then began to sob. 'Papa thinks Elijah is dead. But my brother is living. I *know* he is. Oh, Uncle Freddie . . . I feel so alone, so lost without Elijah.'

Freddie was standing behind my chair, his hand gently patting my shoulder and the quiet defiance in his voice belying the tears that gleamed in his eyes when he said, 'Lily . . . dearest, you are not alone. Have no fears, we shall find your brother, I swear. But for now, I have something that you should see. I wanted to show you, that visit before, but the opportunity never arose . . . not after those sordid events in Cremorne. God knows, Augustus had every right to be angry with me and take you home. I've always been too liberal. I've . . .'

Breaking off, going back to his desk again, after opening up another drawer, Freddie withdrew a small brass frame, and when he had placed that in my hands, I gasped – to see my mother's face. I knew it was her, you see. There was not a moment of doubt in my mind, and without even thinking I said the words, 'She weeps alone for pleasures not to be . . .'

'What?' Freddie looked bewildered.

'It's from the engraving . . .' I pointed towards the end of the room. 'From "Isabella . . . The Pot of Basil".'

'Oh, yes, of course. The poem by Keats.' He wiped a hand across his brow and then returned to his fireside chair, sitting down while repeating, 'Six years, six years! And now you are grown as lovely as she.'

The face in the frame was beautiful, my mother's eyes as brown as mine, her hair very much like Elijah's, waving, dark and lustrous. Once, I would have smiled at such praise. Once, when I was very small, I might have crawled on to Freddie's lap and pressed my ear against his chest, closing my eyes while drifting off to the reassuring slow beat of his heart. But such things were no longer appropriate. And whether from the strain of emotions, or exhaustion from all the day's travelling, I felt sick to the pit of my stomach, and then, after swiftly standing, I said, 'Freddie, I really must go to bed.'

'Why, of course.' He reached out for the bell by the hearth. 'We are both overwrought and the hour is late. The maid will show you to your room . . . the same room that you had before. Nothing has been changed.'

I thought, *But it has. Far too much has changed.* I glanced down at my mother's likeness again, the picture frame still in my hands, and found myself wondering aloud, 'How do you come to have this? Is she alive? Do you happen to know where my mother is?'

'I have not seen her since Gabriel's death. That miniature is a self-portrait. Among other talents, she was a fine artist . . . perhaps the source of your brother's skills. She intended it as a gift for your father, to celebrate their wedding day . . . an event that was never to occur. She left it behind when she disappeared. I suppose I should not have kept it. I should have shown it to you before, but . . .'

What was this, when Freddie also stood, reaching forward and touching a hand to my cheek, then drawing me closer in his arms. Could there be something more than affection in those shuddering breaths, that thudding heart? Whereas once I would have responded now I felt myself to be compromised – though I did feel guilty to have such thoughts, because this was Freddie, and surely my uncle would never think to betray my trust. Still, I confess it was a relief to hear the gentle knock of the maid, when he lowered his arms and I stumbled back, and still avoiding my uncle's eyes looked down at the painting and plaintively asked, 'May I keep her picture? Would you mind?'

*

I turned the key in the door that night, locking myself inside the room, where gold flocking swirled over red chintzy walls, still as garish when glistening with light from the flames that blazed high in the marble hearth, that flickered and flashed across the glass of the miniature propped upon the stand, and behind that the face of the mother who I had never known – except for one time when she'd visited me – an occasion I'd always kept locked in my heart, not even telling Elijah so much. And that was something strange in itself, for I told my brother everything.

We were very young, about six years old and by then quite at home in Kingsland House, though, not long having moved to a separate room, I still grieved to spend my nights alone, longing for the warmth of my brother's flesh, and my brother's breaths upon my face. But that dawn, when the strange event occurred, when he lay oblivious next door, I thought I heard someone calling my name, and it seemed to come from the gardens outside. So, bleary and yawning, I climbed from the mattress and, pulling back the window drapes, I noticed a moth on the other side, its battered brown wings all dusty dull with the faintest of powdery residues; their feeble beating a whispered percussion, and that whispering only enhanced my fear, until –

'Lily . . .' There! It came again. Someone – something – *was* calling my name, and so clear and so near I could almost imagine that lips were pressed against the glass. And yet, there was nothing to see, any view obscured by the ivy leaves, and against that darkness my own small reflection, and my own reflection gave a gasp when I sensed something move inside the room, a presence shifting around on the walls, floating through shadows that seemed to be swaying as if the air was water, and that air too fluid, too thick to breathe.

Turning around, very slowly, I pressed my palms against my eyes, afraid to witness what was there, too curious not to take the risk of spreading my fingers to peep through the gaps, to see that every rosebud wall had now become a glistening red which danced in the light of a fire that was burning in a white stone hearth, and I swear I could feel the surge of its heat – even though no fire was really lit, my own little iron grate quite cold.

I blinked, and those phantom flames were gone. My room was still and 'empty' again, as was my bed with its crumpled quilt, and, jutting below, my chamber pot, and hanging on the wall above, the sampler once made by our grandmother, embroidered with birds and flowers and leaves that twined around the curling words: '*Suffer the Little Children to Come unto Me*'.

Cautiously tiptoeing back, heading past my big doll's house, I wanted no more than to crawl into bed and pull the covers over my head, to wish my vivid dreams away. And perhaps they were only dreams after all, and perhaps it was nothing more than a breeze that caused the ivy to rustle and sigh, that lured me to glance at the window again, where a lingering image was burning – no longer my face but that of a woman, a woman who I felt I knew. And even though her mouth was closed, in my mind I heard her speak my name, and when I answered, I said, *Mama*.

That night, when I lay in Burlington Row, as I drifted off to sleep in a room where red shadows danced round the walls, I remembered that face at my window again – the same face I now saw in a little frame – and how it had slowly disappeared, the features unravelled like ribbons of mist before they had simply ceased to exist.

The maid knocked at nine, then turned and rattled the knob of the door – the door that remained locked up all night.

When I rose from the bed to open it she came in with some coffee for me to drink. I tried some but found it much too cold, thick and silty, black as mud. I wondered whether she had simply poured what was left on the tray from the previous night – though she looked too honest and open-faced to have done such a thing maliciously, bobbing and blushing nervously when she said, 'Mr Hall is already downstairs. He's waiting for Mr Beresford. Do you want me to make your fire up? Do you want me to help you wash or dress?'

I said no, I should manage quite well on my own, and the

moment she'd gone I was hurriedly splashing my face with some water grown chill in a bowl near by. A brief shivering glance in the mirror above and I pinched my cheeks and bit my lips, trying to bring some colour in. I tied back my hair in a plain brown knot before snatching up clothes thrown off last night, fumbling to fix the corset clips and cursing while securing the bustle, hoping those ribbons would stay at my waist, and with them the lump that padded the rear. There was a cartoon I'd once chanced to see in Papa's copy of *Punch* magazine. It was captioned 'A Woman's Humiliation', with the woman concerned quite unaware of the bustle that slipped from beneath her hems, with gentlemen sniggering behind when she seemed to be laying a giant egg. The thought of it haunted me still, whenever I wore the wretched thing – but there was no time for such petty concerns as I rushed down the narrow flights of stairs to join Freddie in the dining room, though again I felt much too anxious to eat, only taking small sips from my coffee cup, that beverage now being fresh and hot, though most of it was left undrunk when I heard sounds of hooves and the rattle of wheels, and a sudden loud knock at the house's door.

Samuel Beresford did not come in but waited to greet us beneath the porch while, in something of a rush, Freddie and I bustled round in the hall donning our hats, my cloak, his coat, before heading out to the waiting cab, its wheels soon splashing through rain-swept streets, the two men sitting opposite me, and me all a quiver of anxiety as to what the coming day would bring – or was that simply the state of my nerves after meeting with Samuel Beresford, or was it that coffee which buzzed through my blood to make me feel giddy and nauseous?

When I was only fourteen years, when my blood had fizzed with Cremorne champagne, my behaviour had been precocious. Now, I could barely bring myself to meet with Samuel Beresford's eye when I finally summoned the courage to ask, 'Mr Beresford, did you happen to see my brother on his latest visit to London?'

He said, 'No, only that day in Cremorne.'

Do you remember me in Cremorne? I glanced up to appraise Mr Beresford's looks, to compare this new version with what I recalled, when he must have been of a similar age to that which I had now attained. His attire then had been very gay, but today he wore a black top hat, a dark jacket, a plain white-collared shirt, knotted at the neck with a grey cravat. His face was still clean-shaven, and his hair still hung long to his shoulders, still a gleaming chestnut brown, the same with his eyes, intelligent, kind and full of an earnest intensity – just as they'd been when he kissed my hand and I'd thought I should drown in his smiling charm. Had that previous attraction been mutual, when he'd stood at my side in dusked gardens – or had I been foolishly naive, my overexcited female mind interpreting London etiquette for something more akin to romance?

Such frivolous yearnings were soon put aside when Freddie began to make complaints regarding how fruitless his posts in the press, which had garnered no news of Elijah at all, to which Samuel answered in serious tones, 'There has been some gossip going around, about Osborne returning from Italy because of a violent incident . . . something involving a studio assistant.'

'What sort of violent incident?' Such a horrible sense of dread I felt, though Freddie's response was calmly made, 'I don't give a fig for such tittle-tattle unless there is actual proof. And, without any proof, let us hold our tongues or risk up-setting Lily more.'

My answer was one of blunt indignation. 'But I want to know *everything!*'

'Well . . .' Samuel Beresford paused for a moment, as if torn between humouring Freddie or me, 'I dined with my mother only last night and certain matters have reached her ears. There *may* be another route of persuasion . . . some rumours pertain-ing to book illustrations now come to light in Holywell Street, and their value so much greater these days with my cousin's reputation grown.'

Uncle Freddie was musing, as if to himself, 'Hmm, Holywell Street, you say?'

'What illustrations?' I was abrupt. 'Do they have anything to do with my brother?'

'Nothing to do with Elijah at all!' Freddie gave his friend a very stern look before offering his explanation. 'There are vendors in that part of town who specialise in . . . how shall I put it . . . in salacious types of literature.'

Samuel Beresford went on, 'There is talk that when Osborne was younger he became involved with a decadent crowd, providing images for books, so shocking they might well ruin him now *if* come to the public's attention . . . and that's not to mention the wrath of the law . . . the Immoral Publications Act.'

'Can you be sure?' Freddie enquired, his voice grown cold and very low.

'Oh yes! On the best authority. *The Times*'s art correspondent has long been a friend of Mama's. He has had the story at hand for some weeks, suppressed out of consideration for her . . . for our family connection. But he thought it best to alert her, and I shall alert my cousin in turn. We might come to an understanding, for Osborne to give any news of Elijah, in return for which I shall furnish him with the name and address of this dealer so that he may then purchase the items himself. If nothing else, Osborne is proud. He won't want to have his name dragged through the gutters.'

Freddie continued to quibble. 'Is there really any point in bringing up such historical facts?'

'But why not,' I protested vehemently, 'if they lead to some news of Elijah?'

'Miss Lamb,' Samuel Beresford touched my hand, 'if your face doesn't prick my cousin's heart . . . if he has the brass neck to see you and . . . well, who knows, he may tell us something, if only the day and the time of your brother's disappearance . . . or what he was wearing, or what form of transport he might have used, anything that might help us with identification.'

'Identification?' That word was used when describing the dead. Reluctantly, I drew back my hand and turned my eyes to the window, trying to hide my own distress when hearing

Freddie spit his threat, 'If that boy has come to any harm, then Osborne Black will rue the day he made an enemy of me!'

While speaking he shifted about in his seat to rummage in greatcoat pockets, from which he pulled a box of cigars, a cutter, a small silver tinder box. The paraphernalia sorted out, he finally lit the smoke in his mouth while puffing away to make it burn. The tip glowed red. His cheeks flushed dark and, almost like a child with a lollipop, Freddie's temper was quickly soothed, his lips puffing out grey plumes of smoke, so thick that I edged towards the door where some draughts of fresh air were blasting in, and, as I did that, through the folded crush of my cloak and skirts, my legs pressed against Samuel Beresford's. I must have turned red as a beetroot, and all I could do was stare at my lap in which my hands were tightly clasped. Meanwhile, Samuel Beresford started to cough, which made me think yet again of Cremorne and the sneezing attacks that had plagued him there. He proceeded to wind down the window, through which a sleety rain drove in, and I thought how selfish Freddie was, to keep blowing out that acrid smoke when it clearly caused his friends upset.

Brushing specks of ice from my burning cheeks, I persisted with my questioning. 'So . . . you think Osborne Black will be at home? You think he will actually . . .'

Uncle Freddie removed the cigar from his lips. 'Whether that man is there or not, the thing is to try and get Pearl alone. Mark my words, *she* holds the key.'

I heard a voice, a voice in my head, repeating the words I'd seen last night – '*He knows. He lies. He is here.*'

And then, we were '*there*', and Samuel Beresford tugged on the string to alert the cabman to make a halt, parked in a narrow country lane where he then asked Freddie to sit and wait, hoping that way for more success – considering Freddie's lack before – and my uncle seemed happy enough to comply, already lighting another cigar to add to the dirty fug around.

Having descended from the cab, Samuel Beresford took my arm. We both sheltered beneath one umbrella, and really on any other day I might have believed my giddiness the result of such close proximity, by the fact that his breaths froze and merged with mine while around us a circle of silver dripped, and through that veil I saw a church, and above its grey tower the snapping of wings, gulls screeching, whirling, soaring. And what was that assault on my nostrils, a distinct aroma of sewage and fish and something else I didn't know, a sweet malty odour that Samuel explained was the waste from a brewery built near by.

Elijah had mentioned a brewery. Hard to think that any factory could exist beside dwellings as lovely as those that we passed while walking along the Mall, all red brick façades and black balconies and beyond them flowed the River Thames, though its dimpling surface of gunmetal grey was grim and cold and forbidding that day, as were the puddles through which we splashed. By the time we arrived at Dolphin House my skirt hems were sodden and dragging, but rather than lifting them up I was far more concerned with gazing about, trying to picture my brother living in such a place.

Just as his letters had described, Dolphin House was set apart from the rest. Looming high above its walls were the wintery skeletal branches of trees. Tall gateposts were topped with stone dolphins, and between them there hung two iron gates, which that day had been left to stand ajar as if we were expected.

'Has Osborne Black always lived here?' While making our way up the gravel path I looked at Samuel Beresford. His answer was barely a murmur, as if fearing we might be over-heard. But I noted the tone of reproach in his voice. 'He inherited it from his mother. She and my mama . . . her sister . . . were raised in this very house, but then it was empty for many years when both of the sisters married . . . my mother to a banker, and Osborne's to a clergyman who hailed from Manchester himself and considered London to be no more than a hotbed of sin and iniquity . . . so much so that the sisters rarely met, a rift growing up between them. My mother despises him to this day, even if the man is dead.'

By then we were standing beneath a porch and Samuel shook his umbrella down, a pool of raindrops dribbling round as I whispered my question back at him, 'Then, how did you and Osborne meet?'

'He left home to study in London. By then my mama was widowed and glad of the rent that he could pay. He lived with us for almost a year, though his father strongly disapproved, considering his son's chosen career as being akin to the devil's work. But later, when his parents died – an unfortunate incident with a fire – Osborne went on to inherit the bulk of his mother's not insubstantial estate, which meant that he could then pursue any goal or career that he wanted to. Before that, he had been involved with your uncle, illustrating some of the magazines . . . which was how I first came to meet Freddie myself when he visited our house one night. I was no more than a boy at the time, but all of their talk of the publishing world . . . well, I knew that was what I wanted too, pestering Freddie remorselessly until he agreed to take me on.'

As I listened I stared at the gleaming green door, its brass knocker shaped like a mermaid, only with a tail that split in two, curling up on either side. Upon that seemingly decadent form Samuel Beresford's hand played a loud tattoo; so very insistent it made me start. Surely no one inside could have failed to hear – unless they happened to be stone deaf – unless they pretended to be elsewhere.

While we waited my stomach cramped in knots, more so with every second that passed. Samuel stepped back along the path and raised a hand to shield his eyes from the constant drizzle of the rain, through which he appeared to be studying every window in the house, and a sigh of frustration when he returned, knocking a final rat-a-tat-tat, though I had despaired of an answer by then – until we heard some shuffling feet and the tinkling of chains and the scraping rattle of turning keys, after which the door slowly opened up, and there in its frame was an elderly woman who blinked and then screwed up her eyes, squinting to see who we might be – who had dared to knock so aggressively.

'I'm sorry,' she gave a breathless response, 'Mr Black is not at . . .'

All at once her fearful expression changed, and she smiled with recognition. 'Why, is it young Samuel Beresford? How long can it be since you came to the Mall . . . and your mother? Is she well?'

'It's been almost seven years, Miss Preece . . . since before Osborne travelled to Italy. I had not expected to find you still here.'

'Oh, I'm still here, and shall have been fifty years next spring, though many things in the house have changed . . . and most of them last summer.'

When she stood back and allowed him to enter I found myself oddly reluctant to follow, to meld with the dinge of that big square hall where the atmosphere smelled of rot and damp, where the air was as mizzled and grey as the mists that hung low and ominous outside. But when Samuel Beresford glanced back at me his expression was so encouraging and, meanwhile, the old woman was prattling on, 'He's married, you know. But, of course, you must know, with such things written up in the papers, and all his Academy success, but . . .' she frowned and began to look confused, 'he didn't mention expecting you. I hope I've done right by letting you in. He's been so taken up of late, what with having the care of his invalid wife, attending to her every whim . . . and none of us servants allowed to go near, to disturb *her* peace and solitude. I've never known a man so devoted, feeding her tonics continually, and thank goodness she's up on her feet at last after all these weeks of moping around. I must say it's raised his spirits no end. They're working in his studio now.' She jerked her head back towards a door that led off from the farthest end of the hall. 'Well, down in that grotto of his.'

'Grotto?' Samuel Beresford looked bemused.

'Oh yes, he's had the builders in. The excavations and

158

tunnels they've made! You'd never believe what's gone on in those cellars . . . though how he can see to paint a thing! And the damp can't be good for anyone's health.'

On that pronouncement she tugged a cord that dangled in one of the corners, setting off a jangling bell which echoed somewhere low in the house – which brought me to my senses again, and I found the courage to look around and to see through a door that was standing ajar a space that must be a parlour. It possessed a severe formality with its dark panelled walls being relieved by what looked to be French porcelain plates – but those next to ghoulish African masks. There were several chairs around a hearth, some draped in oriental throws, whereas others were covered by plain white sheets as if the house remained halfway between being shut – or opened up. Curiosities were cluttered on tabletops; glassy orbs, silk flowers and stuffed birds in domes. In pride of place on the mantelpiece were ivory elephants, Chinese jars, and many-armed brass Indian gods, which made me think of Elijah, that day Pearl came to Kingsland House, when my brother was taking my photograph. I had to blink and swallow hard, looking away from those ornaments to the desk which held paper, inks and pens, and there at its side, in the window bay, what must be a very great treasure indeed – a tall black onyx pedestal and atop that two marble figurines; Leda's arms caressing the neck of the swan.

Such a blatantly erotic scene. My eyes closed and then refocused upon the hall's blue walls, and those hung with so many paintings that I could not begin to count. The watery mood of every one was enhanced by the liquid sounds outside, the rain's pitter-patter on window glass, the thin splashing gush of the gutters which formed the most fitting accompaniment for all those exquisite landscapes – the streams, and fountains and rivers and pools – and nothing that you would think to relate to the character of Osborne Black. But they were his. There was no doubt. I saw his name quite clearly daubed.

Such minute attention to detail. Such precision in every stroke of the brush, where even the smallest blade of grass

159

might be plucked from the canvas and held in your hand. And perhaps there really was dew on that grass. And perhaps those canvases really perspired with what looked like some form of moisture because, down below, where the skirtings were fixed, the plasterwork was blown and wet.

My eye next fell on the peacock, the stuffed bird that Elijah had written about. And from there to a marble Venus who was rising up from a scallop shell; that figure between two luxuriant palms. But Elijah's letters had not described what lay on a circular table, its base on a purple velvet cloth, a thing that made my stomach churn, reminded again of the freak in Cremorne – though this artefact was not ugly, for the contours of its wooden face were painted to look like living flesh, but with no biological origin, being one of those clockwork constructions with moving parts that mimic life – what they call an automaton. I found it eerie and sinister, having such an uncanny resemblance to Pearl, and not Pearl the woman I'd recently met, but Pearl as the girl once seen in Cremorne.

I shivered. I could not drag my gaze from the glassy green eyes that stared my way. I felt the damp brush of a draught on my cheek, and I thought I heard Elijah's voice. But wishful thinking, that's all it was, for when I looked round it was not him, only Samuel Beresford, still engrossed in interrogating that maid, who was growing increasingly reticent and evasive in her answering –

'. . . all I know is that he was dismissed. We miss him around the place, we do. Mr Lamb was like a breath of fresh air. But really, I shouldn't be saying. What goes on in this house is no business of mine. Mr Black is a very private man, and . . .'

'And what brings my cousin here today? What business is *he* engaged upon?'

Osborne Black's deep voice echoed through the hall. He stood in the now open door at its end. 'You can go.' He curtly addressed the maid, who wasted no time in scurrying off, her feet tapping along the passage until, at its end, she plunged from view: a little white rabbit who falls down a hole. Much like

Alice, I wanted to follow her, to hide from the heat of Osborne's glare, for such a charmless greeting he gave when rapidly striding towards us then, calling out, 'Good God . . . my cousin Samuel! What can you want, coming here today? If I wanted trivial gossip then I would have invited you for lunch. But I have no such inclination.'

What insults. My jaw almost dropped to the floor. How on earth to respond to this insolent man? In the months since our meeting at Kingsland House his beard had grown wild as a hermit's again, and lower, the matted dark hair of his chest protruded through his undone shirt, where the flesh was flabby, gleaming with sweat. His aroma was animal, musky and thick, combined with the smell of turpentine – and something else; festering, fishy it was. And as on that day when he'd been in Cremorne there were streaks of paint all over his clothes, more glistening wet in his auburn hair, a deeper tone of purplish red, and when he lifted a hand to his brow, to push some strands of hair aside, that colour was smeared on his fingers too, a stain I thought too much like blood.

Thank goodness for Samuel there at my side, quite unfazed by his cousin's semblance. 'Dear Osborne, forgive our pestering. We have no wish to detain you long . . . our visit only being to enquire as to the whereabouts of Elijah Lamb.'

'I imagined as much, with his lily-livered sister cowering there at your side.' Osborne Black's lips curled in a grimace. Meanwhile, he dragged a bench from the wall, its ebony fretwork inlaid with gold; surely what my brother had described as being an ancient marriage chest – upon which this ungracious groom proceeded to sit and cross his legs, his booted feet planted heavily on the turquoise blue glaze of the Eastern tiles that were laid across the hall's expanse. I found myself admiring their beauty, some illustrated with birds, some trees, some purely geometric shapes, though my drifting attention was quickly regained when Osborne Black continued with, 'If you've something to say then spit it out. I've nothing to hide. Not from you, or her . . . or anyone else.'

Samuel Beresford took a deep breath and proceeded to reel off his blackmailing threats, nowhere near as composed as he'd been in the cab. Even so, his cousin's dark features paled as he stared through the webbings of dreary light to swear that my brother had not been dismissed but had simply disappeared one day, no one having seen him since the night he left Chiswick for Burlington Row.

Burlington Row? Did my uncle know more than he let on? Through a sense of confusion I found my voice. 'But Freddie made no mention of this.'

'You must take his things. He left his things!' A different voice now, soft and trembling as its owner emerged from the very door through which her husband appeared before, and I felt as if time was winding back to that day when she came to Kingsland, except that now the perfect Pearl looked too thin and drawn and ill, a condition that could not be disguised by the finely embroidered wrap she wore, which was clinging to every angle of which her frail body was made. Her hair fell loose, greasy and lank. Her milky complexion was roughened and marred by scaled and flaking patches of red.

Osborne made to stand and looked back at his wife. 'This meeting is no concern of yours. Go upstairs. You need to rest.'

Without giving any acknowledgement she came forward and walked right past him, I presumed to obey his stern command when she began to climb the stairs. But once she had disappeared from view there came a fast drumming of footsteps above, as if she was running from room to room – after which she returned, breathless and panting, her green eyes glittering wildly when she gazed back down from the stairs' balustrade, where her arms held a bundle of what looked to be clothes – which she suddenly flung high into the air, and as those items scattered round I recognised my brother's things. How callously she discarded them!

Falling down on to my hands and knees, I was trying to gather those garments up when Osborne Black began to speak, his voice no less steely or controlled, though I feared that at any moment the man's temper might well explode, glancing back to see white-knuckled fists, above them shirt cuffs, oily and frayed, streaked black with smears of charcoal, and such a contemptuous sneer on his face when a fine spray of spittle fell over mine, which, combined with the rancid stench of his breath, almost caused me to retch in sheer disgust, inwardly quaking when he snarled, 'Take what you want and get out of my house. As you can see, my wife is unwell. The last thing we need is visitors.'

My eyes lifted to Pearl, still looking down, her gaunt features strained and running with tears. I wanted to get up and run to her side, to keep her safe from this monstrous man. But I felt a restraining hand on my shoulder. I heard Samuel Beresford's steady words, 'Lily . . . we really should think to leave.'

He helped me to stand and we made for the door, though only halfway across the hall when he paused to stoop down, to pick up a shirt and next to that a package of papers, all secured with a ribbon binding.

'What's that?' Osborne Black was at his side, the bulk of the man deceptive again, his movements as swift as a coiled spring when he snatched at what I recognised; all the letters I'd written from Kingsland House.

'Leave them alone!' Defiant anger made me brave when my eyes locked firm with Osborne Black's, seeing his burning, red-rimmed with exhaustion — or was it guilt I witnessed there? 'Those are the letters I wrote to Elijah. They are mine. They have nothing to do with you!'

The artist chose to ignore me, proceeding to flick through the first few sheets, staining the white with the paint on his fingers, his features full of a sneering contempt for whatever he'd happened to witness there — after which those papers were thrust at me, an act so abrupt and violent that I stumbled against the table upon which the automaton lay.

From deep within the mermaid's bowels there came the sound of clicking and whirring, her mechanism jolted to life, and that was when Pearl began to laugh — high pitched it was, hysterical — during which she raised a thin white arm, pointing down at her husband and shouting, 'Look at the red . . . the red on his hands? What more proof do you need of what he's done? Take those letters. Read the truth, and then go and tell Mrs Hibbert too. Mrs Hibbert has papers to set me free, to stop him putting me away . . . another ghost in Chiswick House.'

When that distressing tirade was done Osborne Black groaned and closed his eyes. His shoulders slumped forward as if in defeat, his voice gruff and weary when turning to me. 'You can see how things are, what she has become, why I try to maintain our privacy. Now please . . . I've told you all that I know. Won't you go? Won't you leave us both alone?'

The horses' wet coats were still foamed with sweat. The driver's leathers glittered like jet. Icy rain still dripped from the big black umbrella beneath which Samuel guided my arm, the weight of my body pressed hard to his as I struggled to climb into the cab, clutching that bundle of clothes to my breast and within them the stack of letters.

For five minutes or so I sat there stunned, exhausted and on the verge of tears as the carriage trundled on its way, and when Freddie broke the silence and enquired as to what had occurred in the house, Samuel Beresford placed a hand on my arm and answered his friend with a shake of his head, as if suggesting he wait to hear. But then, what was there to hear? We'd been left with more questions than answers. We had no more news of Elijah. We only knew that Osborne Black had reverted to his brutish self, as offensive as he had been in Cremorne. And how strange was Pearl's behaviour; her awful dishevelled appearance, and—

'His wife is quite mad. There's no doubt of that.' Samuel's curt statement took me by surprise.

I rapidly came to Pearl's defence. 'She wasn't like that a few months ago. It's him . . . can't you see? It's Osborne Black. Oh, Freddie . . .' I turned to my uncle then, my words coming fast and rambling. 'We have to do something to help. Pearl looks as if she is in Hell and I'm sure she knows more than she dares to say . . . and she thinks Osborne Black will put her away. She mentioned an asylum. She mentioned a Mrs Hibbert. She said Mrs Hibbert would help her.'

Freddie inhaled very sharply. Samuel Beresford went on, 'Lily, I'm sorry. I don't mean to upset you. But what option would any husband have but to seek some form of medical care. It's more than apparent that Pearl is ill. Why, all this talk of Chiswick House! I went with my mother when I was a boy. We attended a garden party there. It is a private residence. Most certainly not an asylum.'

It was then I recalled the letter, when Elijah had also mentioned that place, the house surrounded by glorious grounds in which Osborne Black's latest painting was set.

Could Pearl be deluded, after all? I felt confused and agitated. I said, 'I don't know about that, but I find Osborne Black far *too* rational. I find it most peculiar that having employed my brother to work with him in his very own house he now displays so little concern as to Elijah's whereabouts.'

A quick pause for breath to regain my composure, and then I told Freddie every word of what had been said in Dolphin House, all about Pearl's wailing distress, and that clicking automaton that had filled me with such an ominous dread, almost believing it might be alive, mocking us, mocking Pearl's despair – at which I glared at Samuel. 'I dare say that such observations will now cause you to question *my* sanity!'

He did not give an answer. Uncle Freddie looked stony faced, a vein at his temple throbbing fast when he lit another cigar, creating yet more of that choking fug, at which Samuel rolled the window back down, and as we re-entered the city's streets the freezing air that blew back in was not as fresh as it could have been, a dense swirling fog, gritty, yellow and grey, and a taste that was almost sulphurous, that stung in my eyes and burned my lungs. Samuel Beresford was coughing again, a handkerchief pressed against his face, but that could not disguise his wheezing breaths.

'Dear chap . . .' Now Freddie was all concern, his cigar

thrown out of the window. 'When we get back to Burlington Row, I'll have the maid bring a kettle up . . . get you inhaling some steam in those lungs. We'll soon have them clear and working again.'

But such an offer was not taken up. By the time we arrived in Burlington Row Samuel Beresford was all but recovered, saying that he must return to the office, a meeting he'd planned now overdue.

With the office standing opposite he did not have very far to go, but I felt a vague sort of yearning inside, a wish that he could have stayed a while – that we had not argued over Pearl – that I had replied when he said his goodbye, when his hand extended, seeking mine – when I deliberately looked away, though I did sneak a glance when he turned from me, to make his way across the street, all too soon lost in the drifts of fog that obscured many other houses around, encroaching yet more with each moment that passed, so that by the time Freddie had trudged up his steps and jangled his keys to unlock the door we might be the only souls on earth.

Before we went in, Freddie glanced at me. 'Samuel seems to be rather fond of you.'

'Oh . . . do you think so?' The observance surprised me, suddenly wondering, *Could it be true?* But then I quickly dismissed such thoughts, still finding myself to be outraged at Samuel's condemnation of Pearl, my response very curt and certain. 'Well, I'm not so sure that I care for him.'

To this, Freddie gave no more reply, merely arched one knowing brow when he ushered me into the warmth of the hall, and there, with that bundle of clothes in my arms, with my eyes strained and itchy, my throat dry and sore, I said I would go to my room to rest, at which Uncle Freddie only urged, 'But you must try to eat something, my dear . . . at least let the maid bring a cup of tea.'

I nodded, simply to placate him, for Freddie looked exhausted too, his voice croaking and tense when he called up the stairs, 'If you need me . . . I'll be in my sitting room.'

166

'Will you write to Papa?' I looked back down from the landing rail and thought again about Pearl Black, when she'd stood above us in Dolphin House. 'Will you let him know how things go on? I know he will be worrying, and waiting for news of my return.'

'Of course.' I'm sure Freddie's smile was forced. 'I'll send Augustus a telegram. I'll assure him you're perfectly safe . . . with me.'

In the bedroom I dropped that bundle of clothes on to the rug before the hearth. I went to stand at the window and peered between the undrawn drapes, looking through swirling drifts of fog at the house on the opposite side of the street. Faint yellow glimmers of gaslit rooms were shining through cracks in the shutters below. The upper floor was in darkness – though I could have sworn that through the gloom of whatever room must lie behind, a man's pale face was staring out – straight into the one in which I stood. Was it the ghost of my father? Or was it Samuel Beresford? Whatever my previous indignation, my heart began to race as I lifted my hands against cold glass, where my breaths formed a misting gauze of lace which, when I had smeared it clear again, revealed that my eyes had been deceived. But for the trailing fingers of fog that spread and dissolved before my eyes, that window was devoid of life.

With a heavy sense of loss in my heart I made my way back to the chair by the hearth, where the atmosphere was close and warm from the fire that burned so high in the grate, and soon rendered sleepy and listless by that, I stared a long time at Elijah's things, the muddle of fabrics at my feet. Not much to show for the loss of him. Reaching forward and snatching at one of his shirts, I pressed it hard against my nose, inhaling sweat and turpentine, the same fragrance I'd noticed on Osborne Black, but without the stench of rot that had per-meated Dolphin House. I sniffed and sniffed at that cloth in my hands like a dog in search of a lingering trace that might lead to my brother's whereabouts. But the clue I needed was not found there.

Next, lifting the stack of papers, rubbing in vain at the stains of red paint, once the ribbon's knot had been released I flicked through every letter I'd sent – which numbered a great many pages. And there was the sketch Elijah made when I had been sitting beside the stream, a young woman whose eyes were moist with tears. But then came the pages I had not expected – some photographic prints of Pearl, all steeped with a decadent mystery, even those where the edges appeared to be cracked, curling away from the paper's edge, so fragile the collodian when it coated the glass of the negative. But within every frame was the model's perfection, and I could not begin to look away from that glamorous, mesmerising spell. I might have been back in the tent in Cremorne, knowing myself the unwanted voyeur yet lost in the magic of monochrome shadows.

Below those sepia photographs were a number of sketches Elijah had made: scratched inky flowers, insects and leaves, and as more of the stiff white pages turned, again and again I saw Pearl's face. Pearl's eyes. Pearl's hair. Pearl's nose. Pearl's mouth. Pearl's hands. Pearl's breasts. Pearl's strange webbed toes, even that other more intimate part which looked like an oyster in a shell, or the opening bud of a fragile rose – that left me ashamed and shocked to see.

But then, I had never been meant to see. As my fingers traced the lines he'd made I saw my brother's love progress. Its first manifestation was delicate, shy, the stroke of his nib light and tentative, but those later portraits, they were more knowing; strikingly bold and passionate. And there, at the very back of the pile, I found the words he had written down – that formed a kind of story – a story Elijah had never told in the letters sent back to Kingsland House. It began with a tale of forbidden fruit – though even that word 'began' is a lie, for it had started long before, when a boy saw a girl, in a tent, in Cremorne.

ELIJAH'S DIARY

*A person unacquainted with the process, if told that nothing of this
was executed by hand, must imagine that one has at one's call the
Genius of Aladdin's Lamp. And, indeed, it may almost be said, that
this is something of the same kind. It is a little bit of magic realised.*

William Henry Fox Talbot on the Art of Photography

September 12th 1870

*A pineapple – Ananas sativas. What an exotic thing it is! Freddie
says it is ripe. I should eat it soon. But how to begin, with those
spiked green leaves, the rough scaled plates of its armoured skin.
Tomorrow, if Osborne spares me the time, I might try to make a
photograph to capture the essence of this fruit. A photograph that is
formed as art. A still life like a sepia painting. If only a picture
could capture its smell; sweet, and yet oddly acidic.*

  *How strange that I'd never seen one before. I wonder what Lily
would think of it? I long for my sister's company. So often I look at
that sketch I made, that last day when we sat beside the stream,
but I would not think to invite her here. Osborne Black is an
inhospitable man. Still, Freddie insists she may go to him. He asks
after my sister most earnestly, and both of us wished she'd been
here today. How Lily would have smiled to see how brazen Freddie
was when he plucked that little pineapple as if Kew Gardens were
his to own and then, after making a bow to a scandalised couple
strolling past, to set the fruit on top of his head, concealed within
the very hat that he had doffed and then replaced. He insisted
that's what all the best fellows did – 'My dear boy . . . you should*

know that President Lincoln used to keep all his letters and documents beneath his stovepipe hat.'

The hat Freddie chose to wear today was a thing of history itself; the tallest concoction I've ever seen, and only he could pass it off with such a swaggering nonchalance. He does have some odd eccentricities. Those occasions when I have left Dolphin House to visit with him in Burlington Row he has come down to breakfast in monogrammed slippers, still wearing that old red tasselled cap. To be honest, he looks ridiculous, like some decadent Turkish potentate. But then, he clearly has 'the knack' when it comes to attracting the female sex.

One evening he took me to Wilton's, a dubious East End music hall, a place that might generously be described as having a varied clientele. I'd never been anywhere like it before. Such a clamour of bodies. Such heat they gave off, and the smell of the place. Sweat and perfume and alcohol. The shouting. The laughing. The fug of cigars. The sparkle of mirrors set around which reflected, not only the audience, but also a huge crystal chandelier, beneath which, in the flaring of the limes, I was as dazzled as a hare when caught in the beam of the poacher's lamps. But a glass or two of Freddie's 'phizz' did somewhat alleviate my nerves, soon admiring the glints of light that caught on the balcony pillars around. Very finely made of brass they were, like sticks of sugar-barley twist. I wished I had my camera to capture such a scene, though Freddie frowned at that remark. He said we were there for fun, not work, and pointed up to the stage near by where a monocled swell was walking on, beginning to sing some bawdy song. Freddie was having the best of times, joining in with the chorus – calling to other acquaintances, or raising his glass to some women who blew kisses down from the balcony, one leaning so very far forward that her breasts dangled loose from her bodice. ''Ello, Freddie,' she screeched, 'ain't sin you in a while. Fancy a suck on me bubbies tonight?'

I had the impression they'd met before.

Very soon, she appeared at our table and perched on Freddie's knee, suggesting many indelicate things. I fear he was disappointed to see my lack of interest. But all that I could think about was that afternoon we'd spent in Cremorne. A child with tawdry yellow curls, with crude daubs of paint on a knowing face. I was not inclined to follow his lead and, to be fair, when he saw my reluctance he sent that 'lady' on her way, concentrating instead on the 'tableau vivantes' then being paraded across the boards – naked women who posed as if made of stone.

One – Botticelli's Venus – was stood in a papier mâché shell, with two or three nymphs crouching down in the pit, shaking twists of blue satin, like rippling seas. The next display was Lady Godiva, naked white legs astride a white horse, though those squeaking wheels set in the hooves could have done with a little oiling. In places the stuffing was poking out. A more moth-eaten sight would be hard to find, and the audience seemed to think the same. Like pandemonium it was, all that whistling, hooting and booing. But Freddie insisted the acts would improve, one particular singer he wished to see being hailed as the very next Jenny Lind. She came on in due course and trilled out some popular aria while the audience whistled and clapped and stamped, whipped into a frenzy all over again. And Freddie was equally impressed, saying he must interview the girl (who could not have been more than sixteen years) to appear in his latest magazine, one devoted to stars of the London stage, a world in which Freddie seemed quite at ease, until someone new appeared at our table to whom he extended a chiller response, his smile fallen into a sullen grimace through which he simply stated, 'You!'

The 'You' gentleman tipped his hat and replied in a lilting London drawl, 'Indeed, it is I, Mr Hall. I spread my net very wide these days. Catch all manner of bits and bobs that way.'

He proceeded to make himself at home, pulling up a chair and sitting down, expressing how sorry he was that Freddie had not been content with his wares, taking it as a personal slight that his very best whore had been sent away. He asked, 'Has my friend's personal preference changed? Is Cock Alley not to your taste these days?' At that he gave me a lascivious wink, and while awaiting Freddie's reply spent several tortuous moments arranging the folds *of his overcoat, which was made of black velvet and very long. His whole persona was quite unique. He had straw-coloured hair held back in a ribbon, hanging halfway down his narrow back. He had the most distinctive moustache, the hair on his face unusually fine, like silk ribbons those tusks drooped each side of his jaw. Added to that were his pursed rouged lips, and the frothings of lace at his collar and cuffs, and the flaring waistcoat beneath his coat, embroidered with mermaids, flowers and shells, all of which rendered his style to be that of some antique dandy conjured up from a bygone century. It transpired that he also had a taste for certain sorts of literature, suggesting that Frederick Hall might like to renew his professional interest in those 'special publications which were always in such demand with the punters'. At that he leaned forward, appearing more earnest, elbows propped on the tabletop, the palms of both hands pressed together hard and the fingers steepled, as if in prayer. And that was when I noticed his nails, most being well over an inch in length, some tips being filed as sharp as knives, the others jagged where broken off. And above that most unnerving sight his clear blue eyes were narrowed to slits, which caused the thick layers of powder he wore to flake and split where wrinkles creased when, while awaiting Freddie's response, he made a sly sideways glance at me. 'You must tell me the name of your pretty young friend. Is he another protégé, a new writer employed by Hall & Co.?'*

Was I naive or the victim of pride when so freely offering my name, my employment being an artist's assistant, and also a photographer – to which boast he said I would be amazed at the sort of prices being paid for portraiture of 'the intimate kind'. Next thing, he asked for whom I worked, and when I mentioned Osborne Black the queer fellow became all ears, his eyes widened, positively gleaming, when sitting back in his seat to pronounce, 'What a serendipitous event! So the prodigal has returned at last.'

And that was the point when Freddie broke in, sternly insisting that my sort of work would be of no interest to his friend, standing abruptly and looking flushed when he told me that it was time to leave, that the evening was late and he found himself bored with the entertainment then on show. But before I could gather my wits to rise and follow on in Freddie's wake that other fellow grabbed my arm, long nails digging down through the cloth of my jacket, and surprisingly strong for one so slight when he drew me near and murmured low, a smirk stretched over weasel cheeks, 'Won't you see to changing the old cove's mind? There's special perks for special art, particularly where Pearl Black is concerned. I should very much like a picture of her . . . for nostalgia's sake, if nothing else.'

The whole incident could not have lasted for more than five minutes or so, and yet it unnerved me greatly. And when I found Freddie out in the street he remained in a very dour mood. Neither one of us mentioned that fellow again. And yet, I do wonder at Freddie's connection – and how odd that the man claimed to know Pearl Black.

The enigma has been in my mind all week, only forgotten in Kew today, after which Freddie pressed me to go back to London, to dine at Bertolini's again. I laughed – 'so that you can do your best to persuade me to live in Burlington Row?'

I must say his persistence is admirable. He asks me every time we meet, and although he makes no specific claims, I suspect he has no liking at all for the character of Osborne Black. And yet, it was at his suggestion that the artist came to seek me out.

Not that I needed persuading to come. For years I have felt London's calling, but stronger now is the other thing, the siren song of Dolphin House, the fact that Osborne is married to Pearl, and most men would accept any offer he made if only to look at her each day. When I saw her in Kingsland I knew her at once – the girl I had seen in the freak-show tent. She is the reason for me to be here. It is nothing to do with Osborne Black.

Does Freddie see through me? I think he does, just as Lily did before. Today he was teasing that I must be either homesick or lovesick, for what else had caused me to grow so thin?

I suppose it is true. I have lost some flesh. I blame the regime here in Dolphin House, where every servant is gone by six and none back again before nine in the morning. The former is when

*Osborne likes to eat dinner, and no food permitted between that
and breakfast when the maids creep around us like frightened
mice, their master resenting each squeak and bump. There is no
familiarity, and when not engaged in assisting his work I find
myself rarely ever disturbed. On occasions, when Osborne works
alone, he and Pearl confined in his studio, I have taken to walking
the river paths, more at home there than ever in Dolphin House.
Most rooms here are cold and unwelcoming, full of relics as if a
museum, such an air of concealment and mystery. I stay in my
room on the attic floor and only use the service stairs, though
whenever the maids come up to clean, rattling buckets, changing
sheets, I overhear their hushed complaints, that 'his' and 'her'
bedrooms are rarely cleaned, because Osborne hates anyone going
near.*

*He is a private, closed-up man; a man of plain words and plain
habits who shows little interest in anyone else; a man who likes to
be in control, who sits at his table in glowering silence,
admonishing his wife if she should dare to ask for more than the
meagre portions that he, personally, dishes up on to her plates, as
if she is somehow incapable. As if she is a child.*

*I don't want to eat when she may not, all hunger lost when
witnessing hers, forced to observe Osborne's bullying ways, how he
stuffs his own mouth while berating his wife for being too greedy,
for growing too fat – when there is not one ounce of spare flesh on
her bones. I see her humiliation, the way she lowers her eyes while
he gloats, growing more and more flushed from the whisky or wine
which renders him drunk and insensible.*

*Often, when she has gone on to bed, he wakes from his stupors
and claims to have witnessed the visions which will then inspire
whatever new painting he has in mind – and every painting is of
his wife – his wife and water. Nothing else. At such times he will
rouse her from her sleep and have her pose throughout the night. A
few times I have woken at dawn and come downstairs to find her
still sitting, in his studio. She looks in wretched spirits; drawn and
exhausted, strangely old, her lovely brow puckered and wincing at
the sound of her husband's snores – with him sprawled at her side*

on a tattered old chaise, his brushes dropped to the ground at his feet, and there, on his easel, some half-formed creation, the latest depiction of his wife – a thing so unlike her reality. Or is she half human after all, this vision who floats in a liquid world, in realms as far removed from the truth as that automaton in the hall?

Osborne boasts of commissioning Phalibois, a famed Parisian artisan. The doll is a thing of genius. Its resemblance to Pearl is uncanny to see – Pearl's eyes, Pearl's mouth, Pearl's arms, Pearl's breasts. And yet, as in most of the paintings here, that oh so exquisitely modelled doll has a mermaid's tail in place of legs – and it may be illogical of me, but when Osborne winds the mechanism, when all of that clicking and humming begins, when the mermaid lifts a shell to its ear, I feel myself chilled to the very bone. For some reason I always think of Cremorne, the freak-show tent, the fainting girl. Does that girl remember me?

Pearl and Osborne must have gone out tonight. The house was still when I came back in. I stood with my back against the door and listened a while as it rattled shut, staring through the dusky gloom to look at the landscapes hung over hall walls – the paintings he made 'before Pearl', which are empty of any human soul, all desolate beaches, expanses of oceans, rivers, lakes, streams in woods. He uses pure colour, squeezed straight from the tube. It is striking, this impression he makes. It is something vibrant, raw and exciting. When you stand close by those pictures are blurred, as if being viewed through a misty lens, but if you take a few steps back all of the fractured brushstrokes merge, thus creating a magical 'whole' where light and shadows are flickering, every leaf and flower glistening. Does it sound too foolish of me to say that they exude some 'energy'? Or does that vitality only come from Osborne's automaton as she watches me through her cold green eyes. Eyes like Pearl's. Eyes nothing like Pearl's. Or is it the lingering odour of drains? Or is it something animal?

I notice it more and more in the house. The very first night I slept here I had the strangest dream, unsure if I was awake or asleep but all too aware of that noxious smell, an invisible, physical entity *that crept beneath my attic door, a black stain that melted over the boards. Like a serpent it slithered beneath the sheets. Its tongue was an oily bristled brush which painted its excrement over my belly, smearing my chest, my neck, with slime, trickling in between my lips, gradually filling up my lungs, causing me to gasp for breath when I stumbled from the bed to the window, where I lifted the sash to breathe fresh air, and then drank a whole jug of water down, trying to wash away the filth that I was convinced still clung within.*

I know it is ridiculous, but was that dream a warning – a warning that will not go away? Even now I can smell it still, that rancid cloying fishy stench infused with the pineapple's ripening, a smell too thick and sweet and moist, almost a thrumming sound it has, like the droning of flies round rotting meat.

September 27th

A day spent in the Eden of Chiswick House gardens – until our peace was disturbed by those troubled souls imprisoned there.

It was late in the afternoon. Osborne was still immersed in his painting. I was at work with the camera, directed by him to make pictures of Pearl, who lay on the grass by a circular lake while acting the part of a sleeping nymph. Her feet – her feet, which are strangely webbed – were dipped beneath the water's skin. Her legs were uncovered, the flesh quite bare, the same with her shoulders and her breasts – her arms slipped free from the narrow straps affixed to the top of her cotton shift. She kept the same pose for hours on end and never once voicing any complaint. But her eyelids closed only when Osborne demanded, for she passed the time with reading a book which she'd propped against a stone near by, only lifting up one languid arm whenever a page needing turning, during which moment she raised her eyes, she smiled at me, and I smiled back – and wished she might read all the faster.

When Osborne allowed her to rest and stand, her feet were wrinkled, white as wax. She walked stiffly, as if her legs were wood, and I thought of the automaton again. Does he ever see

Pearl as she really is, a woman made of flesh and blood, not another mechanical toy to be wound so that he can dictate every movement? I try, but I cannot work it out, how this couple ever came to be married, for no signs of affection do they show. And if they met in Italy – if she really did live there so many years – then how did she come to be in Cremorne? It <u>was</u> her. I know it was.

I was pondering such a question while staring again through the camera's eye, when something unexpected appeared in that world turned upside down upon its head. A group of women, all dressed in grey, were walking across the grass-green sky.

At first, being so absorbed in his work, Osborne did not notice them. When he did, he showed no surprise – anger perhaps, but not surprise. But then, it transpired he had known all along that the house was leased as an asylum, being run by a man called Cruikshank, who soon appeared in pursuit of his patients while taking great pains to apologise for any disturbance they had caused.

Why had Osborne not mentioned this before? I am taunted by the nagging thought that he is playing some sort of game – and yet this is a sport from which he appears to derive very little pleasure. His mood is increasingly surly. Or do I malign the man too much, my judgement warped by jealousy, the fact that he has Pearl, not me.

Every day I am tormented. Every time I look through the viewing lens. Osborne wants more and more photographs. The production is like a small factory, with hundreds of prints pegged up on the ropes now strung above the washing trays. And so many plates do I have to prepare that even with windows opened up I find myself coughing and breathless from the constant inhalation of fumes. Sometimes I have to go outside, hardly able to draw any air in my lungs. But such a discomfort is far outweighed by that precious moment of alchemy, when the printing frame is retrieved from the sun, in that singular moment of perfect exposure when the picture that has materialised is judged to be exactly right – before the paper grows too dark, before the whites all blur and melt. At times I must try again and again, and even then I cannot relax until the image is fixed and washed. And those are the moments I feel like a god, in control of my life, in control of my art, to see what bobs up through the water towards me – to see Pearl silver-lustred, a shimmering ghost. Pearl's torso wrapped in bindings of silk. Pearl with both arms lifted over her head, or lying in grasses, curled into herself, or sitting and reading a book by a window, the light permeating her muslin gown. When she reads she tilts her head to one side. She bites down hard on her bottom lip – and what can justify that charm when the best that these monochrome pictures can show of the bloom in her cheeks is grey, the same with her eyes and the gold of her hair?

I gaze on these reflections of Pearl without fearing the heat of Osborne's stare. I have even brought some prints to my room. At night, when sleep evades me, twisting and turning for hours on end, I stroke my fingers over the paper, touching her eyelids, as fragile as shells, and her skin which glows alabaster white when caught in the candle's muted flame. I look and I ache to touch real flesh. I touch myself and pretend it is her. And I wonder what Osborne might think to do if he knew of my obsession for Pearl, of the wanting that rushes through my veins, clawing and writhing until it is free, my groaning desire at last released. I wake every day exhausted with longing. My eyes are burning, blurred and sore. And how can I ever confess such thoughts? One wrong step, one false move, and Osborne Black would surely dismiss me from his house.

I feared he was going to send me away when I photographed the pineapple and then, on a sudden whim, thought to offer the reproduction to Pearl. She was fully dressed that morning, though her hair hung loose as usual. She was posing on the dais that stands at one end of the studio. On either side of that platform were two enormous potted palms, their colour echoed in the cloth upon which the artist's model lay; the yards of velvet and green damask upon which were scattered shells and weed; the smell of the sea still lingering. I waited for Osborne to lay down his brushes and then approached to show the print, only to find it snatched from my hands, screwed into a ball and thrown to the floor. All the while he *was shouting – a maniac. 'Do you know what that fruit represents . . . do you? Fecundity and lust! I forbid such an image in my house!'*

I was speechless. I had no idea what to do in the face of such a reaction as that. It was Pearl who sought to calm his mood, standing up and rushing to his side, taking his hands in both of hers, imploring, 'Osborne! Osborne, please . . . I was always told that a pineapple is the symbol of hospitality . . . hospitality and friendship. Nothing more than that.'

He pushed her aside, and so very roughly she stumbled back against one of the palms. It went toppling down with a banging crash. Soil and roots were flung about and the knife-like shards of the china pot were barely an inch from where she sprawled.

The blood was boiling in my veins. It was all I could do not to strike the man. But something restrained me. I'm not sure what. Was it the way Pearl shook her head, eyes wide and glazed, quite terrified? Or was it because I have come to suspect that this is what her husband wants?

As every day passes I grow more convinced that he is laying out a trap, that he takes perverse pleasure in watching me – as I watch his wife – as she watches me.

September 30th

Freddie came to visit in Chiswick again. As usual we met at the Bell. I made no mention of Osborne's behaviour, only listened to my uncle and all of his enthusiastic talk about new authors and new publications, all the scandal and gossip of his world – and the regular suggestion pressed that I write and ask Lily to visit with him, and I said that I will, but not just yet. I have no desire to distress Papa.

After eating we walked the towpath again, this time as far as Syon House, and not back at the Mall until well after seven, when Freddie suddenly professed that the heat had brought on a headache that required he take an early night. I thought it may have been the wine, a great deal consumed along with our lunch.

But I also felt exhausted, with the weather so very oppressive, unseasonably warm for the time of year, what they call a real Indian summer. There may even be a storm tonight. The air in my room is stifling. I have dragged the bed to the window frame in the hope of relief from a cooling breeze. Outside, bats are flitting round chimney stacks. House martins dip and swoop from the eaves, which are barely a yard above my head. I see over the gardens, right down to the river, where a shadowy form glides through branches of willow, suddenly disappeared.

October 1st

Last night something happened. It cannot be undone. It was Pearl who I saw in the garden. I'd never seen her alone before, not without Osborne at her side.

I went downstairs to his studio to see if he might be working there, but the room was quite empty, no candles lit. The garden doors were all locked up.

I left the house through a side passage door and made my way to the riverbank. The gardens around me were humming with insects. Birds called a poignant evening song and my nose filled, not with the stink of drains, but the malty sweet scent of the brewery. In places the river's grey surface was darker, as if it had been slicked with oil, but the water was calm, no traffic there to disturb the tide's gentle suckings and slappings, the occasional splash and quack of a duck. A rowing boat covered in dusty tarpaulin was moored upon an iron ring which chimed like a bell as that vessel rocked, as if it to announce my arrival there – though at first Pearl seemed quite unaware.

She was sitting alone at the top of stone steps that led down to the shore when the tide was out. An embroidered shawl was draped at her back and beneath it no more than her nightshift. Above that one ear might be a shell behind which some tendrils of hair had been pushed, the rest hanging down like a curtain, gleaming white gold in the fading light.

I trod on a twig. The snap of it made her gasp and turn, a look of alarm upon her face before she offered the faintest smile, when she said, 'Oh . . . it's you! Osborne's gone out for the evening . . . to dine with that Cruikshank man. His doctor friend from Chiswick House.'

'You did not wish to go?'

'Osborne did not want me there. He thinks I am safely locked in my room, no idea that I have a means of escape. But,' she gave me a quizzical look, 'what are you doing here tonight? When you left the house this afternoon he said you would go to London, to stay with your uncle, Frederick Hall.'

'That was my intention. But Freddie has not been feeling well.'

'What would he say if he knew?' She smiled.

'If he knew?'

'If Osborne knew that you were here, that we had already met before.'

'You do remember . . . the mermaid tent!'

She made no response, looking back out at the river again before speaking, almost mechanically, 'They called me the child of a mermaid. That's why I like to sit here by the river, to think about her . . . my mermaid . . . my mother . . .' She lifted her legs, straight out in front. Her naked feet circled around in the air. 'From whom I inherited these toes.'

I made no response – what could I say? Did she really believe her mother a mermaid?

She heaved a great sigh before going on, 'I can't even swim . . . and I dare say that she couldn't either. Not much of a mermaid to go and get drowned. I think she intended the same for her child because that's how they came to find me. A bastard floating in the Thames.'

So, this was the truth. I crouched on the grass, much closer. 'You know, I was orphaned too. My grandfather found us . . . Lily and me. We'd been left at the Foundling Hospital.'

She lowered her eyes at that, pressing the tips of her fingers together as if in an attitude of prayer – a motion that unnerved me, reminded too much of that fellow in Wilton's, the one who'd expressed such an interest in her. But before I could think to mention him, Pearl went on, a slight tremor in her voice. 'I was raised in a brothel. The House of the Mermaids on Cheyne Walk. It was owned . . . it may very well still be, by a woman called Mrs Hibbert. The woman with me that day in Cremorne. I wish I could see her. I wish I could tell her . . .' She broke off for a moment, her voice filled with longing and sadness. 'Cheyne Walk overlooked the river too. When it was summer I would sleep with my windows opened up, listening to the creak of the boats on the river, and the creaking of springs in the beds below. Sweet lullaby music of water and sin.'

Shocked at such candour, my mind filled with thoughts of the Wilton's whores and the man who purported to be their pimp. Had Pearl really belonged to such a world?

'I knew there had to be something wrong, with all those stories Osborne told . . . when he said you were raised in Italy.'

She bit down on her lip, in that way she has, confusion written over her face as if wondering whether to trust me or not. 'But we did . . . we did live in Italy. We stayed there for several years. While there he called me daughter. But now, he tells everyone I am his wife . . . for the sake of respectability . . . for the sake of his career. But I am not a real wife, no more than some glorified slave to his art . . . a slave he wants to keep as a child. Can you imagine how that feels,' her voice was higher, louder now, 'to feel as if time is suspended, to feel _I_ am suspended. Is that normal, do you think? Is that natural?'

I thought it was not. And yet the only thing I said was, 'All the paintings he makes . . . they are . . . you are beautiful.'

She shifted her weight, shuffling on to her knees, her face now turned and level with mine. 'But I want you to see me for what I am.'

'What are you, Pearl?'

'Not a mermaid.' She spoke with such vehement passion. 'That's only how he wants me to be. It's the very worst thing about being . . .' I thought she was going to say 'his whore', but Pearl was far from being that, and I did not deserve what she gave that night; freely, of herself, for me. For then, she broke off and stared up at a sky that was bruised with clouds of purple and grey, through which a pale moon was shining down; its twin a wavering orb in black waters.

Pearl asked, 'Do you know the tale of the mermaid who fell in love with a man, who sold her soul to a wicked witch, in return for which her tail was shed and replaced by a pair of human legs? But every step she walked on land caused the mermaid to suffer agonies, as if she trod on the points of knives.'

She glanced back over her shoulder again. She said, 'I would walk on knives for you.' A tear spilled from her eye and rolled over her cheek, down her neck to the soft indentation that formed a hollow at its base, and there it became a miniature pearl, and I longed to lick it, to lick her clean, to forget everything she'd said before, only wanting the taste and the touch of her skin, which was perfumed with lemon and musky rose – nothing like those other girls I'd known, who lay on their backs in fields of straw, who smelled of hops and cider and sweat.

I lifted one of Pearl's feet in my hands and kissed the small scar that marred its heel. I kissed the flesh between white toes, translucent and marbled blue with veins. I lifted up the folds of her gown, exposing her body's fragility, no mermaid's tail but pale lithe limbs, hips and ribs that might be carved ivory, above which her eyes were agate glazed, and her hair spread like coiling twists of gold, the same as the curls between her thighs, which opened up beneath my hands, her back arching, her moans and sighs coming urgent, her belly rising to meet my weight, and I wished I could drown in that sweet embrace, though almost as soon as my thrusting began I felt the resisting barrier, and that was the moment she cried in pain, and I came with an all too swift release.

But I felt but no sense of emptiness when I lay with Pearl cradled in my arms, as she clung to me, as I nuzzled her neck and pressed my cooling flesh to hers, and would have done more – but for the church's tolling bell which made me feel like a man condemned when my lover let out a small sigh of dismay and drew away from my embrace, sitting up, dragging fingers through her hair, unsnagging the leaves and grasses there.

*Every window was still steeped in darkness when I followed her
to the far side wall against which an ancient wisteria grew, and
there she made her sudden plea, the words I had least expected to
hear, 'Elijah . . . you must stay away from me. You must leave this
house. You must go tonight!'*

'Why?'

'Because of Osborne.'

*'If I go, then I'll take you with me! How could I leave you
behind with him?'*

*I had never felt surer or braver, exulted at such a chance as this,
my hopes only dashed when she lowered her face. 'But Osborne
will try to hurt us both.'*

'Not if we go to Burlington Row. Freddie will help us and . . .'

*'Frederick Hall?' She spoke his name slowly, until the next
words came rushing out, 'No! I could never do that.'*

*Before I could think to ask her why we heard the dull echo of
footsteps near by, an irregular beat on the pavement slabs as
someone approached along the Mall. Pearl froze, staring hard into
my eyes, as if making a further silent plea before suddenly
hitching up her hems and starting to climb that wisteria ladder, so
swiftly ascending the side of the house that she might have turned
into a monkey. And while standing below, watching every move, I
noticed the stains on the back of her shift, how the white of the
cloth was dark with blood. And then came the groaning of a gate,
at which point I returned to my senses again, re-entering the house
by the side passage door and making for Osborne's studio. And
there, despite my trembling hands, I managed to light a candle, to
snatch up a pen and some paper upon which I started to scribble, to
make the pretence of working. But I need not have fretted. Osborne
was drunk and when finally lurching into the house, he slumped
on the sofa at my side, grunting some words that made little sense
before laying his head on my shoulder; the pillow upon which the
cuckold's head had come to find its sleeping rest.*

*The stench of that man's foul snoring breaths! I pushed him
aside to go on upstairs to hide away in my attic room, but this time
I took the main front stairs and paused a while outside the door*

that I felt so sure must correspond to the window through which I'd seen Pearl climb. I placed my fingers on the knob. I thought to turn it but did not dare, hearing the sound of steps behind as Osborne trudged across the hall. He had woken. He was following me, his tread creeping heavy upon the stairs while I walked on up the second flight.

And here, I have locked my door tonight, consumed with the irrational dread that Osborne might pursue me, relieved to hear a door slamming below, some more dull thuds and then nothing but silence, during which I lit the candle stub, undressed and looked down at my naked self and saw more blood, like streaks of rust that have dried upon my flaccid sex.

October 5th

Three days have passed by. Three days and I have not seen Pearl. Osborne tells me that she is indisposed. He has made some sneering comments regarding 'the filth of a woman's curse'. Was that the cause of the blood, then? Was I deceived into thinking – I don't know what to think any more. Osborne's eyes are cold and interrogating. There is no way to guess the true cause of his mood. It may be, as he claims, that he is simply at odds with himself, impatient to start upon something new and, with that in mind – with his wife being unavailable – he asked if I would agree to pose. He had me kneel on the studio floor, reaching out with my arms, my eyes lifted up to the ceiling above. I complied, but found the experience odd. Despite being clothed, I felt unsafe. I felt myself unprotected, as if his eyes stripped me naked, as if they had peeled the flesh from my bones.

Does he know what happened the other night? Does he see through my questions regarding Pearl's health, what I try to pass off as polite conversation, when inside I am like a man possessed, only yearning to see her face again?

October 6th

Pearl came downstairs today. She looked like a ghost, any glow in her cheeks from those days in the sun when she posed for Osborne at Chiswick House now having faded entirely away. Her eyes were shining, unnaturally bright, as if she had taken some opiate. Even Osborne was moved to comment upon how languid she seemed to be. But his sympathy only went so far, insisting that she sat again – the scene with the nymph beside a lake needing some final adjustments made – a minute touch to the shape of her mouth, to a curl of her hair, to be absolutely sure in his mind that the portrait was done to perfection.

He had her recline upon the chaise and no need for her clothes to be removed while he worked through the whole of the afternoon. I think she slept. Her eyes were closed. And, while watching, with every hour that passed, I despaired of us ever being alone, of touching her with my hands again, until the gods must have heard my plea, when the doorbell rang, then a hammering knock, which caused Pearl to start in some alarm.

Miss Preece, the oldest of the maids, came shuffling in to make the announcement that Osborne was needed to sign for a letter – after which, while cursing to be interrupted, he stormed his way out to the entrance hall.

When alone, I enquired if Pearl was well. She said nothing at first, still looking to be disoriented, and her eyes darting swiftly around the room before she glanced up and whispered, 'He came to my room. He saw the blood. I said it was my monthly curse.'

There was no chance for more. Osborne returned, his presence like a brooding cloud passing over the light of the midday sun. He thumped a letter down on his desk, afterwards staring hard at Pearl and pressing a hand against his brow as if in actual physical pain. And locked in such a posture he announced that his inspiration was gone. He told Pearl to go upstairs again.

She did not come back down to dine and, finding I had no appetite, I excused myself and also retired. I have spent the evening drawing Pearl, her image burned into my memory.

October 7th

When I asked if Pearl was still unwell, Osborne simply shrugged and smiled. All day he has been in the best of moods, examining sketchbooks and making notes for whatever new work he has in mind. While he muttered on in that way he has, I worked in silence, cleaning the brushes and palettes, checking the stocks of all the paints, after which he requested I go to the darkroom and bring back every photograph. Some, those of Chiswick House gardens, he told me to copy out in ink – illustrations he'd promised to supply for some advertising brochure. While I did that he tore many others to shreds, carelessly flinging the scraps to the floor. It grieved me to see my work so abused, to see Pearl's image being destroyed. But those prints with which he was satisfied were carefully dated and stored away in large manila envelopes, every one being marked with notes on the front, listing details of place, and posture, and light – every reference that he could possibly need to select his chosen 'part' of Pearl.

Only now, when I sit here alone in my room, have I dared to admit to the flicker of hope that he may be preparing to let her go. Is this why he had me come to his house, to take so many photographs, so that he can continue with his work should his muse ever happen to disappear?

October 8th

I could not sleep. I waited 'til dawn, then dressed and went down to the studio. Osborne lay unconscious on one of the day beds, an easel knocked to the floor at his side, paint spilled and congealed round a bottle of chloral – a substance of which he is too fond. He disguises its taste in whisky. He says it aids a state of hypnosis, his visions more vivid, more lucid.

I left him to his dreaming. I left the house through the passage door and went to the wall at the side of the house where Pearl's wisteria ladder grew, and only the briefest moment of doubt before I began to ascend myself, flinching at every rustle and creak – in case I fell. In case he woke. But thankfully, those branches held. I finally scaled the parapet gulley and crawled beneath her window.

The moon proved itself my friend that night, its radiance spilling into a room which seemed to be filmed in a coating of snow, a powdery dust on the mirrored armoire, on a chest of drawers, all the trinkets above, all the pebbles and shells that lay around. There was a large mahogany bed, its posts carved with mermaids and dolphins and within them Pearl looked like a princess, lost in a pale enchantment. When I tapped on the glass she did not stir, nor when I pushed to raise the sash, to allow me the space to squeeze beneath before slowly creeping towards the bed, where I knelt, where I gazed at her dreaming face and then lowered my lips against her ear, to whisper my lover's name.

That was foolish of me. She woke in blind panic, rearing up like a creature possessed, her eyes open but not really seeing, her breaths very fast when lashing out, trying to push me away with her arms, crying the same word again and again. It was something like 'tip'. It made no sense, though my only concern at that point in time was that Osborne might hear and discover me there. I may have been too rough, pressing a hand against her mouth, repeating her name until she woke – when the arms that had tried to strike me were now reaching out with affection. She drew me down to lie at her side and how sweet, how slow that silent love – until the dawn came slanting in, when Pearl began to weep again, when she said she saw malice in Osborne's eyes. She begged me to go away again – and was it my guilt, my imagination, or was there a creak outside the door, the slightest groan, the hush of cloth?

October 9th

At breakfast today, Osborne only smiled when he said Pearl was still indisposed and would spend the rest of the day in her room. He seems intent on locking her up and now, more than ever, I must make plans. But Osborne must not suspect my intentions, so when he asked me to pose again I agreed without hesitation. He said we *would work 'below', proceeding to open a hidden door in one of the studio's panelled walls – one I had not previously known to exist. He struck a match and lit a jet to illuminate a narrow hall, a run of stone steps at its farthest end. He beckoned for me to follow. He smiled – an expression sinister, with his beard grown so knotted and wild of late, taking on a strangely bluish hue from the cast of the flame upon the wall. My nose prickled and itched with the mushroomy dampness, beneath which a familiar noxious stench, even stronger that odour of sewage and fish. Could Osborne smell it too? He said nothing. He seemed only excited when, looking back over his shoulder again, he said I was his honoured guest, that apart from Pearl and the cleaning staff, and the builders who'd followed his plans for construction, I was the only visitor to see where his favourite paintings were hung, the ones that he would never sell.*

The lamp threw its juddering rays on mossed walls. I heard sounds of running water, a pleasanter fragrance in the air – of linseed oil and turpentine, the ingredients of any artist's trade. But nothing could have prepared me for that moment the passageway opened out into a subterranean room, in the centre of which was a raised round pool, and around that a circle of hissing jets. Osborne told me those burners were never turned off. 'The flames warm the water for the fish. I observe them for my paintings. But the wretched things keep dying on me.'

Stepping nearer, past marble sculptures of porpoise and turtles, mermaids and nymphs, I saw gliding shapes in the brackish black water. Each one was at least a foot in length, scales glinting metallic when caught by the light which drew out the sheen of white, orange and black. But most of those colours were crusted grey, the spread of some spotting fungus. Two or three of the fish floated dead on the surface, though Osborne did not seem the least concerned, only proud of the engineering feat. 'Ingenious, don't you think! Fresh water is drawn from the house supplies, circulated through grated vents then dispersed along pipes that run down to the Thames.'

I said nothing in reply. My eyes had moved on, seeing a mound of sand in one corner. Perhaps it was white when dry. Down here, damp and clogged, the colour was dark, and it was littered with pebbles and weeds as if naturally deposited there by the tide of some invisible sea. All over the walls were shell mosaics, intricate swirling shapes they made – of stars and moons and flowers and hearts – except for the niches, where paintings were hung, one or two of them being concealed by cloths, but the rest were clearly visible, and every single one of Pearl, her face a pale star shining out through the darkness.

I found myself turning around in slow circles to view the entire collection there, being stunned by their ambiguity. An alluring sexuality suffused with the modesty of a child. A child goddess, a child nymph, a child mermaid, her hair wreathed in flowers and sea snakes and shells, and the luminous glimmer of aquamarine from the water in which she floated or swam, all studded with glistening bubbles of air, with fish like those in the pool near by, all manner of bird and insect life, lilies and ferns and anemones. Every image was something fantastical, yet stunningly honest in tone. A long while before I could find my tongue, to say how wonderful they were, how it was nothing short of a crime to keep such treasures hidden away where surely the moisture would cause them to rot.

'It's dry enough. I light the fire. The work is protected with varnish. I do not paint for other eyes. I paint for myself, and this is my world, modelled on a grotto . . .' He paused, almost wistful when he said, 'The grotto in which my muse first posed.' And then, looking up, with his arms spread wide, he asked, 'Don't you find it enchanting . . . my secret realm, my darkness?'

I said I found it cold.

He laughed and crouched down by a large stone hearth, where a metal basket overflowed with the debris of some half-burned logs. There Osborne lit some kindling. Yellow flames threw dramatic shadows around, flashing over the candlesticks on either side, two tarnished silver dolphins from which wax must have dripped for hours before, thick dribbles of white on the stone-flagged floor creating organic, intricate shapes.

'What do you think of our angel?' With a sudden flourish, he drew back a cloth to show the painting that lay beneath – one in which Pearl was not alone. The mermaid reclined in lace frothings of surf that ebbed at the edge of a sandy shore. There were towering cliffs in the distance behind and on the pebbled beach at her side a small boy was kneeling, bowing his head, as if in adoration or prayer. He might be some raven-haired cupid, but whereas all the putti I'd seen before were adorned with wings of downy white, those on his back might belong to a bat, being rubbery, black and sharply tipped. And the link, or large candle, that Cupid held seemed the crudest of phallic symbols to me, with its base pressed low against the boy's belly, its pillar clutched tightly in one of his hands, and the fizzing of smoke rising up from its wick – what might be a smouldering firework – too suggestive of something carnal.

Osborne did not wait for my response, going on to explain how that boy was modelled on a child who had once shared his home in Italy. 'His name was Angelo,' he said. 'I looked on that boy as if a son. But he grew too precocious and daring in all of his shows of affection for Pearl. It was a shame, but he had to go, though his beauty will always be preserved . . . if only for my eyes, down here.'

I knew – how could I not know – the implication behind his words, that Osborne had guessed my feelings for Pearl – that perhaps he had spied on us last night. And that cloth he drew down from the painting, was it the shawl that Pearl had worn, that night when I found her beside the Thames? Had she left it there? Had he found it?

And yet, still not wanting to draw his suspicion, despite all the turmoil in my mind, I simply did as Osborne asked when he sat behind his easel and directed me to kneel on the sand, in much the same stance as he'd sketched me before – though this time he asked me to take off my clothes, my jacket, my waistcoat, my shirt as well, my naked upper body and arms stretched to the domed rock ceiling. Despite the fire that Osborne made I shivered. I felt claustrophobic, as if I'd been buried inside a tomb. But still, by my show of obedience, by the means of my silent compliance, I hoped to conceal any trace of guilt that Osborne might seek to find in me, even if it was mirrored wherever I looked, my eyes reflecting those pictures of Pearl.

For hours he worked – feverish brushstrokes, swiftly applied, tutting with impatience when, every ten minutes or so, I had to lower my arms to rest. My knees were aching, burning, numb, and when he finally said we could stop it took some considerable effort to stand and work the stiffness out. And Pearl has endured this for years and years.

When he led me back up the steep stone steps, he looked over his shoulder and grunted, 'Only two or three more days of this should be sufficient to see you done.'

I suspected that when this next work is complete, when I am – as he charmingly puts it – 'done', his intention will be to send me away. But I was not prepared for what came next, when he threw back his head and laughed out loud. 'I must say, it's a sight for sore eyes, seeing you shuffling behind. Do you know . . . you resemble your grandfather?'

At that moment I hated Osborne Black – to hear such sneering cruelty for which there was no cause or justification, even less when his taunts persisted, as he reached back with one of his hands and chucked it lightly under my chin, the strangest sorry look on his face when he leaned in towards me, his face very close, when he held my gaze and murmured low, 'An old man with the face of a beautiful boy.'

Tomorrow is a Saturday. I shall spend the day posing as Osborne suggests. In the evening I shall travel to London and visit Freddie in Burlington Row. I have decided to end this charade – this taunting game that Osborne plays – the rules I cannot comprehend. When I tell my uncle all that goes on, surely he will be able to offer advice with regard to this quandary in which I am placed. Freddie will know what to do for the best. Freddie is a man of the world. He holds no affection for Osborne Black. I shall feel no remorse when I steal his wife.

PART THREE

From Observations on Hysteria,
by Rufus W. Cruikshank

'Further to our findings, it is an indisputable fact that a quarter of all women suffer from the ailment of hysteria, the name of which stems from the Greek word for uterus, which is *hystera*. The symptoms of advanced *Female Hysteria* or *Histeria Femenina* affect most civilised women whose dysfunctional or overactive reproductive organs are prone to experience the symptoms which manifest themselves as: faintness, nervousness, insomnia, fluid retention, heaviness in abdomen, muscle spasm, shortness of breath, and irritability, all of which are due to emanations that seep up from the vaginal tract and overwhelm the fragility of the female body and mind. Delirium is a common symptom of hysteria, often constituting the final phases of a classic major attack during which the manifestations of muscular spasms and paroxysm betray a maniacal diathesis. Insanity is beyond any doubt, and the patient's family and doctor will have observed at first hand what the asylum physician will go on to confirm. Many illustrative cases may be found, and only once was a misdiagnosis applied when the inmate, J.D., was later found to be suffering from typhoid. Nevertheless, we consider this a secondary infection, favoured by the condition of the patient, and in every case observed there were marked neurotic disturbances where the diagnosis of hysteria was entirely justified.'

From Aretaeus the Cappadocian:
Ancient Greek physician

'In the middle of the flanks of women lies the womb, a female viscus, closely resembling an animal; for it is moved of itself hither and thither . . . also upwards in a direct line to below the cartilage of the thorax and also obliquely to the right or to the left, either to the liver or spleen; and it likewise is subject to falling downwards, and, in a word, it is altogether erratic. It delights, also, in fragrant smells, and advances towards them; and it has an aversion to fetid smells, and flees from them; and on the whole the womb is like an animal within an animal.'

PEARL

Set me as a seal upon thine heart, as a seal upon thine arm; for love is
strong as death;
Jealousy is cruel as the grave: the coals thereof are coals of fire,
which hath a most vehement flame.
Many waters cannot quench love, neither can floods drown it:
if a man would give all the substance of his house for love, it would utterly
be contemned.

Song of Solomon, Chapter 8:6–7, *King James Version*

It keeps raining, like cats and dogs it is. I lie in my room and all
I can hear is that continuous pattering sound. I think it is going
to drive me mad, as mad as those ghosts in Chiswick House.

I know they exist. I saw them, on one of those last hot
summer days. I lay on the grass with my feet dipped in water,
my head wreathed in the trails of geranium that Osborne had
picked from the gardens around. How he fussed over my pose,
arranging the fall of the stems through my hair, not satisfied
that I held my arms in quite the same way as the day before,
each part of my flesh being placed just so, in just such a way, at
just such a distance from the lake's edge, at just such an angle to
show the same view of the obelisk rising up from the pool and
the temple, the little folly, that stands on the slope at its farthest
edge.

When finally satisfied with me he turned to complain at
Elijah's work, the easel erected in quite the wrong place, as was
the box with the brushes and paints, though Elijah refused to
rise to the bait, lips pursed as he whistled some pretty tune

while erecting Osborne's parasol, so that Osborne could work without being oppressed by the heat or the glare of the midday sun.

I presumed it was the weather that caused this fractious mood. It had changed, almost imperceptibly. There was no mist, but the sparkling clarity had gone. The air was heavy and humid, the sure sign of a storm on its way.

Of course, the English weather could never be predictable, which was why he wanted the photographs to keep an accurate reference, the true nuance of nature in all of its detail for when the leaves and the flowers were gone. But I think it is imagination that makes his work unique, those touches that Osborne always adds when a painting is very nearly done; the malevolent satyrs, the ogres and goblins – though it does seem a shame to me to infuse what appears as a paradise with those leering horned beings, those creatures half formed that crouch to peer out from the bushes and trees. Sometimes when posing, when half asleep, I could almost believe those demons are real, inch by slow inch creeping nearer, watching and waiting, biding their time.

Only once did I dare to tell him that I found them too clichéd, too crudely suggestive. He said he must give the connoisseurs the things they like to see the most: '*a sensual titillation wrapped up in the guise of classical art – to hang high upon the Academy walls*'.

Oh yes! He must hang high. But is he selling his soul to the devil, to be exalted above other artists who may at one time have spurned his work, just as he now derides most of them? He holds a grudge as close as a love. For Osborne, any slight is a wound. It never heals, but festers and rots, eating its way into his heart.

Does Osborne have a heart? I am not sure he does. He works me harder and harder these days. In Chiswick House gardens I was used up, posing from morning until the dusk, legs heavy and aching when walking back home, and Osborne striding on ahead while Elijah followed a way behind with his camera and all of Osbourne's equipment, and the painting secured on top of that below an oilcloth canopy. But it wasn't so very far to go, and pleasant enough by the river path where we passed by the quaint little cottages where donkeys and cows were tethered in yards, and almost a tunnel in places it was, overhung with branches of dripping green where we breathed in the malt from the breweries around, and below us the Thames encroached on mud shores, rising up around the green isles in its midst where nothing ever seems to live, apart from ducks and herons and coots.

'Do those islands have a name?' One evening I spoke my thoughts aloud. 'They look like miniature fairy worlds, with the mists rising up from the river like that.'

'One of them . . .' Osborne stopped. He lifted his arm to point, 'That eyot over there . . . they call that one Oyster Pie Island.'

'Oyster Pie Island!' Elijah chuckled, his mirth so infectious that soon we were all of us laughing at the incongruity of the name – and so seldom does Osborne even smile that I felt the swelling of my heart. But all too soon the mood dissolved, the three of us growing silent again when we came to the house, like an isle of its own, with its walls of high hedging, and the new stuccoed walls, and the new painted door – every ounce of levity sucked away by the dingy gloom of Dolphin House.

However much work Osborne's builders have done, as soon as you walk into the hall the stench of the damp is waiting to greet you, still lingering from the previous year when, by all accounts, there was a flood when the river rose up and broke its banks. There is nothing – no flowers, no scented oils, no fresh air coming in through the windows and doors – that can mask that odour very long. No amount of new plaster and whitewash paint can stop the moisture bubbling up, the salts growing out like wormy threads.

Even worse is the air in his grotto. Sometimes I can barely breathe down there, and yet his obsession with darkness endures, even now, even after all of these years. Goodness knows what it cost to create such a world, and all of those precious artefacts that he had shipped back from Italy, only to hide them away in that dungeon. I begin to think he is a troll, gloating over his treasure hoard while burners hiss and candles dip, gilding his sunless temple while he creates pictures of shadow and light. But none of *those* canvases will he sell. He insists they are '*the Truth of my art, created for posterity*'.

How I prefer to be out in the light. And the Chiswick House gardens were lovely, though Osborne was not so happy there. As the sun arced higher in the sky the perspiration stained his shirt, the linen clung damp like a second skin. His face was flushed. Sweat ran from his brow and into his eyes, which were constantly rubbed with the heels of his hands. The hairs of his chest were matted dark, stuck with sweat to the linen cloth. I thought again of Margate beach.

The heat did not bother Elijah. I watched him through my half-closed eyes and saw his smoothly shaven face, not red, but tanned to an olive brown. The same with his arms where the shirtsleeves were rolled to show the roping lines of veins. How I desired to touch them, to follow the patterns they made on his skin. It seemed that my soul was trapped in a spell, and when he removed the camera cap or gazed at me through his secret lens, or counted the seconds out aloud until the exposure time was done – every one and two and three and four – every beat was a stolen thud of my heart. He captured my image so many times, taking so many pictures from so many angles, in every degree of light and shade. He stared at me because he could, because that was what Osborne had asked him to do. Elijah stared, and Elijah smiled, and who would not want to kiss that mouth, and who would not want to brush their fingers through those curling knots of hair, like the prettiest boys in Italian paintings, like a work of art that has come to life, like—

Where has Elijah gone? What has Osborne done with him? Has he harmed him, just like my sweet Angelo? I dream of that child. Such guilt. Such loss. When the rain trickles over my windowpanes, it mocks me, it hisses, it whispers its song through the new iron bars Osborne screwed to the frames. *You are here. They are gone. They are gone away.*

I whisper back. I tell the rain those things of which I grow surer each day, the truth that I wrapped around a stone when Frederick Hall came to knock on the door, when I found some paper and scribbled my words and flung them down to land at his feet. *He knows. He lies. He is here.*

I meant Osborne, not Elijah. Osborne, who was unaware of what was forming beneath his eyes, immersed in his other painted worlds, at night drinking chloral until in a stupor, collapsing and lying as still as the dead. Now, I wonder – did he only pretend?

I know he lied to the visitors . . . to Elijah's sister, Lily Lamb. I hope she reads those papers – what I found when I went to the attic room and saw Elijah's possessions there. Why would he leave them behind? Why was his work still spread on the table? And that bundle of sketches, such private things with his sister's letters placed on top concealing the secrets under-neath, when he wrote about that blessed night, when he climbed through the window and came to my bed – before Osborne fixed the bars in place.

Now I lie here alone. My sheets are cold. The room is furred with layers of dust. Sometimes I write through that dust with a finger. I write on the mirror placed over the mantel, *Where is Elijah Lamb?* I stoop down and throw a log on the fire, and when the flames roar up again I imagine that heat to be the sun, and the sun is shining clean and hot, just as it shone in Chiswick House gardens, every day during August, and all through September, a St Martin's summer, an Indian summer. Summer of Elijah . . . Elijah . . . Elijah . . .

A fly has landed on one of my arms. I don't even try to push it off. It reminds me of the sweet green grass, and the insects that zithered around us then, and the shimmering oily perfec-tion in the turquoise blue wings of a dragonfly. I think I'd been entranced with that before looking up to see the ghosts.

All dressed in grey gowns, they came floating towards us, and how peculiar they looked, every woman with her hair shorn off; reduced to something asexual. Some of them twittered and squabbled like birds. Others were mute, staring blankly around. They all gathered there on the opposite bank, gawping and pointing, staring at me. But then, like bored children, they turned to move on, heading towards an arched stone bridge across which the man was approaching, the man with his ginger-bristled moustache, his stiffly old-fashioned black frock coat, and that cane with its silver hooked handle – what they call a 'life preserver' – its end tip-tapping along the path.

Until then, Osborne had been oblivious, entirely engrossed in his work. When he noticed he stood so abruptly that his stool was sent rolling across the grass, his brushes following after as he threw them down and started to rant, 'For God's sake . . . has Cruikshank let them out?'

'Who are they?' Elijah calmly enquired, having withdrawn from his camera tent; now also observing that little crowd.

'The lunatics!' Osborne growled his response. 'The women who live in Chiswick House!' He motioned towards the red-haired man. 'Elijah . . . Go and speak with him . . . the asylum super-inspector. Tell him to take his fools away. He guaranteed my privacy. Damn him!' Osborne cursed again, stamping his foot like a petulant child. 'I told that doctor . . . I *must* have peace . . . I cannot be disturbed when I work.'

While Elijah went off to convey such a message, hardly able to conceal my own disbelief, I asked, 'Osborne . . . is this place an asylum? You told me that no one lived here. Why didn't you tell the truth?'

'What need was there? I had not expected to be disturbed. And back in my youth it was a resort, an exclusive idyll for the rich. There was even a menagerie, with elephants, emus and giraffes, all wondering free in these very grounds. Now, the rich place their embarrassments here, those family members they need to cage.'

'Locked up like creatures in a zoo.' As I murmured my answer Elijah returned, followed by the Cruikshank man, who extended his hand to Osborne, a gesture that Osborne rudely ignored while the doctor made his apologies. 'Mr Black, I most heartily regret that you have been disturbed today. The patients were due for their airing, which they normally take on the eastern lawns. But we have a new nurse, and . . .'

'You have broken your side of the bargain. Have I not bequeathed enough to your blessed medical charity?'

'Your support has been most generous.' Dr Cruikshank gave a sickly smile, now knocking his stick on the side of his leg. 'Our reputation is growing fast . . . great advances are being made in understanding the female psyche and . . .'

'That is of no concern to me!' Osborne turned his back disparagingly, at which I thought the Cruikshank man would take the hint and make to leave. But instead he came walking over to me; that cane of his sinking into the grass as he dragged one limping leg behind. When standing directly above where I lay, he lifted the stick into the air and said, 'Do excuse this old soldier's ungainly approach.' His free hand reached down to take my own, though I cringed at the touch of his sticky palm, and I thought his eyes were horrible, as big as saucers they seemed to be, magnified by his spectacle lenses – behind which, when he chanced to blink, I saw thick red lashes brush over his cheek, and when that curtain rose again he looked back at Osborne and stated, in the most obsequious of tones, 'Mr Black, your muse is quite as enchanting as I have been led to believe.'

In the process of reclaiming his stool, Osborne looked daggers over his shoulder and answered the doctor dismissively. 'My *wife* . . . whose pose you have now disturbed.'

'Ah . . . your wife? Well, I see why you hide her away. I must insist you bring her along to the upcoming governor's dinner here. And perhaps you will bring the sketches then, the ones you promised to provide . . . some pictures of the gardens to illustrate our brochure . . . for the advertisements, for the magazines?'

'I have not forgotten,' Osborne snapped. 'The sketches are

but a trifling thing. I shall have Elijah make them. Rest assured, he has talent enough. But for now I must ask you to leave us to work, to gather your fools and go away.'

Osborne's insults were interrupted when another woman appeared on the bridge, a nurse I think she must have been, very neat and pristine in blue and white. She called to Cruikshank, who limped back towards her, the two of them huddled in some consultation before spreading out in separate directions, circling and herding their wards like dogs – and the patients all obeying them, like sheep playing Follow my Leader. But what sad and pathetic expressions I saw upon those women's faces. How fiercely stern was that of the nurse, and how irritating Cruikshank's stick, still making that tap-tap-tapping sound – a sound like the rain on my window right now, an endless percussion that makes me too nervous; the same with all the groaning whines that seep from the bones of this old house. Or do they only come from me, when I think too much on the other thing, the event that caused me such distress – when this morning I looked through the bars at my window and saw a man in the street below, a man with a very distinctive appearance, long yellow hair hanging loose at his back, yellow whiskers that drooped around his mouth, and such an uncanny resemblance to—

No! I must have imagined that. I must have grown delirious, to think of *that* ghost drifted back again. But when I hear the buzz of the fly, when I hear the slow whining drone of its wings and the bang as it bats on the window glass, my heart begins to race. My nerves are like wires stretched to their limits, at any moment about to snap. I look over my shoulder at every small shadow, even though I know *he* cannot get in, even if he climbed the wisteria branches, even if he was able to stare through the window, those iron bars so newly fixed would surely keep Tip Thomas out – just as they keep me trapped inside. Still, I jump at each footfall that comes up the Mall. I imagine clawed fingers pushing the gate, springy steps padding silently up the path as Tip Thomas stands beneath the porch and prepares to rap upon the door, to demand admission into this house, to take me away and—

This is how foolish I have become, because Osborne would never let *him* in. Ever since Elijah went away Osborne insists he will keep me safe. Osborne keeps telling me not to cry. Osborne keeps locking my bedroom door, bringing my meals in on trays, feeding me thin and tasteless broths, pushing the spoon between my lips as if I am an invalid.

He always leaves me hungry. But the sticky brown medicine soothes those pangs, and soon I am lost in its sticky dreams. Last night I imagined I grew very small and squeezed my way through the window bars, and then floated up on a gust of air and landed on Oyster Pie Island. The trees were fruiting real oyster pies, the pastry warm and buttery, the salty rich liquor dribbling out as I crammed more and more of them into my mouth. I swelled to the size of a great balloon, and drifted high into the clouds – on up through the clouds to the shining stars.

If Osborne has his way I shall shrink to the size of a child again. But then, he has always preferred me like that, with my ribs jutting out, and my hips like a boy's and my breasts become shrunken and flat to my chest. And still he complains that I have too much flesh; that the fat is leaching into my mind, now addled with fancies of the mad. And perhaps I have been driven mad by the guilt of the secrets I have to keep – all the things that I did with Elijah Lamb?

How long has it been since he went away? I don't even know what month it is. I only know the time of day by hearing the chimes of the church's bells. Sometimes there is a ticking, but it comes from the clockwork doll in the hall, with her etched silver scales, with her painted gold hair, and her emerald eyes that roll up and down, that swivel to look both left and right, not missing a thing that goes on in this house. I think her repulsive. Osborne thinks her exquisite. He paid a great deal to have her made, her every feature to mirror my own, modelled upon those sketches made when he first bought me, when I was fourteen.

I begin to think there is magic at work, that he's blagged my soul to give to her, that she hates me as much as I hate her. I imagine her slithering down from the table, dragging her body across the hall, on up the stairs to my bedroom door. And there she reclines, like a sentry, a marble eye fixed at the keyhole, and even when I stuff that up so that she will no longer be able to look, at every visit Osborne makes, when his key rattles in from the other side, the rags of my privacy fall out. I hear her fervid whispering. She tells him about Elijah, the things we did, the things she saw—

Listen – that is the whirring scrape! Osborne is winding her up again! It is like the beat of another heart, and then comes the tinkling music in those moments before her arm rises up, a jerking staccato motion it is as she lifts the shell against her ear – just as I once did on Margate beach. And almost like the tide of the sea is the endless accompaniment outside, the drumming beat of this ceaseless rain. And *is* that the tapping of Cruikshank's cane, how *that* would sound if *he* entered the house, knocking on every rising stair, over the boards of the upstairs hall, and then against my bedroom door?

Oh, this is the madness of my condition; to think that my mind can conjure such things, because Osborne would never send me away. I must pull myself together. I must prove to him that I am well, though I'm sure that my spirits would be elevated if he only let me out again, to walk in the garden, to take some fresh air. He could give me some small occupation – a magazine or book to read. He could let me have my embroidery threads, something to deviate my mind and drag me out of this laudanum fog through which my spirit seeps away while my body is stiff, like a piece of wood, a useless mechanical toy who is trained to open her mouth on command, to swallow Osborne's medicine – the potions he swears will make me well. I hope he is right. I want to be well, but I crawl on my hands and knees like a dog. I vomit black bile. My bowels are loose.

I would not want Elijah to find me like this, stinking, unwashed, too befuddled to dress. And Osborne smiled strangely the last time I asked if he happened to know where Elijah had gone and when Elijah might chance to return. He locked the door and left me alone for what seemed to me like days on end, with nothing to eat or drink at all until I was weeping and parched with the thirst, the hunger gnawing like rats in my belly. And when he came back with a tray in his hands, when he offered me that broth to sup, I could not even hold it down. I retched at the bitter vinegar taste. But he forced me to take it, every drop, stroking my brow, soothing my moans with, 'Drink it, my love . . . it will keep you thin.'

Today, when I woke the fire was dead. Why has Osborne not made it up again? Why does he never send a maid? It must be night for the light is dim. Ice crystals cover the window glass. Do I shiver from cold or because of the dream that keeps ebbing and flowing through my mind – remembering how I'd been gasping for air, sinking in cloudy waters, and there at my side was Elijah, a stream of bubbles escaping his mouth, his body slowly circling round and his clothes billowed out as if filled with air while the spiralling currents dragged him down, and the blood that was flowing from his head – that was turning the water from grey to red.

Now, Osborne is standing in the door. No medicine or soup in his hands, only my embroidered wrap held out towards me when he says, 'Get up. I want you to come to the grotto. I want to complete the picture.'

I nod and turn my face to the wall, too tired to care what picture he makes, whatever new pose I have to take, if only the nightmares will stay away.

LILY

In Burlington Row my room was all darkness. I woke with a start in the hearthside chair. The fire's coals had long burned out, now reduced to a smouldering heap of ash. No candles were lit, not a sliver of gold from the hall outside to shine through the crack at the base of the door, though with my room at the front of the house the street lamp did offer some illumination, a watery glow that trickled in through the sides of the half-drawn window drapes. I shivered a little, turning my neck from side to side, trying to work the stiffness out, having slept with my chin upon my breast, having nodded off while reading—

Oh no! My brother's papers! Where could they have gone? His diary, the sketches, the photographs?

Hastily rising to my feet, I scrabbled around on the mantelpiece, eventually finding a tinder box with which to light a candle, then holding that candle high in my hand as I scanned every inch of the room. And that's when I saw Elijah's clothes, picked up from the floor where I'd dropped them, all neatly folded and piled on the chest that stood of the end of the big brass bed. At their side had been placed a tray, and on that a teapot, a plate of cold meats and some buttered bread. But who had brought that supper in? Why hadn't they tried to wake me? And *where* were Elijah's papers?

How happy I was to realise that there had been no theft at all – that the papers had simply slipped from my lap, now strewn on the floor beside the chair from where I snatched up every page, seeing again those drawings of Pearl, so honest, so shocking, and leaving me with little doubt as to what might go on between women and men. With those intimate studies secured at the back, I wound the ribbon round again and was placing the bundle on top of the clothes when I felt a sudden rushing draught as if something had moved behind me; the distinct sensation of being watched, suspecting, however illogically, that whoever had brought that tray of food was still there, still in the room with me. My eyes darted swiftly back and forth. I looked behind the window drapes. I even opened the wardrobe doors, but the game of hide and seek I played was doomed to end in nothingness – until my eyes fell on the little brass frame, my mother's portrait still there on the nightstand, her eyes seemingly intent on me. Or did she stare at Elijah's things?

Perhaps I should hide his secrets away, somewhere discreet from prying eyes? And yet, to show others, to show Uncle Freddie, might actually lead to finding Elijah, for surely his confessions held clues, and surely his words might vindicate my firm belief that Osborne Black knew more of my brother's vanishing than he was prepared to say. Osborne Black was not a man to be trusted. How wickedly he had treated Pearl. And now, in no more than a few short months, she had been altered beyond recognition, humiliated and bullied and starved by the pompous and deceitful man who that very morning suggested her mad – and according to Elijah's notes, Chiswick House *was* an asylum, whatever Samuel Beresford said, and—

What was that sound, that banging? Was it a door or a shutter? I stood very still and then heard it again – a rattling from somewhere low in the house, as if someone was turning a key in a latch.

With the house then muffled in silence that only the depths

of night can bring, those metallic scrapings were all too clear. To my ear they were eerily amplified and, creeping towards the window seat, I knelt on a cushion and strained to look out. Of the sulphurous fog that had drowned the street that afternoon only a few drifts now remained, wafting over the windows of Hall & Co., that house once again all in darkness and above its black mass only heavy clouds, a sky without any moon or stars. But there on the pavement, directly below, the street lamp's sputtering yellow glow shone down on the man who was loitering there, right at the base of Freddie's steps, and with one of his arms resting over the railings he might just be propped at a public bar, so very nonchalant he looked.

My first thought was, *Elijah . . . Elijah is back!* But the hope lasted less than a fleeting split second, for that man's build and stance were entirely wrong, even though it was hard to make out any features. He wore the strangest long fur coat. A glossy top hat was tipped low on his brow, and the muffler he wore wrapped round his neck was extended to cover his mouth and nose which – my heart leapt up in a foolish dance – was something that Samuel Beresford might do, to protect his lungs, to stop his cough – *if* it was him. But it was not. More likely to be some drunkard mistaking Freddie's house for his own, now trying to turn the wrong key in the lock. Or was he an expected guest for, from a door in the basement floor, I saw a figure emerging and recognised the pretty maid, a blanket hugged at her shoulders for warmth. *She* must have rattled some keys in the lock, the sound which had come from *inside*, not out. Perhaps this was her secret lover, about to enter Freddie's house, to creep inside that housemaid's bed, wherever that bed might happen to be. I had no idea where the servants slept, only now supposing it must be down there, never yet having heard the creak of a board to suggest any movements above my head. I also began to surmise, as if filled with the spirit of Ellen Page, that for those who resided in London town, immoral events must go on all the time; that everywhere you happened to look – if you looked hard enough – you would find some proof.

That man, that stranger, acknowledged the maid by slowly lifting one of his hands, seeming to motion for her to step nearer, and as she ascended the basement steps he drew his muffler from his face and appeared to murmur some words in her ear, though nothing that I could comprehend, despite my own being held to the glass, the cold like a prickling burn on my cheek. But I did see the tusks of a pale moustache and some cheeks angled sharply in whippet-thin features, all curtained by strands of long pale hair that fell from beneath the brim of his hat. The sight of that face unnerved me, the strangest sensation of déjà vu, before recalling Elijah's words and the man he had met at the music hall.

I was glad when the maid retraced her steps and disappeared into the house, a thud vibrating up through the building when the basement door was closed again, at which that man walked across the street, his heels splish-splashing through puddled slick cobbles – until pausing midway, where he turned to look back, scanning the frontage of Freddie's house and his gaze very readily meeting my own – the window from which I then looked out, which caused me to gasp and my heart to race, though, in retrospect, it could not have been so very hard for anyone to spy me there with the glow of the candle I'd lit behind luring his eye like a moth to a flame.

While swiftly withdrawing back into the room, hiding behind the curtain's folds, I saw him raise one arm to wave, after which he made a little bow, tipping forward the brim of his hat before resuming his mincing gait towards the other side of the street. From there I heard a low whistle. I saw someone else creeping out from the shadows, another man dressed in a tall top hat and what seemed to be a dinner suit – but a tiny man, as small as the dwarf that Elijah and I once saw in Cremorne. He clung on to the hems of his friend's fur coat, scuttling behind on short bowed legs – like a bridesmaid who carried a veil; a veil just as soon dropped down to the ground to

drag through the slime of the gutters – the same filth I imagined swirling up, passing through my window glass, tainting
my nostrils, filling my throat.

Oh, what a horrible fancy that was. It took some moments to
be released, to come to my senses and wonder why someone had
called at that time of night to converse with one of Freddie's
maids – the very same maid who now knocked on my door,
who still had her blanket clutched around when she muttered
in nervy stuttering tones, 'Miss, I've been sent up to say that a
gentleman has some news . . . something pertaining to Elijah
Lamb. A gentleman . . . wanting to speak with you now . . .
waiting in the street outside.'

'Where is my uncle? Does he know?'

'He's sleeping, miss. I was told not to wake him . . . only
you.'

In hope, in fear, I rushed back to the window, looking down
to catch another brief glimpse of that peculiar couple again, by
then almost come to the end of the street. I had to follow – I
had to go. A moment more and they might be lost, though I
wasn't thinking clearly at all, not even looking for my hat, only
pushing some fallen hair from eyes when I snatched up my
shawl from the floor and rushed down the three flights of stairs
to the hall – my breaths coming fast as I drew back the bolts and
then placed my hand upon the latch, swallowing my fear when I
opened the door, my skirt hems hoisted high in my hands, my
vision obscured by freezing breaths, soon having no clue as to
where I was – only vaguely aware that those grander streets, the
residences with gleaming front steps and doors that mirrored
Freddie's home were now replaced by narrower lanes and the
iron grilles of shut-up shops where, above the shuddering pant
of my breaths, came distant shrieks and breaking glass. Some
sheets of newsprint fluttered past, circling around me like paper
ghosts, and somewhere far off, a voice cried out, 'Falcon . . .
Falcon. *Come on, you early birds . . . come and buy yer* Falcon
'ere.' Somehow I managed to trip and fall. An elbow struck hard
against the kerb, and while I was winded and wincing with pain

a black monster was looming high above – a horse's front legs rearing over my head, great metal hooves stamping down in the street, with me but inches from being crushed – and again by the wheels of the night-soil cart that came skidding behind as I cowered and crouched into a ball, as the driver was bellowing, 'Silly cow . . . why you wanna go and scare me 'orse? Wanna go and get yerself killed, or what?'

Struggling to roll away, to avoid the river of steaming piss that now gushed from the horse's bladder, I lifted my eyes to realise that the driver was standing at my side, helping to pull me up again while I managed to gabble some grateful words. 'Thank you . . . I'm sorry. But please, can't you help me . . . I'm looking . . . I'm looking for a man.'

'Gawd alive, you come out of Bedlam, or what? Most folk in this city are wimmin or men!'

'This one was wearing a long fur coat . . . a little man with him . . . in evening dress.'

'Tip Thomas and his monkey friend.' He answered with no hesitation, pointing back the way he had come, towards more narrow twisting streets. 'I sin 'im all right. Covent Garden way, along with the rest of the fruits. All there 'til the light sends 'em scurrying off. But, if I were you, miss, I'd keep well away from the likes of 'im. If I were you I'd get back 'ome to yer family, to whatever . . .'

Whatever further warning that driver intended to make, I didn't stop to listen. Having had that chance to recapture my breath, I was ducking and diving through the lanes where doors exuded hazy lights through which, now and then, some women spilled, parading themselves on pavement and steps, talking in accents I did not know – and all of them must have been chilled to the bone, dressed even less suitably than me, some in no more than corsets and shifts! My heart went out to one old man who made me think about Papa, who emerged through a narrow creaking gate, his jowly cheeks a lardy white, drenched in a running greasy sweat. He pushed a rattling trolley piled high with a jumble of household possessions: a worn Persian rug, a cat in a cage. I assumed he was going to sell them. I assumed they were everything he owned.

A great many vendors were round about hawking eels and potatoes, sausage and chops. What a cacophony it was between all the towering pillars of stone, as fine a temple to Mammon as anything you could imagine, all teeming with wagons and donkey carts, all loaded with fruits and vegetables. More shouting and singing and laughter too in that echoing riotous rabble of sound in which I felt frightened and lost, and—

There he was, standing straight ahead, that midget last viewed in Burlington Row. Only he *was* a monkey after all, with a chain attached around his neck, and that chain now wound at the base of a pillar below which the creature was happily sitting, its nimble pink fingers dipping into a bag, picking out what looked to be raisins and nuts.

And there was the man I had seen from my window. He would have been difficult to miss, as flamboyant as any gypsy king. But he had not yet noticed my presence there, engaged as he was with the pestering of a girl in front of a flower stall – a girl with eyes like beads of jet within the swollen flesh around, below which three crusted raking lines had been scratched very deeply across one cheek.

Still standing five or six feet away, I was near enough to see when one of his hands was nimbly thrust between the folds of her apron skirts, from which he must have withdrawn some coins, for she pleaded in a desperate voice, 'Just leave us enough for me bed. It's cold. There's bin barely any trade tonight. I'll do better tomorrow. I swear on me life . . .'

'One more night . . . or . . .'

'Or what?' Her ruined features were filled with dread.

'Or you'll take a trip down to the Limehouse gaff. Oh, my sweet, where will you find work again, except for a halfpenny a throw?'

His expression was one of derision as he plunged all but two of those glinting coins into the pocket of his coat, and the few sorry coppers he deigned to spare were dropped to the slabs at the flower girl's feet, where, with all too little dignity, she fell to her knees to save them, her eyes meeting mine when she rose again, her complaint coming hoarse and bitter. 'I trusted you with me life, but you well and truly fucked me, you did.'

'You're nothing more than a bunter. I'd say you were fucked in your quim and your wits long before you ever came my way.' His voice was thick and tense with threat, and I think all along he knew me there, perhaps having seen my reflection in the teary glaze of that poor girl's eyes, for so suddenly did he spin around, and so suddenly did his monkey drop its little paper bag of treats, grabbing at my hems instead, its jabbering screech rising high above the jingling snap of the metal chain, which, luckily, restrained the beast as it lurched at me with teeth all bared.

Only then did I truly comprehend the folly of my enterprise, to be out alone in that hostile place. But there I was, and I must ask what this villain might know of Elijah – though the question stuck like a stone in my throat, only able to gape like some idiot country bumpkin when he smiled and greeted me with, 'Well, well, look what the cat's dragged in.'

I tried to step back, but the monkey's grip on my skirts was firm, leaving me trapped in its master's eyes, around which white skin was heavily dusted with streaking layers of powder and paint, and within pale whiskers his rouged red smile was as thin and as sharp as a razor slash. He doffed his hat and made a bow, afterwards lifting a finger and thumb to stroke down one side of a silky moustache – during which act I could not help but see how long were his fingernails, the ends being filed to jagged tips, and I thought of the scars on the flower girl's face, and trembling, sick with fear by then, I managed to speak to this sinister man. 'I'm looking for Elijah Lamb. I know you've met him once before. I know you went to Wilton's hall!'

'Best you ask me no questions, I'll tell you no lies.'

'What sort of an answer is that?'

'What sort would you care to hear? Little country bee . . . come buzzing around my honeypots, flying in places that you should not . . . though,' he paused and snatched up some blooms from the stall, holding them out as if offered to me while continuing with his menacing, 'you might find your answer by solving this riddle. Will it be violets like these . . . violets for your chastity, or pansies for unrequited love? Or poppies . . . sweet poppies that stand for death?'

I felt the hairs prickle up on my neck as the flowers' sweet odour filled my nose, as I heard the flower girl's crying whine, a high shrill sound like tearing cloth. 'Give me back them posies. Cost us a pretty penny in winter, having to queue in the flower hall and beg for the dregs that's not bin sold. What larks! What fun and games I 'ave, and now you chuck it all away . . . wooing this milky dolly mop.'

Fired by my own frustration and anger, I shouted at our mutual tormentor, 'What do you know? You must tell me . . . now!'

Somewhere near by, a beggar jingled some coins in a cup. The growl of a dog. The cracking of knuckles. And a pair of blue eyes grown wider, and a barely restrained note of threat in his voice when this demon said, 'Tut tut . . . but she is a fiery one. She'll hear more when I'm good and ready to speak, but for now I think she should buzz off before *my* temper is truly riled, before we decide on another game, and one she might not want to play . . . one with a sting, with a bit more bite. Why, my Nebuchadnezzar's growing chill . . . might fancy the warmth of nice new muff.'

Whatever his Nebuchadnezzar was I really didn't want to know. Trembling – from the cold – from terror too – I could hardly believe it to be true when that girl spat out a great gobbet of mucus that fell hot and gluey on my cheek. And, while wiping that off with the back of my hand, trying my hardest not to retch, I saw that the flowers that 'gentleman' proffered had now been dropped to the ground at his feet, stamped to a pulp by his boots' high heels, during which act he was shaking his head and pursing his lips in a whistle – at which order the monkey released its grasp, which I took as the sign to make my escape, to flee, without a backward glance.

Goodness knows how I ever found Burlington Row, weeping and wretched, wandering lost, but eventually, guided by kinder souls than those I'd met in that marketplace, I retraced my steps to Freddie's door, which was just as I left it, still ajar, welcoming any thieves right in. But too tired by then to think or care of any other present threat, it was all I could do to close it, to drag my bones back up the stairs and enter the room where the candle still burned, where, not even attempting to get undressed, I threw myself down on the mattress where pillows were perfumed, white and clean, no matter how filthy I'd become, how rank with the odours of the street. As my rasping breaths and heartbeat slowed, I stared a long time at the gaudy walls which were bathed in the candle's sombre gleam, at the flowery chintz on the furnishings, and the ornately carved rococo frame of the mirror that cast my reflection back – in which I appeared to be wavering, too fluid and insubstantial, and within that moving picture I saw Elijah's diary and clothes, still piled in a heap at the end of the bed.

The last thing I did before going to sleep was to sit up and stretch my arms forward, taking those papers in my hands and stuffing them under the mattress edge. And when that task had been achieved I reached forward again and lifted a jacket of brown velveteen, arranged as a blanket to keep me warm. I lay there and thought about Kingsland House and how when we first went to live with Papa I used to share my brother's bed. I used to breathe my brother's scent, and . . . my eye caught a glinting, mercurial light on the glass behind which my mother's eyes looked out from her little portrait. But how strange her image seemed just then, more like a half-exposed photograph, and how peculiar it was that I did not feel the least bit afraid to hear my mother's picture speak, to see the new grey threaded through the dark hair, and the tracings of lines etched into the brow that, before, had been entirely smooth. And in the way that some dreams have of reweaving the form of our daily lives and embroidering patterns quite different, it seemed the most logical thing in the world for me to believe that somewhere, somehow, my mother still lived and cared for me, for what spirit wraith could ever respond in so lucid and natural a way as when my mother's image said, 'How uncanny it is. You remind me so much of my father. You are so like . . .' She paused as if on the brink of tears, struggling to contain her emotions as she swallowed hard and looked away, muttering, as if to herself, 'Could it be possible?' And then, turning back, her eyes fixed with mine, 'Tell me,' she asked, 'do you have a twin?'

I nodded my response, wondering why she had to ask, watching her lift a hand to her mouth before the next question fell from her lips. 'One twin a girl? The other a boy?'

Again, it was all I could do to nod, silenced by the depth of emotion I saw when my mother smiled and said to me, in the way I imagined all mothers must, 'Rest now, my love. Go to sleep, my love. No one will hurt you any more.'

Her words were a spell I could not resist. My heavy eyes began to close. I felt bereft when I sensed she had gone, sobbing while calling out her name, 'Mother . . . don't go. Mother, come back. Please tell me where Elijah is.'

'She's back. Thank God . . . she's with us again.'

Above the harsh patter of rain at the window I heard the deep tones of a masculine voice. I was squinting to see, my eyes all blurred, eventually focusing on Uncle Freddie, and Uncle Freddie was not alone, another man being close behind and, at first, recalling the night before, my mind was filled with panic. Had I had been followed back to the house?

But this stranger was not the monkey man. This one was dressed conventionally. He appeared to be in late middle age, rather short in height, rather corpulent, with a belly that strained at his waistcoat, so much so that I feared every button would pop. Either side of a moist, somewhat flabby mouth, black whiskers grew from ear to chin, only ending where thick rolls of fat circled like collars at his throat. Higher still, above liverish bags of flesh, were two decidedly hawk-like eyes, both making a long hard study of me, and it came as something of a shock to follow the line of his leering gaze and to find that my breasts were hidden from view by nothing more than my nightgown.

When had I changed into that? I could only recall coming back to the house, lying down on the bed, still fully clothed, with Elijah's jacket pulled on top. Now, I was lying beneath the sheets, which I snatched at and dragged all the way to my chin while my eyes darted down to the end of the bed – to see that Elijah's clothes were gone!

Struggling to sit, I was crying out, 'Uncle Freddie . . . where are my brother's things? Who is this man you have brought to my room? How dare you! How could you? How . . .'

'Lily!' Freddie's voice was full of concern. 'You've been ill . . . you've been sedated for days. That first morning the maid found you raving. You were taken with a fever. We had to send out for the doctor and . . .'

'The doctor?' I looked at the stranger again and noticed the brown leather bag in his hand, and beyond him, just to one side of the door, was the very same maid from the other night, and she might refuse to look my way but I sensed the guilt in her downcast eyes. *What has she told them? What do they know?*

'This is Doctor Evans,' Freddie explained, 'an old and trusted acquaintance of mine. He's only here to make you well.'

The doctor gave an impatient sigh. 'May I re-examine the patient now? I do have other appointments.'

Freddie nodded and moved aside. The doctor stepped forward and lowered his face until barely six inches above my own, so close that I saw the yellowish hue of the whites around his pupils. The greasy coarse hairs of his whiskers. The pungent odours of onion breath through which he spoke in a droning voice – first a few words regarding my colour and the regularity of my breaths, and each observation directed at Freddie, as if I was a dunce with no sentient thought inside my head, until he fixed me in his gaze and said, 'Now . . . young lady, show me your tongue.'

While I opened my mouth and poked it out, one of his hands lifted my wrist. The other held a fob watch high, observing that with a brief nodding 'hmmm'. He then asked me to loosen the neck of my gown, at which Uncle Freddie turned away while the doctor reached deep into his bag, drawing out a stethoscope and placing the rounded end on my breast while pressing the other to his ear. Such a faraway gaze as he listened, until lifting the instrument again when he straightened to give his opinion. 'Her heart is too fast and irregular. Her temperature is elevated. In my view the severity of her condition has hardly abated at all. Do you know where she happened to go that night to get herself in such a state? Is there to your knowledge any cause for this abhorrent behaviour? Any underlying chronic disease? Any history of instability?'

'Instability? No!' Freddie replied without hesitation, but the pompous doctor carried on, 'I regret to say she exhibits the signs . . . a tendency to moods and exhaustion, manifestations of melancholic behaviour, not to mention a less than healthy attachment to these inappropriate objects.'

'What objects? What are you talking about?' At last I managed to find my tongue, this doctor's pronouncements become more alarming with every passing moment.

'Miss Lamb, when I was first called in you were clearly in a state of distress. Your dress was torn and filthy. You had chosen to surround yourself with items of gentlemen's clothing. I wonder, has this inclination of yours become a regular habit, to demonstrate a violent rage when such apparel is taken away? Why, you had to be physically restrained from . . .'

'They were my brother's clothes! Where are they? I want them back!'

Whatever I might have done before, there was no doubt I was raving then, my head twisting and turning around the room as I looked for some sign of Elijah's things, and somewhere at the end of the bed, as if from the end of very dark tunnel, a red-faced Freddie was staring back, trying his best to explain to me – something about laundry and pressing it was – above which the doctor's voice resumed, and so smugly confidential in tone, 'Mr Hall, what we are dealing with here is an advanced hysteria, a common but serious complaint affecting young women of sensitive natures, especially those unmarried, with no outlet with which to relieve their frustrations . . . resulting in fits as severe as this.' He gave a long and sorry sigh. 'I strongly advise preventative measures. There are some excellent private asylums which offer the most enlightened care. I myself consult at one of them, discreetly positioned away from the city and yet near enough for visiting.'

His diagnosis left me stunned, eventually able to protest, 'But I am perfectly sane. I saw a man . . . a man who might know where Elijah is. And then, I was dreaming! I was dreaming about . . .'

Well, what *would* this doctor make of that – if I mentioned a talking portrait! Luckily Freddie broke in to prevent me, indignant when he said, 'Really, Evans. This is ridiculous. I hold your skills in the highest regard, but in this case I fear you misguided. If Miss Lamb has no physical ailment as such then I must thank you and ask you to leave. Whatever the cause of her distress, your presence is only causing more.'

The doctor appeared to be taken aback that anyone dared to question his view. He gave Uncle Freddie an arrogant stare, but no further comment was made. He picked up his bag and snapped it shut, only looking back from the door to add with an unnerving smirk, 'Very well, Mr Hall. But I must advise that you keep her observed. No stimulating literature, no exercise or excitement. And nothing but bread and water to drink . . . with a liberal dose of laudanum should the patient show any signs of relapse.'

Freddie followed the doctor out. I jumped at the bang of my closing door – at every thump of their feet on the stairs, and then the high tenor of Freddie's response, though not every part of it reached my ears. *How dare you imply any family madness . . . misunderstand the dilemma . . . my intentions only honourable . . . never . . . deign to consider . . .*

To be honest, I wasn't trying to listen, more concerned with retying the ribbons that had previously fastened the neck of my gown, and simply relieved that Freddie was there to defend me against that disgusting man who called himself a doctor – a doctor who, far from curing me, had sickened me with the touch of his hands. I didn't feel safe. I wanted to leave, to go back to Kingsland, to be with Papa – Papa, who really was ailing – and how dare that doctor try to imply that I had become hysterical – or was my mind deranged after all? I *had* imagined my mother's voice and I—

'I'm sorry, miss.' The maid was still standing in the room, so quiet I had forgotten her. 'I had to tell Mr Hall . . . that you'd gone out on the streets that night. You really were in such a state. I thought . . . I feared you'd been attacked.'

She was staring down at the frame on the stand, the one with my mother's portrait inside. She said, 'You kept touching that . . . you kept saying "mother", again and again. I once heard Mr Hall with your brother before, saying you'd come from the Foundling . . . just as I did myself.' She looked up and asked very earnestly, 'Do you still have your thread?'

'My thread?'

'The bit of fabric you get to keep . . . the half that your mother pinned on to your clothes when she left you at the orphanage door . . . keeping the other for herself.'

'No . . . I . . . that is, we . . . have never owned such a thing as that.'

'But then, you do have your portrait. My thread is all I've got. My key to tell me what I am. It's nothing special, just some shabby frayed cotton, some embroidery worked into half of a flower. But,' she tilted her chin and looked straight in my eye, 'I shall treasure it to my dying day.'

'I wish I had such a treasure,' I mused, and then added somewhat more suspiciously, 'But . . . if you're from the

Foundling Hospital too, then how many of us has Freddie saved? Does he have you call him "Uncle" too?'

'Not so generous an uncle as he is to you!' She laughed, a brittle ring to her voice, before clapping both hands to her mouth in alarm, as if trying to stop what had just slipped out. 'Oh, miss, I should never have said so much. Truly, I did forget myself . . . and I wouldn't want to offend Mr Hall. As you know, he's very considerate . . . and he always pays a decent wage, and we all have warm beds and a roof overhead. He's never *really* caused us harm.'

Why should Freddie cause her harm? And, now that I came to think of it, why was she opening Freddie's doors to men who came visiting at night? Or had I imagined that as well? I hardly knew what to think any more, what was true, what was false – and was almost in tears when I implored, 'Did I really see you late that night, talking with a man on the basement steps? Tell me I wasn't dreaming.'

'Oh, miss, he was there, all right. I thought he might be Mr Hall at first, having gone out and forgotten his keys. He sometimes turns up, somewhat worse for wear, and we have to get up and let him in, but . . .' She paused again, very serious. 'I never imagined that you'd go off, running around in the dead of night.'

'Do you know him?'

'Oh yes, I do! He is no stranger hereabouts. One time, he used to bring packages, for me to pass on to Mr Hall.'

'Packages?'

'Full of etchings and photographs they were. The devil's work. But really, I should not say a word, not with Mr Hall having those pictures of me . . . and me with no chance of respectable work if they should ever come to light.'

'What on earth are you talking about?'

She looked up from beneath wet lashes. 'It started with that camera club. Obsessed, your uncle was at first . . . taking pictures of every room in the house, even the carriages out in

223

the street. And then, that morning, he came downstairs, and, well . . . what do you think, miss?'

(Really, I did not dare to think.)

'He took a picture of me, you know, when I was lying in bed asleep! At least I was decent, wearing me shimmy . . . but there wasn't much left to the imagination. Screamed blue murder I did when I woke, and he never once tried to do it again, and I always make sure to lock my door, and the other girls, they do the same. But can you imagine how I felt when Mr Hall showed me the result. He called it artistic, so he did. He said I could model at his club, but . . .' She paused for a moment. 'I should never take such a decadent path, for I've seen the pictures delivered here, the ones that arrive in the dead of night, wrapped up in brown paper and tied with string . . . the ones Mr Hall makes into books . . . and those books with flashy bindings of silk and tissue paper to shield the prints . . . the sheerest paper you ever did see, just a breath too near and it flutters and lifts, like the trembling flesh of a maiden. Well, that's what Mr Hall always says. But there ain't nothing maidenly underneath, not what him and his fancy friends like to see, when he invites them round to dine . . . and one of them friends just happens to be the very same doctor attending today, and . . .'

She broke off at my sudden gasp. 'But, surely . . . this can't be true.' I was clutching a hand to one side of my head, which was aching from all her prattling talk. Just how well did I know Frederick Hall? I was trying to add up the number of times he'd actually been to Kingsland House. Fewer than twenty days in twenty years. Fewer days than the number of years in my age. But to think that he could be involved in something so – well – so scandalous, and what was it Samuel Beresford said – those rumours he'd heard about Osborne Black – the stories linked to some Holywell Street and immoral publication acts? Hadn't Freddie been keen to ignore such things?

'But, miss,' the maid interrupted my thoughts, 'I assumed you knew about all that, that you might be involved in some way yourself . . . seeing what was held in your lap, that night when you'd dropped off to sleep in the chair, when I came up here to leave a tray. After all, it's not the respectable thing . . . not for a young lady such as yourself . . . to be staying alone in a gentleman's house . . .'

'What can you possibly mean to imply?'

I knew, of course. I knew what she meant. But I had to ask. I had to be sure, to try to make everything clear in my mind, which at that very moment was nothing but a panicked whirl. When I caught a flash of myself in the mirror I saw something wild, something possessed, my nightgown all crumpled, my hair all in knots, more like one of those women who walked the dawn streets than any reflection of Lily Lamb.

No wonder the maid edged back to the door, looking cowed and anxious when she said, 'A photograph, miss . . . just a photograph.'

Oh, thank goodness for that! She had not seen Elijah's drawings, then. But what if − I had to focus my thoughts − what if Osborne Black − and Elijah too − had been involved in Freddie's trade? No, what was I thinking, to take on the queer fancies of this maid? *She* was the truly hysterical one, to imagine such things between Freddie and me! And then, as far as Elijah went, how could I ever believe such a thing when his diaries were full of his love for Pearl.

I must remain focused and sensible because Pearl was the key to this puzzle, just as Uncle Freddie said. It was Pearl who might lead us to the truth of what had become of Elijah Lamb.

PEARL

He took out the tinderbox and the candle stump, but the minute he struck fire and sparks leaped from the flint, the door flew open and the dog that he had seen inside the tree, the one with the eyes big as two teacups, stood before him and said, 'What is my master's command?'

From 'The Tinder Box' by Hans Christian Andersen

Water: There is a storm tonight. There is such a wuthering under the eaves, such a slating against the window glass – or is that the rattling of keys?

Water: The glisten in Osborne's eyes, the pupils large and much too bright in the glim of the candle that he holds. He stands beside one of the bedposts and stares at me for much too long, his mouth open, chest heaving and gasping for breaths beneath which are muttered evil threats. I can't understand every word his says, but more than enough of them are clear. 'Witch whore. Lying here in these stinking sheets and whimpering like a bitch on heat . . . calling out to your river friends, calling their spirits back up from the Thames, to take their revenge, to ruin me!'

I am frightened. He is a man gone mad. He stinks of shit. He is drenched to the skin. He looks as if he is half drowned with water dripping through his hair, over his brow, his eyes, his beard, puddling on to the boards at his feet.

I watch. I see that water spread. I wonder – is he melting?

Water: I am dragged from the bed and down the stairs. His hands are wet and cold as ice, as cold as my flesh whenever I

226

pose in that grotto of his for hours on end. I think that is where he will take me now, but although the door in the panelled wall is already standing open, when Osborne descends the dark stone steps he leaves me behind in the studio.

My nightgown is snapping and blowing out. A debris of paper is swirling round, whipped up by the icy splintered rain now gusting in through the garden doors, which bang back and forth upon their jambs. When I try and fail to close them up I see silhouetted bushes and trees which appear to be lower than before. And then I realise what's wrong. The river has flooded and broken its banks.

What can Osborne be doing down there in the grotto? Strange sounds I hear, like the gushing of taps, water slapping and splashing against stone walls which echo with curses when he re-emerges, his arms full of canvases dripping with slime, which he props next to others, against the walls. How long has he spent in the darkness, saving these treasures from his cave, all of my mirrors distorted and warped, every painted Pearl now a ghoulish freak? Better he let those mermaids drown than to witness the horrors they have become.

Water: The tears that are springing in my eyes when I kneel before the Chiswick House painting – the one in which I am a water nymph reclining on the banks of a pool. But now, another figure is there, a young man almost fully immersed in the water. Long floating weeds are blinding his eyes. His mouth is wide open, as if calling in anguish. He is reaching up with both of his arms, grasping the lilies and rushes, the stems of which only break in his hands, and no hope that the nymph will aid his plight because all along she is sleeping – unlike the real Pearl tonight. Tonight, for the very first time in weeks, *her* mind is free from the numbing fug of Osborne's dose of opiates. Osborne has been too busy by far with the saving of his other Pearls to have thought to dope the one upstairs.

And have the scales dropped from my eyes, or is it only a trick of the light with the flames of candles drawing long and creating such eerie plays of light when I see a third form in the canvas, some shadowy creature, half man, half fish? He vomits black weed from his thick-lipped mouth. His muscular arms are matted with hair, the elbows encrusted with barnacles. They stretch up. They mimic Elijah's pose. But this ogre is not beseeching the nymph. It is Elijah's life he wants. Stubby fingers lock on to the heels of his prey, dragging him down into the depths, which fester with many horrible things. Fish with protruding, glowing eyes. Coiling black snakes. The corpse of a dog. Waving weeds, like human hair. Bones that are bleached, white as ivory.

My head fills with the strangest buzzing sound. It is almost as if the rain has stopped, as if the wind has blown itself out with only a core of stillness left, a diamond-sharp kernel of clarity. For within Osborne's oily, swirling daubs, his cryptic confession is clearly made. It is written for those who know to look. I look, and I think of Angelo. I look, and I know where Elijah has gone, and why Elijah will not return.

Water: I am running out through the garden doors. The stench is overwhelming now, a rotting, like death, like effluence, like the odour that constantly lurks in the house. But now it is intensified, making me gag, stopping my breath, which, when it finally does escape, is a puffing white cloud on the cold wet air through which I see the rowing boat, bobbing about on what used to be lawns. My bare feet are skidding over the slabs. I step over some battered white feathers, a length of frayed string wrapped round splitting twigs. Like a fetish it is – or a funeral wreath. I have to step past it. I have to go on, feet squelching through icy mud and grass. I have to reach the river and then I will find Elijah. But Osborne will not let me go. I am grabbed from behind. I am dragged to the ground, trapped in the iron grip of his arms as he carries me back inside the house. I scream. I kick. I scratch and bite. He howls like a dog and throws me down. My head hits the wood of the studio floor.

*

Water: I wake to a trickle of warmth on my cheek. I gasp at the throbbing hot sting of the pain when a flannel is pressed against my brow. My eyes are itchy, sore and gummed. It is all I can do to squint through them now, to look up at a dull and dribbling light that creeps through a narrow window, a vertical slit, set very high.

Where am I? What day? What time is it?

A young woman, a stranger, is staring down. Above her head the ceiling is low. A greyish white paint is flaking off. The walls are the same. It is how you'd imagine the clink to be, with no adorning features at all except for the single picture which hangs over the black iron rails of the bed, and viewed as it is from my prostrate position it seems that the world is turned on its head, as if being viewed through a camera lens. I know that the upside-down man there is Jesus. I know that Jesus will save his flock from tumbling over the edge of a cliff. Even so, to my eyes, those sheep must fall – to join me, already cast down by the man who embodies the devil himself, who bullies and wounds with no remorse, who has taken the only things I love.

Somewhere in the distance I hear women singing. Is it Elijah's funeral? It could almost be a hymn or a prayer; that otherworldly, atonal sound, so swiftly shut out by the slam of a door, then the steady beat of footsteps on stone. A female voice comes very stern: 'It is time. Is she washed? Is she decent?'

She wears a dress of starched blue stripes, a white starched hat above grey hair, and a grim grey face, quite expressionless, while she waits for the other to reply.

'The wound is staunched, Mrs Cruikshank.' The springs make a twanging creak when she stands. She is rinsing her cloth at a table near by. The pale pink of the blood trickling into a bowl.

Water: I am surrounded by cold white tiles, tiles that are streaked with smeared brown stains, all running with condensation. A green mould is growing between the joints. There are several wiry curling hairs. Some are black. Some are red.

Neither of the two women attempts to speak, both busy with the methodical task of stripping off my soiled shift. I stand there, shivering, hunching my back, arms crossed at my breasts to cover my shame as my ears fill up with the splutter of taps, the banging rattle of the pipes. While waiting for a bath to fill, the older one prods at my wasted limbs. When she looks down to see my feet and the silverfish scuttling around, she makes the sign of the cross at her breast. She says, 'Lord, save us . . . the proof of sin. They should have smothered this at birth.'

The younger one frowns. 'Her belly is swollen . . .'

'They always swell like that when they take it upon themselves to starve. We'll soon have her eating regular meals, though I dare say we might have to start with the tubes.'

It's strange, I don't think about food any more. The hunger I used to feel all gone, only the throbbing ache in my head, and the water when they plunge me down, scalding hot, burning my skin, reddened yet more where these women scrub. I think they might rub me clean away, erased like a smudging of pencil, a line made in error upon a page.

Don't they know I will never be clean again, never clean enough for Osborne Black? Perhaps they do. The older one's mouth is clamped and unsmiling. She looks as sour as her breath – vinegary, like disinfectant it is, mingled with the rancid gas that hisses from rusty lamps on walls. And then, whoosh, they pull me out of the tub, and I am trembling, cold again, weeping my impotent tears when I hear the snap of the metal shears. Thick clumps of hair fall at my feet. My hair always looks so much darker when wet.

I hear singing again. I think of nuns, those women who give up their hair as a dowry, the forfeit of earthly decadence. And that's when the words escape my lips, as harsh as gravel in my throat. 'Are we back in Italy? Has he brought me to a convent?'

The older one snorts, 'Another one who thinks she's a nun! We've already got us a Joan of Arc . . . not to mention the Virgin Mary.'

'Leave her be.' The younger speaks softly.

The older lashes with her tongue, 'Stupid girl! You must learn to harden your heart. These women are not like you or me. The devil is at work through their madness . . . . cunning harlots every one. Until we have safely driven him out you must not show her any sympathy or he'll try to ensnare you, just the same.' She snatches my wrist, twisting me round, continuing with her brash tirade. 'Come on, take her other arm. Time to get this shift back on.'

'But it's filthy . . . it's wet,' the younger protests, 'and where is the warmth in such a thing?'

'You know the rules. The new ones appear at the initiation in the same state of dress as on their arrival – for an accurate assessment to be written up in the records. So shut up, and do as you're told for once . . . and remember to save and dry that hair.'

They tell me to lift my arms. They lower the shift down over my head. It is like being a child again, being dressed by Mrs Hibbert again. She used to brush my hair at night, one hundred times, 'til it gleamed like a mirror, sparking with tiny flashes of gold. To think of what I have become – and what she would think if she saw me now – and then I am struck by a numbing thought, which is that with my arms stretched up like this I am standing in the very same pose as Elijah in Osborne's painting. Two arms reaching up in search of salvation when there is no hope to be found.

I start to cry, and that's when the older one punches hard, right in the hollow of my back. That does the trick. I am silenced again, so winded that I can hardly breathe.

Water: I sit at a long narrow table upon which a glass of water is set. I long to drink it. My throat is sore. My tongue feels too big and dry in my mouth. But worse than any thirst I have is the fear of being drugged again.

I eye with suspicion a trolley near by. There are cork-stoppered bottles all in a row. There are syringes with long metal needles, all manner of medical instruments, though I cannot begin to imagine their use, so odd and contorted are those shapes. There might be an octopus sitting there, such confusions of rubbery tentacles. Is this to do with my 'initiation'?

I sit very still with my hands in my lap. My eyes are pricking with tears again. I blink and wait for my vision to clear before looking around the spacious room. Gold leaf on the doors and plasterwork. Gilt-framed pictures on the walls, and a ceiling painted to look like the sky with putti cavorting about in the clouds. One of them might be Angelo – but how can I bear to think of him? I lower my gaze to a window instead, and beyond it the spreading gardens, though it is hard to make out any detail with such a heavy mist of fog through which shapes of trees and statues shift, and above them crows are whirling, painting straggling black lines over dull grey skies.

My eyes return to the glass on the table. I stare through the crystal-clear liquid within and see everything on the 'other side' as if fractionally warped, as if unreal. The glass is so full that the skin of the water appears to be domed, stretched from rim to rim, and I tell myself if that skin doesn't break then nothing here in this room exists, and if nothing in this room exists then how can those sitting opposite actually do me any real harm: Osborne, and two other men, and the stern grey-haired woman with stern grey eyes?

One man is fat with black hair and black eyes. One man has eyes unnaturally large, magnified behind his spectacle lenses, through which he stares intently at me from beneath a thick hatch of crinkled red hair. He has a wiry red moustache. His lips simper in a scarlet grin, and then a slight dribbling sheen of saliva, which extends like glue from lip to lip, only broken when his words spill out. 'Mrs Black . . . are you listening? Are you aware of your whereabouts? You and I have met before. Do you remember who I am?'

Hot air blasts through vents in the skirtings, causing my shift to flutter out. I look down at the moving fabric and try to recall who this man could be. There is something familiar about him but my head is too befuddled. All I can think about is a cat, a big ginger cat in Cheyne Walk. It would let you stroke it and then, without warning, lash out with its claws and tear your flesh. But I know that is not the answer he wants and so I simply shake my head, and I swear I can feel the air vibrate with the purring hum of his smug satisfaction, half expecting this man to lick his paws and rub them against his whiskered cheeks, instead of which he leans forward, his forearms pressed flat on the tabletop, its dark surface gleaming like that of a mirror through which he speaks to me again. 'Surely you haven't forgotten that day? Well, well, Mrs Black . . . this is not a good sign.'

I hear him, but I am looking at Osborne. Osborne's eyes are lowered, avoiding mine. He has changed his clothes since last we met. He is wearing a jacket, a clean white shirt, a blue silk choker wrapped at his throat. But he could not have looked in the mirror or he would have noticed the streaks of mud now caked and rusty on his cheeks, and the way his dirty hair has dried, standing up in the most peculiar way.

'Mrs Black?' The man with red hair repeats my name.

My answer is made, but very slow. 'I would rather you did not call me that.'

'Call you what?'

'Mrs Black. It is not my name.'

'So, Mrs Black . . .' The fat man breaks in, ignoring my protestation. His furrowing brow looks simian. His chin is lost in the doughy flesh that splurges across his collar's wings. It wobbles slightly when he says, 'You would prefer us to call you Pearl. But Pearl what? You must have a surname. We all of us have a surname. Mine, for instance, is Evans.'

Evans? The doctor who examined me in the House of the Mermaids years before, employed in that role by Osborne Black? I shuffle back into my seat and shake my head and watch his response, that quick furtive glance at the red-haired man and a rising note of excitement when he says, 'No family or friends on whom to call, to tell of your altered residence?'

He knows who I am, where I am from. Why is he pretending otherwise? Or have I changed as much as that?

'No. No friends. No family.' I think of Elijah, but he is gone. I think about Mrs Hibbert and Tip, and how Tip had promised to find me one day and take me back to Cheyne Walk. I shudder to think of such a thing. I watch the Evans man lick his tongue over his blubbery greasy lips. He lowers his hands to the table again. Dimpled fingers drum an irregular beat. His gaze is distant and serious, as if he is contemplating the fate of the whole of the British Empire, when in truth it is only that of a girl once sold to be an artist's muse – and that's when it strikes me – the name of the other.

I say, 'You are Doctor Cruikshank! I met you in the gardens.'

'Well remembered.' He speaks as if to a child. 'And *you* would like us to call you Pearl?'

He sits back in his chair with a leisurely sigh. He cracks his knuckles. A horrible sound, after which there is a silence, probably only a moment or two, though it feels more like a year to me, during which a thin ray of sunshine breaks through the sky's thick layer of cloud, slanting through one of the windows, making rainbows appear in his spectacle lenses when he suddenly turns the other way, to place a hand on the arm of the woman, who, despite the heavy silver cross that hangs from the chain around her throat, shows little Christian charity in a face that could freeze the fires in hell. Was that cross at her breast when she struck me before? I suppose it must have been.

He says, 'This is my wife . . . Mrs Cruikshank. She is the matron here, in charge of the hospital's daily routine . . . much like the role of a housekeeper, such as those you have known in your previous life.'

'My previous life?' My tongue can hardly form the words, so parched that it sticks to the top of my mouth.

'From now on, Chiswick House will be your home. You must not be afraid of us. We treat every inmate as our guest. Our only hope is to make you well – to be happy and comfortable again. In return, we ask you to show us respect, obeying any rules set down . . . in which Mrs Cruikshank and myself will do our best to educate you.'

'You must also trust to our medical skills,' Dr Evans carries on, 'being well read and versed as we are in all of the latest practices for treating unfortunates such as yourself. We will train you to be meek and compliant, less tormented by abnormal desires and . . .'

'I don't want to be locked in this deadlurk place. I have no abnormal desires.'

My heart is beating much too fast. My head is throbbing. I feel sick. I am staring hard at Osborne Black – and still he will not meet my eye. 'Osborne . . .' I plead, my voice as shrill as a child's now, 'you can't mean to ding me in this place . . . to throw me like carrion to these crows?'

The fat man replies in Osborne's place, 'That is not what your husband tells us. He is most concerned at your lack of control, the deviancy of your activities . . . and how for some time he has been obliged to keep you locked away from the world . . . the world of sin and temptation, to which one as blighted as yourself will always find herself drawn back. It is all in the nature of the beast. It is all in the nurturing.'

'We are here to make you well.' Mrs Cruikshank echoes her husband's words, cracked lips barely parting to let out the caution issued in flat monotones, 'to guide you in the righteous path, for which I shall be your guardian. As such you shall find me strict but fair.'

The Cruikshank man rises up in his chair. Its legs scrape across the wooden floor, creating a screeching, like that of a rat. I want to shrink and disappear when his cane comes tapping across the boards, travelling the length of the table until he is standing behind me, so close that I can feel his breath tickling soft on the back of my neck, and the things he half-whispers, half-purrs in my ear, 'You must learn to trust us, Mrs Black.'

I can bear this no longer, standing abruptly, turning to face him and lashing out. His cane goes clattering down to the floor, over which sound my objection is made. 'I am not Mrs Black. I am perfectly sane. It is *he*,' I point at Osborne Black, '*he* is the one who should be locked up. That man is a wicked murderer. I have seen his guilt in the paintings he makes, the ogres and devils who live in the water. You should have him hanged and set me free.'

At that my knees buckle. I slump to the floor, pressing my aching brow on the chair as I mumble my sobbing, desperate plea, 'Won't you go to the House of the Mermaids and tell Mrs Hibbert where I am?'

'Who is this Mrs Hibbert?' Dr Cruikshank is questioning Osborne, a note of caution in his voice. 'What is this place, this Mermaid House? Does it actually exist? You assured us that Pearl has no other kin . . . no one who might think to interfere.'

'She does not,' Osborne snaps. 'I have no idea what she's talking about. There is no living family. She was orphaned when her parents died, while she was still living in Italy, which is where I met and married her . . . before we returned to England.'

Oh, how he lies! And his conspirator, this Evans man, he only smiles when his colleague goes on, 'But a Mermaid House? We must be sure. We cannot risk . . .'

'It is a brothel!' Evans replies with a snorting laugh. 'A house of carnal pleasures. What respectable woman would ever know of such an establishment as that?'

'Only respectable men like you!' I shout back. I cannot help myself, though silenced when looking at Osborne again, whose hands are trembling and clenched, a sudden tic beside one eye when he exhales a weary sigh, and admits, 'Yes. It is a brothel. I fear that my wife has learned of such things from the lips of a previous assistant of mine . . . a sordid, contemptible young man who has since been dismissed from my employ. He was much too fond of visiting whores, relating his exploits back to her, playing on her venal propensities. You see what she has been reduced to. She no longer knows fact from reality . . . believing herself a prostitute . . . believing *me* a murderer! I have tried my best to carry on, but gentlemen . . .' he pauses a while, 'you see the way things are.'

'I am *not* your wife! I never was. Where is the proof? Show me the proof!' A terrible anger is welling within me. I try to keep my voice even and calm, to sound as if I am rational, even though I can sense the futility. The net is tightening around. Dr Evans and Osborne must be in cahoots, and I wonder how much my 'husband' has paid to make sure that he is rid of me, grown tired of what I have become, no longer his angel or virgin child, but a woman . . . a woman who, if she was free, might very well seek to ruin him.

'Do not reproach yourself.' Cruikshank speaks, and I think that pitying tone for me. 'It is indeed a tragic event when a loved one loses her reasoning. But, dear man, you cannot blame yourself. This delirium is a common thing, and bordering on the psychotic when affecting nymphomaniacs, which, from what we have heard today, would seem to describe your wife accurately. A simple examination, and then we may clarify the thing . . . that intimate matter we touched upon in our discussions earlier? I know it is distasteful to you, but I do think it best if you stay and observe. Patients presenting with symptoms like this are prone to be cunning and devious, not above making false allegations.'

While he speaks, the matron comes closer. She mutters in my ear, 'Stay still, you little vixen. Sit down and spread your knees.'

'No!' I gasp in disbelief. A cold sweat is trickling over my brow, stinging my eyes as they cast round the room, searching to find some means of escape. But the big double doors through which I was brought are firmly closed on the rest of the world. The window is high above the ground and blocked by the bulk of the Evans man, who shakes his head, who smiles at me, who groans when he stoops to reach under the table, retrieving some garment hidden there. Meanwhile, Mr Cruikshank limps to the trolley, a tinkling song of bottles and jars when he wheels it close beside my chair. And while he is fiddling with a syringe the matron moves to grab my arms, to hold me still when I call

237

out, imploring Osborne to make this stop. But something is clamped across my mouth. The fat man's hands are grasping mine, wrenched into the sleeves of a padded coat. A jangling percussion of buckles and straps as my arms are forced across my breasts and the garment is secured behind, so tight that however I twist and buck there can be no escape from this firm embrace, or the sting of the needle jabbed into my thigh, after which I am pushed back into the chair. But I am still able to reason and think, to feel someone cupping and lifting my chin, someone else lifting the hems of my shift. And when the examination begins, Dr Cruikshank looks up to smile at me – perhaps only meaning to reassure, but I start to laugh. I can't help it. I am thinking about the fairy tale where a soldier climbs down through a hollow tree and comes across a giant dog sitting on top of a treasure chest. That dog had eyes, big as saucers – just like the ones looking up at me now, the big round eyes of the Cruikshank man. The Cruikshank growls some medical terms as his fingers prise and poke and stab, just as the Evans did before when confirming my virginity. I feel the same humiliation and pain, a degradation mingled with fear, when Cruikshank glances over his shoulder and dictates his findings to his wife, as she sits in the chair at Osborne's side and takes up a book from the table there and starts to scribble down some notes, her pencil scratching over the page as fast as Dr Cruik-shank says – 'Hmm . . . this violent trembling and thrashing of limbs, the heat of the sexual organs . . . a sexual paroxysm, I think . . . all the signs of erotomania. Perhaps, Mr Black . . .' He strains to look back at Osborne now – Osborne, whose face is as rigid as stone, as white and cold as marble. Not a trace of sympathy remains in that darkly penetrating gaze, through which I hear Cruikshank chanting on, '. . . these past months you will also have noticed a lack of appetite for food, an excessive production of mucus and tears, the permanent state of arousal occurring in those so afflicted, for which . . .' He pauses, extracting his hands, letting out a slight groan when he stands again, holding his arms straight out ahead as the matron sets down her writing tools, returns to his side and removes some gloves, and a snap like the break of elastic during which he nods and then concludes, 'We will first employ the water cure.'

'But, if that fails,' Evans addresses Osborne, a lascivious smirk upon his lips, 'as it very often does, may I suggest a more radical cure, something that Cruikshank and I find ingenious in its simplicity. In short, a clitorectomy, removing the evil at its root. In the past five years we've had great success, and only the loss of two patients here, both of whom had underlying infections, their demise no result of the surgery. But all the rest have been restored to a childlike docility, returned once again to their husband's care. Only in one case did the problem persist, when the woman had to be returned and a hysterectomy performed – the total removal of sexual organs. A month or two to convalesce and that patient was never again oppressed by the dangerous wanderings of the womb.'

I don't understand what he's talking about, but I see Osborne's mute complicity when the Cruikshank starts to speak again, when he confirms my virginity lost – though what natural husband would be surprised to hear such a thing about his wife! And that diagnosis is all it takes for this lying and unnatural man to give me up, to sign the forms, to have me committed a lunatic.

Water: Are there tears – is that guilt in Osborne's eye, or is it only the glazing of mine when he stoops forward to kiss my cheek? I smell the paint and turpentine. I see the streaks of charcoal dust that stain the cuffs above his wrists, and beneath those cuffs is the thick dark hair that marks him out as an animal, though he sounds more like a lover when crooning softly in my ear, 'You will always be *my* mermaid.'

Thus we began and thus we end. No other word of goodbye for me, though he stops for a while when he reaches the door, to look back and enquire of the others, 'Her hair?'

'You shall have it, of course,' the Cruikshank replies with a simpering grin, 'I have not forgotten your request.'

And then, there is only the slamming of doors to tell me that I am abandoned here. I panic. I struggle, but not for long, because Cruikshank's drug is numbing my brain. Overcome with a tingling lethargy I no longer notice the pain in my head, or the cramp in my arms; only find myself slumping down in the chair, my chin falling forward on to my breast as I quickly lose touch with all that's real. I sink, like a stone, into water.

A LETTER FROM LILY TO KINGSLAND HOUSE

Saturday, December 2nd

MY DEAREST PAPA,

You must not worry that I have not written over these past few days. Freddie assures me that he has sent word while I have been somewhat indisposed, but only with a winter chill and now I am quite myself again, despite the weather in London remaining so bitterly cold and wet.

I hope you are warmer in Kingsland House. I worry. I miss you, and Ellen too. Truly, if it were not for the fact that today there has been a 'development' then I would have considered coming home.

But, at long last, there is some news, with Freddie's advertisements in the press resulting in a direct response. Earlier this morning, while Freddie was out, a letter arrived, right here at the house, and I know you will think it wrong of me, to open Freddie's personal mail, but the envelope was clearly addressed 'to those with an interest in Elijah Lamb'. And I do have an interest, after all.

The note inside was very brief: 'From the House of the Mermaids in Cheyne Walk to those who are seeking Elijah Lamb: Come this afternoon at 3 o'clock.'

The House of the Mermaids, Papa! Surely the name is fortuitous, when I think back to that book you wrote, and all of Elijah's drawings too. For the present, I know no more than this and shall have to set my pen aside and wait for Freddie to return, and whatever the rest of the day may bring, dearest Papa, you shall soon be told.

Until then, I hope with all of my heart to have news to bring some joy to yours.

Your own most affectionate granddaughter,

LILY

It was true, a letter had arrived, and I thought it best to inform Papa, who must surely be wondering how things went, even if my news was deliberately vague, skimming over the details of other events occurring in the past few days – Elijah's papers – what I really knew of the House of the Mermaids – my foolish nocturnal wanderings – Uncle Freddie's scandalous books.

The thought of those books would not leave my mind. I was hardly able to meet Freddie's eye when, after the doctor's departure, when the maid had also left my room, he returned with a mug of sugary tea and a plate piled high with toast and jam – as if all that sweetness would make things right, would make me forget what I'd learned about him; though, of course, Uncle Freddie was unaware of what secrets his maid confessed that day.

He looked at me through tired, bagged eyes, and then sat down on the mattress edge – just above where Elijah's papers were hidden – reaching forward to take my hands when he said, 'Oh, my dear girl . . . what on earth possessed you to go running off through the streets like that? Why, anything . . . anyone . . .' Seeming unable to find the words, his hands cupped my shoulders, drawing me close as he sighed, then said, 'I honestly thought I'd lost you too.'

So tense that I could barely breathe, my mind was reeling with panic by then, recalling what the maid implied, imagining all sorts of scenarios – indecent things of which I'd read, those stories where simpering raddled-out lechers were intent on the ruin of innocent virgins. It came as a very great relief when Freddie said he must leave for a while. 'I'll be gone a few hours at the most . . . just at the office across the road, attending a meeting with one of our printers. But I shall return in time for lunch . . . at liberty for the rest of the day to sit with my Lily and see her get well, entirely at her disposal again.'

I don't know whether he noticed how cool my disposition, how my hands lay unresponsive in his as if they were made of nothing but wax. But to think of Freddie at my side while I lay in that bed for hours on end: I really couldn't bear it!

The moment he left I got up and dressed and started to pack my things away, fully intending to leave that day and make my return to Kingsland House – when there came a sharp knocking upon the house door, a banging very urgent it was, and thinking the maids must not have heard, that perhaps it was Freddie come back again, I ran down the three flights of stairs myself and opened the door to find no one there, only a blast of winter air seeded with sleet as hard as rice. And then, with the door closed up again, while brushing those melting slivers off, I happened to see what lay on the mat, just below the letterbox.

That stationery looked fit for a queen, the envelope as smooth as silk, and no frank mark or stamp to mar the front where the edges were cut as if made of lace, the borders within embossed with shells. Reading the mysterious inscription – *To those with an interest in Elijah Lamb* – I wasted not a moment more in breaking the seal upon the back, which was black, and formed a capital 'H'. Such a delicate fragrance wafted out from the flattened violet placed inside, reminding me of the market- place when I had been offered just the same. *Violets for chastity.* Leaving that flower quite untouched, I extracted the page in my unsteady hands and read the brief contents of what it contained, all the while thinking of Elijah's diary, and how Pearl had said she'd been raised in a brothel – a brothel called the House of the Mermaids. It was surely too coincidental that this missive arrived from the same address.

In a state of some confusion I walked back up the stairs, heading for Freddie's sitting room, where I looked at the envelope again, and this time I lifted the flower out, flinging bruised petals on to the fire, where they shrivelled and hissed among the coals, smoking like purple poison. Then, with the envelope still in my hand, I went to sit at Freddie's desk, using Freddie's stationery to scribble my letter to Papa, and about to address an envelope when disturbed by the swift tread of feet on the stairs, and then Freddie calling my name, his face lit up like the rising sun when looking in at the sitting-room door. 'Ah, Lily, dear girl . . . there you are!' Retreating to the landing, he peered back over the bannister rail, conversing with someone still below. 'Well, come on up, then, if you must. Don't dawdle about down there all day.'

Wondering who could be visiting and hoping the doctor had not returned, I stood up and smoothed down the folds of my skirts and glanced in the mantel mirror, wishing I'd thought to brush my hair, at least to tie it neatly back. But such regrets were all in vain, for in no time at all the guest was there, his hat grasped firmly in his hands, his voice deep and earnest when he said, 'Miss Lamb . . . Lily . . . I do hope you are feeling recovered. Freddie told me how unwell you've been. He thought it best I did not come, but I felt myself to be somewhat at fault for trailing you out and about in the rain . . . and I wanted to apologise for any upset I may have caused, after our visit to Dolphin House.'

Just what had Freddie divulged of my 'illness' to cause Samuel Beresford such concern? I felt myself growing hot and embarrassed, my words rushing out, too tart, too sharp. 'Mr Beresford, you flatter yourself to assume such degrees of influence . . . that your views might affect my state of health!'

In reply, he looked flustered and ill at ease, and I felt a sudden pang of guilt, going on while trying to force a smile. 'It is kind of you to come, but really I am perfectly well . . . a little tired and bad tempered, that's all.'

'Good!' Freddie interjected. 'In that case Sam can put down his hat. A medicinal sherry for all of us, to restore our spirits as well as our health . . . and then perhaps a spot of lunch!'

Very soon, he was holding two glasses out, though mine was immediately refused, knowing I had to keep a clear mind for whatever the day might happen to bring, regarding the invitation of which Freddie was still in ignorance – but not for long.

Drawing the letter out of my pocket, I thrust it underneath his nose. It was neither polite nor ladylike but what did I care for etiquette, only the ticking down of the clock with every second nearer to three – which made it a matter of urgency.

So long Freddie stared at that envelope. It really was excruciating, during which Samuel Beresford lifted a book down from the shelves and, seeing him flick through its pages, I felt a slight tug of doubt in my mind as to whether he was also involved in the making of Freddie's 'other' tomes – the ones compiled of pictures, not words. I found myself shivering yet hot. I went to stand at a window, where the glass was etched white with webbings of ice, and when my hand was tracing there my thoughts were expressed somewhat casually, though inside my emotions were anything but, when I said, 'Look at these patterns, so like ferns . . . like the ferns by the stream at Kingsland House. Water is the strangest element, don't you think? Sometimes it is quite magical . . . to take on so many varied forms.'

Samuel set down his book and offered me a tentative smile. 'My mother has fallen victim of late . . . to this fern craze, this Pteridomania.'

'Pteridomania? What a word! It sounds like a kind of madness.'

'Well, yes, I suppose it is in a way. Charles Kingsley coined the phrase, you know.'

'Mr Kingsley who wrote *The Water-Babies*?'

'Yes, indeed. He claims his daughters have gone insane to become so obsessed with collecting ferns. My mother is just the same . . . any new species, she simply must have it! Goes all over the country searching them out and then grows them in Wardian cases at home. But she does not have the greenest of fingers. They all seem to shrivel and die in the end.'

'She could always ask Freddie to steal some . . . the next time he goes to visit Kew.'

'Kew?' Freddie asked, glancing up from the letter.

'Yes, Freddie . . . Kew! You visited there with Elijah one day. He wrote and told me about it. My brother tells me everything . . . unlike the secrets *you* like to keep, hidden away underneath your hat.'

Samuel Beresford was frowning by then, looking distinctly uncomfortable. 'Freddie,' he said, 'would you like me to leave?'

'You may as well go.' I gave him my airy reply while sweeping back towards the fire. 'Freddie and I have an appointment to keep . . . at the House of the Mermaids, at three o'clock.'

'Oh, in that case,' Samuel set down his glass, the sherry inside it barely touched, 'I *am* interrupting. I must be on my way.'

'No, stay!' Freddie responded with passion, his cheeks growing very florid. 'You are a dear and trusted friend. Would you cast an eye over this note for me? Tell me what you think of it?'

Having passed the letter to Samuel, Freddie then appealed to me. 'I cannot take you to such a house. If you knew what it was, then . . .'

'But I do! It's a brothel. It's where Pearl Black once lived as a child, before she was sold to Osborne Black.'

'A brothel? But Osborne met her in Italy.' Samuel lowered the page in his hands, confusion written all over his face.

'He didn't,' I answered bluntly. 'That was a convenient lie. Your cousin is *not* a respectable man.'

Freddie downed his glass in one, his eyes then fixed on the fire's flames while speaking in strained but measured tones. 'Lily, you should not have opened my post. No niece of mine . . .'

'But I am not *really* your niece, am I!' My voice was raised, almost a shout. 'And that letter was *not* addressed solely to you. It implies some news of my brother, and like it or not I intend to go and hear what the author has to say.'

Freddie sighed and visibly paled. 'Don't let your feelings excite you, my dear.'

Meanwhile, clearly shocked by that earlier disclosure, Samuel

246

Beresford glanced back at the window, as if seeking to find an answer there when he mused, 'She came from a brothel . . . not Italy? I would never have thought that of Osborne. Could Pearl be lying, do you think? Could Pearl be imagining such things?'

For a moment I was speechless, because what if Samuel was right, what if Pearl had fabricated it all – deceiving Elijah, deceiving me? My ears started ringing. I felt very strange. I heard Samuel saying, 'Freddie . . . Lily looks rather feverish. Is the doctor coming back today?'

The thought of that doctor was more than enough to restore me to my senses again, saying, 'I am not ill, and I am not mad!'

But, really, I was not myself at all. My limbs were shaky, my chest tight and sore; my head as thick as cotton wool. I *had* to try to think clearly, to prove that my mind was rational, and, suddenly heading for the door, I ran upstairs and into my room, where I lifted up the mattress edge and grabbed at the papers stashed beneath.

'What's all this?' Freddie asked when I brought them back down, pushing the bundle into his hands, feeling as if I was floating in air, simply watching in silence as Freddie read until, with another weary sigh, he set the papers down on a table, looked up and moaned his loud dismay. 'Oh, my dear, to think you saw such things.'

'I'm sure there are worse things to see.' I was thinking of Freddie's secret books. 'The main thing is, this House of the Mermaids . . . Elijah knew about its existence, and now whoever lives there is claiming to know about him in return. We *must* go. We cannot ignore this chance.'

'*If*. . .' Freddie raised his voice yet more, 'if *anyone* in Cheyne Walk has information regarding Elijah then you may be assured I will find it. God damn it!' He thumped a fist on the table, his empty glass then tinkling as papers went floating down to the floor, and though his next words were calmer they were no less emotional. 'I encouraged Osborne to hire Elijah and for my own selfish reasons. It is I who should now be responsible for discovering what has been going on. But really . . . this note . . . the most likely outcome is blackmail, some deceitful means of extracting more money. You can't begin to understand what these sort of people are capable of.'

Blackmail? Had 'these people' written to Freddie before? I wondered what he could be hiding now. I stated categorically, 'I insist on coming with you. There is no point trying to stop me. I know Papa would want me to . . . after all, they have news of Elijah, and I'm only here to find him . . . and then I hope to take him home and *never* return to this place again! Everything Ellen said is true. London is nothing but vice and sin!'

I thought of my brother's love for Pearl, how her life with Osborne had been an illusion, and Elijah now trapped in that web of deceits. I *would* go along to the House of the Mermaids, whether Freddie liked it or not, however desperate the gleam in his eye when he said, 'Lily! I never thought you so stubborn. If your grandfather knew how ill you've been . . . if he thought I would let you be defiled, to enter a house of prostitutes!'

'Look!' I pointed down at the papers. 'I am no longer so innocent, and if you won't take me, I'll go alone. I'll find this place and . . .'

I broke off to watch Samuel Beresford gathering the fallen pages up and placing them on the tabletop – and he may well have glanced at those pictures of Pearl, and he may have read some of Elijah's words, for his cheeks had bloomed with spots of red and he gave an awkward sort of cough before saying, 'Freddie, if you genuinely fear some blackmailing plot, then I think you should tell the constabulary.'

'You might think so.' Freddie offered his friend a tight forced smile. 'But I have my reputation to think of, and that of the business too . . . and everyone in my employ, not to mention the names of Elijah and Lily. I prefer to keep this matter discreet, which is why I shall visit this house today and *if* Lily persists I shall take her too. In the meantime, Sam, would you be so kind as to wait here until our return? If we are not back by eight o'clock then, by all means, I give you my blessing to inform every constable in town.'

The last time I'd been that near to Cremorne, it was summer, we'd made our trip on the river, with Elijah and Papa and—

This time, it was bitterly cold. Sitting in the carriage at Freddie's side, I hugged my arms to my breasts for warmth. I leaned very hard against the door, and despite the fact that a draught blew in I preferred to endure such discomfort as that than to find myself pressed too close to the man of whom I had grown so suspicious; confused as to precisely what and who our Uncle Freddie really was. At least he did not think to light a cigar, though I'm sure the prospect entered his mind, as he automatically pushed a hand into his overcoat pocket, drawing out the silver box in which the offending items were kept. But after a rapid glance at me the container was swiftly put away. From that point on Freddie twiddled his fingers, exhaling the weary sighs of a martyr. His breaths created a fug all their own, the air in that cab become just as dense as the mists of rain that hung outside, above which the clouds were thick and low, almost engulfing the roofs of the houses, sucking up grey plumes of smoke which rose from most of the chimney stacks. A sleety rain glistened over iced pavements which shone in the glow of the carriage lamps, and the gutters that lined the sides of the road bubbled with froths of marbled slime.

It seemed to me that all of London was made of nothing but water and ice when I stood next to Freddie beneath an umbrella, as he tugged on a bell affixed to a wall, set next to some gates where a polished brass plate was engraved with the curling letters that spelled out the name of our destination: *The House of the Mermaids.*

My eyes squinted up to the top of a wall in which jagged shards of glass were stuck, beyond which the paint at the windows was peeling, and windows were draped with more grime than lace. I imagined a spider lurking there, hiding in dark dusty corners, luring innocent flies to its web. But all such reflections were soon interrupted when we heard the running patter of feet and then the sound of a key in the gate. And when that barrier opened up, a maid greeted us from the other side.

In late middle age, she was very plain, dressed in immaculate black and white, and needing no umbrella herself, being sheltered by the canopy that covered the path all the way to the door. A swift bob and she asked us to follow, to enter a hall where the milky sheen of black and white tiles was soon to be marred by our muddy feet. And, yes, I was more than nervous by then, beginning to question the sense of the visit, and wondering up *what* garden path Freddie and I were being led.

Freddie set his umbrella down and while he was shrugging off his coat the maid reached out to take my cloak, both of those items soon hanging damp on the large brass hooks of a chiffonier, all marble and mirrors, as grand as an altar, upon which she also placed our hats, while glancing back over her shoulder to say, 'You're late. The appointment was made for three.'

'We were delayed by the weather.' Freddie's answer was equally abrupt.

'Tell me about it!' She raised her eyes to imaginary heavens. 'As if business isn't bad enough.'

'I told you. They're after money.' Freddie was muttering under his breath.

I didn't dare to meet his eye or I might well have turned on my heel and run, instead of which I followed the clicking of the maid's as she led us both across the hall, around which many candles had been lit, exuding a pungent aroma which mingled with that of the fragrant white lilies arranged in a vase of crystal glass, the smells you might find in any church.

We were led into a reception room, anything but religious in tone. On the walls either side of the double doors, which creaked behind us like rusty jaws, were a pair of wooden mast-heads, each one a bare-breasted mermaid. On top of a piano-forte where the ivories were cracked or stained there was a white cockatoo in a cage, though those gold metal bars were no longer needed to contain what was clearly stuffed within. There were Chinese screens, and carvings of jade, and glass epergnes placed upon lacquered tables, and one of those tables was set for tea. The pot's silver was burnished and shone like a mirror, reflecting the tiny embroidered glass circles that glinted in spangled throws around, all the reds and greens and purples and golds that were draped over many low divans. On closer inspection those fabrics were worn, here and there frayed away into little holes. Behind them the walls were panelled in wood that extended from skirting to dado rail, and much of that veneer was chipped but, oh, to see what lay between the dado and the ceiling's cove – what transported me to another world; a vision of sand and coral and weeds that swayed round the limbs of the half-drowned men embraced in the arms of their fishy loves, bound for the whole of eternity in the flowing ropes of those mermaids' hair.

Lowering my gaze from that sensual scene, I tried to concentrate instead on the jewel-like colours in Turkish rugs which were scattered most everywhere over the boards, and only looking up again when Freddie swept past me to sit himself down. His long legs were crossed, and his face very strained as he stared straight ahead at some more double doors – just then beginning to open up. The slight whine of hinges, the rustle of silk, and a sight which caused me to gasp out loud, for I had seen that vision before; the black-veiled woman in Cremorne. Now, she emerged like a chrysalis from the clear cocoon of glassy light of the orangery spreading wide behind, in which more candles were flickering as if dancing along with the patter of rain, the rushing of silver rivulets that streaked over transparent ceiling and walls. A magical fairy grotto it seemed, with statues and fountains and palms and ferns, and the smell of vanilla – like Freddie's cigars – which caught in my throat and made me cough, and I lifted a hand to one side of my head where I felt a sudden stabbing pain.

Somewhere else in the house, a clock chimed the half-hour. The woman closed the double doors and stepped farther into the mermaid room. From top to toe she still wore black, and through the gauze that hung over her face not a hint of her features could be glimpsed. I wondered whether she could see us at all – me being half frightened out of my wits, and Freddie like a wooden doll popping in and out of a weather clock, for no sooner was he sitting down than he was standing up again, extending a hand in greeting, though with very little enthusiasm.

Our hostess ignored his gesture, remaining entirely motionless, her arms held rigid at her sides. 'Mr Hall . . .' Another step closer. 'It has been many years since we met, and yet I see you are hardly changed.' Her voice was husky, thick with French accent.

'Mrs Hibbert.' He pronounced her name 'eebair', and his voice was measured but also curt. 'I might very well say the same of you . . . if only you removed those veils.'

She laughed; a throaty chuckling sound. 'I doubt you would think the years so kind if you saw what lay beneath this disguise.'

It was then I had a ghastly thought, wondering if she wore those veils because of scratches on her face – like those that had scarred the flower girl. Or could she somehow be deformed? There was surely a monster's soul inside, to have thought to sell Pearl to Osborne Black when she was barely more than a child.

Freddie did not seem to care, lacking his usual vivacity, only offering the weary response, 'Some of us are older and wiser now. Having been bitten we are twice shy.'

What history did he have with this woman? What would I learn about him next? While I pondered that, he spoke again. 'I don't know what game you are playing, madam, but we have only come here today in the hope of some news of Elijah Lamb. Or was that correspondence of yours no more than a tantalising lie? Pray do tell. We are all ears!'

His stance was too rigid, his tone too aggressive. I found myself crying, 'Please, Uncle Freddie. We must wait to hear what Mrs Hibbert says.'

'Uncle?' Mrs Hibbert echoed me, that word said in barely a

whisper, after which I heard a long, deep sigh, saw the tremble of muslin, which shifted out before being sucked to her lips again.

'Not a real uncle,' I quickly explained. 'Freddie is a family friend. He is helping me to look for Elijah . . . Elijah Lamb . . . my brother . . . my twin. I beg you to tell us whatever you know . . . whatever it is, however small.'

While I pleaded and struggled to hold back the tears, Freddie harrumphed, sitting back down, flicking some speck of imaginary lint from the pristine grey cloth of his jacket sleeve, during which Mrs Hibbert came near to my side, not sitting but reaching out with her hand, silk fingers gently caressing my hair. A strange thing that was, and a strange thing that I did not recoil when, really, I should have felt disgust at the touch of that black widow spider. But all I could do was to gaze back up, still trying to see through the layers of gauze, attentive to every silky word when she spoke more softly than before. 'You must not fret. We know exactly where he is. Elijah Lamb is safe . . . for now.'

For now? Alarm bells were ringing in my mind. 'What do you mean . . . for now?'

'Do not be distressed, ma chère. You will see him very soon. So long as . . .' Again, her words broke off, interrupted now by another voice, from the man who came in through the hallway doors where, as they slowly creaked behind, I saw right through to another room that was set on the opposite side of the house. No mermaids to adorn those walls, but there was an enormous mahogany desk with more drawers and doors than you could count, and rows of elaborate shelves on top. What a mess it looked to be, with papers scattered everywhere or crumpled in piles on the floor round about. Truly, you'd think a bomb had gone off. But when the doors had closed again my concentration was wholly fixed on the lilting voice and flashy garb of the man I had chased to the marketplace. He wore a purple silk cravat, below which there gleamed a large brass key that dangled from a chain at his neck. Seeing that, another memory flashed into my mind – that same gold around Mrs Hibbert's neck when we saw her in the mermaid tent.

Despite being indoors he still wore a coat, and a long black velvet one it was this time, the hems skimming over the tops of his boots. On his head was a grey felt hat, the brim wrapped around with mauve ribbons and violets. I felt my gut wrench to see those blooms, my cheeks burning hot in his iced blue gaze, and the leer of his narrow oiled red lips, below which barbed fingers tugged and stroked at the ribbons of his pale moustache. When he'd done with that little performance he took up where his friend left off – 'Yes, you will see Elijah Lamb, so long as you do as we request and bring our precious Pearl back home. *That* is the price on your brother's head.'

What could I say to that? Through my confused consternation I heard the rustle of black silk skirts, and the thrash of the rain on the glasshouse roof, and then came another creak of doors, the tinkling of little bells, a blur of grey fur and pale pink flesh and that horrible monkey scampered in, sitting right next to Freddie's feet, where it started to play with its private parts! All the while it was chitter-chattering as if in self-congratulation, baring its blackened dagger teeth, which glistened with bubbles of spittle and slime. Thank goodness that vile occupation stopped when it spied a bowl on the tabletop, its fingers then reaching for sugar cubes, stuffing a great many into its mouth, lips pursed in wrinkled sucks of delight which turned to a violent screech of alarm when Freddie kicked the beast away.

'Disgusting, filthy creature!' His contempt was loudly voiced. 'And you, Tip Thomas . . . what do *you* want? Will you deign to speak plainly for once in your life and tell what you know of Elijah Lamb?'

'Not much of a welcome, Mr Hall.' Tip Thomas whistled and then reached down, scooping the monkey into his arms, soothing it, stroking its wrinkled cheek while it picked its fingers through his hair, as if it was searching for lice or fleas. And perhaps it had found some for, now and then, those busy fingers poked back into its mouth and rubbery lips appeared to move, as if in mastication. Quite unembarrassed by such a show, Tip Thomas continued his smiling reply. 'I expect more respect from my business friends, no matter how previous our dealings here. I am hurt, Mr Hall . . . really, I am. I thought Lily Lamb might like to play at guessing a little riddle or two. But,' he sighed, 'if neither of you will pander to me, perhaps I shall pander to you instead. Yes, I think I should come straight to the point and repeat what you do not seem to have heard. You bring Pearl back home to the House of the Mermaids and I will give you Elijah Lamb.'

It was only then beginning to dawn, leaving me breathless and faint with the tension, asking, 'Elijah is here? Is he in this house? You *must* let me go and see him . . . now!'

'All in good time.' A sharp finger was lifted to greasy lips, waiting a moment before he went on, 'You must understand what is at stake.'

'Will you come to the point!' Freddie shouted, but this man, this Tip Thomas, would not be rushed, pausing to twist a whisker again. 'Oh dear, *where* to begin? Perhaps a good place would be this very morning when a doctor was brought into your house . . . a house around which I've loitered of late. We chanced to meet when he came out, and having some previous acquaintance I found him not at all discreet, revealing his patient's condition and how such ailments of the mind were these days his speciality . . . often venturing as far out as Chiswick way to work in a private asylum there, where his skills are usefully employed in . . . how shall we put this tender point . . . in certain surgical procedures. Why, I asked if he might be lured out east, to mend and darn a few holes of my own, to repair time's nasty wear and tear . . . though,' he turned to give me a wink, 'I would hazard *that's* not a problem for our little shrinking violet. Anyway . . .' he was grinning at Freddie again, 'being such a gossip, this quack of yours, he spilled ever so many secrets into my own little shell-likes, and not only Miss Lamb's fragile state of mind, but . . .' He paused before

255

continuing. 'But that of another delectable girl who he hopes to get his hands on soon, an inmate of the asylum, and one committed recently, and going by the name of Pearl.' His voice grew deep and threatening. 'Now *that* I found most grievous news.'

I gasped. 'Osborne Black has put her away!' And then, thinking back to Dolphin House, all the pictures I'd seen in its dingy hall, when looking again at the mermaids adorning the brothel walls, I found the style familiar and asked in disbelieving tones, 'Did Osborne Black paint these?'

'He did indeed,' Tip Thomas replied. 'No doubt they are worth a small fortune now, with the artist achieving such recent fame. If only we could find some way to remove the plaster, to frame it up and sell it on. But alas, he has diddled us there as well.'

'When were they painted?'

'Once upon a time, long, long ago, before *you* were a twinkle in *anyone's* eye. He'd taken a fancy to one of our whores, quite a favourite with several young artists about . . . though most would not care to admit that now, become such *respectable* gentlemen.'

Tip Thomas walked towards one of the walls, scratching a talon over its surface. 'This one, this is her . . . the one Osborne Black was obsessed with then.'

Half hidden between some rocks and reeds I saw a mermaid, staring out, her eyes a vivid emerald green, her waving hair like strands of gold which glistened around the shell she held, holding it cupped against one ear. Really, it was remarkable, how much she looked like Pearl, but an older Pearl, more voluptuous.

'So,' I was trying to understand, 'was this mermaid, this woman, related to Pearl?'

'She gave birth to her and then she drowned.' Mrs Hibbert's answer was brusquely made, to which I gave my shocked reply, 'You sold her child to the very same man who had also painted the mother before . . . a man who paints nothing but mermaids and water?' I was thinking again of that tent in Cremorne and how Pearl had swooned when she saw the tank – the mermaid within like a mummified corpse, like something exhumed from a watery grave. I tried to imagine what Pearl had been thinking – when Tip Thomas's voice slashed thin and sharp, 'Things in this house are different now. It's time to bring our mermaid home.'

He laughed with his mouth, but his eyes were cold when he spat on the carpet and pursed his lips, making a sort of kissing sound. His monkey then rolled back its lips. It might have been smiling in sheer delight, chirping, singing a pretty song. And while that display was going on Freddie was looking murderous, standing again, his voice booming out like a great bass drum, 'Where is Elijah? I must insist you give him up. If not, I will see you both in court.'

Such an outburst made the monkey cringe, its tiny hands lifted to cover its eyes.

'Will you calm yourself, Mr Hall!' Mrs Hibbert's voice sounded different then, somehow less guarded, less composed. 'Are *you* so pure and righteous a man? Could you swear to *that* in a court of law?'

For a moment, Freddie looked confused, staring hard at the apparition in black, and meanwhile Tip Thomas carried on, 'I dare say that many would be shocked to hear of Mr Frederick Hall's involvement with the literature available in shops in Holywell Street . . . some fine examples of which reside on this establishment's bookshelves, very popular with the clientele. I myself like a bit of *The Lustful Turk*. For Miss Lamb I might offer *Fanny Hill*. But then who is to say what is moral, what not, and who are the most respectable . . . those dealers in the galleries who pimp naked flesh to the great and the good, or the book vendors who ply their trade somewhat more illicitly. Oh, the quandary of such hypocrisy!'

Freddie's mouth was gulping open and closed, like a fish being dangled on a hook. His response was simply to sit back down almost as if he'd been physically winded, pulling a handkerchief out of his pocket and rubbing it over his brow and neck, where the flesh now gleamed with beads of sweat.

'Gentlemen, please . . . *Comportez-vous!*' Mrs Hibbert snapped to break the spell, as irate as a governess admonishing two disobedient pupils, after which she said more levelly, 'Tip, show some manners instead of contempt. Will you pour Mr Hall a cup of tea . . . or something stronger if he desires. Stay here and entertain our friend while Miss Lamb is escorted to visit her brother.'

'Take as long as you want,' Tip Thomas replied. He sounded just as sly as rat. 'Mr Hall and I will be happy enough discussing literature and art. And while on the subject of storybooks I might sit here beside the fireside and tell Mr Hall a tale or two. There might even be a ghost involved; a death still haunting him today, the soul he thought buried away in his past. What a white-knuckle business this living can be . . . don't you agree, Mrs Hibbert?'

Mrs Hibbert stiffened and then replied, 'I believe we have had revelations enough!'

'Ah, well. All in good time. But the truth has a habit of outing itself, whether sooner or later, who can tell? First, we must take care of Pearl.'

The truth? What could this villain mean, and why the vicious smirk on his face when he arranged the folds of his coat as he sat in a chair beside the hearth, pushing the monkey down to the floor and withdrawing an object from one of his pockets. At first I thought it to be a knife with which he meant to threaten us, but he only used it on himself, one dull ridged side of that metal blade rasped back and forth between his hands as Tip Thomas filed and sharpened his claws; a vision sinister, threatening.

Meanwhile, a soft black hand took mine and led me away from those muralled walls, back out into the gloomy hall, where I followed Mrs Hibbert as she began to climb the stairs, a labyrinth winding up through the house, where many small landings had rooms leading off, from which women stared out from doors ajar, and those rooms exuding pungent aromas, so dense that I felt myself dizzy and sick. It was like being trapped inside a dream, all thoughts of Tip Thomas forgotten by then in the anticipation of seeing my brother – my brother, in this very brothel.

The low hissing gleam of lamps on walls offered much too little light, and more than once I stumbled, my feet snagged by holes in the runners worn through by how many feet before, though Mrs Hibbert seemed to know exactly where to place her own, floating above me quite effortlessly, leaving me gasping and panting behind, my lungs become too constricted, and that pain in my head growing worse every moment, much relieved when we finally came to a halt – having reached the last of some narrow stairs and then passed between two Chinese jars, with thick velvet drapes hanging either side. It was there, in a dark narrow corridor, that Mrs Hibbert paused and turned, and I had the distinct impression that she might be about to reveal her face, for her fingers played at those black veil hems before dropping down to her sides again.

I asked, 'Why do you hide yourself? You have been in mourning a very long time. When I saw you before, one day in Cremorne, you were wearing veils then as well.'

'You saw me in Cremorne?' There was a question in her voice before she went on more forcefully, 'I mourn because of the curse of deception . . . because of the stain of sin.' And with that cryptic pronouncement made she walked towards a door near by and said, 'He is here. But he must remain calm. Your brother has been most gravely ill.'

'What is wrong with him?'

'He was found by the mudlarks late one night, wandering the shore beneath Battersea Bridge. He kept repeating the same three words . . . "black" and "Pearl" and "mermaid", which caused his finders to assume that he had some association here, carrying him to our very door. Who knows how long he spent in the water, what filth was swallowed down from the sewers. And there is a wound to one side of his head.'

'A wound?' My own head was pounding when I demanded, 'How long have you had my brother here?'

She placed a hand upon my arm, the lightest touch, hardly there at all. 'For weeks . . . for months. At first, he was often insensible, not even knowing who he was. But Elijah is strong. He recovers well. I have prayed and God sends us a miracle. But . . .' She paused. 'The devil is never far off. Tip only decided to let him live thinking Elijah would lead us to Pearl. He knew him, you see. They had met before. And now . . . with this news about the asylum, Tip's need has grown more urgent.'

She let out another heavy sigh. 'I cannot bear to think of her there . . . but never imagine that Tip has a heart. He wants Pearl for the wealth she will bring to his coffers. Your brother is nothing more than her ransom. Tip would have thrown him back into the Thames if not for this bartering game he plays. I cannot say what he might do if . . .'

'If what?'

Her answer came slow and resigned. 'If you fail to bring Pearl back again.'

'But you sold her before, to Osborne Black. Why do you suddenly want her back?'

'Since she left us the business has faltered. With Pearl, Tip will lure the best gentlemen back. She will be the House of the Mermaid's jewel.'

'When I saw her, last week in Osborne's house, she mentioned your name. She said you would help. She said Mrs Hibbert would set her free, and she spoke of some papers . . .'

'Papers? Ah, that explains it. Tip has turned this house upside down with his searching.' She leaned closer and whispered in my ear, 'Let this be our secret. Tell nobody else. If there are legal documents, then . . .' She seemed to be trying to work things out, as if her memory failed her. 'Then he may have no need for Elijah.'

'But then he would give my brother back!' The hope I felt was soon depressed when her answer came so stridently. 'No, I have told you . . . you *must* believe. Tip Thomas does not have a heart. You could cut it out . . . he would not bleed.'

I was afraid, hearing those words. I can hardly describe the turmoil I felt, at first barely able to do much more than to press my forehead against the door – the door that would lead to my brother's side. I spread my fingers against the wood and listened for any signs of life, hearing nothing but silence from within. Was he really there? Or was this a trick? Mrs Hibbert and her accomplice, Tip, intending to lock me up instead, to blackmail Freddie for *my* release? You do hear of such things going on. Ellen Page had warned me often enough – and thinking of her and Papa again, both of them waiting for news of Elijah, I stifled my panic and gathered my courage and placed my hand on the cold brass knob.

It was like being six years old again, standing perfectly still in that doorway, looking into the room where my brother lay, but inhaling those scents of the sickroom, the faint tangs of vomit, ammonia, carbolic, and something else, something cloying, metallic. The room was very dim indeed, though leaking faint through some bars at the window there dribbled the last of the dreary day. A fire burned low in a small iron grate, the occasional hushing of a coal, the crackle and spit of a flaring log that afforded my eyes sufficient light to register the rosebud walls – so like my own in Kingsland House – and the shelves full of books and magazines. Hanging on a hook to one side of a mirror was a little circlet of flowers and shells. When taking a step farther into the room I noticed some pictures pinned to a wall, and recognised one immediately – a scene from *A Christmas Carol* it was, which Papa once read to us every year. Another two were posters to advertise days out in Cremorne; one depicting the flight of a hot-air balloon floating up high in a starry sky, the other the sketch of a pleasure boat, emblazoned with a legend that read, *The Citizen Boat Company*. That jaunty vessel was decked in flags, and much like the one we'd travelled in – that day when we visited Cremorne – that day when my brother's fate was sealed – my brother now lost in a shadowy gloom as dark as that in the mermaid tent.

I made out a table. A jug. A bowl. A razor. A towel. A bar of soap. A bottle half full of some syrupy mixture which I guessed must be an opiate, for it looked like the potions prescribed to Papa. There were brown sticky stains on the sheets of the bed, where some of that liquid must have spilled, beneath which lay a sleeping man – but a man who was a stranger to me – not my brother – not Elijah at all! Since when was Elijah so pale and gaunt, the bones in his face much too prominent? Since when was Elijah's hair cut short, one area having been shaved away, a fur of new stubble growing in through which you could clearly see a scar, the livid wound above one ear extending almost to the crown – where I'd felt such a stabbing of pain in mine. That man looked like a living corpse, with the dark bruising hollows beneath closed eyes, and his breaths so shallow that, as I stepped nearer and dared to peer down, I really did think him already dead, jumping back in alarm when his lids flickered open, eyes blinking before they closed again. But that was enough for me to see, even if they were swollen and rimmed with red, shining too bright in that wasted face; those eyes still belonged to my brother.

My heart gave a lurch to see them. I lifted both hands to my mouth, stifling a sob while crying out, 'Oh, Elijah! Elijah! What have they done?'

He answered by giving a heavy groan, parting lips crusted white with saliva, and when his eyes opened up again he seemed to be afraid of me, trying to rise on the pillow when beset by a sudden coughing fit, and his brow breaking out in a running sweat. He was straining to catch any breath in his lungs. I didn't know what to do to help, looking back in a panic to see Mrs Hibbert, who walked to the other side of the bed, where she lifted a cloth from the metal bowl, wringing it out, then dabbing his brow, her voice soothing and mellifluous. 'Ssshh. There is no one to harm you. It is not him, not Tip. It is Lily. Lily, your sister.'

'Elijah . . .' I said his name again, taking one of his hands in mine as he slumped back down on the pillows, and although his coughing abated, from somewhere deep inside his lungs there came a squeaking, scratching sound, as if a rat was trapped there, scrabbling around in the cage of his ribs, trying to escape through his living flesh. I placed my other hand on that breast and felt the fast beat of my brother's heart. I said his name again and again, at which he looked up and answered, 'Pearl?'

'He has forgotten me!' I looked at Mrs Hibbert again. 'Can he really be as ill as that?'

She sighed. 'It is the medicine. Tip doses him, to keep him subdued.'

Elijah struggled again, raising himself on one elbow now, his free hand reaching out to me as he spoke in a voice that was hoarse and cracked. 'Lily, you came! You found me. I saw her. I saw our mermaid. She saved me . . . she saved me from drowning.'

'What do you mean? What has happened to you?' I feared that wound to my brother's head had caused some damage to his brain.

'Osborne wanted to paint a drowning man. He said he needed to see how it looked. That last night . . .' He broke off. My brother was panting, inhaling deep breaths before going on, 'He asked me to lie with my head submerged in the pool, in his grotto. But I wouldn't. The dead fish. The noxious slime. So he asked me to lie in the river instead. It was high tide when we went to the gardens, and once by the water I lay on my back, holding my breath with my head submerged while Osborne observed me from above. But then . . . I don't know. He must have attacked me. I felt a dead weight pressing down on my chest and opened my eyes to see his boot. He was holding a rock in one of his hands . . . I remember blood all over his hands. I was sinking down into blackness . . . and that's when I saw her. She looked like Pearl, but she wasn't Pearl. She reached out to hold me in her arms, and then I was rising up again, able to grab at the rowing boat. I hid there, underneath the tarpaulin, until I was sure that Osborne had gone, until my body and mind were numb. I must have lost consciousness again. When I woke I didn't know where I was. I remember a bridge . . . and then this room.'

I hardly needed to ask, but I did, the fury rising in my breast, 'Osborne Black tried to drown you . . . to murder you?'

A slight nod, then his mouth fell slack again, and all too soon his eyes had closed, and I watched him like that for some moments more, and I could have stayed and watched all night, but then came the tug upon my sleeve and Mrs Hibbert was telling me that it was time for us to go.

'But how can I leave my brother here! He needs some proper medical care.'

'Our doctor has seen him often enough, but Elijah is in no state to move . . . even if Tip would allow him to go.'

'Then when will he be well enough?' I was trying my hardest not to shout and cause Elijah more distress. Her reply was only silence, and I knew that she was right, for then. For then, my brother must stay in that bed. For then, I simply lowered my lips, and kissed his cheek and promised him, 'I'll come back, Elijah. I swear I will.'

Was it only the beat of the rain still thrashing on the windowpanes, or was it those shifting coals in the grate, or the rustle of Mrs Hibbert's skirts as she led me back down through the house – or did I really hear those words, my brother's hoarsely whispered plea: 'Lily . . . help Pearl. Save Pearl.'

When Freddie and I were preparing to leave, collecting our things in the entrance hall, Mrs Hibbert was standing a little apart. Hard to say who she might have been looking at but I think it was probably Freddie, who was causing quite a commotion then, cursing and muttering under his breath while struggling to don his damp overcoat and complaining of how unhappy he was at not having seen Elijah too – to which Mrs Hibbert made her reply, clearly at pains to contain her emotions, 'Happiness is not a right, Mr Hall. Sometimes it is stolen. Sometimes it must be stolen back.'

While she said that, I heard some steps behind. I cringed from the touch of Tip Thomas's fingers, like claws they were upon my arm as he brought his face very close to mine and hissed where the house madam left off, saying, 'Steal Pearl back for me, and don't delay . . . my little shrinking violet.'

'Why don't you go and get her yourself?' What gave me the courage to spin around, to face Tip Thomas's snaky smile, around which I saw every crinkling line where the thick white powder fractured. I felt instinctively repulsed and yet was fascinated too, by his eyes, which were neither blue nor green but steeled with such malice when holding mine, when he answered in the softest tones, 'Oh, we've tried, little violet . . . we really have! I myself have written to Osborne Black. I have written to the asylum too and made my case, most plaintively. But it seems that it has been ordained that Pearl should receive no visitors. And Osborne Black's word – as her husband – is law.' While speaking, he lifted a hand and picked a few pins from beneath my hat. The metal chimed thin when it hit the tiled floor. Some loose strands of hair fell over my face, which he then pushed aside, very slowly, as his fingertips lightly scratched my cheek, where his breath brushed warm when he said the words, 'If those quacks mar one single inch of her flesh, if they harm so much as one hair on her head . . . then I will not be accountable. An eye for an eye. That is the rule we live by here, all those in the House of the Mermaids. You have one week to bring Pearl home. If you fail . . .' He paused. His hand dropped down and drew a line across my throat, 'Well, *someone* will have to pay the price. And don't think about going behind my back. Half the coppers in London come visiting here to smoke on the whore pipe now and then and . . . well, much like your Mr Hall, they don't care for adverse publicity.'

'You wouldn't dare!' Freddie was glaring through the gloom, and again I saw that sheen of sweat pricking up in the lines of his worried brow.

I was too stunned to speak or move when Tip Thomas gave his crude response. 'Don't dare me . . .' Such guile there was in his voice. 'I never could resist a dare. It would only blight your Lily flower . . . or perhaps you've already ploughed her soil. After all, she is your type, *n'est-ce pas*? Don't you agree, Mrs Hibbert?'

At that Mrs Hibbert hissed, *'Tais-toi!'* Tip Thomas pushed me towards Uncle Freddie and then pressed one taloned finger against his pursed and whiskered lips, and it seemed the whole house was holding its breath as the air around us clotted thick, and with more than the stench of white lilies in vases, but the odour of desperation too; the fear in the stench of stale sweat that reeked from Freddie's every pore when I followed my uncle to the door, beside which Mrs Hibbert was standing. Freddie strode past her and down the path, but I chose to linger a moment more when those silky black fingers reached for mine. And where Tip Thomas had threatened to scratch, her lips brushed soft against my cheek . . . veiled lips smooth and slippery as a ghost's.

PEARL

I am – yet what I am, none cares or knows;
My friends forsake me like a memory lost:
I am the self-consumer of my woes;
They rise and vanish in oblivion's host,
Like shadows in love's frenzied stifled throes:
And yet I am alive – like vapours toss't.

Into the nothingness of scorn and noise –
Into the living sea of waking dreams,
Where there is neither sense of life or joys,
But the vast shipwreck of my life's esteems;
Even the dearest, that I love the best
Are strange – nay, rather, stranger than the rest.

From 'I am' by John Clare

I am naked, outside in the gardens. Pine needles prick at the soles of my feet. My toes keep snagging the hems of the sheet that is clutched around my shoulders. I stumble again when looking back. And there in a window – is that a face? Has anyone seen me leave the house?

I am trying to find my way to that place where last summer I lay upon the grass and dipped my feet into a pool, the water like a mirror then, reflecting the temple folly behind and the clear blue skies that shone above. The memory hurts me. It stabs into my heart like glass, a shard from a broken reflection which once showed Osborne at work with his paints, and Elijah behind his camera lens, and then, on the very last afternoon, those ghosts who foretold my destiny – though I did not know it at the time, when I saw them approaching, over the lawns to stare at me from the other bank – exactly where I am standing now, lungs heaving, mouth gasping, throat burning with fire.

Will they find me again – those ghosts? Will they follow and watch when I walk on the water? Look! I am doing it now. You might think me mad to say such things but my thoughts are as clear as the beads of light that gleam on the stone of the obelisk, that sparkle like gems in bare branches of trees, so bright that I have to lift my hands to protect my eyes from the glare of the sun – the white jewel that has turned the whole wide world into this dreamland of ice and stone – the spell that the Cruikshank man might break, just as he does the silence – the way he keeps shouting out my name, and how oddly it echoes through the air, and louder every moment as he makes his way across the lawns, that stiff leg of his wheeling out to one side. He might be another mechanical toy.

I have to escape him, to be with Elijah. Is Elijah under this water, his arms reaching up for mine? I throw down the sheet, like a carpet it is upon which I kneel to rub at the ice, trying to see through that opaque film to the blackness of bubbles trapped beneath. The cold burns. The skin of my fingers splits. The blood is a splintering cobweb of red in this glass which will not show Elijah's face. But the Cruikshank's face is all too clear, because now he is standing beside the pool, berating the woman at his side, her own turned purple from the chase. 'She has no clothes! She'll die of exposure! You should have watched more carefully. What if the ice fractures? She'll freeze. She'll drown!'

Doesn't he know that's what I want, why I stand now and edge my way farther along, stamping down hard with my devil's feet? My toes burn as bloody and raw as my fingers. My ears fill with the ice's snapping crack and above that the voice of Cruikshank's wife, her protests a flurry of rasping breaths. 'She was taking the water cure. I only turned my back for a moment.'

What she tells her husband is true enough – only a moment she looked away from where I was sitting in a tub, draped like a corpse in those sheets of wet muslin, those sheets which draw all the heat from your body. You shiver so much that your teeth click like marbles. Your skin bloats and wrinkles, goes white, then blue. You think you will die from the pain of the cold – and then comes the numbness of body and mind when you start to slip into a swoon and you want to sleep and never wake – which is when they drag you out again and force you to drink all those glasses of water – gallons and gallons of water, it seems, and your belly swells as tight as a drum and you fear it will burst – which is when you are plunged into the bath, and the water there so shockingly hot every nerve end sears with a needling pain. And then, it is back to the sheets again, all freshly dipped in buckets of ice – the buckets that stand outside the door – the door Mrs Cruikshank left open while sermonising that I must endure, that she will drive every demon out, purifying my body and my soul. And, just to make sure that I understood, she added the iron pinch of her fingers, more bruises for my mottled flesh, more stinging hot tears to well in my eyes – like the ones that drip on to the ice right now.

Will my tears be able to melt this ice?

The Cruikshank's breath is warm and moist, a spreading net as he crawls out towards me on hands and knees. The ice creaks and groans beneath his weight. A great bang, like a pistol shot it is, as it splits apart and opens up, as his cane – that life preserver of his – thrusts out to hook on to my ankle as he stops me from falling and drags me back, clutching me tightly in his arms as we lie together on stiff hoared grass, as I stuff a fist into my mouth, trying to stop the screaming sounds. I look up. I see his wife's grey eyes. The white lace of her cap is quivering, caught in a little breeze. Or does it only look like that because of all my trembling?

'Pearl . . . Pearl Black!' Dr Cruikshank looks up from behind the long table upon which is another glass full of water, in front of which he asks me to sit. He asks whether I am feeling well.

He says he is sorry, 'very sorry indeed at your deviant behaviour yesterday'.

'Is she eating?' the fat man, Evans, asks. 'God knows how she managed to run anywhere. Alarmingly pale as well. Are we recording her menstrual flow? Has she seen any blood since arriving here?'

'None!' Mrs Cruikshank's statement is blunt. She stands like a guard at the gilded doors.

Evans gets up from his chair and walks around the table's edge. He says, 'When she does, you must measure the menses . . . record every ounce in her medical files.' He places a great doughy hand on my arm and pats it when he carries on, 'You must eat, my dear . . . keep up your strength. You must eat, or . . .'

'I would rather die!'

'Oh, come, come. You could be so pretty, and then . . . who knows? Every house needs a pet to pamper and spoil. But unruly pets must be chastised.'

He strokes a finger over my cheek, over the upper lip of my mouth. But when I bite he strikes me hard. I see blackness and stars. The chair rocks back upon two legs, suspended for so much longer than the laws of physics would seem to allow – but still, enough time for the Cruikshank man to scrape back his own and limp to my side, taking the back of my chair in his hands, all four legs once again upon the boards.

Twice he has saved me from falling now. But foolish to think he cares. My value is more alive than dead. My value must be in the chink for my board, for what these men proffer as medical care. Long ago, in the House of the Mermaids, the services offered were different. But I understand the ways things work. And yes, I must live for them to be paid, and for me to live I must be fed – and that is what will happen next while Mrs Cruikshank sits down to observe and writes the details in her book, just as Mrs Hibbert wrote before when she composed her Book of Events. But what is Mrs Cruikshank mumbling? Can it really be a prayer? Surely, she is not saying grace?

The fat man pushes the trolley near. Black rubber tubes, a funnel, a bowl that is full of some thick brownish substance, into which he dips a finger, which he licks with the tip of his glistening tongue, afterwards screwing up his nose. 'Hardly an epicurean feast, but then you should be better behaved, my girl. You shall be fed and your strength regained, and this time next week when I return we shall cut the root of Eve's madness away.'

I am back in my cell. It is dark again. My breaths form little clouds of ice, and yet I feel hot and feverish, a horrible cramping ache in my belly. A stinging sweat runs from my pores, soaking through the cloth of the dress I still wear. To breathe is a labour. To cough is a nightmare, but cough I must to spit out the clots, all the bleeding caused by those rubber tubes. Even though they were oiled, it hurt so much when they forced them down into my throat, and nothing that I could do to fight, gagging, thinking I would drown, constrained by the pacifying coat, until every sense of feeling was gone – and I think it must have numbed my mind because, afterwards, when they were done, when I was taken back to my room, I thought I had turned into water, become so transparent and slippery I might melt away through the gaps in the boards, down through the drains to the sewers.

I want to sleep but I cannot, tormented by distant whimpering cries. I wince at the pain of my blistered toes when I stand and creep towards the door. I look out through a metal grating. Wall jets burn like the baleful eyes of dogs. I don't *think* those dogs can see me, but still I duck down when I hear the whining of hinges near by. A solid thump, then a shadow looms closer, the overlong and distorted form of a man who is limping towards stone stairs that lead to the house's upper floors. I wait and I listen long after he's gone, when the whimper becomes a keening cry, a heart-rending, pitiful sound it is. I can't bear it. I have to go back to the bed and bury my head in the blanket there, pressing my hands against my ears, not

271

daring to draw them down again until it is quiet, until it is dawn, and only the hissing rush of air that blasts through the vents built into the walls. By that clock, I know it is time to rise.

Mrs Cruikshank comes in with a tray. She stands very close at the side of the bed. 'Just look at the state of your pillow,' she says, 'all these bloodstains! How is the laundry to keep up? Well, let's hope you've learned your lesson now. I want to see you eat this toast . . . or is it to be the tubes again?'

My throat is cut into ribbons of flesh. How can I swallow? The thought of toast brings tears to my eyes. Could she really be as cruel as that?

I think the sound is inside my head, but no – it is out in the passageway, a shriek that rebounds off hard stone walls, then the scuffling patter of running feet, and the younger nurse appears in the door. Her voice is rushed and panicky. 'Mrs Cruikshank, you must come at once. She's gone and taken awful bad. I think . . . I think . . .'

Mrs Cruikshank drops the tray to the floor. An echoing, clanging crash it makes. The other nurse kneels to clear up the debris – or so it seems to me. But no, she is bowing her head in prayer, her words punctuated by sniffling cries. 'Oh, dear God, have pity on her soul.'

Mrs Cruikshank gives her a face a slap. 'Won't you shut up, you stupid girl. Go upstairs and fetch my husband . . . and then come back to clear up this mess!'

Mrs Cruikshank sweeps out. The young nurse goes scurrying after her, clutching a hand to her reddening cheek while I press mine to my aching chest and swing my legs off the side of the bed, and slowly, very slowly, I make my way to the open door – which neither one of them thought to lock.

A shaft of light is shining out from the farthest end of the passageway. I move closer. I smell something putrid and sweet. I see another metal bed and the woman who is lying there while Mrs Cruikshank draws back a sheet, beneath which the patient's nightshift is bunched up high around her waist. Her legs are spread wide and between her thighs is a bloody mass of swollen flesh, a gash suppurating with thick green slime. There are ugly black stiches, criss-crossed and knotted, ends dangling loose like pubic hairs, though all of her own have been shaved away to leave a mound of nude white flesh – much like the pudenda of classical statues, those forms that Osborne so admired.

Here is nothing to admire. I am transfixed. I am horrified. Is this the operation, then, to remove the root of lust and sin? My voice is a croaking whisper. 'What have you done to her?'

Mrs Cruikshank speaks, but does not look round. 'Blood poisoning . . . an infected wound.' There is a sobbing in her throat when both hands grasp hard at her crucifix and Mrs Cruikshank starts to chant, 'Our Father, who art in Heaven . . .'

Oh dear God, what is to become of me, for wherever Our Father might happen to be, I do not think it can be here.

LILY

When Freddie and I left the House of the Mermaids I felt myself almost torn in two, hating to leave Elijah there, desperate to escape from Tip Thomas's touch – the scrape of those fingernails on my cheek, not to mention the implications made about Freddie's relationship with me. In the cab was a stony silence, only broken by the beat of the rain and the splash of the wheels through slush and ice, and Freddie's breaths, too heavy, too loud.

Elijah's had been too feeble.

I was restless and fractious, my nerves strung too tight, tempted to ask Freddie to try to be quiet, so that I could think, so that I could plan – but then I noticed the tears in his eyes, which captured the sheen of each street lamp we passed. And when he took my hand in his I let it lie there, limp and chill.

More dazzling light in Burlington Row, where Samuel had waited as Freddie requested, still in the upstairs sitting room, where he'd clearly made himself at home, surrounded by books and magazines, trays with pots of tea and cake – and Elijah's papers, there on the table.

Had he read them? In his place I think I would have done. But even so I did not ask, and he did not tell when, without a word, I picked them up and took them upstairs to my room again to replace them beneath the mattress edge.

On my return, he and Freddie became most attentive. I was urged to sit beside the fire, though nothing could thaw my dismal mood when Freddie related the tale of our day, and Samuel Beresford listened, intent. I sat there very still and mute – which quite belied the turmoil inside; I was breathless with the anxiety of knowing how ill my brother was, and the wicked fate befallen Pearl. But the hold that Tip Thomas exerted on Freddie, that part my uncle did not relay – though it was the books, of course it was – the threat that caused Freddie such distress.

I looked straight into Samuel's eyes, my own no longer as coy as before when I stated, 'Freddie was right . . . when he mentioned a blackmailing plot. Only it is not money that they want. Unless we bring Pearl to the House of the Mermaids they mean to take my brother's life.'

'What?' Samuel Beresford actually laughed, turning to Freddie in disbelief. 'But this is ridiculous! The stuff of penny dreadfuls! You can't leave Elijah locked up in a brothel. Why, it's illegal imprisonment. You must tell the police . . . immediately!'

'Things have gone too far for that.' Freddie was looking very grim. 'I will be frank with you, Sam. If I go to the law then I shall be ruined . . . my name, my business, everything. Tip Thomas will tell of events from my past, things I once did that would shame me now. I prefer that you . . . and Lily too . . . should never have the need to know.'

I made my passionate retort. 'I might know more than you realise. But what do I care for your shameful past! My only concern is my brother, and because of that and that alone we must not speak of this to a living soul.'

'Lily, dear girl,' Freddie's voice was raw with emotion, 'to think of your brother in Cheyne Walk, in that house full of murderous thieves and whores, the very place from which . . .'

He broke off, the silence remaining filled by me. 'The worst offender is Osborne Black. It was he who tried to murder Elijah, and whatever that Mrs Hibbert may be, she seems . . .' I struggled to find the right words, thinking back to the time I'd first seen her, that day in a hot dark tent in Cremorne. 'She seems kinder . . . kinder than I would have expected. She has cared for Elijah and . . .'

'She is unnatural and devious,' Freddie cut in, his voice brutally hard. 'She is as cunning as a fox. She would tear off your head and not give the matter a second thought. And, as for that Tip Thomas, as I have learned to my detriment, he is not a man to do business with. That simpering smile is all a mask. He is a fiend in human form.'

'I do not trust him either, but what choice do we have in the matter? We must do as he says or else risk the revenge he might think to take, finishing what Osborne Black began. And, believe me, Elijah is in no state to protect himself from any harm. They have doped him near senseless with opiates. He needs a doctor . . . he . . .' The seed of a plan took root in my mind. 'Your doctor, Freddie . . . what about him? The doctor who came here this morning. Did he not speak about an asylum? Did he not tell Tip Thomas that he'd seen Pearl?'

Freddie sighed and shrugged, his shoulders hunched forward. He looked like an old and broken man. 'He may possess some influence. But what favours will Evans do me now? I fear that we argued most dreadfully regarding his views on your own state of health.'

'Exactly what action do you suggest?' Samuel's interruption was stark. 'Lily, you can't knock on an asylum's doors and leave with an inmate on your arm. If the committal forms have all been signed then there's really no way around it. Only Osborne, as Pearl's lawful husband, can have any say in the matter.' He stopped short, and looked thoughtful a moment or two, going on with, 'I should approach him again. Osborne may be more reasonable if *I* tell him that Elijah is found . . . and in what state, and how others may soon come to hear our suspicions.'

'No!' I shouted in reply. 'Osborne Black must *not* be told. He cannot be trusted. What if he takes Pearl somewhere else?' I stopped and closed my eyes for a moment, wishing the throb in my temples would fade, continuing in meeker tones, 'What evidence do we actually have? Nothing more than my brother's word, and what would such accusations be worth with Elijah hardly fit to speak?'

'Lily, please!' Samuel Beresford's next interruption caused me to sit back in shocked alarm, for all at once he was kneeling before me, his arms holding mine in a firm restraint, his eyes lit with gold by the fire in the hearth, which in turn caused my heart to flicker up – that flame all too soon being doused again when recalling Freddie also there, seeing my uncle's scowled response to this over-familiar display, and my face growing hot with embarrassment when caught in that disapproving glare. After all, not twenty-four hours before I had been chasing through London's streets with no concern for decency. And then, on that very afternoon, I had willingly entered the doors of a brothel – the doors through which Pearl might be compelled to return and begin a new life as a whore – the commodity of flesh and blood – the bartering chip for my brother's life.

Bang, bang, bang! I almost jumped out of my skin at that sudden knocking sound below, and then the jangling ring of a bell. Freddie looked momentarily stunned and then wondered out loud as to who it could be, grumbling at the tardy maids when Samuel rose from his place at my feet and proceeded to make his way downstairs.

Freddie was calling after him, 'Tell whoever it is to go away. We want no visitors tonight.' And when I heard the door's dull slam I imagined any caller gone, that the only feet thudding back up the stairs belonged to Samuel Beresford. But, at Freddie's sudden intake of breath, I glanced up to see Mrs Hibbert again, standing there in the door like Death's harbinger, still dressed all in black, still disguised by her veils.

'I thought it best to bring her in,' Samuel explained, looking flustered. 'This lady claims to have some news . . . something vital regarding Elijah Lamb.'

Freddie was most unwelcoming. 'Mrs Hibbert. To what do we owe such a visit? I thought today's business settled and done.'

'Oh no, Mr Hall, *my* business with *you* is far from done.'

Freddie groaned. 'Will you say your piece and be gone. Out with it, madame . . . then out with you! As you know, there are plans we need to make.'

'Any plans *you* have made I will unmake.' Mrs Hibbert lifted an arm from which there dangled a reticule. Its jet beads glistened with red from the fire, and then a white flash as some papers emerged, and I noticed a whiff, like musty old books, exuding from the scroll in her hand, which, despite being held out for Freddie to take, he seemed determined to ignore.

She lowered her hand, a weary sigh, to which Freddie responded impatiently, 'Well, what is it? What have you brought?'

'Thanks to Lily's reminder this afternoon I have found this document. It bears the name of Osborne Black, made at the time when Pearl was sold. There is a clause in which he agrees that should he ever throw her off, then I . . .' She faltered, before going on, reciting the words as if memorised. 'Then *I*, Mrs Hibbert of Cheyne Walk, being Pearl's legal guardian, may take her back into my employ, caring for her accordingly . . .'

'Is this true?' Samuel asked, his voice hard-edged with doubt.

'You did not say so this afternoon,' Freddie went on with equal disdain.

'I . . . I had forgotten. Tip Thomas had not. But he did not think to look in this bag. If he had,' she lifted the paper again, 'then he would have no further need to consider the fate of Elijah Lamb.'

'But,' Samuel spoke slowly, as if thinking aloud, 'would the asylum accept this draft as proof without seeking confirmation from whoever drew the contract up . . . that is *if* it was legally drawn up.'

'I suspect the lawyer now lost or dead, otherwise Tip would have gone to him. But *you* may use this against Osborne Black. It is the only hope we have.'

Freddie countered sharply, 'But Osborne claims to have married Pearl. If he could produce such a contract then it would supersede your own.'

'But he lied about that. They were never wed!' I made my vehement protest.

Mrs Hibbert's veils swayed back and forth as if she was shaking her head beneath. 'We can but try. We can but hope.'

'That's naive!' Freddie was standing now, his hands pushed back through silver hair, pacing up and down the room. 'What if Osborne Black disputes your claim, discrediting any agreement that you so conveniently come to hold? Why, we'll have the next Jarndyce and Jarndyce; the case dragging on for years . . . every lobby in Temple filled to the eaves with scheming whores and lunatics.'

'Lunatics?' My question came strained and querulous – and that's when something snapped inside, my mind crystal clear when I announced, 'I know *exactly* what to do!' I held Freddie's gaze for a moment or two before more words came rushing out. 'Your doctor's diagnosis of me! He said I was hysterical. He said I needed treatment. You can write and tell him that you agree. You can have *me* committed a lunatic too. That way, we might gain some access to Pearl. We might find some opportunity to . . . Oh, I don't know . . . we'll work something out. There must be a way to achieve the thing!'

All at once I was terribly tired, that dull ache in my head setting up again, in the very same place as Elijah's wound, and my voice sounded very far away when I pleaded, 'It must be possible. We *have* to do something! We have to act soon. It is my brother's life at stake!'

'What you suggest is ridiculous. Anyone would think you already insane!' Samuel's words were filled with derision. 'What might become of your future? Have you not considered the stigma of being connected with such a place . . . how it might affect your own good name and any future prospects?'

'What prospects can you possibly mean?' Freddie intervened. 'You are too forward, Samuel! I can't say I condone Lily's reckless plan but it's surely the lesser evil here. And speaking as your employer, this business affects your future too. The reputation of Hall & Co. is in the direst danger.'

Samuel's stance was rigid, his expression very serious when looking directly into my eyes, speaking in an earnest voice. 'Lily, forgive me. I have no desire to be unkind. Your motives are perfectly admirable, but this headstrong nature you possess . . . I cannot agree with Freddie.'

Mrs Hibbert broke in, speaking starkly, 'If Lily enters such a place then we must all hope that Frederick Hall does not forget and leave her there. That would be a careless oversight . . . an innocent woman left to rot for the sake of *his* reputation.'

'What on earth do you take me for?' Freddie snapped back at the woman in black, his features distorted and menacing, and meanwhile Samuel pondered on, 'But what if this Thomas fellow lies? What if Pearl isn't in the asylum?'

Mrs Hibbert sighed and simply said, 'Tip Thomas does not lie.'

I felt sick and exhausted the following morning. When I dressed and looked into the mirror my eyes were dark circled, my cheeks too wan. But then I had hardly slept all night, my mind turning over a thousand times, knowing the folly of my endeavour, wondering whether Samuel Beresford had intimated some personal intent – some intent as yet half spoken that would only be withdrawn if I continued with my plan. And yet, when compared to the peril in which my brother lay, how could I think of a future life? How could I think to waver?

At breakfast – which neither one of us touched – Freddie hunched over his coffee cup, his expression harrowed, his colour grey and only a nod when he heard me announce that I was determined to go ahead.

A letter was written, a maid dispatched to the home address of his doctor friend, who sent an immediate reply – a brief note that Freddie read aloud, its contents indicating that with so recent a diagnosis no further consultation would be deemed necessary. Freddie should take me without delay to the Chiswick House Asylum, where Evans was due to be visiting on business that very afternoon. My admission could be swiftly made with the least inconvenience for all.

How easy that imprisonment. How many women were so condemned without access to judge or jury or friend? Samuel Beresford – was he my friend? Had he come to visit us that morn then he might have persuaded me to stay. But he did not, and so I departed Burlington Row and travelled with Freddie to Chiswick again, arriving at another house well hidden behind some high brick walls, behind which the pale rays of a wintery sun made glittering jewels of the gravel drive, or glanced off Italianate pillars which supported a looming portico, with steps rising up on either side – that looked like a gigantic stage. Adjoined to that elegant stone visage was a less prepossessing red-brick wing, something far more recently built and from which many windows drew my eyes, one of them being tall and arched, glinting more flashes of wavering light.

A telegram had been sent ahead, and Uncle Freddie was also armed with the letters that proved him my guardian, and nothing about them contrived or forged, for I had not realised before but, apparently, at our adoption, he and Papa had reached an agreement, whereby should Papa fall ill or die then Freddie would guarantee our care. All had been drawn up legitimately.

A nurse in a pale blue uniform received us at the entrance door and then requested we sit and wait. A brochure was laid on a table near by, its cover adorned with a sketch of the house and the lovely gardens all around – and to see that I felt such a lurch in my breast, for surely it was Elijah's hand. And that should have strengthened my resolve, but even with Freddie there at my side, his promise that I should come to no harm, so many doubts were rising up, bubbles of panic that popped in my mind as I took a deep breath to steady my nerves.

In the ceiling above us I saw painted cherubs cavorting through azure skies, as if playing hide and seek in the clouds. A plump-faced boy held a bow in his hands. I supposed he must be Cupid. He looked very much like Elijah to me, when Elijah was still a little boy. I glanced from that scene to a great stone hearth. The marble was carved with the face of an ogre. He might have been modelled on Osborne Black. And then, the third player in this little drama, this triangle of twisted love, when, through the gap in some half-closed door, I saw two more blue uniforms and between them a woman dressed in grey, looking as limp as a child's rag doll, and being barely sensible, she suddenly slumped in a heap to the floor. The nurses struggled to pull her up – and then they were gone, and I saw nothing more but the filthy soles of two webbed feet being dragged across the polished boards.

Pearl! I clamped a hand to my mouth to stop myself calling out her name. I would never have known her if not for those feet. Her hair, her glory, was shorn away. She had the look of a starving wraith. Some blood was trickling from her mouth, around which her face was a papery grey, and her lovely green eyes looked glazed and blind. But, despite the shock of seeing her – Pearl like a ghost, as fragile as glass – and despite Uncle Freddie's gasping, 'Oh!', I managed to gather my wits enough to lift a finger to my lips, to warn him not to say a word.

We were soon called in for my interview, what the nurse called my 'initiation'. What on earth could that be? I was petrified. I saw through barely focused eyes that loathsome Dr Evans, who smiled when he saw us enter the room, though his elbows remained on a tabletop, his chin cupped in blubbery dimpled hands. I kept my hands tightly clasped in front. I heard Uncle Freddie's shuddering breaths, as if *he* was the one to be put away, while another man, Dr Cruikshank his name – the same Cruikshank of whom Elijah wrote – introduced us to his wife, and rather fearsome I thought her to be, especially when she caught my eye.

I was asked to sit at a long narrow table upon which a glass of water was set. I kept staring at that, and I don't know why but I thought of the stream at Kingsland House, and the time when Elijah fished with a jar. I kept thinking of Pearl and her misery. I hardly noticed any talk going on between Freddie and those men, during which some forms were being signed, after which Dr Cruikshank called my name.

His spectacle lenses were very thick, making his eyes oddly magnified, and who knew what emotions lay behind when he spoke of my condition then. 'Sick fancies' I understood well enough, but those other terms he was using, what could they possibly mean? Words like *'frenosi pellagrosa'* that rolled off his tongue like poetry, while the moist lips of Dr Evans pursed, his brow lowered and beetled into a frown when he sighed and shook his head and said, 'Mr Hall, we must only hope that your ward has not been compromised after her nocturnal wanderings. She is best kept safely secured away until this restlessness abates. We shall strive to do our best, to nip the condition in the bud.'

I sensed danger. I gave a small cry of alarm. 'Oh, Freddie, what will they do?' But no doubt that only helped to confirm the extremity of my 'nervous state', and Freddie probably misconstrued, thinking it all a part of my 'act', reaching out for my hand and calmly assuring, 'Lily . . . my dear, the doctors will take good care of you. I shall come back tomorrow afternoon. I shall come and visit every day until you're completely well again.'

'I'm not sure that would be advisable.' Dr Evans was gruff, shifting in the chair, which creaked beneath his heavy weight. The straining seams of his trouser legs were pulled so taut over mountainous thighs that the cloth formed furrowing pleats, like knives.

Dr Cruikshank spoke softly but firmly. 'We recommend

no visits for at least the first two weeks. Ideally, I would say a month . . . as much for the patients' sakes as our own, to enable them to settle down – to grow used to all the establishment's ways.'

If Freddie was not permitted to visit then how would our plan be realised? 'No . . . no, do not leave me,' I shouted then, tearing my hands through my unbrushed hair – the knots deliberately left in place to enhance the appearance of distress, at which Freddie gently restrained my arm as he turned to the doctors again and said, 'Gentlemen, to place Lily in your capable hands will relieve my mind of the greatest weight but I *must* insist on visiting. I owe as much to her grandfather. And then, of course, more selfishly, I might chance to learn more about your work.' Freddie leaned forward towards Dr Cruikshank, conveying a serious intent. 'I have read almost all of your papers. I found the studies riveting, deserving a wider audience. Perhaps you might yet be persuaded to consider any future works being published by my company?'

'Why, of course! We prophets have need of disciples.' Dr Cruikshank was smiling benignly, his ego well oiled by Freddie's bribe. 'Tomorrow, then, we might talk at more length. Perhaps you will join me for afternoon tea?'

At that Dr Cruikshank rose up from his chair. 'But for now, and to set your mind at ease, I suggest a tour of the house, so that you . . . and Lily . . . may be quite sure that she will be left in the kindest of hands.'

The doctor led the way to the doors, limping a little, using a stick. It made a horrible tap tap tap which echoed off the wooden boards.

Dark, though still early evening it was when I lay on a narrow iron bed in a room that could not have been less like the one where I'd slept the night before. Plain walls. No mirrors. No drapes at the windows, where the latches of shutters had all been locked. Even if I could have opened them up I would need to have sprouted wings to fly, being so high, on the second floor.

I lay very still. I was listening hard, my breaths coming slow and rhythmic – not at all like Freddie's had been when he finally said goodbye to me. We were in the patients' drawing room, and quite pleasant it was, quite homely, with comfortable seating all around, and the potted fern beside a piano, and the set of French doors – both then closed up – which led on to a small veranda. From there, stone steps approached the lawns, where croquet hoops were silver-hoared, almost like little arches to fairyland. I thought I should have to tell Papa. But, right then, Papa and his fairy tales seemed farther away than ever before. That place contained no frail old men, though there was an old woman asleep in a chair, a framed picture of Queen Victoria clutched in her swollen veiny hands, her head lolled on one shoulder, her mouth catching flies while she snored away at the fire's side. She put me in mind of Ellen Page, making me more nostalgic for home with every single second that passed, until diverted by the girl who knelt on the rug at that old woman's feet, who began to hum a nursery rhyme while fitting some pieces of puzzle together. She had a moon face, two small blue eyes and a beaming smile through which issued a gruff and lisping voice. 'Hello, Doctor Cruikshank. Have you brought a new friend to play with me?'

I smiled back and registered that both she and her older insensible friend were dressed in gowns of plain grey serge which were fastened from neck to hem with a long line of ugly black buttons. When I saw Pearl she'd been wearing the same. It must be the asylum uniform. But where were the other patients? Were these the only ones fit to display?

Almost as if he could read my mind Dr Cruikshank took great pains to explain, 'At this time of day most of the inmates rest in their room before coming down again to dine. We always eat early in winter months. The darkness can so oppress the mind. We like to adhere to what my wife calls her "governess hours", with plain and simple nursery food to keep the digestion regular . . . to keep everyone settled and calm. It's very well known that spicy recipes can lead to attacks of hysteria.'

He was tapping his cane against his thigh while sidling closer to Freddie and speaking confidentially. 'Women are so like children, you see, in their appetites for unhealthy food. It is the heat and overexcitement that causes most of the trouble . . . not to mention this modern obsession with reading books and magazines. You will note we have none available here. Why, half the women in my care would probably be entirely sane but for the stimulation brought on by the use of literature. I dare say that might be the problem with Lily? Hmm,' he turned to smile at me, 'an inflamed imagination encouraging our young somnambulist to go out and about in search of romance, going to places where she should not!'

As Freddie's business was publishing books was he now considered responsible for creating a spate of insanity in half the women of England? Really, I almost laughed out loud, but Freddie appeared to have been struck dumb, his mouth opened wide, no sound coming out – though when recovered sufficiently he brought his lips very close to my ear, where his breath was hot and smelled of cigars and the whisky he must have been drinking last night, all the rank odours of his wrath when he murmured, 'Just say it . . . just say the word and I'll take you away from this ship of fools.'

'No! Go.' I pushed him off, fearing he may persuade me yet, for by then all bravado was falling away and I wondered what folly we might have begun. But start we had, and must go on – for the sake of Elijah, and also Pearl – and as far as Freddie was concerned, to safeguard his business and his name. But whatever he might have done in the past I had to trust my uncle now, just as I trusted Samuel, who, before leaving the house last night, had finally agreed to help, despite all reservations posed – though regarding Mrs Hibbert's part, without whom the enterprise was doomed, well, of Mrs Hibbert I could not be sure.

It was clear that Freddie despised her. The best that I could do was hope, though hours after Freddie had gone away, when I lay in that narrow asylum bed, my mind was still a flurry of doubt. I was chilled to the bone by the cries and moans that came from other rooms around – like the souls of the dead in a listless sea.

Which one of them, if any, was Pearl? Did Pearl lie as still and as mute as me?

My hair was now cut as hers had been, though still falling just below my ears. All bindings and pins had been removed, along with the laces that tied my boots, anything – so the nurses who did it explained – that might lead a patient to harm herself. 'We had one . . . oh, what a thing it was, coming in that morning and finding her dead, having gone and hung herself from the bed.'

'Who'd even think it possible!' another went on with morbid glee. 'But she used her hair as a noose, you see. And after that we had new rules. Doctor Cruikshank insisted. All hair cut short.'

'How terrible!' I said, trying to imagine what desperate plight might lead to such an act as that.

'It was,' said the first, 'and to tell you the truth, we never thought her mad at all, more likely to be an inheritance job, stuffed in here while the rest of the relatives got their grubby hands on the family wealth. We get a fair number of them . . . and the alcoholics . . . and the syphilitics . . . and the ones who've gone mad after giving birth. But then you'll see everyone for yourself. You'll meet them tomorrow at breakfast. For tonight, Doctor Cruikshank wants *you* kept quiet. You'll eat your dinner up here in your room.'

That dinner had long since come and gone. A greasy mutton stew it was that lay heavy in my belly for hours. It was eaten by the light of a flame that swayed and guttered constantly, its sooty plumes rising up to the ceiling, and every spoon that passed my lips was noted down in a little book by the nurse who'd brought the bowl in on a tray. Even my use of the pot was recorded. Even the water I drank, and when I said I'd had enough, when she took that tray away again, she made sure to lock the door. No candle or fire was left to burn to counter the oppressive gloom, only the occasional blast of hot air that blew through some ventings in the wall. *Hush*, it seemed to say to me, as hot and damp as Freddie's breath when he'd planted his goodbye kiss on my brow, when he'd held me so firmly in his arms as if to crush out every ounce of fear, stroking my cheeks with his trembling hands, saying, 'Lily, my brave, my dear little Lily. I swear I'll make it up to you. Your prospects . . . your future is safe in my hands.'

But, whatever Freddie's assurances, my mind was anything but soothed. What future could he want with me?

Tossing and turning for hours on end, I started at the howl of a dog, then the tolling of a distant bell. And, I tell you this because it is true, I wept that night when I came to fear that my mind had truly been possessed by some feverish, dark aberration. For long before being claimed by sleep my thoughts turned to Samuel Beresford, and my fingers touched the secret place that I'd never known to exist before – before seeing those scandalous pictures that my brother had made of Pearl.

PEARL

I think I am forgotten here. No one has come to force toast in my mouth, or to make me drink gruel through a rubber tube. The Cruikshanks are out in the passageway, and a right old ding dong going on. Something about a loss of funds, and what should be said when informing the 'trust', and whether in future the Evans man should continue with his work or not.

Their voices eventually fade away. Soon after, the younger nurse appears. The door is unlocked and there she stands, in her arms a great bundle of grey and black. She says I am to take the air while the basement floor is being cleaned. She gives me some heavy boots to wear, a grey overcoat, a grey knitted hat, some black knitted gloves and a muffler. She says I must behave myself. I am not to go running off again, or she can't say what Mrs Cruikshank will do, 'particularly with the mood she's in'.

She crosses herself and bows her head when we pass by the door where a short while before I saw Mrs Cruikshank and heard her pray. After that, more corridors. More doors. Stone steps sprouting mushroomy fungus. The lawns are spangled white with frost upon which some other women are walking. I shuffle behind them. My legs are aching, as heavy as lead. My shift keeps twisting between my knees, and my feet in these boots, already sore, are rubbed into more stinging blisters. I couldn't run away if I tried, though I wish I could escape the mad. Some have fingers as sharp as Tip Thomas's were. They point. They thump. They snatch. They pinch. But others, they keep away from me. They have no curiosity – no apparent interest in anything. They look lost. They look dazed. They look how I feel.

If I close my eyes against the wind I see the dead woman's face again, the flesh tight, sheened white, like a carnival mask with her black sunken eyes and the dead blue lips around the gaping hole of a mouth – an orifice almost too intimate. I try not to think of the wounds below, feeling sick again and tasting bile, and when I open up my eyes the vision is stubborn; it lingers on. I can still smell the sour chemical stench that mingled with waste seeping out of the corpse. I can still see those bloody rags on white tiles, and the shelf with the bottles containing pale fluids; and in some of those fluids there floated strange objects, like fleshy pears or pickled plums, and one – a tiny human form. A baby, drowned and floating. On a metal tray, metal instruments – knives, scissors, scalpels, spools of gut – the same black thread that bound her wound. Oh, her terrible wound!

Tip Thomas once told me a story about the women stitched back up, sold on as virgins again and again until they wished that they were dead. Yesterday I wanted to die, but I do not want to die like that. *I do not want to die like that.* Those words might be a magic spell. If I try to say them often enough then Dr Evans will be dismissed and I will be safe from his meddlings.

'What are you saying? Why are you sad?' Someone is tugging on my sleeve. She speaks with a lisp. Her face is round. Her forehead is bulbous and very high, sprouting tufts of orange hair. But this squinting child has a radiant smile. I think she is an angel.

'Are you new, like my friend, Miss Lily?' She looks away and lifts her arm and waves at another woman, one who stands in the shade of a cedar tree.

Lily? Could I be dreaming, or is that really Lily Lamb – and dressed like me, like the others here? She walks nearer, so close that we almost touch, but instead of saying anything she gives a little shake of her head as if to implore my silence, and then she takes the child's hand and leads her back across the lawns, stopping beside a statue there – a crouching stone sphinx upon a plinth. Does it guard us, that demon sent from Hell?

From there, she looks back at me and nods, and when I start to walk forward again she whispers in the young girl's ear, and the girl gives a high-pitched screeching laugh, shouting, 'Hide and seek, hide and seek.' In no time at all there is quite a commotion with Lily calling to a nurse and pointing at the running girl, who lumbers her way through the rows of green hedges. Several more patients go scurrying after, squealing and hooting with all the excitement, while others are crying out in alarm at this unexpected turn of events. But such a diversion gives Lily the chance to grab my hands, to look in my eyes, to tell me that she has come to help. It is hard to understand each word. There are too many people running past. Lily is speaking much too fast, or is it that my thoughts are slow? But I do hear Mrs Hibbert's name . . . and how Mrs Hibbert is coming for me. It might be tomorrow. It might be today. She must know what room I occupy . . . at the front, or the back, upon what floor?

My answer is croaked, barely audible. My throat is still closed and sore – and now, the nurse is here again, saying that I must go inside – back to my dark damp underworld.

In my dream I see maggoty corpses, bloated like whales as they float down the Thames, and I am floating in between, not sure whether I am alive or dead. And here is Tip Thomas, rowing a boat, hands dropping his oars when they grab for me, nails digging sharp into my flesh as he drags me up and out of the water. I am the fish on the end of his hook. I am the child cradled in his arms, wrapped tight in the folds of his velvet coat as he rocks me and sings his lullaby, *God bless your sweet little orphaned soul. Did she think I was going to let you go? A gift from heaven you are to me. A pearl dropped into me waiting hands.*

'God bless your sweet soul'. The Cruikshank man is at the door. The Cruikshank man is asking, 'Pearl, are you asleep? Can you hear me?'

I lie very still, my head under the blankets, my face pressed down into the pillow. The heating vents are hushing and hissing, over which I hear sounds of cleaning near by, the swish of brooms, the water pipes gurgling, banging, ticking time like clocks – like the tap-tap-tap of Cruikshank's stick when he walks into the room, and then the dull clang when it drops to the floor, when he says, 'I have something for you, Pearl . . . to make up for this morning's regrettable scene, the horror that you witnessed here. Dr Evans's methods are too crude. He does not have the skill or artistic touch so necessary for this business of ours. That is why I am here to assure you now. That butcher will not lay his hands on you.'

I let out a sigh of relief when he reaches below the blanket's hem. He strokes the stubble of my hair and traces the outline of one ear. But my blood runs thick and cold again, to hear, 'No one will cut your flesh but me.'

And now, he is drawing the covers back, and now he is pulling my body around, and when I finally dare to look the picture I see is ludicrous, for balanced there in the palm of his hand is a china plate, with cakes with jam, with cakes with cream, all dusted with sugar – sparkles of sugar that look like ice.

He holds the plate closer in front of my face and my stomach gives a heaving flip as if begging for me to lick and taste. But my throat feels as if it is slashed by glass. How can I think to eat again?

'My dear, you *have* to eat,' he says, his weasel voice sneaking, wheedling. 'You know what must happen if you don't. We'll have to use the tubes again, and I only want to make you well, to cherish you, my Pearl . . . my queen.'

I think of a nest of swarming ants, and the queen that lies at its centre, her belly all swollen, her posture immobile, and always, always, always in darkness – the darkness he punctures yet again with the sugary barb of his poison tongue, when he coaxes, 'Why not one little taste? You know it will make me happy. Don't you want to please me, Pearl?'

I see my reflection in spectacle lenses where my eyes are as big as saucers now, almost as big as the plate in his hand, and my mouth moves slowly to form the words, 'I want . . .' I might say 'my freedom', but there is a sudden whisper of fabric, the fast click of footsteps outside in the passage, and Mrs Cruikshank appears in the door, one hand at her breast where she clutches her cross, her eyes very wide, as if in shock, flinching back when her husband shouts, 'I told you . . . I am not to be disturbed!'

She seems cowed, but then rises to her full height. She takes a deep breath to remonstrate, 'There are some guests. Mr Hall has come to see Lily Lamb. And there are two more . . . to visit *her*.' Her finger points like a quivering arrow. Its tip is aiming for my heart.

'Is it Osborne Black?' her husband asks. 'Really, this is most inconvenient. I don't believe an appointment was made.'

'No, it is not Mr Black.'

'Well, who else could it be? Good God, woman . . . don't tell me you've let them in? What if they see the coffin here? How are we to explain that death away?'

'The coffin has been disposed of.' She is obstinate. She tilts her chin. 'I'm afraid these people refuse to leave. There is a lawyer. He has legal papers. And the woman come with him . . . a Mrs Hibbert . . . she is making all sorts of threats, talking of bringing in the police, of taking her story to the press.' His wife's voice is desperate, high and shrill. 'I must insist you come upstairs. I cannot deal with this myself.'

He sets the plate of cakes on the table. He groans and bends forward to pick up his cane. His jaw is clenched, the sinews taut, too visible through red-bristled jowls when he says, 'Take this woman and her lawyer to wait in the initiation room. Tell them I will meet them there. Well, go on, woman, what are you waiting for?'

'I will do as you say, because you are my husband, but,' she looks at the picture above the bed where all of those sheep will soon fall to their deaths, and from there her eye lowers to gloat on me and I see the brown of rotting teeth when she draws back her lips in a smiling grimace, and mutters, 'the Lord is my conscience here. *He* is my one true master. On your own head your own crimes shall be.'

Left alone again, in this cell again, I sit with my knees drawn up to my chest, rocking slowly back and forth as I stare at the unshuttered grille in the door, wondering, wondering whether it is true – if I really did see Lily Lamb – if Mrs Hibbert could have come. How long I wait I do not know, suspended in this awful state of hope intermingled with gnawing dread. Has Mrs Hibbert come with Tip?

And then the clatter of feet on stone interspersed with the knock of the Cruikshank's cane. The turn of a key, the creak of the door, and he glances at me, then back again, at what I cannot see behind. He speaks through tetchy tuts and sighs. 'Pearl, you have two visitors. It really is most irregular. Even so, they make unusual claims . . . about which your husband must now be informed. It is only under the *greatest* duress that I have agreed to this meeting. No more than fifteen minutes, mind,' he glares back out at the corridor, 'during which the door will be locked up and Mrs Cruikshank will wait outside . . . to witness whatever is said or done.'

He leaves the room. I hold my breath. A black apparition comes gliding in. Mrs Hibbert, the woman who haunts me still. And is this the devil in her wake? *Don't look at him. Don't make him real.* I drop my eyes, afraid to see, even though I can feel his on me, staring, intent, from his place at the door, his back pressed up against the grille, which means that for anyone peering in the room's view must be all but obliterated. And there he remains, quite motionless, while Mrs Hibbert approaches me, and when she takes my hand in hers, I am weeping. 'No, not Tip . . . not Tip.'

Silky black fingers stroke my brow, caressing my cheek when she murmurs low, 'Oh no. Not Tip. He is not here.'

Her voice is somehow different, but then it is nearly seven years – but not so long that I forget what lies beneath the muslin veils. And when she starts to lift them I have to look away. I cannot bear to see that face, though my own must be just as shocking, because Mrs Hibbert sighs and moans, 'Oh, Pearl . . . my bella . . . my sweetness. What have these monsters done to you?'

I feel ashamed and bow my head, but when she drapes the muslin there it seems that I am being crowned, and not with a circlet of tinkling shells but in the mantle of a ghost.

LILY

It is further imperative that the doctor nurtures trust in his patients, developing the intimacy that past isolation may have irreversibly fractured. When contained within the asylum walls, however distracted the female may be, her recovery is dependent upon the comfort and the kindness of masculine guidance, no longer daily present in the form of a father or husband.

From *Observations on Hysteria* by Rufus W. Cruikshank

After the ring of the dawn alarm I was told to wash and dress myself, then trudged down several flights of stairs with twenty or so other grey-gowned souls, all varying ages, sizes and shapes, all resembling nothing so much as nuns when we entered a dreary breakfast room. At the table we had to bow our heads while Dr Cruikshank's sour-faced wife stood at the end reciting 'grace' – though for all her impression of being religious I thought her only sadistic, seeing how, when her prayer was done, she snatched at the sleeve of a woman close by, a woman with darting, fretful eyes who was fidgeting, swaying from foot to foot – until Mrs Cruikshank pinched her arm, and I heard the spite in her vinegar voice. 'Must I tell you *every* day? Stillness is a virtue!'

The woman's eyes welled up with tears, blinking at the tormentor, who, having let go of her victim at last, was now standing erect and breathing hard as she stirred a great vat of steaming grey porridge, its contents spooned into plain white bowls, each one being passed down the table's line, each one of us offered just enough to bring some warmth to our bellies and

296

bones. But I couldn't eat. I felt too sick, watching an old woman dribbling, spit from her mouth, snot from her nose, rheumy pale eyes gazing into thin air – though she smiled when Dr Cruikshank appeared to read a short text from the Bible – *The lips of the righteous feed many: but fools die for want of wisdom* . . .

I was very glad when that Bible closed, when he limped his way out of the room again, leaving his wife and six other nurses to sit there as miserable as the patients. Mrs Cruikshank's lips were tightly pursed as she stared at the closed refectory door. But I – I breathed a sigh of relief, no longer feeling his eyes on mine – just as they'd been when I woke in the night and saw him standing in my room.

He'd been holding a candle in his hand. He brought his face very close to mine, which scared me almost out of my wits, though in the event he only smiled, a smile not kind but menacing, owing to his eyes being made so large behind the thick glass of his spectacles. The candle's gleam made them glimmer and flash when he lowered his bristle-whiskered lips. 'You must not be afraid. I often do the rounds at night. Every patient's welfare is my concern . . . so important for us to become well acquainted. Is there anything you need? Anything I can do to comfort you?'

I was shaking my head. I was speechless, outraged at this lack of privacy – but then came a wail from a room near by, the sound of singing, a nursery rhyme, a tuneless, mournful, wretched sound. He gave a sharp sigh of exasperation and then stood up and made to leave. Not another word was said. The rattle and click as my door was locked, after which the singing came to an end; a pathetic percussion of whimpers instead, punctuated by grunts and slapping sounds.

After that, I could not sleep a wink. My heart was thudding in my ears. My ears listened out for the tap of a stick. My eyes strained through darkness towards the door – in case it should open up again. And all the next day that memory plagued me, and I thought that I should have to leave whether our plans were successful or not, whatever the outcome might be for Pearl

– for what if that man came back to my room? What if nothing occurred to divert him?

It was later that morning I found her. It was when we were being 'aired', condemned to the freezing gardens, at peril of catching our deaths of cold. But all such discomfort was forgot when I saw how pitiful Pearl looked, even worse than I'd found her in Dolphin House with those sores now spread and weeping, crusted around her lips and nose, and her cheekbones so sharp they might break through the flesh. Still, I'd managed to contrive a disruption so that she and I could speak alone, which was when I was able to ascertain where about she was being kept in the house – a fact passed on to Freddie in turn when he visited me that afternoon, so that when Mrs Hibbert and Samuel arrived – she armed with the papers to prove her claim as legal guardian to Pearl, he charading as a lawyer to confirm the plea's veracity – Freddie could tell them where to search, should Dr Cruikshank choose to object, should our friends then find that they had need to take matters somewhat more firmly in hand.

Desperate needs require desperate measures. But in the event no violence was used. At least, not then. Not on their part.

At a little after half past three Freddie arrived in a covered cab. From the drawing-room window I watched him alight, and soon he was sitting at my side, with the moon-faced child, my pliable friend, happily playing her own little game. She was acting as 'mother' to us both, pouring out imaginary cups of tea, offering plates of imaginary cake which Freddie then pretended to eat – seeing how much it pleased her to please him. Such a way, such patience, with children he had, such a warmth that glittered in his eyes, and I felt a sudden surge of emotion, recalling his visits to Kingsland House and – though why that should enter my mind just then I really couldn't think to say, but so vivid was the memory of when we'd said goodbye one day, my heart full of sadness to see him go, as heavy and dark as the dusk's purple shadows that hung around Kingsland House like veils. I remembered running down the drive, seeing Freddie about to climb into a cab, and begging my uncle to take me too. He turned to me with tears in his eyes before scooping me up into his arms, saying, 'Lily . . . dear Lily. I'll visit again. And yes, one day you shall come with me. You shall live in my house in London. You shall . . .'

I couldn't remember any more, overcome with a dizzy exhaustion through which I heard Freddie speaking. 'Lily, I could not sleep last night for thinking about what best to do when this horror is finally over and done. I mean to repent of the wrongs I've done. I have plans to invest in a studio where Elijah can forge his own career and you . . . if you also chose to stay, then I should like to cheer you, my dear, to see you laugh and smile again. I should like to adorn you with clothes and jewels and take you out upon my arm.'

It was then Freddie lifted my hand to his lips and I simply stared in disbelief when he kissed it, his eyes still fixed on mine. Surely, this was not a proposal? Freddie was my 'uncle'. Freddie was old. Not as old as Papa, but even so. And it might be that others still found him attractive – why, Ellen Page, she always had, and that nurse now standing at the door, she fluttered her eyes and smiled his way as if she was playing love's young dream.

It made me feel decidedly queasy to think of the presents he'd bought before – the clothes, the jewellery, toys and games. And that doll's house, exactly like his own. Was I now the doll that played the wife rather than being a favoured child? Or was it even worse than that? Did he want me as a mistress? Had I given him some secret sign, an intention unknown even to myself, some false impression of desire in the kisses and touches so often exchanged in the years when he came to Kingsland House – and that day when we went to Cremorne; I had been fourteen years old at the time, some kernel of sexual awakening already flickering inside – but that was for Samuel Beresford – the man who now made it all too clear that he thought me no more than a headstrong fool, already halfway to a lunatic!

I was certainly close to hysterics then, dragging my hand

from Freddie's grasp, saying, 'Freddie, don't be ridiculous! You know I must go back to Kingsland House . . . and if God should choose to spare him, then I mean to take Elijah too! Please, don't ever mention such things again.'

Freddie said nothing in return. I saw the sadness in his eyes, but right then that only irked me more – as did the giggling grunting sounds being issued by the moon-faced girl. I started at the slightest sound – the snapping of logs on the drawing-room fire – the dreaming snorts of the sleeping old woman who seemed not to have moved one inch since we had first seen her yesterday, except that I knew she had, having been seated beside her at breakfast, and her slurping and farting and tugging my arm, asking over and over and over again what time the Queen would be visiting.

Freddie now sat mute at my side as I stared across the gravelled drive, and the closed-up iron gates at its end – holding my breath when they opened, when a hansom cab came rolling through and crunched to a halt before the house, where two darkly clad visitors emerged. I don't know about Mrs Hibbert, she saw us looking out at her when she made towards the asylum doors. As always, her face was concealed by veils. But Samuel, he did. I know he did. His eyes briefly lifted to meet with mine.

It seemed like for ever we waited then, though in truth only half an hour elapsed, during which our younger friend grew bored with playing at making tea and returned to her puzzle on the floor, and Freddie's smiling mask soon fell, his features drawn in deep strained lines, his breaths too fast and panicky. I thought my nerves should fray away – at the clicking of needles as one woman knitted, at the humming of the moon-faced girl, and that tune too familiar, too recently heard. I knew then that child had been struck last night, her pain the price of my release, and while looking out of the window, seething at the thought of that, wishing to take Dr Cruickshank's stick and beat him with it 'til he bled – that was when Samuel reappeared, leaving the house by the main front steps, and perhaps it was all of Freddie's talk but he looked just like a groom to me, and there on his arm a black-veiled wife.

The fine drapes of muslin that covered her features suddenly rose in a gust of wind, and how delicately he pulled them down, and how tenderly he held her when she staggered and fell against him when, for a moment, their bodies pressed close – and I felt such a pang of jealousy before my senses were gathered again, when I turned to Freddie and gave a nod to confirm that 'the thing' had been achieved.

Looking back, I saw another nurse. Like a bridesmaid she followed in the wake of the pair who now stood by the covered cab. Her face was lowered to the ground, concealed by the white of her bonnet's lace, but I knew it to be Mrs Hibbert – her posture erect and slender, and when she neared the carriage door, into which the others by then had climbed, she reached up to take the cloak passed down with which she covered her uniform's blue, drawing the hood up over her head before taking Samuel's outstretched hand and joining him and Pearl inside. The door of that growler was slammed with a bang. The driver whipped the horses' backs – and another ten minutes or so went by, during which we remained in the drawing room, both Freddie and I on tenterhooks, afraid of raising any suspicions, of doing anything at all that might chance to hinder our friends' escape. My fingers possessed a life of their own as they plucked at the rough grey serge of my dress, right through to the flesh of my legs beneath, encased in those woollen stockings, worn through by who knows how many before, being frayed and darned at the heels and knees. My feet in thin slippers shuffled on boards, creating a rasping, hushing sound – over which came Dr Cruikshank's shouts, his voice very urgent and loud it was, calling for someone to 'Fetch Osborne Black . . . from Dolphin House. Be as quick as you can. His wife has gone!'

A nurse went scuttling down the steps and headed towards still-open gates. My eyes met Freddie's. This was our cue, and I finally cried in faltering tones, 'Oh look, Uncle Freddie . . . your cab, it's gone!'

'Dear God, so it has!' Freddie leapt to his feet in mock alarm, an impressive rendition of shock on his face.

'What's gone?' the nurse asked, coming to peer at what Freddie dramatically pointed to. And then, striding out from that room to the hall, with me and the nurse trailing in his wake, he stormed to Dr Cruikshank's side, where his wife was also standing then, and in such a state you would not believe, her hair like rats' tails, hanging loose, and wearing no more than her corset and shift!

'Cruikshank! What on earth is going on?' Freddie put on his most haughty expression. 'First my cab is appropriated, and now I find you cavorting out here with this woman . . . this woman in dishabille. Is this an asylum or is it a brothel? Sir, you should be ashamed!'

'You don't understand.' Cruikshank tried to explain, his spectacles misted, almost opaque. 'There has been an abduction. One of the patients. My wife has been assaulted and . . .'

'They accosted me,' Mrs Cruikshank broke in, quite breathless with indignation, 'when I opened the door to let them out . . . when they said they were done with the visiting.' She clutched at the big silver cross that hung at the sagging flesh of her breasts. (I could swear it was smeared with jam and cream.) 'They dragged me in . . . knocked me down on the bed, and then . . . that man stripped the clothes from my back. Oh, I thought I should be defiled and killed. I thought . . .'

'It is true.' Dr Cruikshank now joined in. 'I found my poor wife in this dreadful state, with one of her stockings jammed in her mouth, the other binding her hands to the bed.'

'What a tale! What a fabrication!' Freddie gave a snort of derision. 'The fact is that you permit your wife to run around in such a state, looking like something from Bedlam's worst nightmare. Little wonder that you dissuade visitors. Why, what else goes on when the doors are closed? I am shocked, Doctor Cruikshank, truly shocked. I mean to remove my ward forthwith. I shall visit my lawyers this very day. I shall sue you for fraud and misrepresentation.'

And yes, it was as easy as that, and no idea of the bloodshed to come; not only in the asylum, but also the House of the Mermaids. For then, we climbed into the remaining cab which drove past the man who manned the gates (well tipped by Freddie previously to forget to close them up again).

Sitting close in that draughty rattling box, Freddie and I barely said a word, and once we were back in Burlington Row I ran straight upstairs to my room again, to lock the door and wash myself and to strip off that drab grey uniform, flinging it down in disgust by the door, thinking it only fit to burn. I dressed and packed my portmanteau – with Elijah's papers stashed inside, drawn from beneath the mattress edge. I struggled to carry that down to the hall, the case bumping hard on the steps behind and I set it by Freddie's, already there, so that we would be able to leave the house the moment Samuel sent word.

We planned to meet at his Kensington rooms when he had returned from the House of the Mermaids. Too risky to stay in Burlington Row. The Cruikshanks might well divulge Freddie's name. Osborne Black might then come visiting. And, Tip Thomas, what would *he* think to do – when he knew of the theft we planned to make?

Well, how could we think to give him Pearl?

PEARL

True! – nervous – very, very dreadfully nervous I had been and am; but why will you say that I am mad? The disease had sharpened my senses – not destroyed – not dulled them. Above all was the sense of hearing acute. I heard all things in the heaven and the earth. I heard many things in Hell. How, then, am I mad? Hearken! and observe how healthily – how calmly I can tell you the whole story.

From 'The Tell-Tale Heart' by Edgar Allan Poe

I cannot see a thing through these veils. Sounds are all muted. Shapes are blurred. Mrs Hibbert insists I keep them on. She thinks me safer in disguise, in case we are stopped along the way. We are not stopped, but the journey is long and I find myself rocked into a trance, slumbering like a baby with my head against Mrs Hibbert's breast, the ebbing and flowing of her heart like waves that are breaking on a shore. It is comforting, to be cradled so. Such a kindness she never showed before.

I wake with a start when we come to a halt. Without a word she lifts my head. She takes my hand in one of hers and guides me out of the carriage door. We enter the House of the Mermaids – and even though I wear these veils I would know it by the smell alone: musk and rose, and those deeper notes. The brown smells of wax polish. The brown smells of men – their oil, their sweat, their need, their lust.

I lift the muslin from my face. Looking around, I am over-whelmed to be back in the house where I lived as a child, where the black and white tiles are still buffed with milk, so soothing and cool beneath my feet – my feet which are completely bare.

I watch Mrs Hibbert ascend the stairs. The cloak she was wearing has been thrown off, and the trailing skirts of her stolen gown are fading from blue to dirty grey. Should I follow, or does she want me to wait?

Glancing back, uncertainly, I see the man I had feared to be Tip. He is nothing like Tip, so much larger. And now I recognise his face from that time when he visited Dolphin House, when he came with Lily to search for Elijah – Elijah who has gone away – Elijah whose eyes shone like silver.

This man's eyes are brown. They are anxious. They keep darting back to the open door, beyond to the street, where the carriage waits beneath the skeletal branches of trees. Beyond is the looming old black bridge, and the black ribbon river and—

And now the rustle of black silks as Mrs Hibbert descends again. She and I might be twins, born of darkness. In her arms she carries a carpet bag which she places down upon the tiles while murmuring to the brown-eyed man, 'They're not there . . . they're not upstairs!'

Without waiting for any answer she strides to the doors on one side of the hall and pushes them open with both of her hands.

So abrupt is the light now spilling out that I have to blink and wait a while until my eyes acclimatise to see through the drifting smoky haze to the greeny-blue glisten of mermaid walls, not even noticing at first when Mrs Hibbert beckons me.

I hesitate. I am wary, trapped in the nets of past memories, from those times when my head was crowned in shells, when she called me in to her 'gentlemen friends', when she let me feed nuts to the squawking white parrot that bobbed up and down upon its perch and— Oh, there it is – still in its cage. But those pretty white feathers are stuffed, are dead. How sad that is to see.

A woman sprawls on a sedan. Something familiar about her. Scarlet ribbons hang loose from her stays. Scarlet lips suck on the stem of a pipe, its ivory bowl a circle of red that glimmers and fades with her every breath. I notice her arms, the flesh sagged and wrinkled. Her hair might be fair, but hard to tell, so dirty and dull with the grease it is. Her eyes are closed as she mumbles some nonsense, and the heady smoke puffed from her lips flows through the room like water – over the bird that no longer cracks nuts, the dusty piano no longer played, the empty dining table where silver plates of food once gleamed.

Smoke wavers over the muralled walls. I don't remember those cracks before. In some places the plaster has flaked away. It makes the paintings look queerly old, like scenes in an ancient temple of love. But even the mermaid I loved the best, with her long golden hair and her eyes of green – even she is less perfect than I recall, her features too sketchy; not a flicker of light in those staring eyes. Osborne's brush always made my eyes glisten. Osborne Black could make a canvas sing, as potent as any siren's call – and yet, could it be? Is this painting not suggestive of him? Why had I never realised? The style here is cruder, but—

My confusion is interrupted. Mrs Hibbert addresses the smoking whore, 'What are you doing here? Don't you know there will be no trade tonight?'

The pipe is set down on a table near by. The woman elevates her pose, rising up on one scrawny elbow. She opens a pair of glassy blue eyes below which her brows are creased in thought as if she is struggling with a dilemma, and then, from lopsided carmine lips, she slurs, 'Oh, you know . . . while the cat's away. He's sent them all off to a pantomime . . . Cook and the slaveys, all of the pinchcocks. After, if they can behave them-selves, the price of an Argyle dinner too. Generous as Santa, ain't he! But he wanted one friend . . . for company. He says when he's done with you lot tonight we'll go off on the razzle and join them. Mind you, I could be persuaded to stay . . . to climb up the hill to Bedfordshire, looking at what the cat's dragged in.'

A suggestive smile for the brown-eyed man who is standing back by the open doors – until her gaze drifts from him to me, when she claps a hand against her mouth and laughs. 'Gawd alive . . . it's Skinny Lil? Nothing much more than a bag of bones. Don't tell me this is our prodigal . . . Tip Thomas's blessed Helen of Troy! Not even his tossing monkey could fancy dabbing that!'

'Is Tip here?' My voice is shaking now. My head is buzzing. *Buzz buzz buzz.* Isn't that what Tip Thomas used to say?

She answers by lifting a small brass bell. A flick of her wrist and the metal is singing its *Ting-a-ling-ling.* In response there comes a pattering sound of feet from beyond the orangery doors. I see a flash of pink skin, grey fur. I cannot help my sudden gasp, for if this is Tip's monkey – if his creature is here – then surely the master is not far off.

The whore brushes drab curls from a powdered cheek. Her laughter cackles through fugged air. 'Don't we like our little man? Fuck me, beggars can't be choosers these days.'

'Get out, Louisa! You should not be here.' Mrs Hibbert hisses her command while I stand and look on with an open mouth, at last realising who this is – Louisa, who used to be so fat, once sure to net her German count and live in a villa in St John's Wood. She is but a fraction of her size. No more dimpled dewy mounds of flesh. Like an old woman, she groans when she rises, before making a languid progress towards us, swaying, smiling at the brown-eyed man as her loose-skinned body brushes past. But for me, there is only a clicking tongue. No more caresses. No sugary kisses.

I feel a surge of relief when she's gone. I focus on the double doors from which Monkey is peeping out again, through which he as swiftly disappears, replaced by another familiar face – and Sarah the maid gives a strangled cry. 'Oh, Pearl . . . is it you? Have they brought you back?'

She has also grown old in my absence. Her face is lined. Her back is stooped. When she comes forward and makes to embrace me the keys at her waist poke into my belly.

'Where is Tip? He's not upstairs!' Mrs Hibbert's voice stabs just as hard.

Sarah's head jerks back to the orangery doors. She murmurs,

'He's waiting in there for you . . . awful scratchy and jumpy he is today' – to which Mrs Hibbert swiftly replies, 'Watch Louisa, will you. Take her downstairs. Give her more drink if that's what she wants. Lock up the front door. Is the watchman paid off?'

Sarah nods. 'He's gone. Won't be back tonight.'

At that the maid leaves, and I limp my way to the orangery doors. I wince at the needling sting of my feet, but what is that pain when compared to the need for me to face Tip Thomas again – even though it is like falling, to be sucked back into this palace of glass where the air is chill, and the icicles dripping from window frames could be the glittering bars of a cage – the cage from which I never escaped because here I am, back in Cheyne Walk, looking up to see my reflection again, but no longer disguised as an angel with whom I might fly away. Now, I am wearing widow's black, and the sound of the fountain might be my tears, over which comes the click of invisible heels.

I push past some ferns grown very large, but those fronds have turned brown and are brittle to touch. I see Tip Thomas upon a divan, his velvet coat puddled on tiles below. His head is facing away from me, wrapped in a woollen muffler. But he senses me there, and he looks around and— Oh! It is like being in a dream, when things begin to shift and change and nothing is quite what it seems to be – because Tip has turned into Elijah Lamb.

I fall to my knees and hold out my hands. I say his name. It is like a prayer. To think God has given him back to me. When I saw Osborne's painting I thought my heart broken. Now, I think it will break again from joy – until swift as any Spring Heeled Jack the real Tip Thomas comes bounding near, grasping my wrist and holding it firm, and that musical voice I can never forget sings, 'Ooh, la la . . . my precious Pearl.'

Such a hectic colour in his cheeks which may or may not be caused by paint, and I swear I can see the fire in his eyes, the little flames now darting out when his serpent tongue hisses its sibilance. 'What providence, don't you think, my love, for this gentleman to come floating down the Thames? Like Moses in his basket, saved by our Pharaoh's daughters . . . and him the key to the finding of you. What a marvellous serendipity!'

There comes the chirrup of Monkey again, now very close to its master's side, where it lifts a pale and wrinkled paw which Tip then takes with his free hand – the one that is not restraining me. He hoists his familiar up on to his shoulder. He caresses the curve of its snaking tail, but I notice his hand is trembling. In return Monkey's fingers pick through his hair, still very long, hanging loose round his face, though two strands have been plaited above each ear. A strange affectation that is. He looks even more rakish than before. And what is this coat he is wearing? Is it the fur of a cat or a fox that drapes all the way to his ankles, and his crabshells – his shoes – with their silver tips? He is still the dandiest swell on earth, and the dandy looks back to address Mrs Hibbert, a vague sort of tremor in his voice. 'So . . . you really brought her home to me. I must thank you, Mrs Hibbert . . . the most enterprising of madams. To think I ever doubted.'

'Did you ever really doubt me, Tip . . . when you promised my freedom in return?'

I wonder what she means by that, but there is no time for such ponderings because Mrs Hibbert, the black widow spider, approaches through the aisle of ferns and when very almost upon us she pauses a moment and lifts a hand, motioning back to the brown-eyed man. 'This gentleman, the agent of Frederick Hall, has come to collect Elijah Lamb.'

'Mr Hall too much of a coward, then, to come and make the deal himself? Ah well, what's the rush . . . all in good time. Pearl and I must be reacquainted first.' Tip smiles down and drags me to my feet. He makes a jerky little bow, almost like a doll that is hinged at the waist, at which Monkey, less agile than before, despite scrabbling to cling at a fur lapel, is dislodged and falls heavily to the ground, screeching loudly in alarm as Tip tries to soothe him, murmuring softly, 'Are we overexcited, my little friend . . . to see our queen bee buzzing back to the hive?'

I was Cruikshank's queen. I have flown his nest. But Tip's hold has always been stronger. His nails dig sharp through my black silk sleeve, dragging me forward, towards the divan from which Elijah struggles to stand, and Elijah's brow is filmed with sweat when he attempts to counter Tip, gasping, 'Don't hurt her. Don't you dare think to hurt her!'

'Don't you fret your posh noggin, sir.' Tip laughs, pushing Elijah down again. A thing all too easily achieved. Can Elijah really be that weak? 'Why, that is the very last thing on my mind. I intend to protect my investment well, though it's clear that the same cannot be said for those who have cared for her of late.'

Almost tender Tip's eyes when he looks at me, and no more than a tickle his grazing touch when he strokes the strands of hair at my brow, what little stubble now remains, poking out from beneath the heavy veils.

'Ah, such a loss,' he sighs heavily, 'but then hair will always grow back again. We'll soon find a wig . . . get you fattened up. Any damaged flesh we'll stitch in place. In six months you'll be luring the toffs back in. Why,' he grins at Elijah lasciviously, 'we might even let *this* gentleman visit . . . if he has sufficient to pay the fee.' Tip chuckles. He tugs on one whisker and muses, 'Now, how to do this most effectively, to send our hostage on his way?'

'I won't go without her.' Elijah is wheezing.

'Oh, but you really have no choice.' Tip smiles, but his narrowed eyes are cold. 'If I were you, I'd shut your trap. My patience is stretched to its limits tonight. Don't push it. Who knows what Tip might do. He might think to stain you as red as a plum. He might slit your throat and be done with the fuss.'

His free hand digs into the folds of his coat and I see something glint in the pocket there, something metallic, protruding, sharp.

'Elijah . . .' I shout, knowing Tip's threat is no pretence, 'you must . . . you have to do as he says.'

My love struggles to stand, but falls again. What on earth is wrong with him?

Elijah keeps saying he will not go. He will not leave me here with Tip. He is coughing, a hand pressed hard to his chest, and when the brown-eyed man comes near, trying to lift him up again, the two of them fall against the divan, which rattles and squeaks when dislodged on the tiles, almost knocking me off my feet. I stumble hard against Tip's side, and while he steadies me in his arms my fingers burrow in folds of fur and close around the shaft of the file that this creature uses to sharpen its claws.

I think the brown-eyed man has seen. He takes his chance, lunging forward to strike at Tip – who ducks very swiftly to one side, during which, with one wrist still firmly gripped, I find myself being whirled around, caught up in a frenzy of throwing fists. But being so encumbered Tip is too easily restrained, his breaths coming fast with frustration and anger when Mrs Hibbert shouts his name. 'Tip . . . we have you. Let Pearl go free.'

Despite the quandary in which he is placed, his accomplice now his enemy, Tip thrusts out his chin and sneers his contempt. 'Well, well . . . what is this caper? The madam turns thief and demander?'

'As happy to be a thief as a whore . . . as happy to leave *you* here to rot, to condemn you as you condemned me before. And while on the subject of stolen things, give me that key around your neck.'

'It won't do you any good, you know. I've tried every lock in this house. Whatever the key is meant to fit has been hidden away too carefully. But I'll find it. I'm like a dog with a bone. Try to take what is mine . . . I'll tear your throat.'

She suddenly snaps. 'Stop posturing! Give me the key and be done with it.'

'And how am I to do such a thing, restrained as I am by your *gentleman* friend?'

'But Tip,' her voice is different now, softer, exaggeratedly slow, as if speaking to a dullard child, 'I will simply take the chain, and you will release your hold on Pearl, and Elijah . . .' She pauses a little while, as if to ensure we comprehend. 'Elijah and Pearl will leave the house and wait in the carriage still outside.'

This is when Tip begins to laugh, a whinnying peal of derision, still refusing to loosen his grip on me. But the brown-eyed man is holding him fast, and when Mrs Hibbert steps forward her hand dips between his fur lapels, violently snatching the key from his neck. The links of that chain break easily. Metal clinks on the tiles around our feet and Mrs Hibbert retreats again – only just escaping Tip's vicious kick, though it does find the groin of the brown-eyed man, who is winded and groaning, now on his knees – but in the confusion of this new assault I manage to twist and drag away, running at last to Elijah's side.

Tip's eyes are darting around the room – from me to Elijah – from Elijah to Mrs Hibbert again, to whom he is saying, 'Oh dear, Mrs Hibbert . . . this infidelity breaks my heart. What is it makes women so fickle . . . so tricksy . . . so very ungrateful?' He smiles, and creases appear in his cheeks, like the fissures on the muralled walls. 'Pearl is mine. You *know* she is mine, the same as this house, the same as . . .'

I take a step forward, and now I am raging. 'I am not yours! I never was!'

'Ah, but you are, you always were. And before you are crowned in shells once more, shall I tell my sweet Pearl a fairy tale . . . one that never was written down in Mrs Hibbert's Book of Events?'

'Tip!' Mrs Hibbert's voice is low. She sounds less brave than she did before.

'Hush, woman, she has the right to hear . . . to decide if she should stay or go.'

He lifts one foot on to the divan and by the means of that leverage propels his whole body upwards so that he is now towering over us all, standing there as if on a stage, and Monkey jumps on to the iron end and claps its little paws in delight, during which applause Tip's story starts, and with those most clichéd of opening lines –

'There was once a beautiful princess . . . Yes . . . I think we should call her that, don't you? Or shall we describe her for what she was . . . a pretty enough, respectable child who was raised in a pretty, respectable house, down by the docks, down Wapping way. It was shared with her doting parents, and a doting brother too. But everything changed when that girl was twelve, when her father was doomed to lose his luck, caught snitching and then imprisoned, deported off to Australia . . . after which, being so distraught at his loss, her every possession gone with the bailiffs, his wife cast herself into the Thames – or so the rumours went back then. But whatever the truth of the matter was, it was yet another downturn in luck for our siblings, our two little innocents, now left to fend for themselves in the world, and their only hope of survival to enter the doors of the poorhouse.

'I tell you, it was a dreadful place, with the sexes forced to separate, and the girl very soon declining in health, her spirit impossible to raise. But he, the older brother, always being more resourceful by nature . . . he took to learning the ways of the world, educating himself in what had to be done to prosper in that godforsaken place. And soon he came to devise a way out of the bonds of poverty . . . which was to fall back on what was at hand, which was to exploit his sister's looks, trading the gold that shone in her hair for that found in the pockets of wealthy men.

'Yes, yes, I hear your condemning thoughts!' Tip scans every one of us, hesitating when he notes that the brown-eyed man is standing again and glaring at our narrator, who, nevertheless, continues his tale: 'You imagine that brother a rum sort of sinner. But, if not him, then surely another would pimp the girl, and doubtlessly less kindly. His plan was no more than to hire her out as a model for artistic types, her soul still as pure as the virgin snow – unlike his own, as slimy and black as the foulest toad. Oh, such cunning and expertise he'd acquired, acquainting himself with a brothel madam, a widowed lady, always veiled, who owned a house down Chelsea way. Quite a resort it was back then, with its quaint little teashops, and all the bohemians clustered about . . . whose interests were well enough pandered to when that madam brought his sister in, and able to drum up considerable fees on account of her fey and languid looks, being what you might call a regular stunner. More than one of those sots declared his love before his sketch or painting done. But all in vain, for that fair maid set her heart upon the coldest soul – the one employed by the house madam to paint some murals on her walls.'

I gasp. 'It was Osborne! He painted the murals.'

'You think so?' Tip's red lips purse into a kiss, simultaneously drawing his talons down over the length of one drooping moustache. 'Does this also sound familiar – that even when surrounded by cunny and offered his pick of the best of them, this artist's inclinations were not drawn to the pleasures of the flesh, preferring to look but not to touch, preferring his passion to be daubed in the images on these brothel walls . . . scenes which became quite the talk of the town. But then his painting brush was proud, unlike that other flaccid thing always buttoned in his kecks . . . though some sort of prigging must have occurred, the jolly todger raising the flag at least on one occasion before he went and disappeared. Some trip to study art in France.

'Well, you know the saying, the devil goes away when he finds the door shut against him. The abbess who ruled that brothel would gladly have barricaded hers, for being around the place so much, working all through the day and night, that artist's sour and charmless demeanour had been causing offence to the clientele. But, ah . . . the little princess, how she wept, how desolate she was, yearning to hear from the man she loved, who sent no word for months on end, during which time her belly swelled and our beauty hid herself away, refusing to see a living soul, even her loving brother, who feared for her very life when she threatened to follow their mother's lead by throwing herself into the Thames.

'How glad he was when her spirits revived when, around the time of the child's birth – and a child so fair she was doted on by everyone who saw her face – a letter arrived from the artist, returned from his travelling abroad, writing to the sister here and suggesting a visit down Chiswick way.

'Oh, yes,' Tip arches a teasing brow, 'we have another coincidence there! But I'm sure you're impatient to hear the rest, and our tale is almost at its end.'

He grins at me, and then goes on. 'They say absence makes the heart grow fond. The sister had hopes of becoming a wife – to live in a pretty, respectable home and raise her pretty, respectable child. And it seems that when first reunited, she might have had some cause to hope, for the gentleman claimed to have missed his muse, asking to paint her there and then. She dithered. She had not mentioned the child. She knew her body to be much changed, her belly still large from the pregnancy, milky breasts swollen, scarred and stretched. But she had not expected such blatant disgust, the contempt when he saw that his muse was flawed . . . and presuming, because of where she lived, that her morals must be as loose as jam. He told her to leave and never return. He said he would never look again on a body so wrecked by debauchery.

'By the time she returned to Cheyne Walk she was beside herself with grief, though after some hours she grew calmer again, as if by then resigned to her fate – which was to raise her child in a brothel and to take up the trade of a ladybird, with lustful men less discriminating than those prim and priggish aesthetic types.

'Well . . .' Tip exhales a long sad sigh, whether heartfelt or acted I cannot tell, hardly daring to draw a breath myself, being hooked on his every cunning word. 'She *was* resigned, but *not* to that. She tricked us all when late that night she donned her black cloak with the ostrich plumes and left the house by the kitchen doors and made her way to Battersea Bridge, her baby bundled in her arms. And it's quite a way to jump, you know. Even in May the water is cold, as cold as the smack of a dead man's fist. We must hope he knocked her out for the count, and then . . . down, down, down for the swirling dance, with all of the other dead drowned souls in the unmourning ride of the River Thames.'

At that pronouncement, Tip lifts a hand. He looks like a preacher who stands in his pulpit, warning of fire and brimstone to come. 'But that brother of hers would not give up, rowing out on the Thames that night, desperately searching for signs of her body . . . and granted the blessing of finding her child when, by some God-sent miracle, that treasure still lived and breathed fresh air . . . and the rest you know . . . and how she grew and then came to be sold to the very man who had thrown her mother off before, and who has now reneged on the oath he swore to cherish and care for our precious Pearl. And,' I am fixed in his gloating eye, 'that is why she must now return to those of us here in the House of the Mermaids, to live once again with her own flesh and blood – for isn't it true what the adage says, blood is much thicker than water?'

There is a moment's silence, through which Elijah speaks at last, and Elijah's voice is full of shock. 'Osborne is Pearl's father? Could any man be more unnatural?'

I feel as if I am paralysed, unable to move when Tip winks at him, hunching his narrow shoulders high, as if to say '*who knows?*'

'What was her name, my mother's name?' I croak like a frog. I have to know. And it is more than I can bear when Tip licks his tongue across his lips as if to lubricate the ease with which he now declaims, 'What *is* true is that I am your uncle. Your mother . . . my sister . . . my beloved Stella . . . Stella . . . our star, our sun, our moon . . . the very first mermaid in Cheyne Walk. The first, but no longer to be the last.'

Tip sounds inordinately pleased with himself, but I feel such a welling of anger and grief when I say, 'I don't know who is the most loathsome, to have sold me like that, to have done such a thing . . . you, Mrs Hibbert, or Osborne Black.'

I am sobbing with impotence, for every wrong done to my mother before, for everything done to Elijah now, when I take a step forward and spit at Tip, who simply smiles down from his vantage point – and I hardly notice the sudden screech when Monkey comes leaping towards me.

Before I can think to move away bared teeth are tearing the sleeve of my gown. Little pink hands snatch the veils on my head, and the muslin drapes that hang behind are somehow dragged forward, over my eyes – over Monkey's too. And it must be the shock of the darkness, causing the creature to shriek like that, causing me to spin in circles, grunting with the effort of thrusting him off, to send him flying through the air to crash into one of the windowpanes.

A sickening, crunching thump it is. An exploding shower of broken glass. I look down to see a motionless heap beneath black crumpled muslin, and a trickle of red is leaking out, to spread between joints of the black and white tiles.

'Monkey!' Tip cries at the fate of his friend – which might be the only living thing for which this man has truly cared. He jumps down to face me, his eyes filled with murder, and I lift what I've clutched in my hand all along, and when Mrs Hibbert runs to my side I think she must mean to restrain me, grabbing my wrist as Tip did before. But no, her hand is guiding mine. A thud. A deep breath. And then a scream – and that last sound coming from Sarah the maid, now back by the doors and watching all.

'Get out!' Mrs Hibbert turns to shout, and then in a trembling afterthought, 'Sarah . . . go into the office. Find the Book of Events. Put it in my carpet bag.'

I think Sarah goes. I am not sure, my eyes are drawn back to Tip again, my open-mouthed shock a reflection of his, before he looks down at the little spear that is protruding from his breast. A horrible moan when he draws it out, holding it up before his eyes. Mrs Hibbert tells him not to move and then in a voice far more controlled, she says, 'Samuel . . . take Elijah and Pearl.'

'You can't . . . you can't take her.' Tip's words are determined but very faint. 'I saved her . . . I saved her from drowning. She is nothing without me. She owes me her life. This is the house

317

where the mermaid belongs. Pearl . . .' His eyes are beseeching, undaunted to the very end. 'The vice flows as thick in your blood as mine. This blood . . .'

The dripping file in his hand is now being pointed towards my heart. I grow cold. A horrible prickle of fear, some knowledge lurking deep inside like a worm that is gnawing through my bowels, something that squirms through a mire of filth; that creeps out in darkness to pretty its features in layers of white and carmine paint.

'Don't listen to him!' Mrs Hibbert shouts, and her veils bloom out. 'His only wish is to drag you down, to join him in his pit of despair.'

'Ah, Mrs Hibbert! *You* speak of despair!' Tip's mask is cracking a little more, and while watching the disintegration of him the horror comes over me again, when I say, 'You both knew the truth, and still you sold me to Osborne Black? Did he know? Please tell me he didn't know.'

Beneath the streaking powder Tip's face is gleaming grey. A strange sort of sound rises up in his throat. It might be a laugh. It might be a groan. Pressing a hand to the wound again, he looks deeply into my eyes and shudders before slowly going on, 'I always thought it an irony that the thing he once spurned cost him so dear. Oh, Pearl, you were very dearly bought. But then, swindlers all cheat themselves in the end, and I swindled myself when I let you go. Every day since then I have missed my Pearl. Every day I have wished her back again. Don't . . .'

On that unfinished plea Tip's speech comes to its end. Not another word escapes his lips. His voice breaks. Blood trickles from his mouth. His moustaches are stained by the leaking, turned into ribbons of scarlet silk.

I am horrified. I am mesmerised. I am caught in a spell and cannot move, but Mrs Hibbert breaks Tip's curse, her murmured voice echoing his. 'Very dearly brought indeed.'

And with that, she is suddenly possessed, grabbing the file from his hand, slashing it down through the flesh of his cheek, slicing off the tusks of his moustache. An awful emasculation it is, and nothing for the victim to do but to lift pointed fingers, to clutch at his wounds, and I fear he might tear his whole face away to reveal some festering truth beneath, much as when Mrs Hibbert first lifted her veils – when she told me that I was lucky to leave, to go and live with Osborne Black.

Oh yes, blood is thicker than water. Blood can splatter and splash like a fountain, pulsing little sprays of red, the rain through which Tip is staggering, feet crunching on broken glass and ice before skidding and slipping against the divan – from there on down to the floor below, where he sits with both his legs splayed wide. He looks like a doll with the stuffing knocked out; this greasy wet stuffing that leaks too fast. His bowels must have loosened. The foulest of smells. It is like the stench of Dolphin House, when the river rose and the drains backed up. Still, I kneel and reach forward to cradle his head. I swallow hard and hold my breath while staring down at his upturned eyes, which almost look green in this candlelight. And such is my doubt that I *have* to ask – for Tip to speak my father's name.

He shakes his head. He makes a moan. I lower my ear and it might be a word, but nothing that I can understand, all meaning lost in the frothing pink that bubbles around what was his mouth. How long I wait, I do not know. I am hoping for an answer still. Is it a second, a minute, an hour before the last sigh, when the bubbles melt?

Someone covers his face with a velvet throw. It seems oddly fitting, that fancy shroud. And now, with his eyes hidden from mine, I look up and I see Elijah's instead, like glittering diamonds, like suns, like moons, like the stars that will guide me away from here. But I know that however far I go I will never escape from what I am – the spawn of a mermaid, a mermaid dead. Dead mermaids must reek of rotting fish.

LILY

A lovely boy they stole from me, a boy I had kissed, but not kissed to death.
He is once again among humans.

From 'The Ice Maiden' by Hans Christian Andersen

What revelations we learned that night – enough to drive any one of us mad. The waiting alone was torturous, with Freddie and me in his sitting room and the tock of the clock on the mantelpiece grown louder with every second that passed, or was that the thumping of Freddie's feet, pacing up and down so much it was a wonder they hadn't worn through the weave of the Turkey rug below. He was smoking another of his cigars – short anxious sucks, just as soon puffed out to envelop the man in a hovering cloud.

I got up and moved to a window where the air blowing in around the frame was decidedly fresher than that in the room – but so icy I found myself shivering while trying to see the street beyond. Now enveloped in dusty falls of snow, our hansom cab was waiting still. I held my breath when a man walked past. He wore a tall hat, a long flowing coat and, just for a moment, I thought him Tip Thomas, overcome with a queasy sense of doom when I looked back at Freddie and suddenly asked, 'Why do we wait so long? They must have reached Samuel's rooms by now.'

Freddie's eyes were fixed on the clock's brass hands, which by then were saying a quarter to seven. Almost three hours since our return. It was too long. Something must have gone wrong. In answer he rattled off a cough, flinging the stub of his half-smoked cigar down to the fire in the hearth. 'There may have been unforeseen events, in which case Samuel will go elsewhere. We must be patient . . . await his word.'

Another five minutes. Still no message came, and Freddie was tugging the stock of his collar, the bow of his tie become crooked and loose, a wild expression on his face when he turned and blurted out the words, 'You're right. We should have heard.' And then with great vigour and certainty, 'Lily, we must go to Cheyne Walk . . . or,' he pondered for another moment, 'would it be better to leave you here? No!' His resolve was reborn. 'You're safer with me. I'll write a note . . . have one of the maids take it to the police. God forgive me, I should have done this before. If things have gone badly then help may be needed. We must only pray we are not too late.'

It was then, glancing down at the street again, that something occurred to make me shout, 'Oh, Freddie . . . but there's no need. They're here!'

The growler cab was drawing up. The sound of its wheels had been muffled by snow, but there on the other side of the road, directly in front of Hall's offices, Samuel Beresford now stood in the street, raising his arms to lift Pearl down, after which he assisted Elijah – *Elijah! My brother was here, was safe!*

Rushing past Freddie, I flew down the stairs, my heart in my mouth when I opened the door, and no care for the ice that coated the steps, or the sleety snow that fell around as I rushed into my brother's arms and hugged and squeezed him with all of my might. Oh, I cannot say how happy I was to have Elijah back again, even though he was somewhat doddery, even if his garb was ridiculous, with that muffler tied around his head in lieu of any sort of hat, and the long velvet coat, and the garish checked trousers that flapped at half-mast below his knees – for Elijah was so much taller than the owner from which they'd been borrowed. But what did that matter? Who cared what he wore, or how feeble and pained his movements were. My brother was smiling, alive and free.

Having followed, and now standing quite still on the

pavement, Freddie did not seem to share my delight. At that point, he showed no emotion at all and very serious when he called, 'What took you so long to get here, Sam? Why did you not go to Kensington?'

'I'll explain when we're all inside.' Samuel sounded gruff and exhausted but I paid very little attention to that, following my brother's gaze when he turned back to look for Pearl – Pearl, who still wore Mrs Hibbert's black dress over the grey of her hospital gown – and such a queer thing when she glanced up at Freddie and suddenly cried, 'Him! Is this it, then? Have I been duped . . . about to be passed to another man?'

Elijah said gently, 'Pearl, you've no reason to be afraid. Don't you remember . . . I told you that Freddie would help us?'

She seemed to accept Elijah's word, becoming more subdued again, but almost as if she wasn't there, as if she was turning in on herself, as if she might dissolve in snow. And when Mrs Hibbert climbed down from the carriage, a carpet bag in one of her hands, the other reaching out for Pearl – Pearl only shuddered and backed away. Pearl looked to be afraid of her.

Freddie paid off both carriage and cab and then he and Samuel aided Elijah, helping my brother up the stairs and on into the sitting room – though the progress made was very slow, with Elijah needing to stop for breath at almost every other step. And as I watched that, while leading Pearl, I almost forgot Mrs Hibbert was there.

She stood in shadows beside the door, watching as Freddie busied himself with the pouring of some 'stiffeners', of which only Samuel accepted a glass – and that set down on the mantelpiece while he threw some wood upon the fire. It must have been very dry for the flames surged up, great blasts of heat from which he rapidly backed off, and I noticed the slivers of ice in his hair and some of them caught in his eyelashes too, sparkling as they melted. I wanted to reach out and brush them away but that would have been too presumptuous. Instead, without even thinking, I touched a hand to my own head as if seeking to suck on a strand of hair, if any length of hair remained. And if – as Ellen Page once warned – any hair *had* wrapped around my heart it was surely squeezing tight right then, aching with joy when I looked at Elijah – though to see my brother so reduced, what could I do but avert my eyes, sitting and looking down instead at the hands then clasped in the lap of my dress where the fabric shimmered like water, colours all melting from purple to red when bathed in the rippling light of the flames. From there I looked up at a window, beyond which dark skies filled with flurries of snow, flakes fatter and rounder than before and already sticking against the glass, almost as if we were being cocooned from everything in the outside world. But the ice ferns, they were still visible, looking like black paper cut-outs – like fingers with sharply jagged tips.

I trembled to think of Tip Thomas again. I noticed my brother was shivering too, despite the sofa on which he was sitting being drawn up very close to the hearth. And he'd made no attempt to remove his coat, or the muffler still wound around his head. And, how distressing, the sound of his breaths, laboured and much too quick they were – when all he'd done was climb the stairs!

Pearl nestled limply in his arms, her face an almost luminous white against the black of the gown she wore, except for those roughened red patches of skin, and the darker red spots that stained her hands. I had no idea what they could be and Pearl seemed to be oblivious – her eyes staring into the depths of the fire, wide open but lacking in any expression, like those of the automaton that was placed in the hallway in Dolphin House. She looked very old, and also young. She bore all too little resemblance to the beauty she had been before. And yet how tender Elijah's hands when he stroked the fine stubbling growth of hair that covered the dome of Pearl's small head.

Meanwhile, Samuel and Freddie had settled themselves in the two green chairs that were placed either side of the mantelpiece. I dare say to anyone glancing in we looked the most contented group, with Freddie's eyes grown fond and damp when he smiled at Elijah and almost sobbed, 'Dearest boy, to see you back home again. I simply can't tell you what this means. But . . .' He glanced swiftly up at me as if expecting some reprimand, and from me to Samuel Beresford, of whom he then demanded, 'Why here, Sam? Why not Kensington? Should we be thinking of moving on . . . to your rooms, or perhaps to find a hotel?'

'There is no need.' Samuel was blunt. 'Cruikshank won't risk any adverse exposure. And Tip Thomas won't bother us any more.'

'How can you be sure?' Freddie asked – which was when Mrs Hibbert stepped forward, announcing through the sway of her veils, 'Because Mrs Hibbert has murdered him.'

When she spoke that way, as if in the third person, the hairs prickled up on the back of my neck.

'Murdered!' Freddie looked back in alarm. His hands gripped the chair's velvet arms.

'Is he really dead?' I asked.

'Yes,' Samuel Beresford curtly replied. 'Everyone has had the most terrible shock. It's probably better we talk in the morning, when we have all eaten and rested . . . when we can decide what's best to do.'

That was when Pearl began to sob, and that was when I noticed the smell. It seemed to grow stronger with every moment, what with all the flesh warming and all the ice melting, and there in the dancing glimmer of flames I saw the rusty-coloured streaks that were staining Mrs Hibbert's gloves, a match for those smeared on the folds of Pearl's gown, over which, now and then, she wiped her hands – her hands which were splattered with – what? Was it blood?

When Pearl shifted position her skirts rose up and I saw that she wore no stockings or boots, that her feet were naked and crusted with filth, beneath which were blisters, and scarring cuts.

'Pearl . . . your feet!' While trying to keep my voice calm, I asked, 'Freddie, do you have any bandages? I must fetch some water . . . some towels. Look at her feet. Look at the blood.'

Before he could answer I'd reached the door, from which Mrs Hibbert stepped aside, allowing me to run out to the hall, from where I fully intended going on up to my room, to bring the jug and washing bowl. But I'd only reached the base of the stairs when I heard Freddie's voice, such arrogant tones. 'Madam Hibbert. I think you should leave this house. A brothel keeper turned murderess is hardly fit company for . . .'

'Mrs Hibbert is not in this room,' she broke in, and again she spoke of herself as through another person's mouth, to which Freddie swiftly responded with, 'By God, are you now turned lunatic! Why, if only we'd left you in Chiswick House then all of our problems would now be solved . . . instead of which,' his expression was filled with venom, 'you have added yet more difficulties. I respectfully ask that you leave us in peace. Go back to your life of depravity. Why, I'd call the police and have you arrested if not for the hatred I felt for Tip Thomas. For his demise, I applaud you!'

Elijah began to protest, consumed with a new-found energy. 'But, Freddie . . . where can Mrs Hibbert go? Whatever she might have done in the past, this woman has helped to save my life.'

'Elijah is right,' Samuel interjected. 'Surely Mrs Hibbert deserves our thanks . . . a roof over her head, if only tonight, until she can make some other arrangements? If you will not extend that charity then I most certainly will!'

At that point, I was thinking that Freddie was right – about Tip Thomas's death, that is. I was thinking, *Good riddance to bad rubbish! I for one am glad he's dead, whatever the method of his end.* It was a wicked thing, I know, and perhaps my heart had turned to stone, as villainous as his had been. But, honestly, I cared not a jot as to whether Tip Thomas lived or died – only glad that Elijah was here and safe, *whatever* the cost of his freedom had been. If I'd had to, I would have done it myself. I would have killed with my own bare hands. We should sing and dance to celebrate, for the world was a far better place without *him*, and—

What happened next, what a shock that was! I had to clutch on to the newel post to stop myself falling to the ground – when I heard what I did, when I saw what I did, the drama unfolding within that room, when Mrs Hibbert shouted out, 'Frederick Hall, are you deaf as well as blind?'

A swift rustle of silks as she set down her bag, and then raised her hands to lift her veils, during which act Pearl was pleading, 'No, Mrs Hibbert, no . . . not that!'

Mrs Hibbert's hands slowly lowered, and another scent of that bloody tang when she walked to the farthest end of the room, very near to the engraving, 'Isabella . . . The Pot of Basil'. A glint of light flashed over the glass, just as it had when I saw it first, and Mrs Hibbert leaned closer – and Mrs Hibbert raised her hands, taking hold of either side of the frame, then flinging that picture to the floor, where the fracturing glass rang out like a bell then snapped beneath Mrs Hibbert's feet when she turned to walk back towards the hearth, when she started to raise the veils from her face, when Pearl lifted her hands to cover her eyes as if she could not bear to look and see what horror now approached.

At that point, from where I was standing, I saw no more than the gauzy black fabric still draped at the back of the woman's head. But I could see Freddie well enough, and the dread expressed on his features then, and how he recoiled and staggered back, almost stumbling into the grate – at which Samuel cried, 'Dear God, Freddie! Whatever's wrong? You look as if you've seen a ghost!'

Such dramatic reactions. I knew not why, but my ears had registered something odd, and that was Mrs Hibbert's voice – quite different when she had shouted at Freddie, still tinged with a foreign accent but the intonation no longer French – though what it was, I could not tell, listening hard when she carried on, 'If you wish to know my name then you need only ask Mr Frederick Hall, who has,' she turned to face him again, 'indeed seen a ghost rising up from his past.'

'Who are you?' Pearl asked, her hands no longer concealing her eyes, which were full of shock and confusion. At her side, Elijah stiffened, a high colour flooding through gaunt cheeks while he stared at Mrs Hibbert and asked, 'You and Freddie . . . you were acquainted before?'

I wanted to say, *Of course they were! Don't you remember that day in Cremorne?* But Freddie was already speaking, such disbelief in his groaning voice. 'Dear God. Can it be? What witchcraft is this? They told me you'd died. Tip Thomas . . . he told me himself. I never had reason to doubt him.'

'*You* deserve to die, the same as him, for the life you both condemned me to, when you threw me out of this very house and took me to that brothel . . . when I was still grieving for Gabriel Lamb, the man I loved and would have wed.'

'You were only to stay until after the birth.' Freddie's response was petulant, like that of a child who has knowingly sinned but remains indignant at being discovered. 'I did more than most in such circumstances. I paid for your confinement there, a doctor and midwife to attend. You know very well, it was all arranged. The child to be sent to the Foundling, and you to start your life anew . . . released from the stigma of your shame.'

A child being sent to the Foundling – just like Elijah – just like me? I could hardly begin to take this in, staring with an open mouth when she fell to her knees and began to weep. 'To live without shame . . . when they made me a whore! They took my babies away from me. They told me they had died at birth, when I'd seen them move, when I'd heard them cry, when I'd looked into their open eyes . . . the boy's so like his father's had been. But I was ill with the loss of blood. They said I was delirious. They said I had been dreaming.'

She broke off for a moment, taking a deep and trembling breath before being able to carry on. 'They brought another child to me, one whose mother had drowned in the Thames.

327

They forced me to suckle that child as my own until *she* was taken away as well. Tip Thomas was jealous of anyone who dared to grow too close to Pearl. But it broke my heart to lose her too, when he moved me to that Limehouse slum. Things happened there. Things I could never speak about. But nothing was worse than my grief for Pearl, for my children who'd died, for Gabriel, the man I'd loved . . . after which only hatred grew in my heart,' a black finger was stabbing at Freddie then, 'for you, Frederick Hall, for that devil Tip Thomas, for what the two of you did to me. All of these years my only wish has been to see you burn in Hell. And now one of you is already there.'

Her voice was meeker again when she asked, 'Can you imagine how it feels . . . to think that my children were living when I always believed them dead, when you left me in such misery? What had I ever done to you . . . to deserve that fate, to be left alone, enduring a life that no woman would choose if she had any say in the matter!'

Freddie was visibly moved. The heel of one hand was pressed hard to a temple. His voice was deep and strained when repeating, 'But Tip Thomas . . . he told me . . . he said you were dead. You have to believe I speak the truth! I would never have left you in that place. My conscience . . . my affection would never permit it. But as far as the children were concerned . . . you must realise, I had to think of the company, to consider my reputation!'

I heard breaths that came too loud, too fast, though by then I was hardly able to tell which were his, which were mine, which Elijah's, which Pearl's – all of us equally shocked at this news, though Pearl was the first to recover enough to ask in a voice small and tremulous, 'But I don't understand . . . where is the *real* Mrs Hibbert? Why did you imitate her voice? Why do you wear her clothes . . . her veils?'

The answer was blunt. 'Mrs Hibbert died. Tip said it was shortly after you left. He said she was riddled with syphilis, that she'd lost her wits as well as her strength. He showed his true compassion then when he left her to rot on the steps of the Lock.'

'The Lock?' Pearl frowned with confusion.

'The Lock Hospital,' Samuel curtly explained, his gaze still intent on this story's narrator – that is, when not glancing from her to me. 'For those who suffer venereal disease, where most of them go as a last resort, though rarely to emerge again, except to be buried in unmarked graves.'

Pearl moaned, 'Oh . . . poor Mrs Hibbert.'

The woman whose name had still not been said – though I knew it, of course I did by then – now continued to explain, 'Since you left Cheyne Walk the business declined. Many felt they'd been duped at the time of your sale. Many never returned again. All that was left were some lonely old men who liked to gamble more than whore, who treated the house as a gentlemen's club, dining with the veiled madam, listening when she read from her filthy books. In the end Tip feared he would lose them too . . . the revenue they still brought in. He needed to find a new Mrs Hibbert to pretend that things carried on as before. *I* am educated. *I* am literate, well able to mimic her Gallic tongue. I am as French as *she* ever was!'

'But why did you do it?' Samuel asked.

She exhaled a long sigh. 'That first year Tip kept me locked away. That was when he had me caring for Pearl. And then, later on . . . well, what could I do? Where was I to go? I had not a penny to my name. He said he would find me . . . he'd ruin me. But then, I was already ruined. Tell me, what was the alternative? To starve, to sell myself on the streets? And, more recently, playing Tip's madam, I was free of those other depravities, though,' her voice was raised and passionate, 'I would gladly live through every year, every second and minute of my disgrace, for if I had not been in Cheyne Walk I would never have found my son again, when they carried him in, half dead, half drowned, when little by little I came to learn how Frederick Hall saved infant twins from being raised in the Foundling and then sent them to live with Augustus Lamb . . . Augustus, the father of Gabriel . . . Gabriel, my own betrothed.'

At that, she swung round to look at me, and when I stared back at her unveiled face everything else in that room seemed to fade. This was the face I once saw as a child, when I woke and heard someone calling my name, when my window glass reflected the eyes of the woman I thought my mother's ghost. But she was no more of a ghost than I, and we both found our eyes spilling with tears, Elijah's the same when he cried out, 'I should have known. I should have guessed . . . those times when you nursed me without the veils . . . the resemblance to Lily. But I thought I was imagining things.'

His muffler fell as he struggled to stand, that movement causing a little draught, and the fire's flames went surging up, casting a sudden flashing of red to illuminate Freddie's features, revealing the desperate panic there – such emotion that I had never seen in a man as confident as he – except for that night when I'd first arrived, when coming to look for Elijah, when Freddie had spoken about Isabella, when he'd given me her miniature.

Freddie did something dramatic then, holding his hands out beseechingly as if to embrace both Elijah and me – and I almost stepped forward, towards him, but was blocked by Isabella, from whose mouth fresh truths were gushing out as she held me in her moist dark stare. 'Lily, you must not be deceived . . . this man tried to creep into my bed when Gabriel's body was barely cold. And when he discovered my pregnancy . . . what desire or compassion did he show? This so-called benevolent gentleman cast me out without a day's warning.'

She was panting, sobbing, hands clutched at her breast. Silver beads of spittle flew from her lips when she looked at Freddie again and cried, 'This man is the liar and hypocrite who claimed *my* condition might cause *him* disgrace!'

'But, Isabella,' Freddie retorted, 'can't you try to see how it was for me . . . how gossip would compromise the firm? Only later did I realise how foolish . . . how hasty I may have been, that if you had lived I would make you my wife, and raise your children as my own. But I was deceived as cruelly as you when that fiend Tip Thomas arrived at the door, telling me that you were dead, handing over two sleeping newborn babes.'

At that, his eyes met Elijah's. 'How could I manage? A man alone! What if you woke and started to bawl? I did consider farming you out, but there are such tales of extortion and blackmail, of infants doped, then left for days . . . dying from thirst, starvation, disease.'

Elijah was sitting down again, all colour draining from his cheeks as he stared at Freddie through bloodshot eyes. 'Whatever change of heart you might claim to have suffered afterwards, you condemned our mother to misery, to the vilest of any human trades . . . when you had every means to support her, secretly, if you so wished, with no shame whatsoever. Instead of which you made the choice to hide her away in a brothel. And then you hid us in an orphanage!'

During this accusation, Freddie's face had grown yet ruddier, his voice choked and breathless when he said, 'For which I deserve to be lashed! For which I pray your forgiveness now.'

Next, he was imploring me. 'Lily . . . You *must* listen. You *must* understand. When they told me that Isabella was dead I simply didn't know what to do. I should have informed Augustus then, but my mind was too confused. I paid a maid to pose as your mother, to take a letter that I forged and apply for your care at the Foundling. Afterwards, I became a patron there. In time, I visited every week, always searching for a familiar face until Providence brought you back to me, and what a glorious day that was! How could I bear to leave you there? I knew that Augustus would raise you both, never questioning your identity . . . not when he saw Elijah's eyes, being so very like Gabriel's . . . the very mirror of his wife's.'

He paused to let out a lingering sigh. 'Well, the rest you know quite well enough. I wrote to Augustus. Augustus came . . . and what happiness you brought to his life. I confess that did somewhat relieve my guilt, to see you growing safe and well and,' at that Freddie's eyes fused hard with mine, 'every year you have come to resemble her more, the woman – *this* women,' he looked at Isabella again, 'a face which has haunted me for years.'

I felt such a thudding in my head. Had Freddie only been biding his time? Had he only ever wanted me as means of replacing the lost Isabella?

'Oh, Uncle . . .' My brother suddenly groaned, his pallid features drenched in sweat. 'Did Papa know anything of this . . . how cruelly you dealt with our father's betrothed, when she was in need, when he might have shown compassion and taken her into his home as well?'

A mournful look there was in his eyes when Elijah stared at Freddie then, his next words barely audible, 'I used to admire and respect you. But now I see what a monster you are . . . no better than Osborne Black in your way, both of you con-scienceless, arrogant men.'

'Won't you be merciful, dear boy? Don't you know that you have crushed me?' However poignant Freddie's plea, he must have known the argument done, draining the dregs of his brandy glass then grabbing the bottle near to hand, bowing his head for a moment or two before he headed for the door, where he paused beside Isabella, a trembling hand reaching out for hers, as if wishing to hold it or kiss it perhaps, while, through heavy breaths, his next question was asked. 'Who saw you? Who saw what was done to Tip Thomas, apart from the others here?'

'Only Sarah, one of the maids.'

'And she knows who you are . . . who you really are?'

Isabella gave the slightest nod, after which Freddie departed the room.

There was a long shocked silence, and then Samuel Beresford followed him – and I followed after the both of them, coming close to the younger man's side when he stood beneath the house's porch, looking down to the pavement where Freddie was standing, wearing his coat and tall silk hat and holding his travelling bag in his hand. He looked dazed, indecisive and lost, staring out through the drifts of snow towards the building opposite; the offices of Hall & Co. Once again it was steeped in nothing but darkness, as empty and cold as a grave.

Freddie must have sensed us watching then, glancing back with the bleakest of smiles on his lips when he said, 'Goodbye, sweet Lily. And Sam, dear friend . . . may I trouble you with one more request? Would you stay with the others, here, tonight . . . take care of the business during my absence? There are matters to which I must attend. They have been too many years delayed.'

PART FOUR

PEARL

Before we left Cheyne Walk I looked at the mermaid on the wall – the one whose hair was studded with pearls, green eyes staring back through the splintering plaster. I felt something snapping inside my head – like a rushing of air – like water. I ran out of the house and over the road, down the steep run of steps to the jetty below, where I saw such visions from my past, with the story from Mrs Hibbert's book coming to life before my eyes, with Tip Thomas holding a child in his arms, and her toes were webbed, the same as mine – and I had to struggle against the compulsion to throw myself back into the Thames, returning to my mother's arms.

My life was once saved, but at what cost? If Tip Thomas had never found me that night he might have let Isabella go. Isabella might never have been deceived into thinking her natural children dead, giving suck instead to an orphaned babe. And it is only thanks to her that I am here in Burlington Row, Elijah lying at my side, my love sleeping deeply though I do not. My feet are burning. My throat is sore. But in time these little wounds will heal. I worry so much more for him. I count every wheezing breath he takes – holding mine when I see the door opening.

At first, I think it is Tip's ghost coming to visit me again, to sit on this bed and bring me gifts. But no, it is Isabella, her face haloed with light from the candle she holds. One lingering look and then she is gone. The door is closed. All dark again.

I feel bereft. I want to call out, disentangling my arms from Elijah's, and while he sleeps on I creep from the room, out into the hall, where a chill draught is blowing up through the house. A carpet of snowflakes gusts over the floor, the dado and picture frames above.

From the porch I see Isabella, standing outside on the pavement, and Samuel Beresford is walking towards her, approaching from the end of the street where he must have gone to hail a cab. A hansom is rattling in his wake, the clip-clop of hooves, the rattle of wheels, all hushed by the carpet of white beneath. And when it pulls up he offers his hand to help Isabella climb inside.

'Don't go!' I cry out. My voice is as plaintive as a child's, and when Samuel Beresford glances back I feel myself too conspicuous, my nightgown blown hard against my flesh – what little flesh there is these days. I am ashamed to be so exposed, to feel the heat of the driver's leer, whereas Isabella's smile is sad when she looks at me from the open cab and answers in the softest voice, 'If I stay I will only blight your lives. If it is known what I have become . . . your names would never be free of stain.'

'But I am as stained, as guilty as you.'

She lifts a finger to her lips. Perhaps she fears the cabman's ears; the risk that my words might incriminate. 'No . . .' she says, 'not you. Not you.'

She mumbles to Samuel Beresford. What she says to him I cannot hear, only able to watch when he calls to the driver and gives an address in Kensington. And just before the cab pulls off, Samuel reaches into a pocket and gives Isabella some coins and notes, and something else, something glittering. It might only be a set of keys but the sight of her hand closing over that metal reminds me too much of the House of the Mermaids. I shudder at the clang of the door, at the driver's whip as it cuts through the air in a slashing hiss, a sound that leaves me mesmerised, still seeing Tip Thomas's ruined face, and I see it long after the cab has gone, only restored to my senses again when Samuel Beresford climbs the steps to stand at my side beneath the porch. He wipes a handkerchief over my cheeks. I had not known I was crying. He stares down at me through mournful eyes, 'She said you must try and understand. She said the carpet bag is yours.'

We go back into the warmth of the house. I find the bag she left behind, still there on the floor by the sitting-room door. Inside I see the Book of Events, and the key that was snatched from the chain at Tip's neck. I have no idea what that key unlocks. I am tempted to burn that book on the fire, to destroy every one of its wicked lies. But something stops me. I don't know what. Perhaps that whispered voice in my head, *Ma chère, pour toi . . . pour toi.*

I am wearing one of Lily's gowns. It falls around me like a sack, even though I have eaten all that I can, buttered potatoes, soups, porridge and rice – anything I can easily swallow down.

Elijah looks like a scarecrow too, in those clothes Lily saved from Dolphin House, supplemented by some of Samuel's. Everything once belonging to Tip has been burned, along with the asylum gowns. My love will have nothing of Frederick Hall's – except for some shoes, and those he must, for their feet are of a similar size and Samuel's are much smaller, though when Samuel travelled back to his rooms he returned with a hat, and an overcoat, and divers items of underwear.

We waited most eagerly for his return, all three of us hoping to see Isabella. But Samuel arrived alone, and then he only shook his head. He said Isabella had stayed one night but now she has gone, and who knows where, and all that was left was a note of thanks, and that message again – to forget her.

Lily took this news very badly. But when recovered sufficiently she wrote a letter to Kingsland House – completing the one she had started before, saying that we would be travelling soon. But before Samuel went out to post it we all agreed that Augustus Lamb should never know the real truth, nothing concerning Frederick Hall, nothing to say Isabella was found.

And now, even though Elijah is still coughing and somewhat feverish, we have driven through streets of rotting black straw, of melting black slime, of slippy black slush – all that remains of the once white snow. We have boarded the Leominster train, with the tickets that Samuel Beresford bought. There is barely any luggage to take, only Isabella's carpet bag, which I insist on carrying, and Lily's travelling portmanteau, which Samuel heaves on to the rack, during which act the whistle blows and with our departure imminent Samuel takes his hurried leave, wishing us well for our future lives. Lily smiles tightly and thanks him profusely for everything he has done to help. She stands at the window and waves him goodbye, her cheek pressed hard against the glass. She stands like that for a very long time, long after the train has pulled away. When she comes to sit down, she is crying. Elijah holds her in his arms.

I did not cry then. I do not cry now. I am blessed to be loved by Elijah Lamb. I am happy here in Kingsland House, a place where I never thought to return – and that visit last year seems a lifetime ago. But I am tormented by the fear that the scales might yet fall from Elijah's eyes and then he will come to resent me, and all of the woes I have brought to his life – me, and the artist, Osborne Black.

I fear Osborne might try to find me here. But Elijah says that he will not – that he has no rights – that he would not dare. And Elijah says he could never resent me, that if not for the House of the Mermaids he would never have found his mother again. So some good comes from evil in the end.

But I wonder at that; to have found Isabella, and then to have lost her all over again, to have learned what we have of her suffering.

In the case of Augustus Lamb, though I only saw him once before, his suffering upsets us all. What ails him nobody seems to know. He is stricken by a creeping paralysis that makes his limbs tremble alarmingly, no longer being able to master the most basic of his toilet needs, with Lily and Ellen holding him up to piss or shit into the bowl. And his breathing is often laboured, almost as bad as Elijah's was until his lungs grew strong again – though at times my love still struggles for breath. But it is only now and then, mostly when he needs the opium. Tip Thomas dosed him too liberally during those months of captivity, and with more than Mother's Blessing. Without the drug he is overcome. He shakes. Perspiration stands out on his brow. He tells Lily it is but a fever. He does not wish her to know of this curse. But the doctor here, he understands, just as he does with Augustus Lamb.

The old man's mind is so much worse, being plagued by visions – things not there – and even when Lily holds his hand, patiently talking of times gone by and hoping that way to lure his thoughts back into the realms of reality, the very next thing he forgets her name. He thinks her an angel, or fairy child. Twice now he has called me the mermaid.

But Elijah he forgets the most. When we first walked in through the door his grandfather did not know him at all. And Ellen Page, the housekeeper, there was a moment when she stood and stared, a narrowed squint, her mouth open wide and her jaw falling slack while shaking her head in disbelief. So thin and ravaged was my love. But then it was all hallelujahs and joy to see Elijah home again and she wasted no time in hobbling off to fetch the doctor to the house, and though I never thought to trust another medical man again, the one in this village has proved to be kind, and such a regular visitor that he is quite the family friend. He has cared for Elijah attentively, very often called in at the dead of night when, during the bitterest winter

341

months, what had started out as a sniffling cold came to settle on congested lungs. We took it in turns, Lily and I, to care for him during the hours of day, though at night he was mine, cradled close in my arms, only thinking occasionally of Tip and how I once held him the same; in those final moments before his death.

I have not told Elijah but sometimes at night I still see Tip's face. He lurks in the shadows from which he peers, blue-green eyes brimming over with jealousy. Sharp fingers try to snatch the ring that I wear on my left hand these days, a token of marriage that never was bestowed on me by Osborne Black. This gold band once belonged to Augustus's wife, and though I have not been wed as such, Elijah says we shall be soon.

It does for the sake of propriety. And yet, I think it may bring bad luck, with her having died when her son was born. Will I also die, when my child is born? The doctor says my time is near, the conception having been last year, in that Indian summer in Dolphin House. But the doctor thinks there is something wrong. My ankles are swelling and painful. The flesh there is stretched as tight as a drum, to which he applies the leeches, to thin and purify the blood. I hate the way the skin blisters up, and how the bandages ooze with blood. But he says this letting may clear my mind, for Augustus is not the only one to be taking on queer fancies. I try to keep them to myself. I lie meek and mute upon this bed which once belonged to Lily, which is so much larger than the one in Elijah's old bedroom next door. Lily has cleared all her things away; and the big doll's house and the toys of her youth are boxed away in the attics now, though perhaps we shall bring them down – in time.

Lily sleeps in a room above. It once belonged to her grandmother. Often I hear her rise in the night, her footsteps creaky, creeping on boards before padding downstairs to the drawing room. That is where Augustus sleeps, no longer able to manage the stairs, his mind sedated by opiates that the doctor comes to administer, prompt every evening at six o'clock.

Before being confined to this bed I used to spend hours at

his side; my feet raised high upon a stool while attempting to sew some baby clothes. But my fingers are fat and clumsy, and really, there is no need. Lily has found some tiny things in an old chest of drawers on the attic floor. They must have been worn by Gabriel. Such intricate smocking and stitching they have. I could never make anything so fine.

Now I only lie and read. Elijah brings books from the study shelves, many once published by Frederick Hall, as were the magazines they've kept, the same as those I used to keep beneath my pillow in Cheyne Walk – before I became an artist's muse.

And now, I am a muse again. I pose for Elijah's drawings, though I really can't imagine why anyone should want to see a woman who sprawls in her bed all day, who is growing as bloated as a whale.

But Elijah does – that is when he is not out and about, working with his camera. And if she does not go with him, and if Augustus sleeps peacefully, then Lily comes to sit at my side, such smiling amazement in her eyes when I say, 'Look, Lily!' and lift up the sheets, and show her the little thrusting kicks that poke beneath my belly's flesh. This child of mine twists and turns so much. Lily thinks it may be dancing. I think it is due to the weather – so warm it is this May.

I wake at dawn, too restless for sleep. Where Elijah's hand is cupping my breast, a tiny white glistening pearl of milk is dripping from the nipple. How can I not think of Angelo – the painted cherub, the libertine, who reached out to touch a mermaid's breast which was dripping with crystals of water?

The memory disturbs me, as does the drumming pain in my head, and I have such a sudden yearning to hear the sound of water again, to see it, to feel it lap my flesh, to soothe this aching in my legs.

I leave Elijah sleeping fast, his brown cheek against the white pillow, his brow as untroubled as that of a boy and no signs of the trauma befallen him, except for the grey growing into his hair. He is so very beautiful, a regular Adonis. If only I had the talent to draw, every picture I made would be of him; my love all-consuming, too clinging, too selfish. Does that make me too much like Osborne Black?

Osborne. I wonder what can have gone on in his life since that night on the Mall when the Thames flooded up. I wonder, is it wrong of me to find myself thinking about him still? But I lived with the man so many years. At times, there was almost happiness, those early days on Margate sands when I lay in the warmth of the dawning sun, before his vision grew too dark, before he was taken up with the madness of hiding his mermaid away from the world.

Has he found me in this hiding place? Sometimes I feel the heat of his eyes, observing, scrutinising me. Sometimes, I swear, he speaks to me. Can you hear him now? He whispers through the rustle of leaves, through the hushing of my cotton gown as I make my way down through the gardens again. More impatient are his sighs when I push through the tangles of shrubbery, and the dangling lace of a willow tree, where I kneel among yellow marsh marigolds, and the lovely purple hyacinths, and the unfurling fronds of luxuriant ferns uncoiling like snakes in the warmth of the sun. You can almost taste the pollen spores from the cow parsley, daisies and dandelions that make up this posy in my hands, the stems wrapped in ribbons of long green grass. You can almost hear the creaking of sap rising up through the wood of the branches – or is that the scratch of Osborne's pen?

I glance around, breaths trembling, my pulse a gushing in my ears, as loud as the ocean sucking on rocks, through which Osborne tells me to lift my hems and step down from the bank to the velvet-mossed stones, to step down from those stones on into the stream, where, at first, the water is a shock, so cold it almost takes my breath. But the tingling sensation soon turns to a numbness, and I think I should like to submerge my whole body – but then lose my grip on the ragged bouquet, petals floating all about as I try to find some purchase below, spreading my fingers through buttery sludge – though I hope to avoid

344

any broken shells that lurk there like razors to cut my flesh. As sharp as Tip Thomas's fingernails.

Buzz buzz. Do you hear that sound? Is Tip Thomas really the devil incarnate? Do you only have to think his name and 'ta-da', here he is, conjured up again? *You* might say that thrumming vibration of air is caused by a hovering dragonfly – the one with the glowering face of a woman, bulging red eyes and a wide red mouth, and veiled wings of black netting on either side. But I know I have entered some magical world where people are insects, this one Mrs Hibbert. And look! Here is Tip Thomas again, shilly-shallying his way across the weed, disguised as a water boatman he is, a green beetle propelled by two paddling legs which look like the oars of a boat, like the boat that Tip rowed when he fished on the Thames, when he found himself a mermaid's child.

The Thames is dirty. This water is clean. This water will wash my sins away. I shall soon be too slippery for Tip to hold. He shall not blag this child of mine. But, oh, how dizzy I become, and slowly, slowly the mud sinks beneath me. My mouth opens wider and liquid seeps in and while gazing up through a swirling lens I feel a violent stabbing pain.

My little fish's time has come!

Gasping to draw breath into my lungs, I drag myself to the shingle beach and crawl into a nest of ferns, grinding my teeth, rocking back and forth, at last looking up to see a face.

Elijah is here, but upside down, like Jesus on an asylum wall – and, like Jesus, Elijah will save me now, splashing towards me through the waves, shouting, 'Pearl . . . what are you doing here?'

Where am I? Is this Margate? For a moment, I cannot think. My world is nothing but sensory touch, dampness and greyness and cold hard stone, and the glisten of shells beneath velvety moss, and the patterns they make – like stars, like moons.

And then I remember. This is the grotto. I say, 'I am your mermaid.'

Why does Elijah not reply? There is only the silver of tears in

345

his eyes. There is only the glint of the gold on my hand when my wet fingers twine with his, turning and squeezing, gripping hard when he pulls me from darkness and into the light.

And now, when he carries me back to the house, as Tip Thomas once carried an infant child, I wrap my arms around his neck and nuzzle my face against his breast. I see the vibrant green of the lawns, and the red brick walls encroached with vines, and the crisp white sheets upon the bed. I lift my head from the pillow there, and between bloody thighs is a crowning head, black hair all filmed with a greasy wax. I hear a high-pitched screaming sound, like the wailing of a cat in the night. When I open my eyes I see Lily. She is holding a bundle in her arms. I hardly dare ask, but can't help myself, such a desperate plea when I start to cry, 'Does it have a tail? Does it have webbed feet?'

Elijah sits on the bed at my side. He takes the bundle from Lily's arms and places it gently into mine. He pulls the wrapping cloth away and says, 'Look, Pearl . . . a little boy. He has two legs. He has ten toes.'

What if he is only humouring me? I have to be sure, to look again – but there is no scaly fishy flesh, no flaps of skin between the toes, and when my baby whimpers it is only a moment or two he complains before I hold him to my breast. My fingers stroke his downy cheek. He stares back up, through unblinking eyes, eyes like his father's, filled with light, eyes looking into the depths of my soul, and I feel the first needling prick of love like a splinter of ice that is melting, in its place only sweet warm water.

LILY

A warm July day, late afternoon, and almost a year since Osborne Black had first brought Pearl to Kingsland House. In some ways, it was as if nothing had changed, except we were all of us different – with the sole exception of Ellen Page, no more or less wizened than before, and still pouring out gallons of over-stewed tea which spilled from the cups that rattled in saucers when handed round to those of us who made up the picnic that day on the lawns. Over that came our laughter, the gurgling child, the sweet piercing song of a blackbird that perched in the apple tree above.

What an idyllic scene it made. But real life is not a fairy tale. There are too many painful memories, however the surface is smoothed and glossed – much like the garden in which we were sitting. Since his health had been almost fully restored, some parts had been tamed by Elijah, but the rest remained entirely wild, for without hiring in any extra help – which we were reluctant to do back then, not wanting Pearl's presence too widely known – there was no amount of cutting or pruning could quell the rampant growth that spring, every plant and tree

347

grown very tall as if Nature herself had been intent on creating a fortress around us.

And that is how Papa liked it, Papa whose health would never mend, although there were days when he rallied again, when we walked him out in his big bath chair, in which he was sitting that day of the picnic, dozing beneath the ivy leaves which formed a natural bower of shade, although no roses bloomed just then.

Pearl lay on a blanket spread over the grass, sheltered beneath a parasol. You would never imagine how ill she'd been during those months of her pregnancy, suffering with those 'maternal fits', yet before they began she had seemed so well, considering her undernourished state. She ate. She rested. She grew more flesh. The only strange behaviour at first was her tendency to go wandering off, when Elijah would find her out in the gardens or, more often than not, beside the stream.

That's where he found her the day of the birth, where she might well have drowned or caught her death, lying there drenched and babbling nonsense, her hair and body caked in mud, resembling nothing quite so much as the mummified mermaid we'd seen in Cremorne. But then when the labour was over and done, when she cradled the child in her arms, she smiled, she was calm, she was 'sensible', and the doctor's explanation was that poisons flowing through her blood had caused her mind to hallucinate, before being expelled with the fluids of birth. But to those of us who could only observe, it seemed as if demons had been cast out, and a cherub born to take their place, and I wonder if any child was loved as much as my darling nephew, who was named Angel Augustus Lamb.

The happiness we knew back then, three generations beneath the one roof, bound by the ties of love and affection, was tempered only by the loss of my mother. How I grieved for someone not even dead – and to wake that morning in Burlington Row still expecting to find her sharing my bed, and no message she left, not a word of goodbye. At least I had the memory of those hours I spent embraced by her arms, falling asleep while the candle burned, gazing at Isabella's face, Isabella's breaths falling soft on my cheek, so much more than a dream or a picture then, even if a picture is all that remains, now set on my nightstand in Kingsland House, and the face looking out from behind the glass uncannily like my very own.

I see Isabella every day, whenever I look in a mirror. Every day I think of Frederick Hall and what his pride condemned her to.

Samuel Beresford wrote occasionally, though he never mentioned Freddie's name. The week before Christmas he sent us a gift with a note to explain how sorry he was not to deliver it personally. It was a wicker basket; inside which we found a boiled ham, a plum pudding, two dozen speckled eggs, some chocolate dagrees, spices and jams, and a dozen bottles of champagne – exactly the sort of extravagant gift that Freddie would have sent before, which only made me come to suspect that Samuel was not the true benefactor.

The following day something else arrived, a greetings card in a padded box, and the print on the front boldly embossed with a scroll that said *Santa and His Works*. There were pictures of Santa and his elves preparing the presents and toys for his sleigh, and Samuel Beresford wrote inside that he thought I would like it. And I did, very much – despite the rather juvenile theme, and an all too obvious lack of romance – but I was inspired to take up a pen and concoct some stories of my own – something for the very young to read.

By then, we all knew of the birth to come.

Two more letters followed on, both of them set several weeks apart, their content brief and businesslike, no more than polite enquiries asking after our general welfare and whether or not Pearl's child was born. I suspected he asked for someone else though, again, no specific mention was made, except when he said how busy he was, overseeing the running of the firm in lieu of Freddie's continuing absence, and making profuse apologies for the fact that remittances owed to Papa might be the subject of delay.

Too late did I read that last part aloud, for Papa, who was more alert that day, became distressed at his friend's disappearance, of which until then not a word had been spoken. He fretted I might leave for London again, the great detective that I was, and it took several hours to convince him that I had no such intention. I am not proud to have told a lie, but the masterstroke to soothe his mind was when I came up with some wild fabrication about Freddie having gone travelling through Arabia and India. It was a ridiculous notion, but Freddie must have gone *somewhere*, and *if* abroad then I felt quite sure it would be to exotic realms – Freddie wearing his Turkish sleeping cap! And while I was smiling at such a thought, almost come to believe my own story true, all at once I remembered what Freddie had done and how he had ruined my mother's life, finding myself on the verge of tears and making a silent promise never to think of the man again.

Samuel Beresford I did not want to forget. Very often, when alone in my bed, I tried to imagine him being there, such feverish, dancing, breathless scenes, even worse than Elijah's sketches of Pearl – every one of which had been returned while we were still in Burlington Row, being hidden again in the bundle of clothes retrieved when I visited Dolphin House, and with me putting on the convincing pretence of never having discovered them. But my own secret yearning, that went unrequited. I stopped listening out for the postman's horn, my emotions used up on other things, what with Papa's condition worsening so and, even though she is better now, Pearl's confinement proved a great strain on us all. I confess there were times when both she and Papa seemed to exist in other worlds, when I started to think that Kingsland House had become another asylum of sorts. And yes, I am ashamed to say, but whenever I saw my brother weep I began to think it might have been best if we'd left Pearl behind in Chiswick House.

Looking back, I suppose I was jealous, resenting Pearl – who my brother loved – who had taken my place at our mother's breast. It was something I thought of very much when little

Angel was first born, purring and snuffling at the teat, sucking his mother's madness out. But then, by the day of the picnic, I looked upon Pearl with affection again. How could anyone not be beguiled, to hear the infectious delight in her laugh, to see the shining in her eyes, and her lovely hair almost grown to her shoulders, though never so fair as it was before, and sometimes, when caught in a certain light, it gleamed with deeper auburn hues – though *if* there was a likeness to Osborne Black that was something never spoken of. Who would wish to break the magic spell that had caused Pearl's transformation, the outcome of which now lay at her side, the baby boy, but six weeks old, whose nature was all serenity, who, having woken from his sleep, now cooed like the prettiest little dove and who, so his doting father insisted, had smiled for the very first time.

'That'll be wind.' Trust Ellen Page to take my brother's romantic whim and reduce it to something as prosaic as that. 'It'll be indigestion, or else the bowels. You'll need to change that babby now.'

Actually, she may have been right, going by the odour then wafting round. But Elijah was adamant, lifting the baby up in his arms, exclaiming, 'No . . . look! He's doing it again! He's definitely smiling. Papa shall have the final say.'

At first, Papa only nodded. His rheumy eyes were gazing down at what Elijah held so near, and then in a voice grown reedy and small – 'The image of his great-grandfather.'

'And bound to go breaking many hearts,' Ellen Page was quick to add, giving what I thought a too-knowing nod. But whatever it was she meant to imply there was more than one broken heart that day.

Papa sighed. His head lolled to one side. It was something he used to do all the time – dozing off like that in the blink of an eye – and while Ellen cleared the empty plates and Pearl carried the child upstairs to feed, Elijah and I thought to go for a walk. Normally, we would take Papa, pushing him through the country lanes before the doctor was due to arrive. But that day, we did not disturb him. He looked contented and peaceful.

When I touched his forehead the skin was warm, tinged with pink from the last setting rays of the sun – and really it was not so very strange for his body to be as still as that, for an oddity of his condition was that despite how he trembled when awake, when sleeping, or when newly woken, Papa's limbs would be rigid, as if cast in stone, cramping and painful, requiring great concentration before he could will them to move again.

So, we left him alone in the garden, and only when we came back home did we find Ellen waiting at the gate – and God forgive me, when I heard her news, I thought it was a blessing.

Later, when the doctor had gone, Elijah expressed the same sentiment. He said, 'Lily, do you think it wicked of me . . . to say my first thought was the baby. When I knew it was Papa I felt relieved. And now I will have to bear that guilt. To think I wished dear Papa dead.'

'You did not . . .' I broke off, for a moment unable to go on, trying to swallow back the tears. If I cried I thought I should never stop. 'I hardly know how we shall bear his loss, but Papa suffered for much too long. And Angel brought him joy, I know. A great-grandson to carry on his name.'

We stared a long time at each other's eyes. And then my brother left me alone, to be with his son, to be with Pearl.

That evening, in Papa's study, I lifted the ivory box from the desk, the one full of the 'treasures' we used to collect. I lifted the lid to add one more, that portrait of Gabriel as a boy. And then I went into the drawing room to sit by the bed where Papa lay, his corpse now washed by Ellen Page and dressed in that musty old-fashioned suit that he'd worn when we visited Cremorne – where Papa's hands had trembled so.

They would not tremble any more. They were cold. They were still upon his breast, where I would place the ivory box beneath those rigid fingers, to be buried with Papa in his grave.

But before that final act, I thought to look inside once more, to remove our adoption certificate, and the yellowed old letter from Frederick Hall. Of course, I knew very well by then that Freddie's first Coram encounter with us had not been the shock he pretended. Even so, I was not prepared for the final discovery yet to be made – the thing I would have seen before had Papa not woken from his sleep to find me sitting at his desk, having opened a book's marbled covers and found those papers stuffed inside.

This time, Papa would not open his eyes, or urge me to destroy those things. This time, I would read what I'd missed before, what had been hidden beneath Freddie's letter. The reply that Papa had composed. The answer that was never sent.

Frederick – your letter comes as a great surprise, not to say an insult.

You say I must act without delay with regard to the fate of these bastard twins, which you claim as my responsibility.

Don't you realise I know everything, and have done since the night of Rose's death?

The day I laid her in the ground I wanted no more than to follow. I felt nothing but hatred in my heart when I stood there and watched your show of grief, the man who had seduced my wife and then thrown her off without a thought. Yes, she told me, Frederick. Do not think to bluff your ignorance. She told me with her dying breaths. She told me that you had her swear never to breathe a living word, owing to the great 'affection' in which you held her husband.

Well, was it affection, Frederick? Or was it only avarice, the love of the money that you have made from publishing a cuckold's work?

Can you begin to imagine the shock! To know that I had been deceived, that the child I'd longed for all those years had been fathered instead by Frederick Hall! When she begged me to raise that boy as my own I agreed because of my love for her, because Gabriel looked so much like Rose, her spirit somehow kept alive. Had he borne any stronger resemblance to you I cannot say what I would have done – but perhaps it would have been better for all to have left him with you in Burlington Row, because that is where he went in the end, when you offered him employment there, his precious life then being lost as surely as Rose's was before.

Do you ever think of her today? Somehow I doubt it very much. But I do, every moment since her death. How could I leave her flesh and blood, the grandchildren she should have known, to fester in some orphanage? You may speak of Sacred Providence, but know—

Know what? There the letter had come to its end, uncompleted, unsigned, undelivered. What had Papa written in its place? Had he simply gone on with the masquerade, pretending Gabriel his own? Had there been some sort of compromise with Freddie allowed to visit us, but never more than once a year, and for us never to know the truth? And yet, Papa kept this letter – this letter he'd wanted me to burn – this letter that trembled in my hands, grown damp and spotted with my tears. My breast was racked with heaving sobs – to think of things done, and things unsaid – to think of how selfless Papa had been – to think of affections I'd misunderstood when touched by the hands of Frederick Hall. How blind I had been to the obvious signs, even now to the threads of silver hair growing in either side of Elijah's head!

Had Papa also seen that brand, the sign of the guilt of the changeling child; one of three cuckoo eggs laid in his nest? And yet there was not one ounce of reproach that ever fell from Papa's lips – those lips now silent, marbled blue when I leaned in to kiss them.

I placed the letter back in the box, that secret to go to Papa's grave, my brother never to be told. And then, my long night's vigil began, during which I told Papa many things. I told him I would never forget the kindness he had shown to me. I told him that I loved him best, and I wished his blood flowed through my veins.

PEARL

My name is written in my eyes, if you have eyes to see it there.

From *The Water-Babies* by Charles Kingsley

When Elijah lifted the baby up, he was brimming with pride and excitement. He said, 'Look, Papa! Look, Angel is smiling!'

Augustus was in his big bath chair with curtains of ivy draped around, and I wanted to cherish that moment for ever, as vivid as any photograph. But now I wish I could forget – how Lily stood up from the table, stooping forward to peer at the baby and say, 'Yes, Papa . . . he really is!'

She took the old man's hand in hers, looking into his eyes for any response, although by then it was very rare for Augustus to have any memories left, sometimes not even knowing his name. But gazing from her to Elijah he gave a strangely mournful smile. I felt quite sure that he was 'there'. I sensed the mood in the garden change when he pulled his hand from Lily's grasp, reaching out for the child in the basket instead. I'm sure the others thought it affection, the way his finger wavered so while straining to touch my Angel's cheek – how it jabbed from the baby, then up to Elijah, and then away, into empty air, as if at something invisible. He kept doing that over and over again. He was gulping, dribbling, swallowing hard, and after a little time was spent in working cracked lips to form the words, he finally said in a voice so weak that we had to strain our ears to hear – 'The image . . . of . . . his great-grandfather.'

Lily and Elijah were laughing, caught up in this little game they played. But I did not laugh with them at that. There was something in the old man's tone. It made my blood freeze. My flesh prickled and crawled, for I sensed he did not refer to himself. And yes, I was glad when he fell asleep, when I went on upstairs to feed the child.

Elijah came to say goodbye. He and Lily were going out for a walk. He'd been wanting to pick some flowers that he'd seen growing wild in the lanes before to weave a garland for Angel's head, for one of a series of photographs to complement stories that Lily was writing – all based upon an orphaned babe who'd been left in a forest and raised by elves.

The Lost Children, that's what she called it; and every chapter written down she read to Augustus and asked for advice, even though he did little but sigh and nod. From the random snatches overheard I should once have loved to hear that tale, when I was still a child myself. But listening through an adult's ears, I found it to be somewhat frightening, interwoven with threads of sinister threat, with its witches and ogres who hide in the woods, and caverns which lie in the deepest of oceans where mermaids are caged by monsters with tridents, their tongues cut out, their hair shorn off, never knowing the sun or its warmth again.

Whatever Lily may say on the matter, the story's origins are clear, and Elijah's sketches suit her themes, being dark and tangled and intricate with a melancholy wistful tone. And those works based on Angel's photographs, which at first I was only charmed to see, now they make me fearful for my son. Those pictures are too otherworldly, you might really believe him a changeling child, so fey does my little Angel look – something half human, something half myth, too much like me, or what I had once been when I wore a crown of flowers and shells.

So, when Elijah mentioned that garland I found myself suddenly crying out, 'I want Angel to be a normal child, not made into an object of art and illusion.'

Elijah looked at me queerly then, but only for a moment before he went on to say, 'I'm sorry, Pearl. I understand.'

I'm not sure he does. I know that Elijah loves me. He

humours me constantly. Wherever I am he tiptoes round as if there are eggshells on the floor. He thinks I brood on morbid things. I know he fears for my sanity. But the real seed of my distress is simply the fear that *he* is obsessed. I don't want him to be like Osborne Black, creating the same thing again and again.

And I can tiptoe too. My ugly webbed feet tread so lightly that those eggshells will never begin to break, to reveal the secrets that I hide – and what possible good would it do to tell what I'd read about after the old man's death, when Elijah went off to the undertaker's to make some final arrangements, when he brought a newspaper back to the house, wanting to find the correct address to which to send a telegram, to place an announcement in *The Times* and report on the death of Augustus Lamb – even though Lily was reticent, asking, 'Why should we make it public like that? Doesn't everyone know who needs to know?'

'It's only right,' Elijah responded. 'Papa's work was very popular. There may well be people from his past, professional acquaintances, or friends . . .'

'By which you mean Frederick Hall!' her voice cut in. She was bitter and raging, 'Why should we care if he knows or not? I wish he was dead instead of Papa!'

'Frederick Hall is not the only one who may wish to know of Papa's death . . .' Elijah's temper was barely restrained, 'who might want to attend the funeral. But *if* he turns out to be one of them, it will be his chance to show respect, and why should we deny him that?'

I had never seen Lily behave like that, banging her fist on the table and shouting, 'He is the very last man on earth I would want to come anywhere near this house, after everything he did to Papa . . . to our mother . . . and to us as well!'

'He was good to us once. We loved him. Papa would want us to make amends and . . .'

'Why?' She looked aghast, staring hard at her brother then,

and speaking in such steely tones. 'Because you always loved *him* best?'

'Do you resent my feelings so?' Elijah stiffened and looked away. Lines of remorse dug deep in his brow and his eyes were brimming, full of tears. But it was Lily who sobbed, rushing into her brother's arms, her face buried in his breast while she begged for his forgiveness.

There were no more remonstrations. It was only by chance that, an hour or so later, when Elijah and Lily set off for a walk – to go to the village post office, from where they would send the telegram – I took up that copy of *The Times*. I was greedy to read of the outside world. Samuel Beresford sometimes wrote to us but he mentioned very little of note, and perhaps he had chosen to take the view that ignorance might well be bliss. But now, I know about Frederick Hall. I saw his name in those newspaper pages, the pages through which the others but glanced, their minds taken up with the funeral.

This evening, the weather has changed again. I don't complain when Lily comes in from the post office and suggests that we make up some of the fires, fretting as she does over the baby's health, concerned that he might chance to take a chill. And now, when I sit in the bedroom again, with Angel sleeping in his cot, well warmed by the flames in the little hearth, I feed the fire with the newspaper pages, crumpled twists that hiss and shrink, curled into ashy black ribbons of dust. But when I come to that one page, the one with the name of Frederick Hall, I cannot bring myself to destroy it. I fold it neatly, once, twice, three times, and place it in my pocket. I will keep it there, like the grit in a pearl. I will think on this matter a little more. And then, perhaps – after the funeral—

I have never been to a funeral. The church in Kingsland is small and plain. I like its homely friendliness. I like the smell, of lilies and wax, and the plain wooden pews and the stars that are painted up on the ceiling as if God and his angels are floating there. Is there an angel called Stella?

Elijah looks only straight ahead. Lily keeps looking left, then right, then back through the small crowd of mourners, which is mainly comprised of Ellen Page surrounded by her relatives. Augustus forged no friendships here. But he had several correspondents, and a great many letters have arrived at the house since that day when the notice went up in *The Times*.

One morning when Elijah was out, when Lily answered a knock at the door, I listened from the floor above and heard her give a muffled response, a 'thank you', and then, 'leave it there in the porch'.

Being curious, I went to look down from the landing and saw her holding a small white card. She was tearing it up into little scraps – and when Angel woke, mewling to be fed, when alerted to my presence there, Lily glanced up with a look on her face from which I could only then recoil, afraid of what was in her eyes, which were glittering, angry, bright with tears.

That memory – my trance-like state – is now broken by the vicar's voice as he calls out the number of a hymn. Much rustling of paper pages around me, and then the creaking of the door that leads into the church from the outer porch, where a chill blast of wind comes rushing in, causing church candles to gutter and dip, to send plumes of smoke wafting over the coffin. I hear Ellen Page give a stifled groan, after which she cries out, 'God save his poor soul and send all the demons down into Hell.' And, as if that is not bad enough, when Lily looks over her shoulder again she suddenly thrusts out one of her arms, almost waking Angel held in mine, grabbing at her brother's sleeve and whispering in urgent tones that surely everyone must hear, 'Elijah – he's here! It's Frederick Hall. He's standing at the back of the church . . . by the painting of the Scapegoat.'

I don't believe her, not for a moment. But all through the hymn's duration – the one about Lords and shepherds and sheep – Elijah keeps craning his neck around before giving a shrug and a shake of his head, after which he answers my questioning gaze, murmuring softly in my ear, 'Lily is imagining things.'

I think she is simply mistaken, for when we follow the coffin outside I notice two strange gentlemen who sit in a pew at the back of the church. They do not appear to belong in these parts. They have weary expressions and rumpled clothes as if they have travelled quite some way. Surely, it is they who Lily saw, whose entrance led to that blasting draught.

Out in the graveyard, beside the grave, even the weather sings its lament. The rain thrashes down on umbrellas and hats. Skirts and ribbons are snapping like whips. Hailstones batter loud on the coffin lid, where all of the flowers are flattened and bruised. It is a shame. But then I think those balls of ice look like little diamonds, a blessing, a gift for Augustus Lamb wherever he walks in other realms, and perhaps there are fairies who skip at his side, and mermaids who swim through the oceans of stars, just as they did in the tales he wrote.

A week has gone by since that dreary day when we said goodbye to Augustus Lamb, since when the skies have not lifted once, constantly grey and oppressive they are. The evenings seem to fall too fast, this month of August too dismal and dark. Does it also mourn its namesake's loss?

The gloom reminds me of Dolphin House, so much so that, on occasions, when I hear the scratch of a mouse in the skirtings, or the pattering thrash of the rain on the vine, or its rustling leaves at the window frames, I find myself thinking of Osborne again; the scratch of his pencil on paper. I cannot concentrate to read and no one is here to divert my thoughts – with Elijah gone to Hereford to speak with his lawyers about the will, with Lily locked in her silent grief, still busy at work on her storybook. She says it is peculiar but she senses Augustus dictating the words, which often come faster than she can think.

She does not even notice when I get up to leave the room, carrying Angel in my arms. I go to the kitchen and find Ellen

Page. The old woman's eyes are swollen and red and I fear that we have neglected her, so I sit for a while and chat, chat, chat, and drink some tea and eat the warm biscuits that Ellen has baked. But, oh, how she prattles on, and having heard most of her gossip before I find myself gazing out through the window, dismayed to see clouds growing darker still. I suppose my nerves must be on edge but when the kettle boils again I jump at its whistle, a piercing screech. A wonder the baby doesn't wake. I desperately need to go outside, no matter how damp and unpleasant the day. I want to take some fresh air in my lungs, to stop this suffocation I feel.

I leave Ellen with Angel rocked in her arms and promise that I will not be long, only intending a stroll through the gardens. But such a compulsion comes over me as I walk across the squelching lawns, taking the overgrown shrubbery path that leads me back to the stream again, where the waters are high and rushing fast, and the branches around so heavy with moisture its soft susurration wets my hair, tickling down the back of my gown. More than once my feet slip on greasy mud and send little stones to skitter and fall, splashing down into the brook below – and that's when I notice the wreath in the water, snagged on some twigs caught between the rocks. A funeral garland it seems to be. I think it must be made of wax. No roses could be so perfectly formed. But why is it floating in the stream? Could it have blown all this way from the grave?

Crossing the bridge is treacherous. I have to grab on to the rail for support, those splintery planks so slimed with moss. But my progress is swift on the other side, striding along through the meadow's crushed grasses, the motley green scrub of the dandelions, in no time arrived at the churchyard gate. But the grating whine that I can hear does not come from its rusty hinges. That sound is made by the weathercock, high up on the church's tower. It whirls, first one way then the other, caught in a sudden rising breeze – even though lower down the air is still and a mist clings to gravestones and shadowy yews that guard the narrow gravelled path, at the end of which my eye comes to rest on the grave that has been most recently turned, where all of the flowers laid on top are wilted, their colours dissolved by rain. But then, the whole scene is in monochrome, like an old and faded photograph. And perhaps that is why I don't see him at first, dressed as he is in black and grey, the man who is kneeling on the grass – not at the grave of Augustus Lamb but the one just beside it, the one so much older, the one that contains his wife and son.

The man is placing something down. It looks to be a single rose. And then, he stands, and he walks this way, and without even thinking I slip my fingers into my pocket to touch the worn edge of the newspaper cutting, and I think to myself – *So, Frederick Hall . . . are the twins now to know your destiny?*

LILY

The rain had stopped, but threatened more. The air was too warm and oppressive, the kind of sluggish, dreary day that makes you feel itchy and dirty and ill. I almost wished I had stayed in bed. I was tired. I was restless and irritable, my nights too disturbed since Papa's death, and even when I did drift off, every whine or scream the baby made, that rose up through the floor from the bedroom below, filled me with the illogical fear that he might be the next to be taken.

Oh, how I fretted over that child, his every snuffle and sneeze and fart! How strange that his mother could be less affected, all languor, all fluidity, her surface unruffled and still as a pond. But still waters run deep – or so Ellen says, just as she used to say of Elijah. The stillest of waters, the darkest of secrets.

My brother was out of the house again, this time having travelled to Hereford, to visit Papa's solicitor and attend the reading of the will. I felt no imperative to attend, having seen the copy in Papa's study, knowing by then that the house would be shared, equally, between the two of us, along with the rest of Papa's estate, which proved to be a considerable sum, much more than we could have ever imagined considering his quiet and frugal existence, with no flashy show of material things – so unlike the gloss of Frederick Hall.

I was glad of my brother's absence that day. By the evening, when Elijah returned, I was more settled in my mind, able to tell him of the news that I had learned that afternoon, the news which left me dazed and distraught, when barely five minutes before I had been filled with such levity, having completed my storybook, my one and only remaining task to return to the very first page again and make my dedication there – *In memory of Augustus Lamb. The dearest friend I ever had.*

I set down Papa's silver pen and stretched out my arms and arched my back and looked at the ceiling for a very long time – resolving that when the morning came every one of those cobwebs should be brushed down. I stood up and walked to one of the windows, opening it, pushing back the vine, still obscuring our world with its dull green glow, but not what bloomed beside the frame, very late, but the very first rose of that summer, the greeny white bud almost luminous against the dark gloss of the ivy leaves. Quite perfect it was, as if made of wax, though no doubt when the rain started up again those petals would be ruined.

The wreath that arrived at the house one day had flowers that would never fade. But they were not placed on Papa's grave. I took them down to the stream instead. I flung them into the water, mortified when they did not float away but lodged between rocks by the side of the grotto. What an irony that was, to see Frederick Hall's flowers beside Frederick Hall's shells, the gifts with which he bought our love. And what had he written upon the card – the one delivered with the wreath? Only the tritest of lines – '*With my deepest sympathies for your loss.*'

Our loss! How dare that selfish man presume to imagine the loss that we felt? How dare he send white roses like that when, as far as Papa had been concerned, white roses symbolised his wife. And thinking of that, and how Papa had loved and been deceived, I did not mind the prick of the thorns when I reached through the window to pluck the rose, making my way to the kitchen, meaning to leave through the back garden door to take that flower to Papa's grave – a gift unsullied by Frederick Hall.

With my free hand already on the latch I gave a little cry of alarm to catch out of the corner of my eye a shifting shape in the shadows – feeling foolish to see it was Ellen Page.

Since the day of Papa's funeral she'd come to the house less often. When she did come, she gave us no warning, except for the smell of new-baked bread, or the apple pies she placed in the range – which was where she was sitting that afternoon, her skirts ruched high over saggy darned stockings, and while sniffing the odour of mustard and lard then rising up to greet my nose, I said, 'Oh, Ellen, you startled me. Are your knees sore with all of this dampness?'

Expecting another diatribe on the state of her rheumaticky joints, all I received was a black gummy smile, and then a little jerk of her head to nod at the creature in her lap, who squeaked like a baby bird in a nest crying out for its mother to bring a worm – and as I could never bear to hear the slightest whine from Angel's lips, I asked, 'Is he hungry? Is he well? Shall I go and look for Pearl?'

'You might think to call her to come back in . . . she went out to the gardens, to get some air.'

I thought Pearl might walk to the grave with me; that we might have the chance to talk for a while. She'd been acting very oddly of late, beginning to speak then breaking off. She'd stand in the open study door and watch me while I sat and worked, her fingers plucking at her skirts. I worried she might be getting ill, about to take a turn for the worse, starting up with imaginings again. But in the event I need not have feared – though it was a shock to find her like that – and the man who was walking at her side, both of them coming up the drive as I stood beside the laurel hedge, as still as a statue, my mouth gawping open when Pearl called out, 'Look who I found in the graveyard! He saw the announcement put up in *The Times*. He wanted to come and visit us.'

When Samuel Beresford took my hand the blood was pounding in my ears, and through that beat I heard him say, 'Hello, Lily. You look very well. I would hardly have known you . . . the same with Pearl.'

He glanced at the rose in my other hand, gave a slight sniff and then lifted a cloth to wipe his nose, which was red and sore – just as it had been the first time I saw him when plagued by the pollen in Cremorne. But very soon, he was going on, 'I must express my apologies . . . not arriving in time for the funeral.'

'Frederick Hall was there,' I said, 'though I wonder that he had the nerve. At least he did not have the gall to show his face at the side of the grave.'

'But he couldn't have come,' Samuel replied, brown eyes looking troubled and filled with confusion.

'No, he couldn't,' Pearl interjected, her face grown pale and strained, and such a look of guilt in her eyes when she plunged a hand into her pocket and said, 'I have something that you should read. I thought it was best not to speak before. But now . . . now that Samuel is here.'

She held out a newspaper cutting, very creased it was and the ink all worn in the places where the folds had been, but nothing so bad that I couldn't make out the story that was printed there – further stunned to read the date – the same as Papa's funeral. Who would ever believe such a thing had it not been set down in black and white? But then who would believe I had seen a ghost, for still, to this very day, I would swear on the Bible that Frederick Hall really had been there, in Kingsland church – even though he had died some hours before.

The shock of it caused my mind to reel, dropping the paper, dropping the rose, and the screams I heard I thought my own, not knowing then that Ellen Page had staggered out to find us, the baby wailing in her arms, and so loud he might almost wake the dead.

366

The Cheyne Walk Murder Trial

Yesterday morning the convict Frederick Hall was executed
within the precincts of the gaol of Newgate for the murder of
'Tip' Thomas, a notorious criminal and delinquent. The
capital sentence was executed in the presence of the Lord
Mayor Alderman Phillips, and Sheriff Knight, Sheriff Bref-
fit, Mr. Under-Sheriff Baylis, Mr. Under-Sheriff Crawford,
Mr. Sidney Smith, the Governor, and the Rev. Lloyd Jones,
the Ordinary of Newgate. A limited number of strangers and
representatives of the Press were also present. The gallows
had been erected within the gaol yard, and was peculiar in
construction and appearance; it being roofed over, lighted
with lamps at each end, and having a deep pit, over which a
chain and noose were suspended. In front of the scaffold,
but well away from it, the spectators were placed; and a
picked body of the City of London Police were in attendance
to maintain order if necessary. As the clock of the
neighbouring church of St. Sepulchre chimed the hour of 8
a procession which had been formed within the prison
emerged into the open space leading to the scaffold. First
came the Governor of Newgate; then the Sheriffs and Under-
Sheriffs in their official robes, and carrying their wands of
office; next the convict, with the executioner – Marwood –
by his side; and lastly the Reverend the Ordinary, reading
as he went the opening sentences of the burial service. The
prisoner, who had apparently been dressed with scrupulous
care, bore himself at this awful crisis with conspicuous
fortitude; and as he stepped upon the drop, fronting the
spectators, his handsome features were lighted up with an
expression of resignation. After the white cap had been

drawn over his face, and while the noose was being adjusted, the heaving of deep emotion was distinctly visible through the folds of the cap. The necessary preparations were speedily made by the executioner, and all things being in readiness, the drop fell at a touch or signal with an awful shock, echoing for a moment or two all over the prison yard. The body fell a depth of exactly 6 feet 3 in. – that being, by a coincidence, the convict's own height. Judging from the tension of the rope for some considerable interval after the bolt had been drawn the prisoner must have 'died hard', as the saying goes. After the body had hung the accustomed interval, it was taken down, and with Mr. John Rowland Gibson, the prison surgeon, having certified that life was then extinct, it was placed in a coffin and subjected, later in the day, to a coroner's inquest, in compliance with recent legislation. Towards evening, in accordance with long usage, the remains were buried within the precincts of the gaol, that being an integral part of the sentence. A black flag was hoisted, conformably with the statutory practice of late years, from the roof of the prison to indicate to the outside world that the dread sentence of the law had been carried out. The Governor afterwards read, in the presence of the Sheriff and Under-Sheriffs and the representatives of the Press, a written statement which the convict had placed in his hands at 11 o'clock on the previous evening, before retiring to rest. In that, said the Governor – using the convict's own language – he appealed to the loving kindness of a merciful God that his transgressions might be blotted out, for the sake of that blessed Saviour whom he had so long neglected. He then acknowledged the justice of his punishment, and said he deserved it, though he did not absolutely confess that he had committed the crime. He afterwards expressed his sincere thanks to the Governor and all the officers of the prison for their attention, and to his many friends and relations – known and unknown – who he hoped would think of him in their prayers; and he

368

concluded by commending his soul to the hands of that Almighty Father who was the protector of the widow and the fatherless.

PEARL

'But remember,' said the witch, 'once you've taken human form, you can never be a mermaid again. You can never come back into the water . . . or to your father's castle.'

From 'The Little Mermaid' by Hans Christian Andersen

When Elijah comes home and hears the news his emotions are barely contained. He turns on Samuel. He remonstrates, 'Why didn't you write and tell us before? He was innocent! He could have been saved!'

Samuel remains calm but is clearly distressed, 'You think I have no conscience! You think I have not spent months on end agonising over this? The fact is that Freddie made me swear never to tell you while he lived . . . even though there was always the risk that you might read the stories in the press.'

'We rarely bought any papers. We shut ourselves off from the outside world, and now . . .' Elijah's eyes are damp. He picks up a glass to throw at the wall and a hundred little glittering shards scatter like rain on the boards below.

That act of violence shocks me. I think of a mirror smashed down to the floor in my crow's-nest room in Cheyne Walk. I think of what happened to Monkey, then Tip. I think that since leaving London last year we have lived in a bubble of make-believe, our happiness bursting, about to dissolve. Meanwhile, Elijah is all agitation, pacing the room, demanding to know, 'What happened to Freddie? Did he say?'

Samuel answers glumly, 'Freddie's confession was well worked out; employing those facts that he had learned when we gathered together in Burlington Row. He told me that when he left his house . . . no doubt fired with the heat of the brandy he'd drunk . . . he decided to redeem his crimes, hoping to gain some forgiveness, from Isabella . . . from Lily . . . from you.

'He travelled by cab to Chelsea, telling the driver not to wait when arriving at the House of the Mermaids, and there, when the bell brought no response, and finding the street gate firmly locked, Freddie ventured instead to the back of the house, where he scaled a wall . . . though God knows how, with those spikes of glass being stuck in the mortar. But once that obstacle was breached, despite being somewhat bloodied, he had very little difficulty in finding the broken orangery window . . . at the same time shocking some drunken whores who were wailing over the monkey's corpse.

'When their panic had subsided some, Freddie assured them he meant no harm and asked where he might chance to find their pimp . . . thus testing their intelligence. One said that Tip Thomas must have gone out, that he'd been in an agitated mood before sending them off for a night on the town, and the state of poor Monkey was there as proof. It seemed that none of them had spied the velvet throw on the floor near by, and any scattered blood around they must have imagined belonged to the ape. But Freddie knew what was beneath, and when he saw the metal file . . . well, that was enough to aid his plan.'

Samuel sighs and pauses a while. 'Freddie insisted his mind was quite clear. When he was done with his frenzied attack he pulled off the throw to reveal what carnage lay beneath, and every one of those whores convinced that she had witnessed a murder . . . right there, before her very eyes, the slaughter of a sleeping man. It must have been pandemonium. But in due course the police were called, to whom Freddie willingly confessed, though refusing to say another word regarding a motive for the crime. Later, in court, it was presumed that he must have been subject to blackmailing scams . . . a matter later qualified when some brothel ledgers were produced, with accounts going back for many years.'

Samuel stares down at the glass on the floor, as if unable to meet our eyes. 'Suffice to say, Freddie was implicated in scandalous matters of varying degrees. Some pornographic literature was proved to have been supplied by him.' He wiped a hand across his brow. 'I've done my best. I really have. But the business has suffered terribly.'

Samuel is done. He looks all used up, and the rest of us are dumbstruck – until Lily murmurs, as if to herself, 'But he could have hired the best legal advice. He only had to tell the truth. The judge might have shown some clemency.'

Samuel's reply is abrupt. 'And have Isabella accused of the murder . . . and tell the whole world that you and your brother were born in a brothel . . . shaming your names for evermore! No, there was nothing to be done with a hope of saving Frederick Hall, because Frederick Hall did not wish to be saved.'

Another summer has come around. Mostly, we still live in Kingsland House, though occasionally we travel to London, where Elijah is gaining great success, particularly with his photographs. He has visited Buckingham Palace to capture the royal children. Many portraits of the lesser known are displayed in prestigious galleries – this summer, the Victoria and Albert Museum, and there Mr Millais, the artist, bought the print in which Lily once posed in a tomb, pretending to be Ophelia. The focus was a little blurred but that lent it a somewhat ghostly tone – and it seems that ghosts are quite 'the thing'.

I myself have developed a passion for plants, and sometimes Elijah photographs them. If only he could capture the smells! The gardens in Kingsland have been transformed, no longer such a wilderness, though I did quite like its rambling lurks, all those secret places in which to hide. To have spent so many years living with no one but Osborne Black, well, it is not always easy to adapt to the bustle of family life. But I have two glasshouses in which to grow seeds, where I potter alone to my heart's content. And we have a man who tends the lawns, and this spring he cut the ivy back, which means that the house is filled with light – and the rambling rose is thriving still. Lily says there have never been more blooms.

She keeps herself busy, still writing her stories, which Elijah continues to illustrate, and Samuel Beresford publishes them, having set up a business of his own. His office is based in Burlington Row, and the plaque that once said Hall & Co. now bears the legend Beresford Books. A percentage of the rent he pays is entailed to the Foundling Hospital, following the precedent that was set by Frederick Hall before, who, along with Augustus Lamb, stipulated that all of his earthly possessions be equally shared between the twins. But the house that belonged to Frederick Hall, the one that stands opposite Beresford Books – that property has now been sold. No one wished to live there.

Some books on the shelves Elijah burned; those that had not been taken away and used in court as evidence. But some paintings were kept and now hang on our walls – in Herefordshire, where Lily has one above her bed: 'Isabella . . . The Pot of Basil'.

Elijah has taken a London house for those times when he needs to visit town. It almost feels like the countryside, being south of the river in Camberwell Grove, and I do my best to be content, but whenever we are staying there I find myself missing Kingsland House, the place where I feel protected.

In London, I find myself thinking too much about the artist, Osborne Black. Such things are still said about the man. Such things are said about Pearl, his 'wife' – and sometimes even to my face. But then I bear little resemblance now to the child nymph with the golden hair whose image hung high on Academy walls. I charade as the wife of Elijah Lamb, and *her* hair is a great deal darker. When in town, her husband calls her Blanche – Blanche for the whiteness of her skin, as white as the lustre of a pearl. But, however convincing this new disguise, the gossip and curiosity can never quite be wiped away because so many know that Elijah Lamb was once employed by Osborne

Black, and such rumours are spread about what occurred while Elijah lived at Dolphin House – when the young man disappeared for months, when Osborne's muse had gone insane, thereafter being put away.

Society thrives on such scandals, the delight in the ruin of great reputations. But Blanche Lamb can never be drawn on such things. Blanche Lamb has no wish to indulge in this gossip – to damn the soul of an innocent girl who, in truth, had been tainted by a corruption far worse than the blight of insanity.

But there is one story cannot be denied and that is the fate of Osborne Black, who I find myself constantly yearning to see, though I hardly know why that should be. Not after what he did to me.

We have been in Camberwell some days. Today is Angel's fourth birthday. A trip has been planned to Regent's Park, to visit the Zoological Gardens. But when the time comes for us to leave I profess to be weary and stay behind. It is not quite a lie, I hardly slept a wink all night, and being so big with child again I have grown clumsy, slow and lethargic. It is the perfect alibi, and Elijah says he understands – though my son is less forgiving.

'Mama . . . do come!' he whines at me from the open door, and when I lean forward to kiss his head, black curls are like silk against my lips. I try to keep my voice light when I answer, 'I think you shall see enough elephants without bringing one of your own!'

Angel laughs and skips off down the path, the mention of elephants quite enough to make him forget all about his mama, not even turning to see me wave. I would have waved to Lily too but she is already inside the cab, along with Samuel Beresford, and no doubt they are both deeply engrossed in discussing Lily's latest book, a discussion embellished with touches and smiles. (When we are not in London, at least twice a week he writes to her. You might almost think it a little romance – though if so it is very protracted.)

I have written some letters of my own. I have signed them as from a 'Mrs Lamb – a concerned friend and relative'. And then, last month I received a reply. It came from one of the medical men who work at the Bethlem Hospital. He invited me to visit there, and though I dread to enter those doors I want to look Osborne in the eye. I want the chance to say goodbye – a thing never properly done before.

It takes more than an hour to travel to Southwark. I fear that the cabman might be a buck, intent on diddling the fare. But the jams are very bad today and we make a diversion, along the Thames. I stare at black rippling waters. They look as heavy as lead to me, and it may be due to the imminent birth but I think of my mother so much these days, reliving the tale that Tip once told, the one written up in the Book of Events.

When the cab sets me down I am panting for breath. For a while I have to lean on some railings and when I recover my self-control I tell myself I have legs, not a tail. I tell myself I have lungs, not gills – whatever the others may once have said – whatever the artist Osborne Black was determined to try to make of me. And yet, I do feel like a fish out of water, gasping to see the vastness of Bethlem. How could anyone think to escape such a place with those high front walls like a fortress, and behind them the doming cupola – like one of the Florentine churches that Osborne frequented in Italy. And on either side are the long brick wings that are said to house more than a thousand souls. And one of those souls is Osborne Black.

The corridor is scrubbed very clean. The walls are newly painted. The doctor walking at my side tells me we live in enlightened times. He points to signs above ward doors. 'Aged and Infirm', 'Moderately Tranquil', 'Refractory' – whatever that means! He mentions the homely touches about, such as the flowers on the tabletops, the embroidered antimacassars on chairs. This is not the refuge of years gone by, of which there were horrors and terrors described, being one step away from the fires of Hell, with all those who entered condemned to burn. Even so, I hope every inmate *is* mad, not conveniently, not cruelly, 'put away'.

Now, the rattle of keys and the creak of a door and we enter a spacious airy room. It is an artist's studio! It is immaculately kept. A porcelain sink is gleaming white. Wooden shelves are well stocked with materials, the brushes, the papers, the charcoal sticks, and great piles of manila envelopes, which appear to be stuffed with photographs. There are sheets on the floor to protect the boards. They look like a sea with waves of white. Tall windows stream with a clear northern light. The lower parts of them are barred. The higher ones are opened up, but still there is no escaping the fumes; the pigments of paint, the turpentine.

'Osborne?' The doctor walks on ahead, his tone relaxed and familiar. 'Osborne, you have a visitor. She has been most anxious to visit.'

'Can't you see that I'm working?' the patient growls back.

The doctor tries to reassure, 'We are so encouraged that Osborne is working. Very few of his paintings survived – some damaged by water, some slashed with a knife during one of his psychotic episodes. But here we mean to encourage his gifts, as we do with all our unfortunates. And working helps to keep him calm.'

I know that Osborne hears him. His knuckles have clenched around his brush. But he does not stop his painting. He does not attempt to look around – though if he was a dog you would see hackles rising, instead of which the jacket he wears, an everyday jacket, quite normal attire, as if he is a perfectly normal man, living in the normal world, suddenly stretches and flattens out as the muscles beneath it flex and contract. His undiminished bulk is poised upon the edge of a stool before which an easel carries a canvas, and the form on that surface is clear to see, though the details of her face and hair have yet to be filled with colour. The painting is large and unusual in that its shape is circular, and with Osborne sitting in front like that, his tousled crown of auburn brown is auraed by the greens and blues of the vibrant willow and ivy leaves, and the tiny insects hovering, and the light spilling through, like beams of gold.

Oh, but I had forgotten his talent. So exquisite this new picture is. It almost takes my breath away. But somehow I manage to speak the words, 'Osborne . . . it is me. It is Pearl.'

'What do you say?' He spins around.

I lift the nets that fall at my face and push them back over the brim of my hat. Now, I think – *now* I have you. And yet, his expression is menacing, a look of sheer malevolence, and I find myself clutching the doctor's arm, stepping backwards towards the open door when Osborne shouts, 'Yes, go . . . get out! Get out and leave me alone, will you. All you fat women, you wealthy do-gooders who come here to see the mad artist paint. How dare you try and deceive me! How dare *you* claim to share *her* name?'

'What is he saying? What does he mean?' My thoughts must be spoken aloud for the doctor answers casually, 'A misunderstanding . . . nothing more The name is common enough, of course, but Osborne is overprotective and jealous . . . about his muse, I mean.'

'His muse?'

'Yes, Pearl! And about to begin her long day's work! You have come at the most fortuitous time. You will see how progressive the hospital is . . . permissive of certain liberties. We allow him four hours a day with her. Any more than that and he can become overstimulated. He is still prone to violent moods. You know the facts? You know his crime?'

I nod. The story is well known. A dramatic scandal. A cause célèbre. But my thoughts are diverted by the sound, the clanking jangle of the chain, one end being bolted against a wall, the other a cuff round the patient's leg. Manacled he is, like a wild beast. But then, when the doctor pulls back a drape to show what lies on the other side, Osborne's expression is tender again. Something like a trance washes over his features. There is a tangible shifting of tension as his shoulders relax, as he sighs and smiles, as he says those words that have haunted me, that will haunt me 'til my dying day,

'My mermaid . . .'

All the raging questions and blunt accusations that I had been determined to voice are suddenly lost in a surge of emotion. I feel adrift, hardly able to register the meaning of the doctor's words when he addresses this man as a child, when he asks, 'Would you like me to wind her up?'

Osborne smiles. The doctor smiles at me. He does not know I have seen her before, how I hate the grinding mechanical tick as the automaton stirs to life. The scales of her tail rustle and jerk. A buzzing there is, like wasps in a nest. The head makes a clicking as it inclines. Emerald eyes glint as they catch the light. They seem to be staring into mine, and malicious they are, victorious. But the worst of it is, the thing that makes this Pearl so real, is what falls across those budding breasts. The gleaming waves of molten gold tinged here and there with auburn lights are the hair that was stolen from my head when Osborne Black put *me* away, humiliated and shorn like a convict, left to rot in the bowels of Chiswick House.

I cannot bear to look any more. I shiver and turn my face to the wall. I think of a beach with smooth hard rocks, and the hushing suck of little waves, so cool as they ran through my fingers. I stare at my reflection, now superimposed in veils of cloud scudding grey beyond the windowpanes. What I see through that glassy drifting light is everything that Osborne hates. My heart is thumping. Blood pounds in my temples. A great gush of water breaks from my womb. It smells fishy. It trickles across the white sheeting. It is puddling, sticky, at Osborne's feet.

LILY

The child was not due for another month, though I think we should have realised, with Pearl – or Blanche as we call her in London – become so distracted and restless that morning. There was something about her demeanour that I could not put my finger on, only later reminded of how she had been in the days before little Angel's birth, when she'd wandered off to lie in the stream and imagined herself a mermaid.

This time she gave birth to a girl, and the image of her mother she was – even down to the tips of her malformed feet. But the baby was small and frail in health, which meant that we stayed in Camberwell for much longer than we had intended, which pleased me very much indeed because then I saw more of Samuel.

He was there in the Zoological Gardens when Angel grew fractious and started to cry, though up until then he'd been perfectly happy, quite thrilled to have had his birthday ride on Jumbo the famous elephant. But perhaps that was too much excitement for such a sensitive little boy, for when we arrived at the cage with the bears Angel began to grow upset, obsessed with one beast which did nothing more but lumber back and forth again, its dark eyes intense, intelligent, but seemingly lost in another world. My nephew was scowling, staring hard, his plump little fingers clutching the bars when he called in a mournful piping voice, 'Papa . . . why won't they let him free?'

'Bears can be very ferocious.' Elijah tried to divert his son by lifting him up into his arms, then swinging him on to his shoulders. And while my nephew was sitting there, I said, 'He might try to eat you for tea. Bears are terribly fond of little boys . . . sweet little boys who look like you, who smell of honey and sugar and jam.'

Normally, Angel would have laughed. Normally, Angel liked to be teased. But that day he was only frightened, struggling to get down to the ground again, stamping his feet and wailing that he wanted his mama; a tantrum that showed no signs of abating until Elijah took him home, where he came to be glad of his son's distress, finding Pearl on the point of giving birth, with a doctor already sent for and the house maid explaining the fright she'd had when hearing the doorbell jangling and finding her mistress collapsed in the porch – having only gone out for some morning air when taken with the labour pains.

All of this I came to learn when arriving back well after midnight myself, for when Elijah took Angel home Samuel persuaded me to stay, taking my hand in his to say, 'I thought we might take a trip to Cremorne.'

'Cremorne?' I felt myself torn in two, wanting no more than to have the chance of spending some time alone with him, but the prospect of going back to the place where I once saw that horrible mermaid display, where Papa had been so upset by those whores, where Samuel did little but sniff and sneeze – 'It does not hold the happiest memories,' I finally found the courage to say.

'But it does! It is where you and I first met . . . where we have unfinished business.'

As if the dancing had not been enough (although I could only manage the waltz, and then Samuel had to teach me the steps) we dined on oysters and drank champagne. But, oh, what followed after, to rise up into the heavens like that – the rushing of air – the snapping of fabric, bloated with surging blasts of heat. I was giddy with all the excitement. I felt like a child again, and how I wished that Papa was there, because Papa would be in his element, and what stories he might have concocted – of magic carpets, of horses with wings. It really was the most wonderful thing to be floating so high in that big balloon, to feel ourselves weightless, to think that if we let out one more tiny breath then we might soar yet higher and fly like the birds, our fingers stretched wide and feathery tipped, ruffled by breezes as soft as silk. And then all the fireworks around – even though I have now come to realise that every explosion held danger for us. But we were entranced, only 'oohing' and 'aahing' at all the cascading fountains of colour, colours as iridescent as jewels, like shooting stars in ebony skies, like rubies and emeralds and sapphires and pearls, every jewel mirrored back in the night-time Thames, reflected in mirrors of gleaming black before suddenly fading away to dust.

And with that excitement over and done, when our descent at last began, we leaned on the basket's creaking sides to see all the gardens spread out like a blanket, all silhouettes and glinting lights which gilded the trees and towering pagoda, and the streets filled with horses as small as ants, and the glow of the cinders still wafting around – and perhaps there was floating pollen too because Samuel was dipping a hand in his pocket, at last pulling out his handkerchief, but only a passing tickle it was, or so he was keen to assure me, his arm very casually circling my waist, drawing me closer, into his warmth, so close that I felt the beat of his heart and smelled the sweetness of his sweat, the brush of his hair as it whipped my cheek. And that was the moment we might have kissed, but for the shout of the aeronaut who was pointing to a gathering crowd, just visible through shadows then thrown down by the looming bulk of Battersea Bridge, where a great plume of white was spraying up.

'What is it?' I gasped. 'Did someone fall into the river?' *Something* was there in the water, something that looked like an upturned boat.

'I think it must be the dolphins!' Samuel exclaimed. 'I saw

them mentioned in yesterday's *Times*. There've been sightings in the Thames all week. But nothing as far upstream as this.'

'Dolphins! Real dolphins!' I started to laugh, and from our vantage point, still high, you could almost imagine two mermaids there – the quicksilver glisten, the splash of the tails, and I found myself musing upon Pearl's birth, and the book she'd once secretly shown to me, all the wonders and marvels written down, conjured up by a pimp and a brothel madam who kept a house in Cheyne Walk, which, if you looked east, you might chance to see, if every window were not steeped in blackness with the house closed up and empty now – the house where my brother and I had been born – where Pearl had been raised – where Isabella had cared for Elijah – where Tip Thomas's awful fate was met – where Frederick Hall spent his last hours of freedom before – before—

But to think of such things might drive you mad. So instead, I looked west, and there through a blurring mist of tears my eyes met Samuel Beresford's.

The Opening Of The Osborne Black Museum

The Times – September 27th 2012

This Saturday sees the long-anticipated opening of the Osborne Black Museum at 'The House of the Mermaids' in Cheyne Walk. The museum will display many of the artist's later works, which until now have been in the hands of Broadmoor Hospital, the secure institution for the criminally insane where Black died in 1899, transferred there in 1874 from the Bethlem Royal Hospital, upon which site in Southwark the Imperial War Museum now stands.

The House of the Mermaids has a fascinating history, at one point being used as a Victorian brothel, during which colourful era some murals on the inner walls are widely believed to have been painted by Black in his youth. Far cruder than his later works, these paintings still vividly demonstrate the artist's enduring obsession with mermaids. It is hoped that the murals may be conserved, though the plaster is now in a perilous state. Indeed the whole house has been subject to extensive renovation work, having been closed up for one hundred years, and now gifted to the nation by a descendant of Elijah Lamb, the illustrator and innovative photographer who once worked in Black's Chiswick studio.

The ownership of the House of the Mermaids has long been the subject of some speculation, with the local authorities taking steps towards a compulsory purchase order with plans for demolition. It was therefore quite a coincidence when the Italian actress Isabella Di Marco, who lives and works in America, came forward with 'proof' of ownership. It seems that when she inherited a family home in Italy, she discovered there a leather-bound book, along with a key to a secret compartment concealed within its covers. In that were the deeds to the House of the Mermaids, those documents claiming an ownership transferred from the name of one Mrs Amelia Hibbertson to that of simply '*Pearl – the child who was raised within these walls, who is my natural grandchild*'.

The papers cannot be verified and secure no legal entitlement, but Ms Di Marco's donation to the Osborne Black Trust (an amount as yet unspecified but rumoured to be in seven figures) has persuaded the authorities that the house has historical merit and is, therefore, worth preserving.

Clearly, the link between Osborne Black's muse, who also went by the name of Pearl, is intriguing and cannot be ignored. Yet more mysterious is the question as to how this book and certain other objects which originated in the House of the Mermaids then came to be found in Italy – in the home once owned by Elijah Lamb, Ms Di Marco's great-great-grandfather.

The actress claims no knowledge, but her silence continues the family tradition. Despite all his fame, the glamorous Elijah Lamb could never be tempted to disclose any information regarding his private life. Indeed, he was considered to be even more reclusive than his grandfather, Augustus Lamb, the well-regarded author of Victorian fairy tales, many of which are still in print, as are the stories by Lily Lamb, Elijah's twin sister, who remained a spinster for many years while heading up several charities such as Bloomsbury's Utopia House, where prostitutes were sheltered and given the means by which to reform. At the age of fifty-five, she married Sir Samuel Beresford, the well-known Victorian philanthropist and founder of Beresford Books – still an independent publishing house (which has recently reissued *The Lost Children*, Lily Lamb's book of fairy tales which has long been hailed as a classic, with a Hollywood film currently in production, in which Miss Di Marco will play the lead).

However, what has come to light is that there was a great deal of controversy regarding the extended Lamb family when, around the mid-1870s, a notorious scandal occurred in which a long-standing family acquaintance, the publisher, Frederick Hall, was found guilty of a murder which occurred in the House of the Mermaids. Within a few years of Hall's execution, Elijah, his wife Blanche and their two children left London to live in Italy, where they founded an artists' community – among its members an Italian spinster whose closeness to the artist and constant presence in his house was the subject of much gossip. Indeed, it is presumed that the Lambs indulged in what might today be described as an open marriage, with Blanche also thought to be very fond of another artist in the commune, after whom her son Angel had been named.

Tantalising though such 'tales' may be, it has been impossible to answer all questions regarding the Lambs, particularly with regard to their links to the House of the Mermaids. But the museum will display some photographs and illustrations created during the short period when Elijah worked with Osborne Black, and every one of those images shows an ethereal-looking girl who bears an uncanny resemblance to one of the painted mermaids adorning the brothel walls. The same is said of an antique automaton which again has been generously donated by the Bethlem and Broadmoor hospitals, having been an object that Osborne Black was permitted to keep during all those years of his incarceration.

Among those other paintings on show, Tate Britain has agreed to the temporary loan of Black's *The Libertine*, arguably his most famous work; an image so sensual that it caused an outrage when displayed at the Royal Academy. But surely of most interest will be the unveiling of *The Mermaid's Betrayal*. Considered to be Black's masterpiece, it shows a mermaid reclining on a beach, her tail in a small pool of water, a haunting expression on her face as she glances back over her shoulder, her striking green eyes brimming with tears as they meet directly those of the viewer. It is a most unnerving work, and though it bears the same brooding darkness and water theme ubiquitous in all of Black's other work, this painting is itself unique in that the mermaid is fully grown rather than in pre-pubescent form. She has the swollen belly and breasts of one in the late stages of pregnancy, and another anomaly is that whereas Black's other models all have waving golden curls, this one has hair much darker.

Who is she? There are many who claim that the mermaid's eyes bear a striking resemblance to those of Blanche, Elijah's wife – as do those of every other mermaid that Osborne Black ever painted. Some photographs of Blanche (sadly all of them in monochrome) will be on exhibit alongside the canvas inviting a direct comparison. However, it must be stated that there are some letters on display in which Blanche Lamb categorically denies having ever met Osborne Black. There is also the indisputable fact that *The Mermaid's Betrayal* was completed a good decade after Blanche and Elijah left England to live in Italy, from where she never returned.

A great many of Black's later works were lost when his Chiswick studio flooded. (*The Libertine* was still on display on the walls of the Royal Academy.) It was also at this time that his muse was said to have disappeared, and though no confirmation has been found she was rumoured to have gone insane, committed to a private asylum from which no records have survived. However, contemporary newspaper reports allege that inmates were abused, with talk of some suspicious deaths; tragedies which have since been confirmed when, during renovation works being carried out in the gardens, a series of unmarked graves were found. Whatever the fate of Osborne's muse, the artist's mind was surely

386

affected, leading to the episode when he murdered the asylum's superintendent. The incident was a cause célèbre and involved the victim's walking stick being violently broken into two, upon which the poor fellow was then impaled. Somewhat gruesomely that cane was preserved and is now another museum exhibit – along with a metal file said to have been the weapon employed in the crime committed by Frederick Hall.

For those of a squeamish disposition other rooms contain pleasanter *objets d'art* which survived the flood at Dolphin House. Donated anonymously, their provenance has been verified from those photographs made by Elijah Lamb during his brief employment there. There are also some of Black's earlier landscapes, ceramics from the Middle East, and marble statues from Italy.

Of those antique 'treasures' preserved in the brothel, there are some magnificent four-poster beds, two elaborately carved ship's figureheads, and some early examples of 'stereoscopes' through whose three-dimensional lenses may be viewed mildly titillating scenes – with those pornographic items found now stored in the British Library. More aesthetic is the stuffed cockatoo that perches in a golden cage, and a perfectly preserved little 'crown' made of silk flowers and silver shells.

THE END

The Real Historical Characters Who Have Influenced Those In Elijah's Mermaid

The characters in *Elijah's Mermaid* are all entirely fictional, though there is now and then some reference to real historical personages, such as the writers Charles Kingsley and Hans Christian Andersen, or the artists Millais and Rossetti, who belonged to the Pre-Raphaelite Brotherhood – a school of painters and poets reviled by the surly Osborne Black. Even so – in my imagination – I see Osborne's style emulating theirs, especially in the narrative sense, and the use that many artists made of photographic reference to aid precision of detail.

RICHARD DADD (1817–1886)

Richard Dadd was another Victorian artist. He is not specifically mentioned in the body of the novel, but important none the less because of his obsessional nature and subsequent violent madness, very much in the mould of Osborne Black.

When Dadd entered the Royal Academy of Art he was viewed as mild-mannered and cheerful, generally regarded as being one of his generation's most promising talents. But following a period of travelling abroad in the Middle East as an expedition artist, something occurred to unhinge the man. He came home with manic tendencies and went on to murder his father. When captured, while trying to flee to France, several portraits of other intended victims were found among his luggage – all with streaks of red pigment slashed across their throats as if to signify the fate that Dadd next had in store for them.

The artist was initially confined in the Bethlem (or Bedlam) Hospital, thereafter being moved to Broadmoor, a secure institution for the criminally insane where he lived for many years until dying from consumption. He was cared for by forward-thinking doctors who allowed their patient to practise his art – producing intricately detailed works full of mystical creatures and fairies. Many are now held by Tate Britain and are considered masterpieces.

CHARLES KINGSLEY AND *THE WATER-BABIES*

One of the very first books I read was an abridged version of *The Water-Babies* by Charles Kingsley. The tale of an orphaned chimney sweep who drowns while trying to wash himself clean and then turns into a water-baby is one that affected me greatly – though I must confess to being shocked when I recently read the unabridged version and discovered that the story I'd loved soon extended into a moral rant – which was just as Kingsley meant it to be. The Church of England minister was concerned with social inequality and used his work to 'sermonise', with great lists to condemn those issues of which he strongly disapproved, such as Americans (murderous crows), Jews (dishonest merchants who grow fat on the sale of false icons), blacks (fat old greasy Negroes), and Catholics (popes seen as the world's great bogies – alongside an attack of the measles!). All of which may well explain why his book is no longer so popular.

The Water-Babies, A Fairy Tale for a Land Baby was written between 1862 and 1863, and before being published as a book it was serialised in *MacMillan's* magazine. It was an instant hit, but also the butt of many jokes, such as in a cartoon in *Punch* magazine where two scientists, Richard Owen and Thomas Henry Huxley, are seen peering into a bottle in which a water-baby is trapped – an image that inspired me again to imagine

Elijah and Lily Lamb dipping a jar into a stream when hoping to catch their own water-babe.

There is also a charming story that when Huxley's five-year-old grandson saw this illustration, he wrote the following letter

Dear Grandpater – Have you seen a Waterbaby? Did you put it in a bottle? Did it wonder if it could get out? Could I see it some day? – Your loving Julian

To which his grandfather wrote this reply:

My dear Julian – I could never make sure about that Water Baby.
I have seen Babies in water and Babies in bottles; the Baby in the water was not in a bottle and the Baby in the bottle was not in water. My friend who wrote the story of the Water Baby was a very kind man and very clever. Perhaps he thought I could see as much in the water as he did – There are some people who see a great deal and some who see very little in the same things.
When you grow up I dare say you will be one of the great-deal seers, and see things more wonderful than the Water Babies where other folks can see nothing.

How wise and how very charming!

HANS CHRISTIAN ANDERSEN AND 'THE LITTLE MERMAID'

Hans Christian Andersen was an author of Victorian fairy tales, among them beloved classics such as 'The Snow Queen', 'Thumbelina', 'The Little Match Girl', 'The Ugly Duckling' and also 'The Little Mermaid'. His work was immensely popular, and when on a visit to England he was invited to stay at the home of the author Charles Dickens. But he long outstayed his welcome, and when he had finally gone his host pinned a note to the bedroom wall that said: *'Hans Andersen slept in this room for five weeks – which seemed to the family AGES'*.

The lanky, gauche and effeminate writer had little luck with friends and cultured strange 'love triangles' where his wooing of a sister often hid desire for the brother, as in the case of Riborg Voigt – a letter from whom was found in a pouch on Andersen's chest when he died. But it was Andersen's lifelong love for a man called Edvard Collins (whose sister he also courted) that inspired 'The Little Mermaid' – a story of obsessive longing and pain, inspired by the intense desire to be physically 'transformed' as expressed in one of his letters – *'I languish for you as for a pretty Calabrian wench . . . my sentiments for you are those of a woman. The femininity of my nature and our friendship must remain a mystery.'*

In *Elijah's Mermaid* I have taken many themes from the tale of 'The Little Mermaid', not only to echo Osborne's obsession but also his muse's longing for love. There are some physical allusions too, such as Pearl's feet being webbed and then wounded, causing her enormous pain, much as the Little Mermaid felt when, with every step on dry land, she felt as if she was walking on knives.

The Real Places Which Have Influenced The Settings *For* Elijah's Mermaid

Burlington Row, where Frederick Hall resides and where his publishing firm is based, is an entirely fictional street, though hopefully it is indicative of the large brick-built houses in London's Bloomsbury, an area historically linked with the production of literature – and which is also very near to where the Foundling Hospital once stood.

THE FOUNDLING HOSPITAL

The Foundling Hospital plays a small but significant part at the start of *Elijah's Mermaid*, when Lily and Elijah Lamb are discovered before their adoption.

The orphanage was founded in 1741 when a philanthropic sea captain by the name of Thomas Coram wished to do something to help the abandoned children he often saw when walking through London's streets.

The institution has now been demolished but there is a fascinating museum where some replica rooms have been made up, reconstructed with the original fittings – such as the Committee Room, the Picture Gallery and the Rococo Courtroom. There is a Hogarth portrait of Captain Thomas Coram – alongside works by Gainsborough and Reynolds, all of whom donated to a gallery to lure in wealthy patrons who helped to pay for the children's care.

The museum also houses the Gerald Coke Handel Collection – Handel being an original benefactor, with many productions of his work taking place within the orphanage walls.

And then, there is the Foundling Collection – over four centuries' worth of paintings, sculpture, prints, manuscripts, photographs and other ephemera, such as the tokens given by mothers who left their babes in the hospital's care as a means of identification should they ever return to reclaim them. However, in the nineteenth century – which is when *Elijah's Mermaid* is set – the hospital gave out paper receipts, such as those alluded to in the case of Elijah and Lily Lamb. And just as with my sibling twins, the infants were at first farmed out to wet nurses in the countryside until they were four or five years old, when their education could begin. At fourteen, for the boys, and sixteen for the girls, they would then be released to the outside world, apprenticed into domestic work, general trade or the military.

CHEYNE WALK AND THE HOUSE OF THE MERMAIDS

Cheyne Walk in Chelsea (Chelsea meaning chalk wharf or shelf of sand) is now fronted by the Embankment, constructed in the nineteenth century to create an adequate sewerage system and thus divert such waste from the Thames. But before that engineering feat the Walk's many grand old houses fronted directly on to the river. And this is how I have pictured them in *Elijah's Mermaid*, with the looming carcass of Battersea Bridge – the last wooden bridge to span the Thames – appearing just as it would have back then before, in 1885, it was demolished and rebuilt.

At the time of Pearl's 'finding' in the Thames she is taken to the House of the Mermaids, an establishment very much like the old illustrations and photographs of Numbers 4 and 16 Cheyne Walk; the latter once belonging to the Pre-Raphaelite artist Rossetti.

Entirely imaginary are the murals of mermaids upon the walls, for which I referred to the wonderfully sensual artwork of John William Waterhouse, a Victorian painter who worked

Number 4, Cheyne Walk

somewhat later and was not an actual Pre-Raphaelite, but his images of mermaids and nymphs were in my mind consistently when thinking of Osborne painting Pearl.

When it comes to Osborne's automaton, there was indeed a famed French artisan by the name of Phalibois who constructed such clockwork wonders, uncannily realistic to see. However, I have no idea whether he ever made a mermaid.

CREMORNE GARDENS

The Chelsea pleasure gardens once had entrance gates upon the King's Road and also the river at Cremorne Pier. The artist Whistler, who also lived on Cheyne Walk, depicted some of the night-time scenes in his stunning 'Nocturne' paintings.

In 1877, the resort was closed to the public, having become notorious for prostitutes haunting every path. But before that sorry end it hosted a plethora of restaurants, a Hermit's Cave with a fortune teller, a Fairy Bower and a maze, not to mention a theatre with marionettes. Visitors could dance around the exotic Pagoda to the strains of an open-air orchestra, or rise up in the air in a hot-air balloon with fireworks exploding all around. The walkways were notoriously lined with sideshows of many different kinds, not to mention performing monkeys and dogs – and as far as Professor Beckwith goes, well, he really did exist and often presented the Beckwith Frogs – the human seals who performed in an enormous glass aquarium.

COVENT GARDEN MARKET

In Victorian times Covent Garden was a thriving fruit and vegetable market with more than 1,000 porters employed. The market and its public square were constructed in the 1600s on ground that had formally belonged to Westminster Abbey. The Floral Hall, designed by E. M. Barry, was added in the mid-1800s and must have been spectacular when filled with flowers and plants.

CHISWICK HOUSE

Of other London buildings, the Royal Academy does exist, as indeed does Claridge's Hotel. However, Dolphin House does not, though I have loosely based the Thames Mall address upon the real Chiswick Mall, where some more fine residences over-look the Thames, among them Walpole House, once the home to Barbara Villiers, a mistress of Charles II, and later converted into a school attended by W. M. Thackeray – who used that setting in his novel *Vanity Fair*.

Situated near by is Chiswick House – which is open to the public – with acres of glorious gardens, which surround the grand Italianate villa built by the third Earl of Burlington (1694–1753).

The earl, whom Horace Walpole called the 'Apollo of the Arts', constructed the house in the neo-Palladian style, being an ardent admirer of the Italian architect Andrea Palladio, as well as his follower Inigo Jones. But rather than being an actual home Chiswick House was primarily used as a centre for entertainment, with many lavish parties held during the hotter summer months when guests could escape from London's 'stink' and admire their host's collection of art, or play hide and seek in the ha-ha, or wander across the arched stone bridge, where an artificial river flowed with banks all surrounded by informal planting, the lushness of which was balanced by classical statues, obelisks and columns, and even an Ionic temple which overlooks a small round lake – the very setting where Osborne Black paints Pearl reclining as a nymph.

The house was often visited by Georgiana, the Duchess of Devonshire. It was during the Victorian era that Georgiana's son, the 'Bachelor' Duke, filled the grounds with a menagerie that included an elephant and an elk, emus and some kangaroos, and also a sacred Indian bull.

However, Chiswick House was not always the scene of such glamour. By the end of the nineteenth century it was leased out for medical use – more specifically as an asylum for wealthy male and female patients, with the mad most probably being confined in additional wings built on to the house in the late 1700s. In *Elijah's Mermaid* I have reimagined those wings (even though they no longer exist, demolished in the 1950s) and my inmates are all female, with no characters involved with their care having any factual source at all – although treatments described in the novel, from the use of cold baths to surgery, were genuine methods used at the time for the 'curing' of nervous symptoms, such as female 'hysteria' or those classed with nymphomania. It is also true that in very many cases women with no sign of madness at all could be all too easily 'put away' if their husbands or families were so inclined.

KINGSLAND HOUSE

The house described in *Elijah's Mermaid* with its ivy-smothered windows and walls was once the rectory in the village of Kingsland in Herefordshire. Nowadays it is privately owned, but you can walk the narrow path that leads along one side of its grounds and from there through the field with the iron gate that enters the village churchyard. The pretty little grey stone church does indeed have a Volka Chapel, situated just to the left of the porch, and in that there is an open tomb in which Lily poses for a photograph while thinking of the story she'd heard about the Battle of Mortimer's Cross (at the time of the Wars of the Roses) when a parhelion or 'sun dog' was seen in the sky – a story which is recorded as having been quite factual.

Another local story which may or may not be true pertains to the old rectory again, and the little stream almost concealed by thick-growing shrubs and low branches of trees which forms a natural boundary at the very end of its gardens. The tale of a haunting stems back to the time when a rector and his daughter lived quite alone in the house, when the local gossips would have it that the girl appeared to be with child and all manner of aspersions were cast as to who the father might happen to be. However, no child was ever seen, and the scandalmongers' tongues were stilled – until the night when a poacher heard the cries of a mewling babe and discovered a tiny corpse hidden at the water's edge. In the tradition of these things, it is said that to this very day if you happen to pass on certain nights you might also hear the wailing cry of the child left there to freeze or drown.

The stream in *Elijah's Mermaid* is larger than the real one, and the ferns that grow upon its banks provide a recurring theme in the novel; again an allusion to Kingsley and his coining of the word Pteridomania – or fern madness – a craze which affected much of the nation with enthusiasts travelling for miles around in search of the latest specimens, and some-times with fatal results when overzealous adventurers scaled the faces of dangerous cliffs and fell to their deaths on the rocks below. For those who preferred a gentler chase, there were nurseries that supplied the plants, and public gardens where grottos were built: grottos with pools, even waterfalls, and walls created from rough-hewn rock to give a natural sense of rom-ance – but a lighter, warmer, airier world than that created by Osborne Black in his secret grotto in Dolphin House.

The Grade 1 listed Margate Shell Grotto plays a relatively small part in *Elijah's Mermaid*, being the underground 'cave of shells' in which Pearl first poses in darkness for the artist Osborne Black. But it has a great significance in terms of what her life is about to become – and it is the most fascinating place, which, again, you can visit and see today.

The history of the grotto is by no means certain. It was discovered in 1835 when, while attempting to dig a pond, a man named James Newlove and his son, Joshua, discovered a peculiar hole in the ground. When Joshua then crept inside he found no less than seventy feet of winding underground passages at the end of which was a much larger chamber and, within that, something that resembled an altar. What added to the mystery was the fact that the walls were all covered in cockle, whelk, mussel and oyster shells which form various mosaic designs – which some say depict the Tree of Life, phalluses, gods and goddesses, the horns of rams, a three-pointed star, as well as symbols of the sun and the moon.

Mr Newlove was soon to realise the commercial potential of his find. By 1837 the first paying visitors arrived – and the still ongoing debate commenced as to the origin of the caves. Some thought them an ancient temple, some the home of a secret sect, with others entirely adamant that they must be a Regency folly. But such follies were built on wealthy estates and Mr Newlove's discovery existed beneath common farmland. And then, there is also the fact that had the grotto been constructed as recently as the 1700s then surely some record or map would remain – not least with regard to the enormous industry involved in excavating the passages and creating the exquisite mosaics, with shells numbered in the millions. And yet, there was no local knowledge at all regarding the grotto's existence.

In 1999 English Heritage commissioned an investigation, but its only conclusion was that the grotto was unlikely to have been built during the Victorian period. Carbon dating was a failure owing to the build-up of soot from the use of oil lamps for Newlove's tours. And so the mystery remains.

BOBOLI GARDENS

The Boboli Gardens in Florence are truly glorious. First constructed in the sixteenth century and extending up a hill behind the Medicis' Pitti Palace, they are adorned with grottos, fountains, lakes and pools. They feature many classical statues, including the dwarf on the back of a turtle that Pearl refers to in the book. However, some of the more valuable works such as those by Michelangelo have now been replaced by copies.

THE UFFIZI GALLERY

Also in Florence is the Uffizi Gallery, where an international collection of wonderful artworks and paintings was gathered by the Medicis. The permanent display contains Botticelli's *Birth of Venus*, which Osborne views with Pearl at his side in a scene in *Elijah's Mermaid*.

Other Themes In Elijah's Mermaid

VICTORIAN PHOTOGRAPHY

When researching Victorian photography I visited the National Trust's Lacock Abbey, set in the heart of Wiltshire. This country house with monastic roots was once the home to William Henry Fox Talbot, a pioneering contributor to the English art of photography.

When Elijah Lamb takes up the art I tried to imagine his work as being comparable to that of Julia Margaret Cameron, who created stunning portraiture and illustrative allegories which formed a natural link to those themes explored by the Pre-Raphaelites – among whom, as with many artists, there was a growing trend to refer to photographic work to capture the nuance of nature in paint, in all of its intricate detail.

When Augustus Lamb poses for Elijah I have taken the liberty of alluding to an actual Victorian photograph, 'Don Quixote in his Study': a glorious sepia albumen print taken by William Lake Price.

As far as Frederick Hall is concerned, with his exploits of sneaking up on his maid while she is still sleeping in her bed, I have echoed another real event, when Edward Linley Sambourne, the illustrator and cartoonist employed by *Punch* magazine, developed a passion for photography and took to capturing his household staff – and some, such as his maid, were quite unaware when he did so. Also, when his wife was out of town, he was not averse to hiring young female models from the Kensington Camera Club and inviting them into his home, where they posed somewhat provocatively – some in a manner that might well grace Frederick Hall's riskier publications, for the growth in printing and photography in the Victorian era led to a huge surge in pornography.

During Victoria's reign there was a flourishing trade in magazines and periodicals which supplied a regular supply of serialised fiction, social discussions and features on fashion and food – even the latest music to be played on the family piano or harp. Mrs Beeton's *Book of Household Management* began as a series of instalments – as did the work of Dickens, who also edited a magazine which was known as *Household Words*, later becoming *All the Year Round* – the latter title adapted to create my *As Every Day Goes By*, a magazine owned by Frederick Hall, in the pages of which the young Elijah, Lily, and also Pearl, read chapters of *The Water-Babies*.

HEALTH, MEDICINE AND DISEASE

Wherever possible the medicines referred to in the pages of *Elijah's Mermaid* are based on actual Victorian concoctions. Many of them really did contain potent measures of opium and/ or cannibas. A bottle of laudanum could be found in every household medicine chest, and arsenic was readily available too – an ingredient in Fowler's Solution which was used to get rid of unwanted hair.

Doctors still applied leeches for the 'letting of blood', and a popular treatment for bruises was to apply a paste based on a solution of crushed earthworms.

Without today's more sophisticated means of classification and diagnosis an illness such as Augustus Lamb's might leave a doctor at a loss to know what was causing the symptoms of shaking or loss of memory. In this fictional situation I have drawn on personal experience, a member of my family being afflicted with Parkinson's disease – a terrible progressive condition for which there is still no cure, for which hydrotherapy (or water cures) would be entirely useless – although they were very popular and often prescribed for the treatment of various conditions. Florence Nightingale and Charles Darwin were both said to be fond of this regime to build their strength and calm their nerves. But when meted out in asylums the method could be extreme and cruel.

As far as venereal disease is concerned, just as in parts of Africa today, where AIDS has become so prevalent, there were people in Victorian times who believed that men so afflicted might be completely cured if they chanced to have sex with a virgin girl, when sadly such an evil act might lead that innocent to her death.

BROTHELS IN VICTORIAN LONDON

In the mid-nineteenth century the age of consent was just thirteen, and with no compulsory education for girls until 1870. Women were idealised as 'Angels of the Hearth'. A wife was her husband's possession. If she left him, then, more often than not, she would be spurned by society, or demonised as 'the fallen'.

At this time prostitution was rife, the city of London being the home for countless thousands in that profession (reports are variable but some say as many as 80,000) and for girls who entered the workhouse the fate could be more or less guaranteed.

There were various degrees of trade – those who were wickedly lured into the life (such as in the case of my own Isabella), those who led normal family lives but worked for money now and then, those who walked the streets alone, those who worked in communal lodgings under the 'care' of a pimp or madam, and those in high-class establishments such as the House of the Mermaids, who might hope to make 'introductions' and secure a permanent 'love', perhaps being set up in their own abode.

The risk of sexual disease was high, with treatments painful and primitive, with 'Lock' hospitals taking in the afflicted and keeping them in quarantine. The risk of venereal disease to the health of the general population was deemed to be so very great that in 1864 the first Contagious Diseases Act was passed in

Parliament, from then on making it legal to regulate the movements of prostitutes in cities, garrison towns and ports, where females could be arrested and subjected to brutal examinations. Of course, this freedom might lead to abuse, and indeed more than one 'decent' woman was subjected to great embarrassment.

In the final pages of *Elijah's Mermaid*, where a contemporary newspaper report reflects on the House of the Mermaids being opened as a gallery devoted to the work of Osborne Black, I also make a reference to Lily Lamb's philanthropic work, helping to rehabilitate prostitutes in Utopia House in Bloomsbury.

That institution is imaginary but its concept was inspired by the real Urania Cottage, where Charles Dickens and Angela Burdett-Coutts (a wealthy and generous heiress) set up a 'redemption home' where the fallen but 'not lost' could, hopefully, be led back to the righteous path.

VICTORIAN SLANG

In the earlier narrative of Pearl I have used quite a lot of Victorian slang; language she has learned from Tip Thomas and others who live in the House of the Mermaids. Below is a list of such words, along with their definitions, though hopefully most will be obvious from their usage within the story's frame.

Belly plea – when a prostitute cannot work due to pregnancy
Bene – good or profitable
Blag – steal or snatch
Blow – to inform
Blows up – scolds
Bluebottle – policeman
Bolt – run away
Bubbies – breasts
Buck cabbie – dishonest cabman
Bull – Five shillings
Bunter – near-beggar

Buttered bun – a woman who has just had sex
Buzzing – stealing, pickpocketing

Cant – a present
Caper – a criminal act
Chat – a louse
Chavy – a child
Chink – money
Choker – clergyman, or a neckcloth
Cock Alley – vagina
Cokum – opportunity, advantage
Coopered – worn out, useless
Cove – man
Crabshells – shoes
Crib – house, lodging
Crow – lookout, or doctor
Crusher – policeman
Cunny – vagina
Cupid's kettle drums – breasts

Dab – have sex with
Deadlurk – empty or abandoned premises
Demander – one who gains money by menace
Dial – face
Diddies – breasts
Dillo – old
Ding – throw away or pass something on
Don – clever person
Dragees – confections or sweets

Flam – a lie
Flimflammer – deceiver or cheat
Flash house – public house with criminal patrons
Flak – person easily deceived
Fluefaker – chimney sweep
Fly (on the) – doing something quickly

Glim – light, fire, or venereal disease
Glock – half-wit
Grind – have sex
Gulpy – a gullible person

Jolly – disturbance or fracas
Judy – a prostitute

Kecks – trousers
Knapped – pregnant

Ladybird – prostitute
Lamps – eyes
Lobcock – penis
London particular – a thick fog, also known as a pea-souper
Lurk – place of concealment
Lushington – drunkard

Mandrake – homosexual
Moniker – signature
Muff – vagina

Nebuchadnezzar – penis
Needful (the) – money
Nipper – child
Nobble – inflict bodily harm

On the ran-tan – drinking alcohol

Penny gaff – a cheap show or theatre
Piccadilly weepers – a style of gentleman's whiskers
Pinchcock – prostitute
Plucky – brave
Prigg – have sex
Push – money

Quim – vagina

Racket – illegal tricks
Rasherwagon – frying pan
Rummy old cove – eccentric man

Screever – dodgy lawyer
Slumming – spending time with the poor or degenerate, visiting dubious areas
Snide – counterfeit
Spouts – speaks
Swell – well-dressed gentleman
Square-rigged – soberly dressed
Stumps up – pays
Stunner – a beauty

Tackle – penis
Tealeaf – thief
Tifter – hat

Ugly customer – one who is violent or not to be trusted
Unrigged – undressed
Up to snuff – sensible
Used up – fatigued

Whore pipe – penis
Wrap – have sex

For more information and articles related to *Elijah's Mermaid* and also to *The Somnambulist*, Essie Fox's debut novel, please visit her blog, *The Virtual Victorian* (www.virtualvictorian.blogspot.co.uk), which is full of Facts, Fancies and Fabrications relating to the research involved in her fiction and also, far more generally, with regard to the nineteenth century.